Nagata, Linda.
The trials.

$27.99

DATE			

BAKER & TAYLOR

ALSO BY LINDA NAGATA

THE RED

GOING DARK
(FORTHCOMING)

THE RED

TRILOGY

BOOK TWO
THE TRIALS

LINDA NAGATA

SAGA PRESS

LONDON SYDNEY **NEW YORK** TORONTO NEW DELHI

SAGA PRESS
AN IMPRINT OF SIMON & SCHUSTER, INC.

1230 AVENUE OF THE AMERICAS, NEW YORK, NEW YORK 10020

Text copyright © 2015 by Linda Nagata
Jacket photograph copyright © 2015 by Larry Rostant
For information about special discounts for bulk purchases, please contact Simon & Schuster Special Sales at 1-866-506-1949 or business@simonandschuster.com.
The Simon & Schuster Speakers Bureau can bring authors to your live event. For more information or to book an event, contact the Simon & Schuster Speakers Bureau at 1-866-248-3049 or visit our website at www.simonspeakers.com.
The text for this book is set in Adobe Garamond.
Manufactured in the United States of America
Saga Press First edition
2 4 6 8 10 9 7 5 3 1
CIP data is available from the Library of Congress.
ISBN 978-1-4814-4658-7 (hardcover)
ISBN 978-1-4814-4096-7 (eBook)

THE TRIALS

AGAINST THE BEAST

EPISODE 1:
THE TRIALS

"WE ARE BEING ASKED TO CRUCIFY COLONEL KENDRICK."

My words are directed at my soldiers—the Apocalypse Squad. That's the name the mediots have given us and it works for me. The seven of us who survived the First Light mission are all here, seated around a cheap oval table in the center of an otherwise bare, white-walled conference room in the federal courthouse in Washington, DC. It's the first time in the five months since we stepped off the plane at Dulles that we've been allowed to discuss our case all together, with no lawyers present.

I need to know we are all still on the same side.

I'm James Shelley. I presently hold the rank of lieutenant in the United States Army, but that will change at the conclusion of our court-martial.

"Our attorneys have decided that since Kendrick is dead, he's not going to scream and he's not going to argue when we hammer the nails in. So they want us to testify that the colonel used undue influence to get us to participate in a conspiracy. They want us to claim we were not mentally responsible at the time and therefore it is not our fault."

Our return to the United States was voluntary and we're

widely regarded as heroes. It's a status I've leveraged to get us the privilege of this ten-minute session to confer on our defense strategy. Not a private session—camera buttons are watching from the corners of the room and the ocular overlay I wear like contact lenses in my eyes is always recording—but we're used to that. We're LCS soldiers, and in a linked combat squad you expect to be observed.

"In just a few minutes, each one of you will meet individually with counsel, where you will be advised to pursue an affirmative defense, claiming a lack of mental responsibility."

Travel and communication have been a challenge ever since Coma Day, when seven improvised nuclear devices were used to destroy data exchanges across the country, shattering the Cloud and collapsing the economy. So an agreement was reached to hold our court-martial in the centrally convenient federal courthouse in DC. We are using the facility but not the staff. The army is conducting our court-martial, with a court composed of army personnel and presided over by a military judge.

Our court-martial hasn't started, and we will not be in court today, so we're all wearing the informal brown camo of combat uniforms. Everyone but me is also wearing their linked combat squad skullcaps.

The caps look like athletic skullcaps, but they're embedded with a mesh of fine wires that interact with the neuro-modulating microbeads implanted in the brain tissue of every LCS soldier. Some of those microbeads are chemical sensors that report on our brain state, but others trigger neurochemical production. The skullcap is able to switch them on and off to affect the way we feel.

I don't wear a skullcap anymore because I've moved on to a more permanent setup. I use a skullnet: a mesh of sensor threads implanted on the surface of my skull. Like a cap, it houses a simple artificial intelligence tasked with monitoring and stabilizing the activity in my brain. It could be my get-out-of-jail-free card, if I want to try to use it for that.

I tap my head, where my black hair is trimmed to a short buzz cut. "The attorneys want me to say Kendrick controlled my thoughts, my emotions, my decision-making processes, through my skullnet. They want each one of you to say he hacked your heads through your skullcaps. They want us to argue we were not in our right minds and that we didn't understand what we were doing."

Specialist Vanessa Harvey speaks up first: "Fuck that, LT."

She crosses her arms, fixing me with a glare that could stop bullets . . . almost did, at Black Cross, where she was shot in the face. Her visor took the impact of the slug, and she got away with only a broken nose—but no sign of that injury remains in her sharp-featured, bronze-complexioned face.

Specialist Samuel Tuttle expands on Harvey's sentiment. "Fuck *them*." The rim of his skullcap enhances his scowl as his brooding brown eyes shift from Harvey to Sergeant Aaron Nolan, who must have been his big brother in some other life.

Nolan is six foot one, broad shouldered, with deep-brown skin. He told me once he was half Navajo, half white. Generally, he's a congenial man, but now he drops his chin and coldly informs me, "Those shit-eaters can go to hell."

Little Mandy Flynn, with her green eyes and fair skin, is only a private, but she's more eloquent than anyone else. "No way are we pissing on the colonel's grave, sir."

"Damn straight," Specialist Jayden Moon agrees. Moon is tall, skinny, and dark eyed, the offspring of Asian and European bloodlines mixed in some complicated formula.

He used to have a tan, but our stint in jail has bleached his skin to a pale cream. "LT, this is just bullshit."

I turn to Sergeant Jaynie Vasquez, who sits, somewhat loyally, at my right hand. Jaynie is the ranking non-com in our squad. She's got a lean build and moderate height. Her skin is smooth and black. She tends to regard the world with a reserved expression that perfectly reflects her nature: smart, controlled, determined, and not entirely trusting of my judgment. She answers my questioning look with a nod, letting me know she'll back me up as long as I say the right things.

I return my attention to Moon. "Of course it's bullshit, Moon. It's the same bullshit we LCS soldiers get all the time."

Outside the linked combat squads we are commonly believed to be soulless automatons, emotionless killing machines controlled by our handlers in Guidance. It's a prejudice our attorneys want to exploit.

"But it's a bullshit that can be used to buy you a not-guilty verdict and a medical discharge."

Moon looks confused. His gaze shifts to Jaynie. "I don't get it. That's not why we came back."

He's looking at Jaynie, but I'm the one who responds. "No, it's not why we came back. The crucifixion of Colonel Kendrick is an option we are being offered because both trial and defense counsel are under extreme pressure to limit the scope of our court-martial. They do not want to look into the chain of responsibility—"

"*Lack* of responsibility," Jaynie interrupts in a low growl.

I concede the point with a nod. "They do not want to look into the layers of corruption that forced us to take the action we did. We are here to expose that corruption, to confront it. That's why we came back. But this is not a game. We are facing life in prison, very possibly execution.

If you want to reconsider your reasons for being here, now is the time. Just know that for the affirmative defense to work, all of you will need to agree to it. If even one of you dissents, that will cast doubt on all the others."

Harvey's arms are still crossed, her brow wrinkled in suspicion. "What do you mean, *we* would have to agree? What about you, LT? I thought we were all in this together."

"That's up to you, Harvey. There's no fucking way *I'm* going along with it. But the rest of you can claim your commanding officers exploited your sense of loyalty. Let me know if you'd like me to step outside while you discuss it."

It's Jaynie who reacts to this first, in her own affectionate way. "Take a pass on the drama, LT. We've got nothing to discuss, because I dissent. I'm not participating in a bullshit defense."

"I'm not either," Harvey says.

This sentiment is echoed around the table with nods and murmurs. I use my overlay to launch an emotional-analysis tool called FaceValue, letting it study each member of my squad. The app detects no deceit in the faces of my soldiers, no real doubt. Jaynie is frowning—FaceValue confirms the caution I see in her eyes—but her caution doesn't bother me. She's always been the most thoughtful among us.

The standard way for a story like this to unfold is for at least one, maybe even two, of my soldiers to prove treacherous, cutting a secret deal with trial counsel that will betray the rest of us, while saving their own asses—but Colonel Kendrick preempted that tired plot device when he hand-selected everyone in the squad for a spectrum of personality traits that includes a compelling sense of justice and a group loyalty strong enough to keep us together through two harrowing missions. As I look around the table, I know that everyone remains loyal to this, our current mission.

"So what the fuck are we going to do?" Harvey demands, her sharp gaze focused on Jaynie because she is addressing her question to my sergeant and not to me.

My fist hits the table with a loud bang, and I regain the attention of every set of eyes in the room.

We don't have many options. The charges entered against us include conspiracy, multiple counts of murder, aggravated assault, robbery in excess of $500, and kidnapping, with a general article for abusing the good order and discipline of the armed forces. I get an additional charge of destruction of military property, since I was present when Colonel Kendrick deliberately destroyed an army helicopter.

Moreover, we did in fact commit every act we are accused of during the execution of a rogue mission, code-named First Light, in which we took a United States citizen to face trial in a foreign country for crimes committed within and against the United States. Every moment of that mission, every conversation, was recorded by multiple devices, including my ocular overlay. There is no lack of evidence that can be used to convict us. There is only the question of whether or not circumstances justified what we did.

It's a question the court is desperate to avoid, which is the only reason we've been offered the I'm-not-responsible defense . . . but we're past that.

"Because this is a death-penalty case, our plea is automatically entered as not guilty. That means the prosecution has to prove the case against us, step by step for the public record. We want that. We want the public to know who we are and what we did, but above all else we want them to know why we did it."

I know a hell of a lot more about the law now than I did when we started this. I present my strategy with what any competent attorney would surely regard as an amateur's optimism. "The only valid defense we can make goes to our service oath to support and defend the Constitution against all enemies, foreign and domestic. So what we are going to do is expose those enemies—our domestic enemies—shine a light on them, and examine every link in the chain of command that had a hand in sheltering Thelma Sheridan from prosecution for her part in the Coma Day insurrection. We push the judge on it at every step. We force the scope of the investigation to expand. If it ultimately takes in the president, so be it, I don't give a damn. If it sets off a revolt against the rotten core of our country, you won't find me weeping."

"Burn it all down?" Jaynie asks softly.

I turn to her, wondering at the suspicion in her voice. "No. That's not what I want."

She studies me, like she's trying to see beneath the surface. "Just don't push it too far, sir. You might not like what's on the other side."

We're separated again, each of us scheduled to meet individually with an attorney. I get parked in a small consultation room inhabited by a table and four uncomfortable chairs, where I'm due to consult with our lead defense counsel, Major Kelso Ogawa, along with our civilian attorney, Brandon Shelley—my uncle, who's assisting in our case pro bono because he's family, but also because he's as furious about the Coma Day cover-up as anyone.

The room is soundproof, so there's no noise from outside, no warning the door is about to open. I jump hard when it does, but it's just my uncle Brandon. He slips in and slams the door behind him, loud enough to let me know he's deeply unhappy. "That was one hell of a performance you put on."

He's an imposing presence: tall, with a middle-aged

huskiness camouflaged by his expensive gray business suit. His mixed heritage has combined to give him a heavy brow and an aquiline nose—strong features that instill confidence if he's on your side, and present a sense of threat if he's not. Silver is beginning to encroach on his neatly trimmed black hair.

"The prosecutor—" He catches himself, realizing he's misspoken. "Damn it. I mean *trial counsel*," he says, substituting the military's term, "is throwing a tantrum, and frankly, she's got legitimate grounds. Jimmy, you agreed to present the mental responsibility defense—"

"Which I did."

"Accompanied by prejudicial framing. The crucifixion of Colonel Kendrick? Seriously?"

"It's a metaphor."

"*Jesus*, Jimmy! I don't even know who you are anymore. Here." He hands me the tablet he's carrying. I grab it, and immediately tap to wake up the screen, hunching over the display like an addict over his next fix. My uncle tells me, "There's a folder with your name on it."

"I see it." But I don't give a shit about the folder. I want to get out into the Cloud . . . what's left of it.

"Keep yourself busy," my uncle says. "I'm due in the judge's chambers, where I get to listen to trial counsel complain how you prejudiced your codefendants, convincing them to act against their own best interests." He reaches for the doorknob.

"Hold on! The network connection's been shut down on this thing."

"Of course it's shut down. You know you're not allowed an outside link."

I scowl up at him. "I know I'm not allowed an open link from my cell, but Guidance still has access." I tap my head. "They check up on me every day."

He looks worried as he asks me, "What do you mean?"

My overlay is always on. Everything I see is recorded by the lenses in my eyes and what I hear is captured by tiny audio buds implanted in my ears. A gold line tattooed along the curve of my jaw is an antenna that links me to the Cloud when I'm not locked down—and the army gets to keep the record.

I tell my uncle the truth. "At least once a day, Guidance opens a link to my overlay, to upload the feed."

The record gets sent . . . somewhere. I don't know where. Sent to a filmmaker who edits my experiences, blending them with other records to create episodes of a reality show called *Linked Combat Squad*, which has gotten kind of popular.

"You're not supposed to have *any* connectivity," my uncle insists. "None. That's my understanding. It's part of the security arrangements because Guidance is worried about a hack . . . oh shit."

We stare at each other, sharing the same thought.

"Don't say anything, Uncle Brandon. *Please.*"

Out in the Cloud, running on a million servers but for the most part unseen and undetectable, is a rogue AI that I've come to call the Red. No one really knows where the Red came from. Speculation says it began as a marketing AI, maybe one equipped with an all-access backdoor pass stealth-developed by an American defense contractor because, given time, the Red can get anywhere, access anything linked to the Cloud. It hacked into my head—and rewrote the plotline of my life. That's why I'm here.

"Jimmy, if the Red—"

"*No.* It doesn't matter. It's not hurting me. It's not hurting anything."

I should never have mentioned the uploads. So why did I? Why did I bring it up? That's one of the drawbacks of having been infested with the Red. I question my own motives, even when I know it hasn't been active in my head in months. The uploads are just an automated process.

Outwardly I'm calm, but adrenaline is pumping as I scan the ceiling. "No surveillance in here, right?"

"That would be a violation of attorney-client privilege."

"Then don't say anything. If Guidance doesn't know about this, then they aren't going to be looking at the record, not for a while, anyway."

"It needs to be reported—"

"*No*. If Guidance believes there's been an infiltration, they'll take out my skullnet, and my overlay too."

"You might be better off—"

"I will *not* be better off."

His gaze is hard. He hates the choices I force on him. "I've got to go. I'm late already. Look at what's in the folder. We'll talk about it when I get back."

Again, he reaches for the door.

I tell him, "Trial counsel is right."

He turns back, furious. "What the *fuck* are you talking about?"

"She's right when she says we're acting against our own best interests, because this isn't about us. It never has been. It's about bigger things."

"You know, Jimmy, I liked you better when you were a cynical kid. This true-believer shit gets old real fast."

We trade a glare. Then he jerks the door open and steps outside, closing it again with a thud that shakes the frame. I hope he won't say anything.

Something else occurs to me: If trial counsel hears about an infiltration, she could move to have me declared mentally incompetent because my head has been hacked—a diagnosis that could be extended to my squad, providing an excellent excuse to skip the trial entirely and disappear all of us, forever, into some anonymous psych ward. American gulag. Jesus.

But my uncle has been a criminal attorney for a long time, mostly white-collar crime. He knows how to keep his mouth shut, and even though I've made a habit of pissing him off, I trust him to keep my secrets.

I look again at the tablet.

It's gaze responsive, with a ten-inch screen displaying the date and time in one corner alongside a red X—the icon of network isolation, lockdown, no connections allowed—and, in the center, exactly one folder labeled "Jimmy." There could be libraries of data hidden behind that almost-empty screen, but I'll never find my way into them. The tablet knows who's holding it, and this single folder is all I'm authorized to see.

I blink the folder open. Inside are four videos. Their names identify three as news clips generated by propaganda stations. The fourth is labeled "Linked Combat Squad—Episode 3—First Light." When I read that, I get another adrenaline rush. Ye olde fight or flight.

I'd choose flight if I could, but I can't run away from myself.

PTSD rolls in, and my hands shake. I'm worried I'm going to drop the tablet, so I put it down carefully on the table. An icon lights up in the corner of my vision, indicating activity in the skullnet as the embedded AI automatically adjusts the neurochemical balance in my brain, guiding my mood to a quieter place, taking the edge off my emotions.

I do not want to watch the third episode of *Linked Combat Squad*. I already know what's going to happen, because I lived it—and I don't want to see Specialist Matt Ransom's brains blown out again, or witness Colonel Kendrick's slow, agonizing death, or hear the terror in my

Lissa's voice in the moments before she is immolated on that infinite night above the Atlantic. I hear Lissa often enough already, in my dreams.

The First Light mission was never in our own best interests. Not even close.

I stand up and pace, giving the skullnet time to work. The sound of my footsteps is a soft click as my robot feet meet the floor. My real legs got blown off. The army replaced them with cutting-edge prosthetics wired into my nervous system. It takes only four short steps to cover the length of the room. Turn around; repeat. After a few laps I sit down again and scan the news clips.

The first one shows a large protest rally on the National Mall, a block away from where I'm sitting. Between rows of trees just beginning to leaf out in the spring are tens of thousands of chanting protesters. I sit up a little straighter, remembering how it felt to be part of a crowd like that—empowering, intoxicating—and how certain I'd felt that with so many people demanding change, change must happen.

Too bad the world is more complicated than that.

The words being chanted are hard to make out past the voice-over of a mediot telling her viewers what to think, but the luminous banners floating above the crowd make the purpose of the rally clear:

FREE LT. SHELLEY—AMERICAN HERO

FREE THE APOCALYPSE SQUAD

THE PEOPLE STAND WITH THE LION OF BLACK CROSS

The Lion of Black Cross—that's me.

In the hours after the bombs went off on Coma Day, more INDs—improvised nuclear devices—were discovered in metropolitan areas, rigged to blow if disturbed. The only way to disarm them was with codes held by the enemy in an underground, former Cold War facility called Black Cross. My squad was sent to recover those codes. It was fucking hell in a basement, but it worked. Afterward the mediots tagged me the Lion of Black Cross, and if it wasn't that, it was King David, because God is supposed to be on my side.

First Light changed that.

In the months since, the mediots have worked hard to cast us as traitors. It hasn't really worked. A lot of people support what we did, but I had no idea we'd inspired the kind of passion I see in this rally.

The mediot doing the voice-over tries to make it something ugly. Using critical, contemptuous tones, she informs her viewers that responsible people are helping their country by staying at home, doing their jobs, rebuilding their lives, while these protesters have migrated to the capital to make trouble and demand government support.

Many of them are trying to make their demands anonymously. The faces of at least 20 percent are hidden behind masks—and not cheap Halloween leftovers. The masks I see are works of art, like European festival masks except they cover the whole face, and instead of eyeholes, there's a slot that allows them to be worn with farsights. I don't think the disguises can hide anyone's identity, though—not in the face of dedicated surveillance. A good IR scanner should be able to look right through the masks. But maybe that doesn't matter. Even if a government agency logs people's presence here, that will be just one among trillions of bits of data collected today. The real risk for most people in that crowd is being recognized by an employer—and the masks should help protect them from that.

The other two news clips are different versions of the same story. After I view them, I reconsider the icon for episode three. *Linked Combat Squad* is the product of a skilled filmmaker, one who knows how to tell a compelling, emotional story. Is there some element in episode three that inspired people, that persuaded them to leave their homes and their lives to rally in support of us?

My uncle included the third episode because he believes I need to see what it contains.

I steel myself, and I click the icon open.

It's later, much later, when the door opens. I tense, but I don't jump this time, and I don't look up. I'm hunched over the tablet, holding it in two hands. Episode three is still playing, and mentally I'm not really in the room. I'm back on the C-17. We've just completed our air refueling. The squad is cheering.

"Broken city," my uncle says grimly. "Quit and lock."

He's talking to the goddamn tablet, which listens to him. The screen goes blank. My grip on the tablet tightens until it's about to snap in two. "*Fuck!*" I whisper, struggling to keep my temper contained as our lead defense counsel, Major Kelso Ogawa, comes next into the room.

"You don't need to see the rest of that, Jimmy," my uncle says.

He's right. I don't need to see it, because it's playing inside my head. I hear again the radio hail from a mercenary hired by Carl Vanda. The merc tells me to turn on a phone, and I do it. My Lissa calls me, and lets me know the merc has kidnapped her, to gain leverage with me—but that scheme didn't work. Lissa is dead now. So is the merc. I'm still here.

My uncle steps around the table, pulling out the chair next to me. "I just wanted you to see the big policy shift that takes place in this episode," he says as he sits.

I make myself put the tablet down, gently, on the table.

I slide it over to him like it's a loaded gun. "When did episode three come out?"

Major Ogawa answers as he takes a chair opposite me. "Two nights ago."

The major is nearly fifty, of mixed Asian and European descent, with a narrow face showing some dignified weathering, and curly brown hair just beginning to gray. He watches me through the translucent band of his farsights, tinted gray, so thin and light they seem to float in front of his eyes. "You look shell-shocked, Lieutenant. Are you going to be okay to talk?"

I take a deep breath, straighten my back, square my shoulders. Lissa is dead and I can't bring her back, but if this trial goes the way I hope, then a lot of people might finally pay for their part in what happened. I hope Carl Vanda is one of them. "What happened with the judge?"

My uncle answers, "Colonel Monteiro expressed sympathy toward the concerns of trial counsel, but she refused to sever your case from the enlisted. She's under orders to conclude these proceedings quickly, and conducting separate trials is not going to satisfy that goal. Besides, trials cost money—and given the ongoing state of emergency, I don't think there's a budget to pay for a separate trial."

"So we move forward?"

"We have a tentative agreement," Ogawa says. "Right now, the court-martial is scheduled for Monday."

Monday.

It comes as a shock. Ogawa warned it might be months, but today is Friday. Only two more days. I'm okay with that.

"A tentative agreement?" I ask him. "What still needs to be worked out?"

"Trial counsel has asked Judge Monteiro to forbid the use of skullcaps while court is in session, on the theory that they interfere with individual self-determination."

I want to believe he's joking, but my FaceValue app detects no humor, no subterfuge.

"The skullcaps don't work that way."

"Monteiro has taken the request under consideration. She'll rule before the end of the day. In your professional opinion, as an experienced LCS officer, what will it do to the case if the judge rules against skullcaps—and your skullnet?"

I tap my forehead. "There's no off switch for my skullnet. Unless she wants to send me into surgery, she can't rule against it. And if she bans the skullcaps? That's a deliberate shot at debilitating my squad. It's a move that will put their mental health in danger. Ask Guidance."

"I have. They're preparing a formal response."

"They used to make us turn in our skullcaps before going on leave. They don't do that anymore."

"So you're saying it would be detrimental to our case if the judge ruled against the use of skullcaps?"

"No. It wouldn't affect the case at all, because the use of skullcaps has nothing to do with the case."

"But you think there's a risk of mental breakdown—"

"No." I consider it further. "Not right away. My soldiers will testify regardless, but take the skullcaps away and you put every one of them at risk of severe clinical depression."

"All right. That's more or less what Guidance said."

"More or less?"

"There have been incidents of . . . explosive violence in soldiers deprived of their skullcaps."

"What the fuck are you talking about?" I lean forward, studying him. This is the kind of bullshit the mediots like to chatter about.

"It's an addiction, isn't it?" Ogawa asks. "The more you use a skullcap, the more you need it. The mind forgets how to regulate itself."

"What violent incidents?"

"The usual. Murdered families, terrorized neighborhoods, shopping malls shot to pieces. The link to LCS soldiers has been downplayed."

I stare at the table, wanting to deny what he's telling me, but the truth is, I find it all too credible. "We're okay as long as we have the skullcaps."

"I'll tell the judge. The army got you addicted. It's an unfair burden to ask you to function without your emotional prosthetic during an event as critical as your court-martial."

An emotional prosthetic? The term is new to me, but I can't argue with it. My skullnet is an intelligent aid that files off the worst extremes of my mood and eases the trauma of my memories, keeping me in peak form for the next round.

"So you think we're going forward?"

"Absolutely," Ogawa confirms. "The government wants a verdict before the fallout from episode three has a chance to escalate."

I look at my uncle, then back to Ogawa. "Why didn't they just hold it back? It's been five months since the First Light mission. Why release the episode now?"

"Why release it at all?" my uncle asks. "You can be damn sure the army and the president were both against it, but someone out there is interested in your story, someone who's on your side."

He's needling me, talking around the subject of the Red, because he can't argue it directly while Major Ogawa is here.

"You should be happy," he goes on. "You wanted the eyes of the country on this proceeding. I can't think of a better way to achieve that than to release that propaganda film on the eve of the trial."

"What's going on outside right now is just the beginning,"

Ogawa assures me. "You've engineered a media sensation, all right. I'm impressed."

"I didn't set this up."

Ogawa looks skeptical. "We told that to the judge. You're isolated in here. There's no way you could have been involved in the release of *First Light*."

"Of course." I turn to my uncle. "The policy change you wanted me to see. You meant the Red. This time it's part of the show."

He acknowledges this with a nod. "It was never mentioned in episode two. It's never been publicly discussed—until now."

It's true. In episode one, we didn't even know the Red existed. During the events of episode two, we knew about it, we named it, and it was implied to me that other soldiers had been hacked too—but none of that made it into the show. Now, in episode three, the secrecy is gone. Flashbacks detail the Red's discovery and the speculation on its intent: that it engineers chance and coincidence in the lives of individuals both to derail and to inspire, with none of us immune. Thelma Sheridan speaks of it, Jaynie and I argue over it, and the case is made that the nuclear terrorism of Coma Day was more than insurrection, that it was aimed at destroying the habitation of the Red.

But this is information already revealed to the court. "This isn't going to change anything, right?" I ask them. "It's not going to affect the trial proceedings?"

Ogawa questions me in turn. "Is there any reason to think the decisions you've made regarding your defense have been influenced, against your will, by the Red, as an outside agent?"

I turn to my uncle, wanting confirmation that he's kept our secret. He makes a slight sideways gesture with his head: *Haven't said a thing.* I look at Ogawa. He's watching me closely; I'm sure he's using his farsights to run his own emotional-analysis app, one that's measuring the truth of everything I say. "My decisions have not been influenced by an outside agent."

"The history of the earlier incursions was presented to the prosecution during discovery," Ogawa tells me. "So they can't use the past influence of the Red against you. Also included in the pretrial documentation was an affidavit from Guidance asserting your skullnet is locked down."

I nod. I don't say anything.

"If that's not the case," Ogawa goes on, his gaze never wavering from mine, "as your attorney, I advise you to say so."

"Yes, sir."

He waits for me to say more. When I don't, he nods. "Monday, then."

We all stand up, shake hands, and then I follow them to the door.

My personal security is not entrusted to civilian guards. The army has executed an agreement with the US Marshals office allowing a special detail of military police to stand watch over the Apocalypse Squad. So two of my regular guards—Sergeant Kerry Omer and Specialist Darren Vitali—are waiting for me in the hall outside the tiny consultation room.

It's presumed we have a lot of enemies, so watching over us is considered hazardous duty. Omer and Vitali are rigged for it, wearing body armor and the titanium bones of an agile exoskeleton, the same model we use in the linked combat squads, where we've nicknamed them "dead sisters." The gray struts run up the outside of their legs and along their arms, with a back frame linking them together. Our guards also wear the same helmets we use, though their visors are kept transparent, so their faces are easy to see. The US Marshals office permits them to carry sidearms but no assault rifles, and no grenades or other explosives.

Both salute as we enter the hall. Major Ogawa and I return the courtesy.

I nod to my uncle, salute the major, and turn to Omer.

"Ready, sir?" she asks.

"Ready, Sergeant." I hold out my wrists for the cuffs I am required to wear when I transition between the cellblock and the court offices. Quickly and professionally, Omer puts them on me. I try not to think about it.

We step out together, one MP on either side of me. Our route is through a restricted corridor, with the offices of the federal judges on one side, and on the other, the courtrooms—four on this floor alone. Secretaries and assistants step aside for us. One woman ducks into a judge's office. As I pass the partly open door, I glimpse a tall window on the other side of the room, and beyond it, a vista that looks out across the Capitol Reflecting Pool. To the left, skirted with trees in early-spring green and a pink glaze of cherry blossoms, is the dome-crowned edifice of the Capitol Building. There is no one on its marble stairs or on the lawn in front of it, and no tourists wandering around the Grant Memorial, because security concerns have made this forbidden ground. But on the other side of the reflecting pool, where the vast lawn of the National Mall begins, I see in real time the packed human mass of protesters that I saw on video just a few minutes ago.

The door swings shut. We walk on to the end of the corridor, where an elevator stands open, waiting for us. We step aboard, about-face the way we were taught in boot, and face the doors. Omer touches the back of her left wrist to a sensor plate that reads an embedded chip. With her identity confirmed, the doors close.

The federal judges and their staffs use this elevator to

reach the underground parking garage. We use it to reach the underground passage to the courthouse cellblock.

As the elevator descends, Omer says quietly, "We saw episode three last night, sir. I just wanted to tell you, a lot of us think you did the right thing."

"Don't tell your CO that, Sergeant."

"Yes, sir."

And hope like hell this conversation doesn't show up on episode four.

We reach the basement. The doors open.

"Dead zone," Specialist Vitali reports. "The relay must be out again."

It's an ongoing problem. There are supposed to be network nodes throughout the building, but in this corridor the nodes aren't working at least half the time we come through—and post–Coma Day, no one expects replacement parts anytime soon. A working network would let Omer and Vitali get an all clear from their handlers. Instead, they have to confirm the safety of the corridor on their own.

So I stay in the elevator while Vitali steps out to survey the corridor. This requires more than a quick glance. The space is poorly designed from a security perspective. Square support pillars protrude into the corridor, breaking up the monotony of the walls but providing cover for possible assailants. Omer holds the elevator while Vitali confirms that the staff door to the parking garage is locked, before walking the corridor. We listen to his footsteps recede. After several seconds he calls back to us, "Contact established. All clear."

I look to Omer. She nods permission to proceed and we follow Vitali into the corridor, passing the staff door and, farther on, the prisoner-intake door. Just beyond that is the first set of gray steel doors that secure the jail. Bolts cycle as we approach. An alert buzzes, the doors swing open, and we walk inside to a secure foyer, and wait. The doors behind us close and lock, and then a second set opens in front of us. On the other side are offices, consultation rooms, and a control room. I've been told a side passage leads to a bunk room and a kitchen for the guards. We walk on, to a junction at the end of the corridor where there are three more doors, each opening onto a parallel cellblock.

Generally, only prisoners actually undergoing trial are housed overnight at the courthouse, and given the current state of emergency, most trial proceedings have been postponed. So the inmate population is low, which made it possible for the army to lease cellblock B, the current home of the Apocalypse Squad. The center door buzzes open and we step through into a corridor with glass-fronted cells, six on one side, five on the other. My cell is the first on the right. We stop in front of it. Vitali opens the door.

Across from my cell is the shower, and next to the shower is an empty cell. Sergeant Nolan is housed in the cell next to mine, but the sidewalls are concrete, so I can't see him—not from inside my cell, and not from where I'm standing. I can't see any of my squad. Tuttle and Moon should be in the middle of the cellblock, with the women at the end, but I have no way to tell if they're actually there or not. I'd do a roll call, but sound suppression prevents us from talking to one another. We can converse with someone outside the cell only if they are standing directly in front of the glass wall.

"Sir," Omer says. "Please face the cell door."

I don't move. "Is everybody here?" I ask her.

"All present, sir."

In the oppressive silence, where every faint squeak and groan of the MPs' exoskeletons calls attention to itself, it's easy to believe the opposite. I know that if I don't confirm for myself the presence of my squad, doubt will eat at me all evening. "May I walk the cellblock, Sergeant?"

Omer consults her handler. Then she tells me, "You are not allowed to speak to or otherwise interact with the prisoners, sir."

"Understood."

"You may walk to the end of the cellblock and return."

With my hands still cuffed in front of me, I move past my own cell. Two steps until I can see into the next one. Nolan is there, just like he's supposed to be. He's down on the floor doing push-ups. He looks up, watching me with a tense gaze as I pass. Tuttle is in the next cell, asleep. Directly across the corridor from Tuttle is Moon's cell. He's sitting cross-legged on his bed, reading a paper book. When he notices me, he looks up with a startled expression. The next cells on either side are empty. Then I reach Jaynie. She sees me and gets up from where she is sitting on the bed, stepping right up to the glass partition. I want to tell her we start on Monday, but I can't betray my promise to Omer. Flynn comes to the partition too, and so does Harvey. Harvey tells me, "Nobody changed their mind, sir."

I nod, turn around, and return to my keepers, presenting my wrists to Omer so she can remove the handcuffs. "Sergeant, would you make sure all the prisoners know that the court-martial is scheduled to start on Monday."

"I will do that, sir."

The cuffs come off and I step into my cell. Vitali closes the door behind me. I turn, watching through the glass partition as Omer moves out of sight down the cellblock to deliver my message. When she comes back, she stops in front of my cell and, facing me, she salutes. I return the courtesy and then she and Vitali leave. The steel door closes behind them, and I am alone.

I can see no one, hear no one.

It's going to be one hell of a long weekend.

The cell is six by eight feet, with three walls of solid concrete and one of glass. It's furnished with a narrow bed and
an aluminum toilet/sink combo in the back corner. Meals
are brought to us, and we eat alone. There is no exercise
yard, no library, because this is a courthouse jail, meant for
stays of a few hours to a few days. We have been here for
five months. The MPs do what they can, bringing paper
books if we ask for them, and we exercise in our cells.

I have my own unique routine.

An air-conditioning vent is embedded in the center of
the concrete ceiling. It's eighteen inches square, a tempered
steel honeycomb bolted into place. I imagine the prisoners housed here before me, lying in bed, staring up at that
vent and wondering at the possibility of escape through the
air ducts. Hell, I've wondered about it myself, but when I
jump up and hook my fingers in the steel mesh, I'm not
trying to escape.

It hurts like hell to hold on with just my fingertips, so
as quickly as I can, I swing my robot feet up to the grille
and latch on. The prosthetics hurt too—that's how I know
they're there—but the skullnet helps me regulate the level
of pain, and keep it at a minimum.

My titanium toes curl in a secure grip around the steel
grille. My fingers slip free and, slowly, I let my body uncurl
until I'm hanging upside down like a bat, gazing out the
glass door at the empty shower facility on the other side of
the corridor. Weaving my fingers behind my head, I curl
my body up again until my nose almost touches my trou-
ser legs in the vicinity of my mechanical knees. And then,
slowly, I let my body uncurl again. Down and up, down

and up, in a regimen of suspended sit-ups, followed by work to both sides and to the back.

As always, I'm getting a headache, so I kick loose, execute a half somersault, and land with a thump against the concrete floor. Aerobic sets come next: intense bursts of stationary running, jacks, and push-ups, until I can't do any more, and then I move on to tai chi or yoga, anything I can think of to keep my body—what's left of it—from degenerating. I've issued orders to the squad to work out at least sixty minutes a day, so that's how long I keep going.

I lead by example, even if no one can see me. It's boring as hell, but the skullnet helps me stay focused.

Tomorrow I'll get to take a shower.

At 1900, Vitali brings dinner: a microwaved pasta thing with vegetables on the side. Honestly, it's not bad. It's one of a series of contractor-supplied meals, the same that we consumed at Fort Dassari and at C-FHEIT. A little bit of home.

During my idle time in prison I've worked to improve my cyber-integration. FaceValue is part of the software package for a new overlay I had installed right before First Light. Since then, using the app to get an unbiased read on the emotional state of people around me has become second nature. When there are no people around me, when I'm alone in my cell, I work with my skullnet, training it to better integrate with my overlay.

I use a trained response now, focusing on the word *encyclopedia*. The skullnet picks up the command and signals my overlay to launch the program, faster than I could trigger it with my gaze. I read for a while, all nonfiction.

I tried reading a novel a couple of months ago, but I crashed on the romantic relationship—just not something I can handle right now—and in a flash of temper I deleted all the fiction I had stored.

It's hard not to snap sometimes. But my skullnet makes it mostly bearable, and when it gets too hard I just lie down in my bunk and think, *Sleep*—and my skullnet makes it happen.

I sleep maybe twelve hours a day—an article in the encyclopedia says that's bad for your health—but what the fuck, it's better than banging my head against the concrete wall until I'm bloody.

Sunday comes. Visitors' day. We're allowed one visitor each, but I'm usually the only one who gets escorted to a consultation room. My dad lives in Manhattan. Restoring train service between New York and Washington, DC, was a priority after Coma Day, so he's able to ride in Sunday morning and take a cab to the courthouse. He's well off, so it's not a burden for him to handle the post-Coma inflated fares.

It's different for the rest of the squad. Both Jaynie and Flynn are estranged from their families, while Nolan, Tuttle, and Moon are all from the west, their families too far away to stop in for a weekend visit. Harvey's mom has come in twice from Pittsburgh, but today I'm the only one who gets to leave the cellblock.

The senior MP on shift, Sergeant Colton Haffey, presents himself at the glass door of my cell and right away I get a bad feeling. He's not carrying a sidearm and he's not rigged in a dead sister. He doesn't even have a helmet on, just an audio loop. Behind him is Private Dominic Pasco, similarly unrigged.

"What the hell is going on?" I ask Haffey.

"Special circumstances, sir." My overlay confirms the nervous tension I see in his face. He doesn't like what's going on. He's worried. "Please step to the front of the cell, sir."

I do it. Haffey unlocks the door. "Present your wrists, sir."

I do that too, and he cuffs me. "What special circumstances?" I ask, imagining an assassination squad outside the cellblock.

Why not just shoot me inside the cell?

Maybe they want it to look like I went berserk and tried to escape.

"You have a visitor, sir."

"Not my dad?"

"No, sir."

The steel door to the cellblock buzzes open. On the other side are two men in dark business suits, opaque farsights hiding their eyes. Another man and a woman, similarly dressed, are stationed farther along the corridor, outside the first consultation room.

"Advance," Haffey tells me.

One of the suits intervenes. "We search him first."

Haffey looks at me, apology in his gaze, but he steps away. The shorter suit tells me, "Turn around, Lieutenant. Put your hands against the wall."

I do it and he frisks me, finding nothing, of course. The other one runs a scanner over me. It picks up my skullnet, my tattooed antenna, my embedded audio buds, the ID chip at my wrist, and my titanium legs.

"Why isn't he shackled?" the shorter one asks.

Haffey says, "It's not procedure, and the lieutenant is fully cooperative at all times."

"Unacceptable. I want shackles on those cyborg legs, or I want the legs off."

"No, sir!" Haffey snaps. "I will not allow you to abuse the dignity of an army officer."

"Cuff me to the fucking chair," I say.

The suit nods, and I am escorted to the consultation room. The table has been removed. There is only one chair, and it's been placed near a corner, away from the door. "Sit," the suit tells me.

They make Haffey cuff my ankles to the chair legs, worried, maybe, that if they do it, I'll try to kick their faces in. Haffey finishes the task, then stands beside me, facing the door. One of the suits takes up a post beside the door; the other positions himself halfway across the room.

We wait in silence for almost three minutes, during which I go over the possibilities in my head. When the door opens to admit the president, I'm not even surprised.

The door closes behind him as he comes a few steps into the room.

Like most successful politicians, he's a tall man, six three. He's trim and good looking in a dark business suit, but there's a lot more silver in his thick, wavy hair than on the day he was elected two and a half years ago.

I met him once before, on the night we were evacuated from Black Cross.

His expression is stern as he stands there, studying me with his dark Hispanic eyes. When he speaks, it's with the steady, reassuring tone of his signature voice, the one comedians always try to imitate but never get quite right: "I'm told everything you see, everything you hear, is recorded, Lieutenant Shelley."

"That's correct, sir."

His chin drops as quiet fury enters his voice. "Then let *this* be recorded for posterity. If it were up to me, I would have you hanged. Tonight, Lieutenant Shelley. Your heroism at Black Cross cannot excuse what you've done. During a state of emergency like no other this country has ever known, you chose to strike at the heart of our citizens' faith in government, undermining the effort of countless dedicated individuals who are striving every day to reclaim our future. I would have you hanged, Lieutenant. But I swore an oath to preserve, protect, and defend the Constitution of the United States. I respect our American system of justice, and I trust that system to find you guilty, as it must. As it will."

His outrage is so cold and so real it shocks me. In that moment I know, I absolutely know, that the conspiracy to protect Thelma Sheridan goes all the way to the top. I want to tell him I know he's part of it, that I'm looking forward to seeing him fall, but Colonel Kendrick's ghost is in my head, warning me to keep my smartass mouth in check. So I say nothing.

It doesn't matter though, because the show is over. The president gestures at the suit standing in the middle of the room, and my overlay shuts down. The half-seen icons that float on the periphery of my vision wink out, leaving only a pinpoint red light in the lower left corner to indicate that the overlay exists at all.

From this moment forward, no one outside will ever know what happens in here.

My gaze shifts from that tiny red light to the door. I am sure it will open, admitting the black-ops soldiers who constitute the president's personal army. I wonder if they'll kill Haffey too, and I decide that they will. They'll probably blame him for murdering me. I wait for death, one second and then another, but the door stays shut.

I look again at the president, beginning to understand he plays a more complex game than I'm used to. "Sergeant Haffey," he says.

"Yes, sir!"

"Will you please leave the room?"

I can almost hear Haffey sweat. "Sir, my orders are to stay with the prisoner at all times."

"I am overriding your orders, Sergeant. Get out."

"Yes, sir."

I keep my gaze fixed on the president as Haffey crosses the room. Someone in the corridor opens the door for him. When it closes again, the president speaks. "You have been misled, Lieutenant Shelley. You have been misinformed. I understand you believed you were serving some abstract justice when you helped to kidnap an American citizen. But you did not have all the facts and you do not understand the repercussions. For the good of the country, I want you to stand down."

"That's not possible, sir. This is a capital case. Even if I wanted to, I'm not allowed to enter a guilty plea."

"I am aware of that," he growls, letting me know he's not an idiot. "I am asking you to stand down, to mount no defense. Make your statement if you must—I don't begrudge you that—tell us how you felt compelled to do what you did, and *then tell us you were mistaken!* Fall on your sword. Accept the charges against you without expanding the scope of the evidence, and when you are found guilty and sentenced, I will issue a pardon—and the country can begin to heal."

Colonel Kendrick once called him a performance artist. It must be true, because I believe him. I believe he's speaking from his heart, that for everything he's done, he's had the best interests of the country in mind, and if I do as he asks, he will keep his word.

"I'm not the only one on trial, sir," I remind him.

His eyes narrow. "Your squad will do what you tell them."

He's more confident of that than I am.

It doesn't matter.

"I cannot accept your offer, sir."

I don't want to die. Jaynie thinks that, deep down, I'd put a bullet through my own brain if I could. That's not what I want, and I don't want to be a martyr to anyone's cause—but I'm not going to back down either. Matt Ransom died to see justice done, to see Thelma Sheridan called to account for her involvement in the Coma Day insurrection. Steven Kendrick died for the same thing. And it isn't over.

"We did what we did, sir, because the republic has been hijacked, because justice is for sale—"

"*Don't* play your patriot games with me, Shelley. You and I know it's a complex world, and eighteenth-century philosophies don't work anymore."

"Who is it you serve, sir?"

"Watch yourself, Lieutenant. I am your commander in chief. I hold your life in my hands. Your life, and the lives of your companions. As you were so quick to remind me, this is a capital case. You need to consider very carefully what you're willing to die for."

I've already spent a lot of time thinking about that. "I'm all in, sir. No way out but forward. How about you?"

He doesn't answer. He just stares at me for half a minute or more. Then he turns and walks to the door. It opens for him and he steps out without another word. The two suits follow him.

I'm still shackled to the chair. My overlay is still switched off. After a couple of minutes Haffey comes back in, looking scared. "You fucking pissed him off," he whispers.

I have that effect on people.

Haffey frees my feet. "I've got to take you back to your cell, sir."

"What about my dad? Did he come today?"

"Yes, sir. He checked in upstairs, but orders came down. No visitors."

"The president must have cleared out by now."

"Yes, sir."

"So is something else going on?"

"I'm not at liberty to talk about it, sir. If you'll come with me."

I'm escorted back to cellblock B, where Haffey removes my handcuffs.

My overlay is still off as the cell door is closed and locked, but I'm not too worried about it. Sooner or later, the Red is sure to switch me back on.

There is a network node above the cellblock door. The MPs installed it the day they brought us in. Here, underground, they need the node to ensure their helmets always have connectivity.

I have stood here by the glass wall innumerable times, in the murky darkness of the cellblock at night, gazing at the amber point of the node's indicator light, positioned a few feet above the faint, reflected gleam of the door's tiny, rectangular window. The window just looks into another part of the jail as closed and locked and impenetrable as my cell, but that light is a connection to the outside world. Beyond it are people I care about: my family, my friends, my handlers at Guidance—Delphi, especially.

Soldiers aren't supposed to meet their handlers or know them as anything other than a voice that relays orders and advice through their helmet's audio, but I got to meet Delphi once when Colonel Kendrick included her in a debriefing session. When I first saw her, I had no idea who she was. I admired her: a petite and athletic woman, no older than thirty, blond hair in a ponytail, bright blue eyes. A stranger, until she spoke.

I wish I were linked to Delphi now. I wish she could give me a sitrep, let me know what Intelligence believes is happening outside this cellblock, because I think something out there has gone wrong. For the first time since I've occupied this cell, I cannot see the network node's indicator light. It's been switched off, isolating us in here, and I want to know why.

The night-lights are still on—three-inch round panels in the ceiling that emit a dim red glow from the far end of the visible spectrum—but the only point of light I can see is the red pinpoint in my overlay, telling me I am still shut down. Without the network node, Guidance can't get in to switch me on. The Red can't reach me. What the fuck am I supposed to do without my goddamn overlay?

Sleep.

I should sleep.

But I've already been sleeping for hours; I was asleep long before the lights went out because there is fucking nothing to do in a six-foot-by-eight-foot cage when your overlay goes down. I don't even have a fucking paper book and I have no idea what the fucking time is.

Sometime later—a long time later—I see movement beyond the window in the cellblock door, and then the door opens, admitting a figure rigged in a dead sister, one that advances to stand facing me, just on the other side of the glass door. It's too dark to tell who it is, but then the figure speaks. "You've been awake a long time, Lieutenant."

Master Sergeant Mary Chudhuri.

"The network node is out," I tell her.

"You noticed that?"

"I did. What the hell is going on?"

"Officially? We're on lockdown. Preemptive action to curtail a suspected security hole in our local network— which means we're cut off from direct communication with Guidance. I've got Phelps stationed down the hall beside a landline, but I'm not feeling very secure. How about you, King David? Any insights? Any particular shit we need to be ready for?"

I shake my head. "God doesn't talk to me anymore."

I used to have a sixth sense when it came to impending danger. Matt Ransom wanted to believe it was the voice of God that guided me. It turned out to be God in the form of the Red, but even the Red can't reach me with the local network shut down. I am the sparrow that has fallen out of God's sight after all. That doesn't mean I can't sometimes figure these things out on my own. "Just as a gut feeling?" I tell the master sergeant. "Fuck yeah, something is up. Court-martial starts tomorrow. If a coalition of dragons wants to shut us up"—*if the president wants to shut us up*—"the time to slam us is now. With no network access it'll be easy. No call for help can get out."

Chudhuri is a silhouette outlined in dull red, but I can see the nod of her helmeted head. "Maybe. Or maybe your dragon strike force found a softer target. The mediots are reporting that Thelma Sheridan is dead. They're saying she was murdered in her cell."

I stop breathing. I don't blink. For three seconds I am utterly still, a trapped animal obeying an instinct that tells me if I don't move I won't be noticed and then, maybe, I can hide from the truth—because if it's true, we've lost.

The whole point of our mission, of First Light, was to bring Thelma Sheridan to trial, to expose what she'd done, and to implicate those who had aided her and those who had allowed her to get away with it. The only head of state willing to host that trial was Ahab Matugo, who took custody of Sheridan when our plane landed in Niamey. It was his promise to bring her safely to trial, but if he's failed, if it's true Sheridan is dead, First Light will have been for nothing. We will have delivered an American citizen into the hands of an incompetent kangaroo court and no one will give a shit about our reasons why.

I ask, "Has there been any official confirmation? Has Matugo issued a statement?"

"The news just broke."

I ponder the situation, and because I need some kind of

hope to hold on to, I say, "Matugo is a damn good strate-gist. He might let a rumor like that live for a while, just to cut down the odds of someone else trying to murder her."

"My concern, Lieutenant, is what a rumor like that will do to the odds of someone trying to murder *you*."

I look again toward the node; the light is still out. "What time is it, anyway?"

"Oh four oh seven."

The trial is scheduled to start at ten hundred. Six more hours.

"I don't think you have to worry, Master Sergeant. I think hitting us here was always the backup plan. Better to take out Sheridan than us. Hell, she expected it! Eliminate the possibility that she might testify, while turning her into an American hero, murdered in a third-world jail—and we get to be the bad guys who put her there."

"I'm sorry, Lieutenant."

"Thank you, Master Sergeant, for letting me know."

"Yes, sir." She salutes, then turns smartly and leaves the cellblock.

I continue my vigil, standing by the glass, watching the node, endowing that missing light with more meaning than it deserves. I imagine that if the lockdown is lifted, if the light comes back on, it'll be because Sheridan's death is confirmed—and our court-martial will be a short and certain affair.

But the node stays off.

At 0930 we assemble in the cellblock corridor, each of us with our hands cuffed. We're wearing our dress uniforms, except I'm not wearing shoes; I can't. The shoe inserts I need to make dress shoes fit weren't delivered, so I'm stand-ing in bare titanium feet, just like I do every day. I hope the judge doesn't toss me out of court for not being properly attired.

Major Ogawa stopped by the cellblock early to convey last-minute instructions on courtroom procedure. I used the opportunity to inform my squad of yesterday's encounter with the president and of the reported death of Thelma Sheridan. They understand the implication of these events and they're angry, but there's no going back. The only thing we can do is press on, take our case as far as we can, as far as we're allowed.

I stand at the front of the squad with Jaynie beside me. We form two lines. Master Sergeant Chudhuri has stayed past the end of her shift to ensure we make it into court. She and Sergeant Omer face us, flanking the open cellblock door. They're rigged in helmets, armor, and bones. Both wear sidearms. Behind the transparent shields of their visors, their expressions are stern.

Chudhuri says, "Our local network remains locked down. So Specialists Vitali and Phelps will precede us, taking up positions by the parking-garage door and the elevator, to ensure the security of the basement corridor. When they signal all clear, we will leave the cellblock and proceed without delay to the stairwell. I'm not feeling inclined to take the elevator this morning. I think we can all do with some exercise."

She looks at me for agreement—unnecessary because she is currently in command, but I nod my approval anyway. "Thank you, Master Sergeant."

We march as a unit through the jail, Chudhuri on point, Omer as rear guard. I'm nervous as hell. Maybe it's just a mistake that the network is down; maybe someone forgot to turn it back on. Or maybe it's still down for a reason.

We reach the jail's outer doors. Chudhuri gazes out a tiny window. An alert buzzes and the doors swing open.

We step out, and I can see to the end of the long basement corridor. An MP, anonymous in armor and bones, stands guard partway down, with another stationed at the far end. We advance, hard-soled shoes striking the floor in tight rhythm. I hear the doors close behind us. The bolts slide home with a solid *chunk*.

Chudhuri passes the prisoner-intake door. Jaynie and I follow a step behind her. That's when my overlay finally comes back on. Familiar icons crowd the baseline of my vision and I hesitate, missing the cadence as I try to figure out whether or not I've got an outside link. No one notices my misstep though because the next moment gets erased by the deafening *whump!* of an explosion. The concussion breaches the prisoner-intake door, blasting its bolts and hinges away, and slamming my eardrums. I stagger, dazed, into Jaynie while smoke wreathes the steel door.

At first the door refuses to fall. Then a second, lesser concussion sends it toppling inward. I follow Jaynie, scrambling to get out of the way. Chudhuri is screaming, "Get down! Get down!" A flash-bang goes off, so close it feels like the explosion is inside my head. I lose track of things. When awareness pops back I'm on the floor and I can't see shit. My vision is a celestial war of drifting black shadows and dazzling bright flares. And my hearing is trashed. Ears ringing and everything muffled: the screams, the gunfire.

But when a heavy-caliber weapon goes off above my head, I hear it. It's not Chudhuri or Omer because they only have sidearms, which means they're outgunned.

I don't want them dying for me.

Kicking off the wall, I drive my shoulder into half-seen knees.

My shoulder cracks against a titanium strut.

Fuck. A dead sister?

The shooter staggers, but doesn't go down. Logically, the

next step should involve putting a bullet in my brain, but that doesn't happen. Instead, a titanium hook closes around my bicep in a crushing grip, and I'm half lifted, half dragged toward the blown-out doorway.

My arm feels like it's about to pop under the pressure of that grip but I can bend it, so I reach back—with both hands because they're still cuffed together—and I grab hold of a strut. Though I can't see to confirm it, I assume the shooter is fully rigged in armor, bones, and helmet, leaving only one vital spot for me to hit: the throat. That's what I target. Using the strut for leverage, I swing my robot feet straight up. All those sit-ups I did while hanging upside down pay off as I point my toes and jam them in the general direction of my assailant's throat.

I score a hit.

The effect is dramatic, more than I expect. Flesh tears and blood surges free, a hot rain that splatters my face. I try to get my feet back on the ground, but the shooter is staggering, backpedaling through the doorway and into the garage. And with the arm hook still engaged, I'm dragged along.

Then the hook releases. I let go of the strut and tumble to the concrete floor. The shooter collapses beside me, dropping some kind of assault rifle in the gushing blood. I roll and grab for it, but someone else gets there first, kicks the weapon out of my reach, and then kicks me in the chest with the toe of a footplate. It feels like my chest caves in. I curl up in agony—only a moment and then I'm grabbed by my armpits and hauled to my knees.

"Don't fight it!" a man growls in my ear as an arm, braced by struts, squeezes my throat. "We're going to get you out of here." His grip tightens and I can't breathe; I'm down on my knees, so I can't kick. He's waiting for me to pass out. "Tango!" he shouts. "Let's go."

Tango, wearing the bones of a dead sister, appears on the edge of the rectangle of light that is the blown-out doorway. Details are lost to my addled vision, but I can see enough to make out an assault rifle, held at shoulder level and pointed in my direction. I have a fraction of a second to wonder if anyone in the corridor is still alive, and then the weapon goes off: three fast shots that smack against my captor's visor, *pak-pak-pak!* He goes over backward, releasing me on the way down. Three more shots follow. None hit me, but they set off a hell's chorus of car alarms. I suck in a painful breath between clenched teeth as I scramble behind a concrete pillar. The only thought in my head is, *What the fuck is going on?*

If I had a link to my handler Delphi, I wouldn't have to ask. She'd have a situation report ready.

"Shelley!"

My hearing is still muffled and the voice is competing with car alarms, but I swear to God it's Chudhuri. I'm hit with an ugly suspicion. She stayed past her shift. Is she a partner in this?

"Lieutenant Shelley, are you injured?"

I don't answer.

"Are you armed?"

Why the hell is Chudhuri still alive?

I don't answer, holding out for the cavalry. I mean, this is the fucking federal courthouse, the territory of US Marshals. It's a block away from the Capitol, in a district inhabited by cops from the Secret Service, the FBI, and the goddamn National Park Service. I can't be alone here for long.

"I'm coming after you, sir," Chudhuri warns.

"Whose side are you on, Chudhuri?"

Several seconds pass. Then she says, "Fuck you, sir. Lieutenant, if you are not injured, then get on your feet and get out into the open, before I see that you're charged with attempted escape."

I lean out to look around the pillar. My vision is good enough that I can see a sprawled figure beside a white van. Crouched beside the body is one of our MPs, holding a handgun while rapidly popping cinches to separate the fallen assailant from his rig.

Another MP stands over this tableau, holding an assault rifle pointed in my general direction. Chudhuri, I assume, though her visor is black and I can't see her face.

"Why aren't you dead?" I shout over the car alarms.

She asks me, "Why aren't you?"

"I don't fucking know."

"Are you armed?"

"No."

"Then get the hell inside."

I'm awkward with the handcuffs on, but I get my robot feet under me and slowly stand up. "Who's been hit?"

Every one of us is beat up, but the only one who's dead is the merc . . . the one I killed, the one whose throat I kicked out. I'm standing in the shower, letting her blood wash off me, repulsed by what I did to her. Maybe it was justified, but it wasn't exactly human.

It feels worse because I've since learned that the mercs came at us with a nonlethal assault, using plastic bullets tough enough to knock down even the armored MPs but unlikely to kill. They had only four personnel on their team: three rigged soldiers and a driver waiting in a white van with FBI insignia.

I thought they came to kill us.

When the door blew out, I expected black-ops soldiers sent by the president, or by Carl Vanda, but in hindsight it's clear to me they were amateurs.

And that they wanted to extract me alive.

Nolan is showering next to me, his skullcap in hand as he rinses his scalp. On his chest, swollen tissue and a deep black bruise mark the impact of a plastic bullet. My chest is bruised too, from the kick I took. It hurts to breathe. And where the merc grabbed my arm there's a black bruise like some drunk amateur's tattoo encircling my bicep.

"Who do you think sent 'em?" Nolan asks as he slips his skullcap back on. "You think it was Rawlings?"

"No." Colonel Rawlings is retired army. On the First Light mission he served as our outside contact. Along the way, he tried to turn my squad against me. "Rawlings wants this trial. But if he did change his mind? He wouldn't have told the mercs to rescue me and leave the rest of you behind. Hell no. He'd have ordered them to put a bullet in my brain, before they extracted everyone else."

Nolan considers this, and nods. "Who, then?"

I turn the water off and reach for a towel. Sergeant Haffey is standing watch in the doorway of the narrow shower facility. Technically, he should tell us to shut the fuck up, because we haven't been debriefed yet and we should not be discussing what happened, but he doesn't say anything. Like us, the MPs exist at the center of an arena. A spotlight illuminates us, suggests we are central to the action, but in the shadows beyond the reach of that light, dragons contend. The MPs feel the pressure of it just like we do—hell, Haffey had to face the president and no doubt he's thought about what could have happened if he'd been present for the shoot-out—but the pressure has only made our MPs more determined. They know the job they've been handed isn't to keep us confined, it's to keep us alive, and they've pulled together around us. We've become a cohesive unit, just like any unit under pressure in the field. Haffey doesn't tell us to shut up, because he's on our side.

So far as I'm concerned, he's part of the conversation.

"I don't know who sent the mercs," I admit to Nolan. "Nothing about the operation makes sense to me. Carl Vanda might like to have me alive, but he would have used real bullets, and slammed the rest of you."

Nolan reaches for his towel. "Yeah, it's like whoever it was, they wanted to grab you, without really pissing you off." We frown at each other and I know we're both thinking about the dead merc. "I guess they kind of fucked that one up," Nolan adds.

My dress uniform is ruined, and anyway I think the FBI agents investigating the attack bagged it as evidence, so I put on my combat uniform. Then I'm escorted to the same consultation room where I spoke with the president. I get to spend the next ninety minutes with two FBI agents who insist on going over every second of the attack in excruciating detail even though they have video from the helmet cams of all four MPs, along with recordings made by cameras in the parking garage. They don't ask about my overlay and I don't volunteer the news that it switched on just moments before the explosion. My theory is that the fake FBI van was equipped with a relay already hacked by the Red. As I passed the door, it sensed me and automatically restored me as a node on its network—one more surveillance device among millions, made active again.

The FBI agents aren't volunteering anything either. I ask about the attackers: who they were, who they worked for, what they had in mind for me, but I get no answers, and when it's clear we've all decided not to talk, Sergeant Haffey escorts me back to my cell. "The local network's been restored," he tells me. "Guidance cleared it for use, so we're not isolated down here anymore."

I check my overlay. It's still active, but I'm on lockdown as always, with no outside link. "Any confirmation on the status of Thelma Sheridan?"

He raises a ginger eyebrow. "You heard about that? It's not good news for you, is it?"

"It's not. Is it true?"

"The mediots act like it is, but since when do they know anything?"

I ask Major Ogawa the same question when he stops by in the midafternoon. Haffey allows him into the cellblock, but makes him stand outside the glass wall. I'm up on my feet as soon as I see him, facing him from the inside, wanting answers.

"I haven't heard anything official on Sheridan, but that's not your first concern."

I don't agree, but I have other questions. "So what happened this morning? Who the hell staged that fiasco? What were they after?"

He looks me in the eye. "Nothing happened this morning. Nothing you'll ever be able to talk about. The incident has been classified."

Just like the nuclear terrorism on Coma Day. We've got a pattern going here.

"Okay," I say. "Why? Is it being buried because the FBI is embarrassed it ever happened? Or because they know who's behind it?"

He shakes his head. "All I know is they want it hushed up. Colonel Monteiro demanded to know if any of you had the marks of a brawl on your face. If you did, she would have refused to proceed. As it is, it's safer to go forward. The crowd on the Mall was tallied at two hundred twenty thousand today, and the mood got ugly when news broke that the court-martial was postponed. Smells like bullshit, you know? And no one wants a riot. So we're going forward tomorrow. Opening arguments at ten hundred—"

"Assuming we get to the courtroom."

"You'll get there. The army can't wait to put this case away."

Major Ogawa isn't kidding. At 1721, Sergeant Omer brings the news that a fresh set of dress uniforms has been delivered, one for everyone. There's even a set of shoe inserts for me, so my robot feet can be properly attired. It's a miracle of efficiency to speed the hour in which the Apocalypse Squad drops out of the daily cycle of viral news.

After lights-out I'm lying in my bunk half asleep when an upload link opens in my overlay. Data streams out into the world. It takes several seconds, and then the link closes again. Just like always. The routine finishes with the deletion of yesterday's video.

It's standard operating procedure to have a security AI monitor traffic on any military network. That AI should be logging the nightly uploads. It should flag them if they aren't authorized by Guidance, but no questions have ever been asked. I have a feeling there won't be any questions about tonight's activity either.

Got to admit: After last night's isolation, it's a relief to be in the Red's network again.

The next day we assemble again at the request of Master Sergeant Chudhuri. This time, uniformed soldiers wearing armor and carrying assault rifles are stationed everywhere along our route. Chudhuri says they're on every floor and in the parking garage too. It makes her feel secure enough that she doesn't suggest the stairs, allowing us to take the elevator to the fourth floor. Our handcuffs are removed, and then we wait in a conference room, all of us seated around a table.

I listen with interest as the squad gives me their perspective on yesterday's incident.

"When Chudhuri ordered us to get down, we all dropped," Harvey says. "She needed a clear field for shooting, right? But the mercs knocked her down with their toy ammo."

"They knocked down all the MPs," Tuttle adds. "We thought we were next. Nothing left to lose."

Jaynie shifts, fixing me with a pointed gaze. "Is that what you were thinking when you went after that merc?"

"Something like that."

Nolan says, "When you took her down, when the blood started, her partner froze. So me and Harvey tackled him, and Vasquez went after the weapon."

"Stomped his fingers," Jaynie says. "Broke them, I think. Anyway, he dropped the weapon, but Chudhuri was already up. She got her hands on it before I could."

"She was so fucking pissed," Moon says, wide eyed with the memory. "She pumped rounds point-blank into the merc's chest armor—"

"To calm him down," Harvey says. "That's all." She nods at me. "Then she followed you out the door."

"It went so fast," Flynn adds, "we didn't even know they was shooting plastic till it was over."

"We got lucky," I tell her.

Harvey leans back in her chair, giving me a skeptical smile. "I don't know about lucky, LT, but sure as shit, we're better off than that merc you took apart. I did not know you could do that."

Flynn starts to gush her admiration for what I did, but when the door opens, she breaks off in midsentence.

Chudhuri looks in, her expression somber behind the clear shield of her visor. "It's time."

We enter the courtroom through a side door. I go first, with Jaynie behind me, and the others following in a line. According to Chudhuri's security assessment, the chamber was hardened a few years ago to prevent transmission of radio and cell communications, leaving it isolated from the Cloud. The upgrade isn't obvious. Gleaming maple panels line the walls, with the same wood used for all the furnishings.

The judge's bench, with the witness stand, presides at the front of the room, against the backdrop of a high, curved wall. To the right of the bench sits the still-empty jury box. Close to the box, in front of the bar, is a small table where trial counsel wait: Major Adrienne Fong and Captain Elise Bowen, the two army officers assigned to prosecute our case. On the table in front of them are yellow legal pads and two electronic tablets.

The defendants' table is on the left side of the room. It's actually two long tables aligned in an L shape. Major Ogawa and my uncle Brandon Shelley stand at the end of the table closest to the center of the room. Two assistant military attorneys stand at the opposite end of the L, closest to the judge's bench.

Behind the bar, the spectator seats are full. I see my dad in the first row, right behind the defendants' table. He's a handsome man, a few months shy of his fifty-third birthday, who has always been fond of dressing well. These days though, his face is gaunter than it used to be, and his hair is quickly going gray. As I file in, his gaze fixes on me, a haunted look in his eyes as if I'm already a ghost.

Shock hits as I realize who's sitting with him: Lissa's parents, Joe and Amy Dalgaard. I don't want to look at them.

I make myself do it anyway. I meet their eyes. I know what they've lost. I share the pain I see in both their faces. But they're innocent. I'm not.

Major Ogawa signals me to stand aside, directing the others to file in behind the long defendants' table. I pull Jaynie out of the line because I want her beside me, so it's Nolan who leads the others to their seats—all but Harvey, who hangs back. With a dark look, she sends Tuttle, Flynn, and Moon ahead of her. Harvey likes to be close to the action, so she takes the seat next to Jaynie. Then it's me, and then our lead attorneys.

I sit down. I don't turn around. I'm not supposed to speak to anyone behind the bar . . . but I hear Mrs. Dalgaard's whisper, "Bring the bastards down, Jimmy. Make them pay for everything they've done, and everything they failed to do. For Lissa."

I turn to look at her, stunned to think she might be on my side. Tears shimmer in her eyes as she nods.

Under his breath, my uncle tells me, "Turn around and face the court."

I do it, just as the bailiff calls, "All rise!"

A panel of twelve officers known as the court members files into the jury box. Colonel Susan Monteiro enters next, wearing her judge's robes. Monteiro is Caucasian, in her fifties, with a rosy flush in her cheeks and blond hair trimmed short in a feminine cut. She takes her seat behind the bench. To her right is a large American flag draped around a vertical pole. Mounted on the wall above her is a bronze medallion, three feet across, depicting an American eagle. Judge Monteiro surveys the courtroom with a congenial expression. Then she cocks her head to one side and asks the court members, "Shall we begin?"

When it's agreed we are ready to start, her gaze shifts to the table occupied by trial counsel. "Government, do you have an opening statement to present to the court?"

Major Fong stands. "Yes, Your Honor."

"Then please proceed."

Major Fong steps away from the prosecution's table. She's a woman of moderate height. Her figure reflects the gathering thickness of middle age, giving her a sturdy dignity as she turns in her immaculate Class A's to face the officers seated in the jury box.

The function of the court members is the same as that of a civilian jury: to find a verdict. They are all either majors or captains. Major Fong addresses them with an opening strike that takes me by surprise. "We are in the presence of heroes," she says in a hushed, respectful tone. She half turns, her hand palm-up in a graceful gesture that takes in me and everyone else at the defendants' table. "These seven defendants before us today—Private Mandy Flynn, Specialist Jayden Moon, Specialist Samuel Tuttle, Specialist Vanessa Harvey, Sergeant Aaron Nolan, Sergeant Jayne Vasquez, and Lieutenant James Shelley—are all heroes, rightfully honored by a grateful nation for the extent of their service and for the remarkable actions they undertook on the night of November eleventh, when this country faced a crisis the equal of any we have known in our history. Every one of them is a hero of the action at Black Cross."

She turns away from us, to address directly the panel of officers in the jury box. "It's a tragedy of human nature that heroes can sometimes become larger than life, even in their own eyes. This case does not turn on venal behavior or greed. No, it is a case founded on the arrogance of heroes who came to believe too deeply in their own righteousness.

"This is a case about what happens when good soldiers, acting on limited information, are persuaded to take the law into their own hands. We will show that they conspired together and undertook the brutal abduction and illegal incarceration of Thelma Sheridan, an American citizen neither accused nor convicted of any crime, and we will further show that in the course of this action they murdered four employees of Vanda-Sheridan, and compelled the service of Vanda-Sheridan pilot Ilima LaSalle. This was the so-called First Light mission, which took place from November eighteenth through November twentieth.

"The evidence the government intends to present will show that every one of the defendants knew without doubt the actions they took against Ms. Sheridan and her employees were illegal, that the actions of the First Light mission violated the sovereignty of the United States, and that the defendants expected to face a court-martial for their role.

"The government will also show how the actions of Colonel Steven Kendrick, now deceased, initiated the events that led to this court-martial.

"Primary among the evidence the government will present is the video library compiled by the defendants themselves, documenting the events of November eighteenth through twentieth, and turned over as evidence by defense counsel.

"Another key piece of evidence is a video deposition of Thelma Sheridan, who is prevented from acting as a witness in this court due to her continued incarceration."

I feel Jaynie tense beside me. I turn to meet her gaze. We're both wondering the same thing: Did trial counsel just say that Sheridan is still alive? Jaynie raises an eyebrow as if to say, *Maybe, maybe*, while Major Fong continues to speak:

"The government would like to note two key witnesses we'll be calling during the proceedings.

"First, Blaise—a.k.a. Blue—Parker, presently in federal

custody for his involvement in the nuclear terrorism of November eleventh. Mr. Parker will testify to events occurring at Black Cross that directly influenced the subsequent actions that concern us today.

"And another key witness is Special Agent Eve England, who will testify to discussions she held with Colonel Steven Kendrick following the events at Black Cross.

"We will also be hearing from expert witnesses, among them legal scholars testifying to the meaning and implications of a soldier's service oath, and the limits of action inherent in that oath.

"The government is confident that after evidence is presented, you, the court members, will find that all seven defendants committed the offenses as charged."

It is of course a kind of theater, and we are actors in a play whose script we helped to write. The evidence is already logged and reviewed. The witnesses are known, along with the testimonies they will deliver. Nothing is hidden. Nothing held back. It's only the concluding verdict that's unknown, and even that is fairly certain.

Major Fong nods to her co-counsel. Both seem satisfied with her presentation. She returns to her seat, while the judge's attention shifts to Major Ogawa.

"Defense, will you present your opening statement at this time?"

"Yes, Your Honor." Ogawa stands up, steps away from the table, and turns to the court members, this collection of officers in the jury box. He surveys them slowly. Then he says, "On the day you were inducted into the army, you took this oath: 'I do solemnly swear that I will support and defend the Constitution of the United States against all enemies, foreign and domestic.'" He turns halfway, to look at us. "Every defendant seated before you today spoke this same oath. We will show that the actions taken by the defendants during the First Light mission were taken in defense of this oath.

"We will show that the nuclear terrorism of November eleventh spawned a criminal cover-up involving both government officials and military command. The defendants, through their heroic efforts at Black Cross, were aware of legitimate evidence strongly implicating Thelma Sheridan as a primary participant in the terrorist conspiracy. Lieutenant Shelley, a dedicated soldier who has time and again risked his life in defense of his country, was left with only one way to defend his oath of office." Ogawa nods at me, and then he points to each of my soldiers, speaking their names, "Vasquez, Harvey, Moon, Flynn, Tuttle, and Nolan. You've all heard of them. All of them are heroes of Black Cross whose oath of enlistment bound them to do what they did during the First Light mission. It was not a task they wanted. It was thrust upon them when individuals in authority, individuals within our government and within our command structure, abandoned their own duty to defend the Constitution of this country. First Light was a desperate attempt to secure the justice promised in our Constitution, a document that makes no allowance for exceptional privilege to the wealthy and the powerful. We will show that corruption in the ranks and in the government forced these loyal patriots to a foreign court to find the justice promised to us, but no longer available, under our constitutional system."

What he says is true. We *were* forced to a foreign court, but if that foreign court allowed Thelma Sheridan to be murdered, then we will have failed to deliver her to justice—and after that, what defense do we have left?

Major Ogawa returns to his seat. I scan the panel of officers. A few faces look thoughtful, but most just present stonewall expressions. Everyone here is aware of the cameras recording these proceedings, and these officers know that both the attorneys and the media will be analyzing their facial expressions to weigh the effectiveness of the arguments. So most give away as little as they can.

The media will also be looking at us, the defendants, hunting for signs of fear, outrage, denial, approval—any hint of human emotion. And why not give them what they want? It would be the smart thing. It might get us sympathy from their audience, get the public on our side. But none of us do. It's not our way. We listen, wearing the same emotionless expression as two-thirds of the jury.

The judge is the only one on this side of the bar who looks at ease. She weaves her fingers together, rests her chin on them, and gazes out at her courtroom. "Well. It's nearly lunchtime. Shall we break until the afternoon?"

Assistant trial counsel Captain Elise Bowen spends the opening hour of the afternoon session reading stipulations into the court record. These documents describe the basic sequence of events that took place during the initial hours of the First Light mission, ending at 0132 on November 19, when our C-17 lifted off from Alaska.

We have all seen the stipulations; we studied them, made our changes, and approved them weeks ago. As Bowen finishes each reading, the judge requires every defendant to stand up and verbally acknowledge that they accept these stipulations as fact, and will not contest them.

It's boring as hell, but at least we won't have to waste time and money arguing over the minutiae of the mission. At the end of it, Captain Bowen gets the bailiff to lower a projection screen from the ceiling. It's positioned behind the court clerk, to Judge Monteiro's right, which puts it at a distance from the jury box, but the screen is big, so it doesn't matter.

Bowen projects an outline of the events. Then she expends
another fifteen minutes going over it line by line, just to
make sure everyone is clear on the sequence of our Alaskan
adventurism. She reaches the last line and turns to the court.
"Sixteen hours after fleeing Alaska, the C-17 arrived in con-
tested territory on the African continent, setting down at
an airport in the city of Niamey, where Thelma Sheridan
was transferred into the custody of a provisional government headed by Ahab Matugo—and there she remains."

Captain Bowen really isn't much of a storyteller. She's
left out all the exciting parts about our flight to Niamey. I
scribble a note—*What about the fighters?*—and pass it to
Ogawa. He looks at me like I'm a slow child who's trying
his patience.

"Defense," the judge says, "I believe you have a response?"

Ogawa stands. "Yes, ma'am." He signals the bailiff, and
a new chart appears on the screen. This one details the
incidents that occurred during our flight. "At twelve four-
teen UTC—Coordinated Universal Time—two fighter jets
approached the C-17. These planes then accompanied the
C-17 for many hours. We will be presenting evidence that
these fighters belonged to the United States Air Force. Six
and a half hours after they first approached, the pilot of
one of the fighters ordered the C-17 to land. When this
order was ignored, the fighters began a campaign of intimi-
dation and harassment, endangering the lives of all those
aboard the C-17, including the three civilians. The aggres-
sive actions of the fighters culminated at two minutes after
midnight, UTC, on November twentieth, when one of the
planes fired a missile in what we will show to be an attempt
to shoot down the unarmed C-17 along with the defendants and the civilian passengers. When this attempt failed,
the air force fighters withdrew and the C-17 continued to
Niamey without further incident."

I wait for him to say more, to ask the questions that are critical to our defense: Under whose command were the fighters operating? And who issued the order to shoot us down? But he's done. He returns to his seat, and the judge calls for a half-hour recess.

The mood as we wait in the conference room is glum. "We look guilty as hell," Tuttle grumbles. "Shit, *I'd* convict us."

"We *are* guilty," Harvey snaps. "If all you're looking at is what we did, well, we fucking did it. But that's not what it's about. It's about *why* we had to do it."

I add, "And we get a chance to talk about that when the prosecution is done boring us with the facts everyone already knows. So when you go back in there, Tuttle, don't look like you're scared and don't look like you're worried. If we want to pull this off, we've got to believe in what we're doing."

If Matt Ransom were still alive, this little speech would have earned me an enthusiastic *Hoo-yah!* But the only response I get is a sort-of apology from Tuttle. "You don't have to worry about me, sir. I'll do my part."

Back in the courtroom, lead trial counsel Fong takes over. "Your Honor," she says, facing the judge, "I would like to enter into evidence a video deposition obtained from a witness in this case whose current circumstances do not allow her to be present."

So our first witness is Thelma Sheridan.

I knew about the deposition, though I haven't seen it yet. I lean over, intending to whisper to Major Ogawa, but he's already on his feet, speaking my concerns. "Your Honor, the government has stated this deposition was recorded seven days ago. I ask that the government read into the court record Thelma Sheridan's current status and condition."

Monteiro does not look like she approves of this at all. But if Sheridan is dead, it's better if the court members hear about it now, instead of at the end of our defense. "All right," Monteiro says. She turns to Fong. "Major, are you able to satisfy this request by the defense?"

Fong says, "I'd like to request a short recess before I respond."

"How long will you need?"

"Fifteen minutes, ma'am."

"Granted."

So we file out again, to sit in stony silence around the table in the conference room. When we return, Fong stands again, grim faced. "Your Honor, the government is unable to report on the current status and condition of Thelma Sheridan. We request that we be allowed to proceed with the video deposition, which has been corroborated, and already reviewed by the defense."

"Granted," Monteiro says. "Proceed."

Thelma Sheridan hasn't lost any of her ferocity. Dressed in a gray cotton smock and gray pajama pants, she's sitting on a steel chair in a concrete room with stained walls and no windows. The room's light has a yellow cast. Her chin is tucked. She looks up from under her brow line, a fighter, a cornered predator, poised to spring.

"State your name for the record," a woman's voice says in crisp, accented English. Sheridan's lip curls as if this is something to fight over. But she complies. "Thelma Han Sheridan. I am an American citizen, the victim of a kidnapping, and I am being held illegally—"

"I remind you, Ms. Sheridan, this is a video deposition

intended to cover the events of November eighteenth to twentieth. Your recorded testimony will supplement an extensive video record, and will be used in court-martial proceedings in the United States."

"Yes, ma'am. And I would like to attend those court-martial proceedings, in person. As the victim in this crime, it's my right."

The interrogator's voice is not British, but it reflects a British education, with every word crisply pronounced as she states in a matter-of-fact tone, "Ma'am, it is not presently possible for you to attend, as you are engaged in your own separate legal proceeding. But the United States values your testimony. So could you please describe exactly what happened the night of November eighteenth to nineteenth."

Sheridan's brows are not so well groomed as they used to be, her hair has lost its shiny, metallic polish, but there is still a staggering sense of power in the way she handles herself. She settles back in her chair, squaring her shoulders, and she speaks. "On the night of November eighteenth to nineteenth, a rogue squad of United States Army soldiers, under the command of US Army lieutenant James Shelley, along with a senior officer now deceased, trespassed on my private property, kidnapped myself and two of my employees, stole a two-hundred-twenty-million-dollar transport plane, and used it to convey me halfway around the world—endangering my life multiple times during the flight—before finally delivering me here, where I have been illegally and inhumanely incarcerated ever since. I demand my immediate release and restoration to my country of origin so that I may pursue this case in person, as is my right as an American citizen."

"Ms. Sheridan," the interrogator says in a tone of angelic patience, "you stated 'a rogue squad of United States Army soldiers.' How did you arrive at this identification?"

Her smile is thin and hungry. "Lieutenant James Shelley is no stranger to me. We had met and talked before the night of the assault. I knew him by his voice, even when he was still wearing his LCS helmet."

"LCS?"

"Linked combat squad. Cyborg soldiers. Their wiring ties them together. Where you find one, you find more than one. Lieutenant Shelley had his squad with him. He led them in a criminal enterprise. I believe that's called undue influence?"

Harvey growls under her breath, "Because the rest of us can't think for ourselves?"

I swear Jaynie kicks her under the table.

Discipline in my squad is definitely slipping.

It's late afternoon, but the judge is under orders to get this court-martial done with all possible speed, so there's no talk of adjourning for the day. Instead, Monteiro turns to address trial counsel. "Government, are you ready to call your first witness?"

"Yes, ma'am," Major Fong replies. "The United States calls Blaise Matthew Parker."

For a second, I'm thinking, *Who?* Then I figure it out. Blue Parker, the pretty blond terrorist who blew up America. Thelma Sheridan's fall guy.

There's an angry murmur from the spectators as Parker is led in through a side door, a US marshal on either side of him. He's wearing an off-white collared shirt, slacks, and dress shoes. He could be on his way to the office, except for the leg shackles and wrist cuffs.

It's the first time I've seen him in person. At Black Cross, I only glimpsed him briefly through a video feed when Jaynie and Tuttle pulled him out of his spider hole. He looks different now. His head is shaved to a stubble so pale it looks white. His face is thin, bony. He stares at the floor, his lips parted like he's concentrating hard on every shuffling step as he makes his way to the witness stand. To me it looks like he's on his way to God, and I wonder if he's had a stroke. He pleaded guilty to the long list of charges compiled against him and is presently awaiting sentencing in federal court.

One of the marshals assists him to sit down. His blue eyes are not as bright as I remember. He glances at the judge, and then at the defendants' table, as the bailiff chants the oath. "Do you swear that the evidence you shall give in the case now in hearing shall be the truth, the whole truth, and nothing but the truth?"

Blue Parker turns to the bailiff and nods. "I do, sir. So help me God and Jesus."

He sounds sincere.

Of course, he immolated an estimated ninety-three thousand people, wounded many times that number, and left the entire country in shambles. I imagine he spends a lot of time talking to God about all that.

Major Fong moves in. "For the record, you're Blaise Matthew Parker of Dallas, Texas?"

"Yes, ma'am."

"And you are currently in federal custody awaiting sentencing?"

"Yes. Yes, ma'am, I am."

"And what sentence do you expect to receive?"

"I expect to receive the death penalty, ma'am."

"Have you been offered a lesser sentence for your cooperation in testifying in this court-martial?"

"No, ma'am. I have not."

"Where were you at approximately zero four fifteen—that's four fifteen a.m. on the civilian clock—on November twelfth of this past year?"

He stares down at his hands. "I was at Black Cross, ma'am." He realizes his voice is too soft, and leans back, raising his head, speaking louder. "In the control room."

Major Fong walks back to her table, where she picks up a printed photograph. "Your Honor, the United States would move to enter prosecution exhibit thirty-seven for identification into evidence."

"May I see it, please?"

Fong crosses the floor and hands it to Monteiro, who looks at it briefly and hands it back. Fong then shows it to Blue Parker. "Have you seen this man before?"

Blue flinches back. He squeezes his eyes shut. "Yes, ma'am," he whispers. Then he repeats it louder. "Yes, I've seen him before."

"And where did you see him?"

"At Black Cross. That's Colonel Kendrick. He was in command."

"You mean Colonel Steven Kendrick, who was in command of the US Army soldiers who took initial custody of you at Black Cross?"

"Yes, ma'am."

"Mr. Parker, did you ever see, speak with, or otherwise communicate with Colonel Kendrick at any time other than the morning of November twelfth?"

"No, ma'am."

"And on that morning, did Colonel Kendrick question you regarding your co-conspirators in the act of nuclear terrorism to which you have already pleaded guilty?"

"Yes, ma'am. He wanted to know if Vanda-Sheridan was one of us."

"Are you referring to the corporation Vanda-Sheridan?"

"He wanted to know if Thelma Sheridan and Carl Vanda were part of it."

"Part of your conspiracy?"

"Yes, ma'am."

"And what did you tell him?"

"I told him that . . . that Thelma Sheridan supplied the . . . the nuclear devices, but . . . I only said it because I was afraid. He said he would kill me. And I was afraid."

FaceValue reports that he's telling the truth, and I know he was afraid. He was fucking terrified.

Fong asks, "Were you telling the truth when you told Colonel Kendrick that Thelma Sheridan supplied the nuclear devices?"

His mouth is open; his shoulders are visibly rising and falling as he draws in shallow, shuddering breaths. FaceValue redlines him as he says, "No, ma'am. I was not telling the truth."

"You lied to Colonel Kendrick about Thelma Sheridan's involvement?"

"Yes, ma'am. I did. Thelma Sheridan did not supply the nuclear devices. She was not involved."

He's lying now.

I look at the officers in the jury box. Most of them are looking at Blue like he's a slug they'd love to step on, but none of them are wearing farsights, and by the terms of a negotiated agreement I know that none are equipped with an overlay. So they've got nothing but gut feeling to go on, in deciding if he's lying now.

"Mr. Parker, what company provided the mercenaries used by you for protection at Black Cross?"

"Uther-Fen Protective Services, ma'am."

Fong returns to her table, picks up a paper document in a clear plastic sleeve, and returns with it to the bench. "Your Honor, the United States would move to enter prosecution exhibit forty-nine for identification into evidence."

Exhibit 49 is a document verifying that Uther-Fen is a subsidiary of Vanda-Sheridan. It's as if Fong is trying to make our case for us, except I know she's not. "Mr. Parker, when you contracted Uther-Fen Protective Services to provide security at Black Cross, did you know the company was owned by Vanda-Sheridan?"

Blue is calmer this time, but he still gets redlined when he says, "No, ma'am. I did not."

"Did you inform Uther-Fen that you intended to commit an act of terrorism?"

"No, ma'am. I did not."

"Did you insinuate or otherwise imply to Uther-Fen that you intended to commit an illegal activity?"

"No. No, I did not. It was in the contract. They would not commit or participate in any act that violated the law."

Fong enters yet another piece of evidence into the record: an electronic copy of the Uther-Fen contract, digitally signed by Blue Parker. "No further questions, Your Honor."

"Cross-examination," the judge says.

Major Ogawa is already on his feet. "Yes, ma'am. Mr. Parker, do you have any relatives who survived the assault on Black Cross?"

Parker looks at Fong. If he's hoping she'll object, he's disappointed. "Yes, sir. I do, sir."

"Could you tell us who those relatives are?"

"My wife, sir, and my two children."

"How old are your children?"

"Garrett is four. Josh is two."

"And where is their mother?"

"In federal prison, sir."

"And your children? Where are they?"

"They're with my . . . my wife's sister." He turns to the judge. "Do I have to say where they are?"

Monteiro tells him, "Please state what continent they're on."

"They're in Europe, but they're anonymous. People want to kill them."

Ogawa nods. This is the testimony he was after. "Mr. Parker, did you agree to lie under oath regarding the confession you made to Colonel Kendrick, in order to protect your family from reprisals?"

Parker's mouth opens. He looks horrified. "No, sir. I did *not.*"

Redline.

But hey, the man's already murdered ninety-three thousand people. A few more lies aren't going to make his time in Hell any worse.

"No more questions, Your Honor."

"Okay," Monteiro says. "It's now seventeen seventeen, or five seventeen p.m. on the civilian clock. Is there anything else we need to address today?"

Fong stands up. "Your Honor, the United States requests a brief eight oh two."

There's a whisper of surprise from the spectators behind us. I turn to my uncle. He's already scrawling on his legal pad: *802 = conference.*

"All right," Monteiro says, though she does not look pleased. "Defense, any objection?"

"No objection, ma'am."

"Then we will recess until seventeen thirty-five."

After the judge and court members have left, we are escorted to our usual conference room. I've been sitting down all day, so while we wait, I pace back and forth. Flynn is in the bathroom, and Harvey's waiting to take her turn. Jaynie is standing in a corner, her arms crossed, eyeing the door. Nolan, Tuttle, and Moon are dispersed around the table.

In a low voice, Tuttle says, "I felt the hair on the back of my neck stand up when they brought Parker in. Ninety-three thousand people dead. I was scared somebody in the audience would try to kill him. Set off a bomb or something."

"Court security screens for weapons and explosives," I say. "And after yesterday, they're going to be extra vigilant."

"Yes, sir."

I reach the end of the room and start back, passing Jaynie. She's still looking lean and muscular, despite the months spent cooped up in a tiny cell. My mind flashes back to Fort Dassari. I think about the way she looked fresh after a shower, wearing only panties and a thin T-shirt that didn't hide much. And then I catch myself. *What the fuck is wrong with me?*

Flynn steps out of the bathroom. She plops down at the table next to Moon and leans against his shoulder, heaving a dramatic sigh. "I can't fuckin' wait to go on leave."

"Permanent leave, probably," Moon grumbles. He looks at me. "They're going to kick us out of the army one way or another, aren't they, LT? Whether we get found innocent or not?"

I turn around again. "Yes."

"*Fuck*," Flynn whispers, looking scared for the first time. "Even if we're not guilty? How is that fair?"

It's not about fair and I don't bother to answer, but Moon does.

"Hey," he says softly. "It'll work out, one way or another."

I'm eyeing Jaynie again, thinking about what she looks like under her Class A's. She scowls, and for a second I feel like a kid in trouble. But she's not looking at me. She's looking past me, at Flynn.

I turn around to find Flynn cuddled in Moon's arm, her upturned lips brushing his, like they're a high school couple.

Jaynie and Nolan explode simultaneously.

"*Private Flynn!*"

"Specialist Moon!"

"On your feet, now!"

Chair legs screech across the floor. Both Moon and Flynn look shocked as they jump to their feet, coming to attention, their shoulders squared and their gazes fixed straight ahead.

My sergeants are responsible for immediate personnel issues, for which I am grateful because I am not in a good position to handle this one. I put on my standard-issue stonewall expression and hope no one will see through it, while Jaynie takes the floor. She steps around the table until she's standing right beside Moon and Flynn. "You want to fuck each other?" she shouts. "Because that is some twisted shit. We are brothers- and sisters-in-arms here. Brothers and sisters! And brothers and sisters *do not* fuck each other! Is that *understood*?"

Harvey emerges from the bathroom, her lips parted in awe. The door to the hall opens at the same time and Master Sergeant Chudhuri looks in. Meanwhile, Flynn and Moon bark in unison, "Yes, sergeant!"

Moon adds, in a tone of confusion, "It was an accident, sergeant."

"Accidents don't happen in my squad, Moon."

Chudhuri withdraws, closing the door again.

Poor Flynn is horrified. "What the fuck is wrong with me?" she whispers.

"There's nothing wrong with you," I growl.

"Lieutenant," Jaynie snaps.

"It's not her fault!" I tap my head, but I don't meet her eye. "It's all the time we spend alone in our cells." The skullcaps and my skullnet are always working. No one talks about it much, but one effect is that we start perceiving one another as siblings. Then incest revulsion takes over and there's not much incentive left to try to get into someone's bed.

But it works that way only when we're living together, training together, patrolling as a squad.

"Now that we're aware of it," I add, speaking half to myself, "be vigilant, and don't let it happen again."

We wait in guilty silence for two minutes, and then Chudhuri comes in again. "Let's go. They want you back in court."

"Best face forward," I warn them. "Don't give anything away."

We return to our seats at the defendants' table. When my uncle sits down next to me, I ask, "So what was the conference about?"

He leans close, as if he intends to whisper something, but he changes his mind and writes it down instead on the corner of his legal pad, in tiny black letters: *Carl Vanda.*

The judge sweeps in, the bailiff calls, "All rise." We do it, though I'm still staring at that name as Monteiro takes her seat behind the bench.

As soon as we resume our seats, Jaynie reaches for the pad, dragging it closer until she can read the tiny print. Then she shoves it back like it's toxic.

"The court is called to order," Monteiro says brusquely, and I get the impression she's not happy. "Government, are you ready to call your next witness?"

"Yes, Your Honor," Major Fong says. "The United States calls Carl Reed Vanda."

It's the first time I've ever seen him in person. He's tall and gaunt, with buzz-cut gray hair, a scarred face like a man who's been in knife fights, a crooked nose, and electric blue eyes so bright he has to be wearing contacts or using an artificial pigment in his irises. His shoulders are square, his back too straight—broken and reset maybe, after the plane crash in Africa less than a year ago. He walks with a slight limp, favoring his right hip.

As he takes the witness stand, he looks across the courtroom, and when he IDs me, when those blue eyes meet mine, they make a promise. They tell me they are going to watch while my world burns down around me.

I'm not sure, but I think my glare is promising him the same thing.

My uncle puts a hand on my arm. "Stop it."

This man murdered my Lissa. Carl Vanda. He caused her death as surely as if he'd put a gun to her head and pulled the trigger himself.

"Jimmy."

The icon in my overlay indicating activity in my skullnet is glowing in the corner of my vision, and as my skullnet coaxes my brain to pump comforting chemicals into my system, my rage becomes a colder, more patient thing. I look at my uncle.

Okay? he mouths, while Carl Vanda swears to tell the truth.

I nod.

I kidnapped Carl Vanda's wife. Lissa is dead because of that, because of *me*, because I dragged her into this mess, because I wanted to slam a dragon.

Major Fong begins: "For the record, your name is Carl Reed Vanda and you are the president and owner of Uther-Fen Protective Services?"

"Yes."

She asks him to identify and review the contract for services at Black Cross, and to affirm his acquaintance with Blue Parker. "Does the contract name specific employees who were to be assigned to Black Cross?"

"No. There's no need. All our personnel are fully trained and licensed."

"Did those Uther-Fen employees who worked at Black Cross speak English?"

"Yes. Not well, maybe, but adequately."

"Did Blue Parker request that the Uther-Fen personnel assigned to him be foreign nationals with poor English skills?"

"Yes, he did. The little shit—"

"You will express yourself with decorum, Mr. Vanda," the judge warns, "or be held in contempt."

"Yes, *ma'am*," he answers in drawn-out sarcasm. "Mr. Parker informed me the Black Cross facility was being used to develop proprietary technology and that he wanted to minimize the risk of industrial espionage."

"Did you find such a nonspecific explanation to be suspicious?" Major Fong asks him.

"I find every one of my clients suspicious. Everyone is playing their own game."

"But you did as you were asked, and supplied Mr. Parker with non-English speakers—"

Fong breaks off as a low buzz ignites behind me. It's coming from the spectator seats, somewhere to my left. Everyone in the courtroom turns to look, but there's nothing to see.

"Bailiff," the judge says. "Summon security now."

I'm up. I can't help it. I'm an LCS soldier, trained to think on my feet. My squad stands up too as the buzzing gains a companion sound, like the vibration of some high-speed windup toy against a wooden surface.

"What the hell?" a man shouts, cringing back against the woman seated beside him. Several other people cry out and then a mechanical bug with a cylindrical body smaller than my little finger rises on shimmering, buzzing dragonfly wings. Four limbs, needle thin and curved like pincers, hang beneath it. For a second, it hovers above the audience, pivoting to survey the room with a tiny, gleaming glass eye.

I flash on the fact that the courtroom is sealed against radio transmissions. So either the robo-bug is being controlled from within this room or the device is autonomous. I'm betting autonomous. I'm betting a pattern-recognition program is analyzing input gathered by that glass eye.

My dad and Lissa's parents are an arm's reach away on the other side of the bar. Keeping my gaze fixed on the toy-size drone, I say, "Dad! All of you—down on the floor!"

They drop, while I reach behind me, grabbing the legal pad with Carl Vanda's name printed in the corner.

It's like the little drone was waiting for me to move. It shoots toward me, almost too fast to follow. "Fall back!" Jaynie shouts as I swat hard at it with the yellow legal pad. The pad has a big surface, but I almost miss anyway, because the robo-bug is not coming for me after all. It shoots between me and Jaynie. I barely clip it on one wing, but that's enough to unbalance it. I turn in time to see it spiral into the front of the judge's bench. There's a loud *crack* as it hits the wood. The buzzing stops, and it clatters against the floor.

Behind the bench, the judge is standing up, her expression furious. "No one leaves this room without my permission!" A squad of MPs pours in. She gestures at their sergeant. "Secure the public door. Assign someone to guard the witness." Then she turns to the officers in the jury box. All of them are on their feet. "Members of the court, you will form a perimeter around the spectators. See that everyone remains in their seat until they can be searched and interviewed." Master Sergeant Chudhuri appears fully rigged at the side entrance, catching the judge's angry eye. "Master Sergeant! You are the prisoner detail?"

"Yes, ma'am!"

"Ensure there is a perimeter guard, and then return the defendants to holding."

So we leave. I catch my dad's eye before we file out. He's furious with the MPs yelling, telling everybody to remain seated, to be quiet—"No talking!"—and to put their hands on their heads. But he nods at me and mouths, *Be careful.*

Then we're out the back door. Chudhuri doesn't bother with cuffs. Omer, Vitali, and Phelps fall in around us as we walk fast past the judges' offices. We get on the elevator and the doors close.

In a voice low with fury Jaynie says, "Goddamn it, Shelley, that bug was aimed at Carl Vanda." And with a surreal sense of shock, I know she's right. "They got Sheridan already, and today they came for Vanda. That bug had to be carrying a poison payload. You just fucking saved his life."

"Quiet in the ranks, Vasquez," Chudhuri warns.

But there isn't anything left to say.

Am I too paranoid?

A degree of paranoia is a healthy thing, but ever since we returned from First Light, I've expected to be murdered . . . *assassinated* might be a better word.

On Sunday, I was sure the president's visit would be followed by a visit from his special-ops soldiers, but it didn't happen.

On Monday, I never questioned that the mercenaries who came after us had come to kill me, but I was wrong.

Today, I was certain the toy drone was aimed at me because I've come to think of what's going on around me as *my* story—but there are a lot of stories, there are factions in this drama that I'm not even aware of. One of those factions tried to murder Carl Vanda today. It would have been a public service, but I got in the way.

I wonder that the Red didn't warn me. It's not on my side, I know that. And it's not always present. It's operating around the world, allocating resources to affect the lives of millions, maybe billions, hooking in at critical moments and then disappearing again.

If the Red had hooked into my head before I reentered the courtroom, if it had given me just a hint, a suggestion to stay the fuck out of the action, then Carl Vanda would be dead now.

But I sensed nothing. It's been months since the Red was last inside my head, steering me, offering me guidance. All that's left is the automated nightly upload of my experiences. I've been left on my own. I need to accept that it's going to be that way.

And yeah, when it comes to Carl Vanda, I'm okay with murder. A surviving whisper of conscience tries to make me squirm. It doesn't work.

In the morning, Major Ogawa brings the news that no one was arrested for launching the robo-bug. "No one got into that room without a background check, a full-body scan, and a reason for being there. Afterward, everyone was searched again, and interviewed, but emotional analysis couldn't pick out a suspect."

We're in the cellblock. It's early, and no one is in their Class A's yet, but at the major's request Chudhuri has opened all the cell doors so we can assemble to hear what he has to say.

"So someone planted the device," I say. "Meaning whoever it was, they knew Vanda would be there, even though he was a last-minute witness."

Ogawa doesn't agree with me. "They only had to guess he *might* be there. A microdrone is like a land mine—a cheap and easy weapon. Even something as complex as the robo-bug couldn't have cost more than a few thousand dollars in parts. Make it look like a tube of lipstick or an insulin monitor, drop it in someone's pocket or purse—potentially very effective."

There's a derisive snort from Nolan. Harvey chuckles. Jaynie just crosses her arms and glares at me. Sure—the robo-bug might have been effective if I hadn't gotten in the way.

Moving on to other things, I ask, "Are we on today?"

"Oh nine hundred. Judge Monteiro wants this circus over."

"And Vanda? Is he going to finish testifying?"

"My guess? We won't see him again. Fong put him on the stand as a stunt, but it was a mistake. He doesn't play well with others. But we'll find out for sure when court's in session."

Flynn is still dressed in only shorts and a T-shirt when she stands on her toes to see past Nolan's shoulder. "When do we get to tell our side?" she asks.

"Friday, if we're lucky. Otherwise, next week."

"I fucking want this to be over. I swear I'm going to kill somebody if I don't get laid."

Ogawa is right. Carl Vanda does not reappear in court, and the judge strikes his prior testimony.

Despite yesterday's security breach, the spectator seats are full. I don't see Lissa's parents, but my dad is there, right behind the defendants' table. He's sitting next to a fifty-something woman who looks like an older, darker-skinned version of Harvey—if Harvey were to put on thirty pounds, grow out her hair, and style it in a neat perm. When Harvey nods to her, I know it's her mother, come down from Pittsburgh.

The morning discussion turns to skullcaps and the neural enhancements of LCS soldiers. Before the weekend, trial counsel was willing to let us argue that the skullcaps interfered with our mental processes to the extent that we could not be held responsible for our actions. That story has changed. Three expert witnesses do their best to portray us as efficient, rational soldiers, fully responsible for the decisions we make. Ogawa asks a few questions on cross, all aimed at enforcing this conclusion.

So by the end of the morning session on day two, we have conceded that we did what we are accused of doing and that we were responsible for our actions.

This has to be the easiest case Major Fong has ever prosecuted.

The afternoon is more interesting.

On the witness stand is General Brittney Ahmet, a two-star in the Pentagon's intelligence hierarchy. She's tall—over six feet—and rail thin, with steel-gray hair, dark eyes, and a grim expression.

Major Fong presents to the judge a paper document in a plastic sleeve. "Your Honor, the United States moves to enter prosecution exhibit fifty-six for identification into evidence."

"Prosecution exhibit fifty-six for identification is admitted."

Fong shows the document to General Ahmet. "Could you tell us what this is?"

"It's a printed facsimile of a classification report."

"Could you explain what that means?"

"Yes. When a document is designated as classified national security information, a report is issued indicating the classification level of that document, the reason for classification, and the duration of that status. The report takes the form of an electronic document, but it can be rendered in hard copy, as in this case."

"And who prepared this classification report?"

"I did."

"And what document does this classification report refer to?"

"I cannot name the document or its author in open court, but in a general sense it's a document describing preliminary findings at Black Cross."

"According to your classification report, you designated this document as top secret, is that correct?"

"Yes."

"Why top secret?"

"As stated in the classification report, the document includes facts and information that already carry a top secret classification. In addition, much of the evidence cited in the document is uncorroborated, and may well have been misinterpreted. As I said, this was a preliminary document, and as such it contained extensive errors. I determined that the release of such sensitive misinformation would create a serious security breach."

"General Ahmet, did you classify this document as top secret to conceal a violation of the law?"

"I did not."

"Did you classify this document as top secret to prevent embarrassment to a person or organization?"

"No, ma'am, I did not. I classified the document as top secret for reasons of national security, and for those reasons alone."

Major Ogawa undertakes his cross-examination, polite as always, but he shows no sign of being intimidated by the rank of the witness. "General Ahmet, what led you to conclude the document contained extensive errors?"

"I am not at liberty to talk about that, Major."

"Did you arrive at this decision on your own, or were you advised that the document contained errors?"

"Again, Major, I am not at liberty to discuss classified matters."

Major Ogawa turns to the judge. "Your Honor, the role of the chain of command is material to our defense. With all due respect to General Ahmet, the statement that the document 'contained extensive errors' is insufficient without some indication of how that conclusion was reached."

To her credit, Monteiro accepts this argument with a nod. "General Ahmet, please answer Major Ogawa's question. Were you advised the document contained errors?"

The general scowls. Maybe she's thinking she doesn't want to take this all on her own shoulders, because she concedes to Monteiro's request. "Yes, Your Honor. I was advised of that fact."

"Thank you, General."

Ogawa is too smart to gloat. Keeping his expression carefully neutral, he asks, "Who advised you that the document contained extensive errors?"

"I am not at liberty to reveal that."

Ogawa turns again to the judge. This time Monteiro punts. "I'm not going to compel an answer at this time. You may call the witness again on defense, and we'll decide at that time if there is sufficient cause to conduct a closed session."

"Yes, ma'am," Ogawa says. "Thank you, General. No more questions."

"The United States calls Special Agent Eve England."

I know her name from the witness list: the FBI agent who conducted the initial investigation of Black Cross. She looks to be in her early thirties. The business suit she wears—charcoal slacks and coat—is fitted perfectly to her lean, athletic figure. She pauses as she enters, her gaze surveying the courtroom, lingering on those of us occupying the defendants' table. She looks to be of pure European descent, her fair skin lightly freckled and her dark-red hair smoothed and confined in a short ponytail.

Eve England was Kendrick's contact in the FBI, the agent who warned him that all evidence pointing to Thelma Sheridan had been locked up in a top secret file.

Kendrick knew her. How? Did he use his network of contacts to get in touch with her? Or did he know her already? Was she—*is* she—part of the organization, that network of anonymous conspirators who planned and financed the First Light mission carried out by my squad?

Kendrick told me almost nothing about the organization. I don't blame him for that. He knew the Red was inside my head and that no secret was safe with me. I wish like hell he were still with us, though. He knew about a hundred times what I know about people, about how power is distributed, about who gives a shit for their oath of office and who's just playing the power game to climb up over the fallen bodies and get above the blood.

Eve England is a witness for the prosecution. I wonder what Kendrick would have made of that.

"Special Agent England," Major Fong says, "could you please describe your role at Black Cross."

"I was never at Black Cross, ma'am." Her voice is low and smooth, each word crisply pronounced. "Army Intelligence did the initial on-scene investigation at Black Cross. My assignment was to inventory the evidence for the FBI case file."

"And where did you perform this function?"

"At a secure facility outside of San Antonio, ma'am."

"What sort of evidence did you have access to? That is, what form was this evidence in?"

"The evidence included documents, photos, audio recordings, and video, including video interviews of survivors. Fingerprints. Biological samples of the deceased. Air samples. Weapon inventories—"

"Is it fair to say there was an overwhelming amount of potential evidence collected at Black Cross?"

"No, ma'am. A large amount of evidence was collected, but I would not describe it as overwhelming."

"What was your relationship with Colonel Steven Kendrick?"

"Colonel Kendrick visited my work site on November fourteenth. He had full security clearance, and I was told by my supervisor to answer his questions. He wanted to hear my interpretation of the events leading up to the nuclear terrorism of November eleventh, based on the evidence I'd been examining. I provided him with a verbal summary, and on November fifteenth, I used a secure connection to transfer to him a preliminary report packaging key digital evidence, interviews, and my conclusions based on the same."

"Were you aware, Ms. England, that other investigations relating to November eleventh were under way?"

"Yes, ma'am, of course I was aware of this."

"Was this 'preliminary report' you provided to Colonel Kendrick a sufficient explanation of the events leading to November eleventh?"

"Sufficient, ma'am?"

"Sufficient to prove the guilt of the involved parties, Ms. England. Did this report include evidence to prove without doubt the identities and the roles of those who participated in the terrorism of November eleventh, evidence so profound there was *no* possibility of your conclusions being contraindicated by further evidence that might have come to light by virtue of any of the hundreds of other ongoing investigations?"

England lowers her chin. She leans forward, just a little. "I felt that to be the case, ma'am."

Eve England does not rattle easily, a fact that has Fong deeply annoyed. She paces a few steps away, then turns and asks, "What is your current status with the FBI?"

"I'm presently suspended from duty, pending a dismissal hearing."

"Why is the FBI seeking to dismiss you?"

"My supervisor feels I overstepped my authority when I provided the requested report to Colonel Kendrick."

When the judge invites a cross-examination, Major Ogawa is so eager he springs up, stalking to the center of the floor. "Ms. England, did you inform your supervisor that Colonel Kendrick had requested this report?"

Her pale lips turn in a slight smile. "Not immediately, sir."

"Could you explain that?"

"I compiled the evidence package for Colonel Kendrick. I began working on it shortly after he left, and worked overnight. At oh four fifty-two on November fifteenth, I transmitted the report to a secure digital locker that could be accessed only by myself and Colonel Kendrick. I spoke to my supervisor later that morning. That's when I informed him of the report. He indicated by his reaction that he was furious. He told me he had only just received a warning that much of the evidence gathered at Black Cross had been falsified."

"Did he say what form this warning came in, or who it came from?"

"No, sir. He refused to provide me any further information."

"What happened after that?"

"I was immediately suspended, my security credentials were deleted, and I was escorted from the facility."

"The report, which you left in a 'secure digital locker.' What became of it?"

"I do not have direct knowledge of that since I was no longer able to access the user log."

"But Colonel Kendrick would still have had access to the report?"

"I believe that to be the case, sir."

"Thank you, Ms. England."

Her gaze turns again in my direction, though whether she's angry or just curious, I can't tell. Emotional analysis indicates it might be both.

Of course, Kendrick did retrieve the evidence package she prepared for him. He sent it to Ahab Matugo, to be used in the trial of Thelma Sheridan, a trial that it now seems will never happen, making Eve England just another meaningless casualty in a covert war to limit the political fallout of November 11.

It's early evening. I'm sitting on the bunk in my cell, thinking about Eve England and what she knows, and hoping no one is gunning for her, when the cell door unlocks, popping a few inches open. I lean down to retrieve from the floor the packaging from my recently completed dinner, expecting that one of the MPs has come to collect it. But it's my uncle who appears on the other side of the glass, still dressed in the suit he wore in court.

He crooks a finger at me to come out, barely pausing as he strides down the cellblock. I leave the trash where it is and go to the door, pushing it wider. All the other doors are open. Nolan, Moon, Tuttle: They all lean cautiously out of their cells to look around. And then, as my uncle beckons them, Harvey, Flynn, and Jaynie emerge as well. He turns around to head back up the cellblock. He's not smiling exactly, but his expression suggests vindication: the look of a warrior who has won a hard-fought victory.

"There's news," he announces. "It doesn't pertain directly to your case and maybe it doesn't mean a thing, but you wanted to arouse people's passions. You wanted to force questions to be asked. You wanted to trigger official inquiries. Well, congratulations, you've had your first victory. Minutes ago, in a joint news conference with the president, the attorney general announced she is looking into the handling of evidence in the Black Cross investigation, to determine whether that evidence was tampered with, falsified, or manipulated to protect the identities of some of the conspirators. Whether it will be an honest and legitimate investigation, only time will tell—but it's a start."

It takes a few seconds to process what he's just said, then I catch Jaynie's eye and we trade a grin. "*Hoo-yah!*" Flynn shouts, like she's channeling Ransom, and the rest of us echo the cheer, "*Hoo-yah!*"

Uncle Brandon tells us there's been cheering out on the National Mall too. That around four hundred thousand people are out there, demanding the same thing we're demanding—a full and honest accounting. I imagine the misery they've endured in this protest: the lack of toilets, showers, food, and adequate transportation; the risks to their safety from crime, from terrorism, or from overzealous law enforcement. But they stayed on the Mall, in enough numbers to frighten the president into action. This is their victory.

In the courtroom, no one acknowledges the shift in policy. Day three extends our legal education as Major Fong

calls expert witnesses to the stand to lecture the panel of
officers in the jury box on the meaning of their sworn duty
as members of the United States military, discussing the
implication of the oath of office required of every officer,
and the oath of enlistment which binds the soldiers under
their command.

The last witness is an academic, a bearded professor
steeped in political science, dressed in an expensive suit
my dad would admire, with gold cuff links because he can.
He speaks to the court with the assurance of a man accus-
tomed to being listened to:

"Huge responsibilities are placed on our soldiers. It's
their everyday duty to safeguard the deadliest technolo-
gies known to humanity. Every day, they have within their
reach weapons that could destroy cities, countries, the very
Earth on which all our lives depend—but we trust them
with this duty because they are loyal to the chain of command.

"We do not grant to individual soldiers the right to
decide when to attack—when tanks should roll through
a city, when artillery bombardments should commence,
when a nuclear missile should be launched. Such decisions
must descend through the chain of command.

"When a soldier steps outside the chain of command to
take vigilante action based on limited knowledge, that soldier is in violation of the law. When a soldier colludes with
a foreign power to subvert lawful orders issued by superi-
ors, that soldier is in violation of the law, and is guilty of
treason besides. There are legal means for soldiers to voice
their objection to policies. Vigilante action is not one of
those means."

On cross, Major Ogawa looks thoughtful. "Sir, I believe
you've served as an expert witness before the United States
Senate, where you testified concerning the conflict in Bolivia

and recommended that the United States enter into that conflict."

"Strategic needs demanded it."

"And I believe you testified later that US military intervention in the Sahel was demanded for humanitarian reasons."

"That is still the case. This cease-fire will not hold."

"I believe you occupy an endowed chair at your university. Where does that endowment come from?"

"I don't know what this has to do with my academic opinion."

"Please answer the question, sir. Where does the endowment come from?"

"The endowment is provided by Niall and Jenkins."

"And what business is Niall and Jenkins engaged in?"

"It's a think tank concerned with defense issues."

"And is it also a lobbying firm?"

"I am not sufficiently familiar with all of Niall and Jenkins's business activities to be able to answer that question."

Ogawa nods. "Thank you. No more questions."

Major Fong has no more witnesses. The prosecution rests, and we break for lunch. It's only Thursday, but in the afternoon session, Major Ogawa begins our defense by calling his first witness: me.

"Lieutenant Shelley, on November eighteenth through twentieth you participated in the abduction of Thelma Sheridan, delivering her, an American citizen, into the hands of a foreign power. Is that correct?"

"Yes, sir. It is."

"Why did you believe this course of action necessary?"

"When we stormed Black Cross, we took Blue Parker prisoner. We learned from him that Thelma Sheridan was a central figure in the Coma Day conspiracy and that she had provided the INDs—"

"INDs?" Ogawa asks me.

"The improvised nuclear devices used to immolate and injure—"

"Objection," Major Fong says as she stands.

I keep speaking. "—hundreds of thousands of people and bring down the communications structure of the United States—"

"*Objection!*"

The judge just wants to get this over with. "Overruled."

I continue. "No charges were brought against Thelma Sheridan. She was never detained. She was never officially under suspicion. It was a whitewash. A cover-up by a corrupt command and political structure determined to protect the individual who had long been their patron—"

"Your Honor! This is hearsay. This is *gossip.* The witness does not have personal knowledge of the relationship between Thelma Sheridan and unnamed elements of the command structure."

"They're unnamed," I counter, "because no one has the guts to name them, or investigate who they are."

"Your Honor!"

"Major Fong," the judge says in a tired voice, "the lieutenant is testifying as to his motivations. His beliefs are key to answering this question, whether or not they are based in fact. Please let him continue. There will be time later to dissect the validity of his beliefs—if you should wish to dive deeper into that line of argument."

The way she says it: like she's daring Fong to do it, to expand the scope of our case, to compel witnesses to name those who relayed the order for silence, and to trace that order to its source.

I swear Fong looks wistful, like she's thinking about it,

about what it would be like to shine a light into the shadows, about what it would be like to be the knight in shining armor, facing down a dragon. "Yes, ma'am," she says softly, and she returns to her seat.

I turn again to the jury box and I try to explain to my fellow officers why we did what we did. "We knew the truth. But as the days passed it became clear Thelma Sheridan had used her influence to buy off an investigation, to buy innocence, to buy clean hands. We knew she was guilty of mass murder and insurrection, we had seen the evidence, but no one in authority gave a damn—"

"Lieutenant Shelley," the judge warns, "you will conduct yourself with decorum when you are inside my courtroom."

"Yes, ma'am." I turn again to the jury box. "Silence is consent. We could have done nothing. We could have cooperated in the silence. But then we would have been just as guilty as those involved in the conspiracy to protect Thelma Sheridan. It was our duty to defend the Constitution of the United States. The only way we could do that was to step outside the chain of command and seek justice where we could, and that is what we did."

My uncle calls it true-believer shit.

So fuck me. I do believe it.

Major Fong isn't done with me, though. When her turn comes to cross-examine, she is in control. "Lieutenant Shelley, we have heard testimony from Special Agent Eve England and from General Brittney Ahmet regarding a document that ostensibly links Thelma Sheridan to the nuclear terrorism of November eleventh, but for reasons of national security, this document has not been introduced into evidence. I would ask if you, personally, have seen this document?"

"No. I have not."

"Were you aware of its existence before you undertook the First Light mission?"

"Yes. Colonel Kendrick told me about it. He said the evidence it contained was incontrovertible."

"Did he offer you proof of that? Did he share the contents of this document with you?"

"No. I didn't ask to see it. There wasn't time."

"Because you were deploying immediately on the First Light mission?"

I hesitate, realizing what's coming.

"When did Colonel Kendrick inform you of the existence of this document, Lieutenant Shelley?"

"On November seventeenth, after he picked me up from Kelly Army Medical Center."

"And what time was this?"

"It was around noon."

"Your Honor, I would introduce into evidence exhibit sixty-nine, a certification from Kelly AMC showing that the lieutenant checked out at eleven forty-eight." She turns back to me. "At what time did Colonel Kendrick inform you of this document?"

"A few minutes after he picked me up. We talked in the car."

"So you had roughly twelve hours from the time you knew of this document's existence to the time you deployed, yet you never asked to see the evidence of Thelma Sheridan's guilt for yourself?"

I'm in full stonewall mode and I answer like a robot. "I did not ask to see it, ma'am."

"Was this because, on the night Mr. Parker was taken into custody at Black Cross, you yourself heard his allegations against Thelma Sheridan, and you found his statements a sufficient basis for your actions?"

"That is not the reason, ma'am."

"Lieutenant Shelley, were you even present when Blue Parker made his allegations?"

"No, ma'am."

"So how did you learn of them?"

"Colonel Kendrick told me."

"Lieutenant, what were you doing during the approximately twelve hours that elapsed between the time Colonel Kendrick told you of this document's existence and the time that you deployed with him on the First Light mission?"

"I was with my girlfriend, ma'am. Lissa Dalgaard. I knew I might never see her again, and I was right—"

"Twelve hours, Lieutenant! And not once did you try to verify the evidence against Thelma Sheridan. You wanted to believe her guilty. You didn't ask to see the document because you didn't want to risk even an iota of doubt on your next heroic adventure. Isn't that true, Lieutenant?"

"No, that is not true—"

"Thank you, Lieutenant Shelley. I'm done."

Major Ogawa isn't. On redirect, he says, "Why didn't you ask to see the document, Lieutenant?"

"I didn't need to, sir. Colonel Kendrick was my commanding officer. We went through Black Cross together. I trusted him, and that trust was not misplaced. The evidence contained in that document was sufficient to convince an international court to accept the case. It would have been sufficient to convince any American court to accept the case—but no American court was ever going to be allowed to hear it."

Through the afternoon, the court hears the story of each member of the Apocalypse Squad. They discuss the basis for their actions and their motivations. No one shows any doubt or regret for what we did. Flynn goes last, and by the time she's on the stand, the sincerity of her testimony is making my skin crawl. Even to my sympathetic ears, every one of us sounds like a brainwashed robo-soldier in thrall to Kendrick's cult of personality. True believers, all of us.

It doesn't mean we were wrong.

On Friday morning we dress for court, but Master Sergeant Chudhuri lets us know there's a delay. We stay in our cells. It's 1113 when we're finally escorted upstairs. We're brought to the conference room, where we take seats around the table. A few minutes later Major Ogawa comes in, closing the door behind him.

"Is there a problem?" I ask him.

"No." He paces the length of the room, a picture of pent-up aggression. "Trial counsel tried to get our next two witnesses removed from the witness list, on the grounds that their testimony was not relevant to the issue being considered, that is, your guilt or innocence. We argued to the contrary, that their participation in the events of November nineteenth and twentieth offers clear proof of collusion between the chain of command and Vanda-Sheridan."

I realize who the next two witnesses must be. "The fighter pilots. The ones who tried to shoot us down . . . on the orders of a mercenary."

Ogawa nods. "The judge denied the motion of trial counsel. We get to talk to them this afternoon."

Captain Aaron Gilroy, United States Air Force, is sworn in first. He's midthirties, Caucasian, with a husky build, blond stubble on his scalp. Like most of the officers in the jury box and everyone at the defendants' table, he wears a well-polished stonewall expression.

Major Ogawa asks a few questions to establish Captain Gilroy's identity and credentials. Then he asks, "As November twentieth began you were engaged in an action off the West African coast, is that correct?"

"Yes, Major. The action was part of an ongoing mission. I'd been shadowing a C-17 for many hours, specifically Vanda-Sheridan Globemaster Eight-Seven-Z."

"Who assigned this mission to you, Captain?"

"My commanding officer, sir."

"And what were your orders?"

"My orders were revised several times during the mission. Initially, I was to escort the flight and protect it from foreign aggression. Later, I was to persuade the pilot of the C-17 to land at a secure base."

"Did your persuasion work, Captain?"

"No, sir, it did not."

"At what point did your command issue an order to shoot down the plane?"

"My command did not issue that order, sir. The order came from another combatant. I was told by my command to fire on his order."

"Did you know who this combatant was?"

"I did not. Identification was by code. I assumed he was special ops."

"What happened when you fired the missile, Captain Gilroy?"

"Interference from a foreign fighter drew the missile away from the C-17. Subsequently, the missile's guidance system locked on to a civilian jet. The jet was destroyed, and all aboard killed."

He says it in a voice devoid of emotion, but there is a tightness in his face, a hollow look to his eyes, a hard set to his mouth, that hint at masked emotions: Guilt maybe? Anger? A sense of shame? A sense of betrayal? I want to believe it. Captain Gilroy launched the missile that took Lissa's life away. I want him to hate that fact. I want him to know he was used.

Later, Major Ogawa uses the video record to establish that the "special ops" soldier was in truth a mercenary hired by Vanda-Sheridan. The skullnet icon glows in my overlay as I listen again to the merc's mellow, confident voice speaking poison:

"Ah, Lissa. Your Jimmy doesn't love you as much as we thought. I think it's the wiring that gives him a stone-cold heart."

Maybe it is.

Fuck me, anyway.

After that there's a short recess during which the attorneys consult with the judge. Then Monteiro addresses the jury. "If you're paying attention, you will be asking yourselves who issued the order compelling Captain Gilroy to take instruction from a third party outside the chain of command. That question is beyond the scope of this court-martial and will be taken up in a separate procedure. You need only consider whether the defense has indeed proved that the chain of command directing the actions of Captain Gilroy was compromised, and how that relates to the argument being made by the defense."

We hear the same story from the second pilot. By then it's late, and I expect the judge to dismiss us for the weekend—two more days locked up alone in my cell—but I underestimate the fortitude of Judge Monteiro.

"These are unusual times and they call for unusual measures," she says. "We will meet tomorrow in a Saturday session. Defense, I trust you will be able to complete your presentation within the morning session?"

Ogawa looks startled. "One moment, Your Honor." He consults his tablet, then gets a worried nod from my uncle. "Yes, Your Honor. That should work."

"Then we will hear closing arguments in the afternoon. Is that satisfactory?"

The attorneys seem stunned, but they agree. We finish tomorrow.

That night I lie awake in my bunk, the dim red glow of the cellblock's nocturnal illumination limning the concrete walls and I wonder:

Have we done what we intended? Have we shed a bright enough light on the corruption and the collusion that protected Thelma Sheridan, enough to provoke additional investigations, legitimate investigations that won't get buried?

Maybe.

The attorney general has made promises.

Judge Monteiro has implied there will be an investigation into the origin of Captain Gilroy's orders.

But will anyone ever be called to account? Has anything really changed?

People have to give a shit, or it won't matter.

I'm thinking it won't matter.

If Thelma Sheridan really is dead in a third-world prison the evidence against her will likely never come to light, and the collective memory of this incident will be overwritten by a new scandal or an engineered act of terrorism so that when further investigations go unfunded, no one will notice.

No one will be held accountable.

Same old story.

•   •   •   •

Saturday morning begins with expert testimony filling in details on our case; it ends with legal scholars trying to legitimize what we did.

Honestly, their arguments don't convince even me.

Monteiro calls an extended lunch recess. We won't reconvene until 1400. Chudhuri feels more secure with us in the cellblock than on the fourth floor, so after consulting with Guidance, she decides to take us downstairs. Handcuffs go on, and then we form up as always with Chudhuri, Omer, Vitali, and Phelps surrounding us. We march quickly and quietly down the restricted hallway past the judges' offices. I long for one of those office doors to open so I can steal another glance through the tall windows, glimpse the world outside: the Mall, the Capitol Building.

It doesn't happen. We reach the waiting elevator, step aboard, and about-face. The doors are closing when my uncle appears at the opposite end of the hallway. "Master Sergeant Chudhuri!" he calls in an eager undertone as he hurries toward us. "Hold up! Hold the elevator."

Chudhuri puts out an arm to block the doors from closing, but she's on edge. Anything out of the ordinary is cause for suspicion. "Omer. Vitali. Step outside. Cover the corridor."

They do so, flanking the elevator doors. Their sidearms are not drawn, but their hands rest on their pistols. "Mr. Shelley," Chudhuri says in a cold command voice, "please halt where you are. Do not approach."

I do not need to end this week by seeing my uncle gunned down in a courthouse hallway. "Master Sergeant! He's our attorney, not our enemy."

She ignores me.

Some thirty feet from the elevator my uncle stops, looking confused, then concerned, then annoyed. He's never been an easy man to intimidate. "Jimmy, we've got news. We want everyone back in the conference room. *Major Ogawa's orders.*"

"I need to confirm those orders, sir," Chudhuri says. Then I hear her murmuring to her handler. "What the hell is going on? What happened to procedure? Goddamn, yes, I understand!

"Forward!" she snaps. "We are to return to the conference room."

Major Ogawa is stalking back and forth outside the conference room as he waits for us to file in. "Get those handcuffs off," he orders Chudhuri.

We take seats. Feeling protective, I sit beside my uncle. "What's going on?" I whisper to him.

He nods to Ogawa as the major enters. "Good news."

Ogawa moves to the head of the table. Still standing, he says, "Command has issued an official confirmation: Thelma Sheridan is alive."

There's a general sigh of relief; smiles flash around the table. I'm the only one who's worried. "Is she still in custody? Is she still in Niamey?"

"Roger that."

It's my turn to sigh and shake my head, while my uncle claps me on the shoulder. "Take it easy, Jimmy. I told you it's good news."

"So what's the background? What happened?"

Major Ogawa answers. "There was an attempted coup in Niamey. I imagine Command has been aware of it all week but they've kept it quiet. The bulletin they finally released today implies there was some local collusion, but the coup was staged primarily with foreign mercenaries, using foreign funding. During the initial stage of the incident there was an assault on the prison where Thelma Sheridan was being held, and the rumor that got out was that she'd been killed. Maybe Command knew differently. We'll never know. But the loyalists must have been better organized than the mercs anticipated, because the coup was put down and all participants killed or arrested within twelve hours. Since then, Matugo has reassessed his command structure."

"And Sheridan?" Jaynie asks. "What's her condition? Is she still going to trial?"

"The bulletin notes that during the prison assault she tried to escape—"

"So the coup was a cover?" Harvey blurts out. "Vanda staged it, didn't he? To get her out of there?"

Ogawa scowls at the interruption. "I do not have that information, Specialist." Then he cracks a cold smile. "Though it sounds like plausible speculation to me."

"What's her condition?" Jaynie repeats. "Is she wounded?"

"Bruising and indication of some rough handling according to the official bulletin. A French diplomat was allowed to see her and confirms she is alive and fit and able to stand trial. Despite the week's drama, Matugo is determined to go ahead, and an international panel of judges has agreed to assemble on Monday to begin hearing the case."

"*Hoo-yah!*"

The yell goes up with no one coordinating it.

Thelma Sheridan will get her trial after all, and the evidence implicating her will no longer be hidden safely away behind a top secret designation.

•   •   •   •

As soon as Judge Monteiro calls the court back into session, Major Ogawa is on his feet. "Your Honor, additional information has come to light that would answer an inquiry lodged earlier in this proceeding by the defense. We would like to request that the government provide that information now for the court record."

The lines to be spoken by counsel and by the judge were predetermined in conference. It's now Judge Monteiro's turn to speak her part. "Please state for the record the details of your request."

"Defense requests that the government read into the court record Thelma Sheridan's current status and condition."

Fong has the document on her table. Defense and trial counsel affirm they have reviewed and approved this newest piece of evidence; it's logged into the record. Then Fong reads aloud the bulletin issued by Command, and it's done.

Closing arguments follow. They are passionate, but the faces of the twelve officers in the jury box give nothing away. By 1450 we have retired to our conference room to await their verdict.

For the first half hour it's all restless motion. Nolan brews coffee that no one drinks. We take turns in the bathroom. I pace, until Jaynie tells me to please sit the fuck down. We all wind up around the table. Harvey tries to crack a few jokes—gallows humor—but it cuts too close to the bone and she gives it up. By the end of the first hour we sit in frozen silence, hollowed out by a fear we're pretending not to feel.

This waiting is worse than any mission we've been on. My skullnet icon flickers faintly. I scowl at it, and feel a childish pride when it fades away again, pleased I am handling this on my own.

Thirty more minutes creep past. Then the door opens. Chudhuri leans in. "They want you back in the courtroom."

My heart hammers and I stand up too quickly; the chair legs scrape. I gesture at Chudhuri, palm out. "Give us one minute."

She nods behind her transparent visor—"One minute, sir"—steps back and closes the door.

I turn to my soldiers, still seated around the table. They're silent, watching me with anxious eyes. What can I tell them? We're about to go over a cliff and there's nothing I can do about it.

I try to find words anyway. I hope they mean something. "I want you all to remember that we came back from Niamey for a reason. We could have stayed there, been granted asylum, made a new life, but we chose to come back, not because we expected to be rewarded, but because it was our duty.

"No matter what happens in that courtroom, no matter what the verdict is, know that we did the right thing when we returned home. Be proud of that, today and afterward, no matter what follows."

Nolan stands, straightens his uniform. "Roger that, LT," he says in a somber voice. Tuttle echoes him while the rest of the squad rises to their feet. Moon and Flynn both look scared, but they murmur, "Yes, sir." And then, to my shock, Harvey steps back from the table, squares her shoulders, and offers a respectful salute. "It's been an honor, sir."

I return the courtesy.

Then I notice Jaynie watching me with her thoughtful gaze. "Strange, isn't it?" she says. "That the Red was never part of this trial, never mentioned in any of the arguments?"

"It's not so strange. They had Colonel Kendrick to blame. Why complicate things by introducing the Red?"

"So you think it's still out there?"

"I know it is, Jaynie. It's not going away."

"I hope to prove you wrong on that, sir, but however it turns out, we did what we had to do." She snaps off her own salute. "No regrets."

In a resigned murmur, the sentiment is repeated by everyone but me: "No regrets."

No regrets.

I turn and open the door. Chudhuri is standing just outside, her back to the wall, looking invulnerable in her armor and bones, but when she turns her head to look at me, the face behind her visor is wearing an anxious expression.

"Thank you for the time, Master Sergeant. We're ready to go."

My dad is there in the first row, as he's been every day. Sitting beside him is Harvey's mom from Pittsburgh. We file around the defendants' table and take our seats, only to rise again as the judge comes in, and then the panel of officers charged with bringing in a verdict in our case.

I study their faces as they file into the jury box. I see ambivalence, resentment, a lingering anger. They won't look at one another or at us.

We are allowed to sit, and then Judge Monteiro addresses the officers. "Have the court members reached findings on each charge and specification before them?"

A major, seated in the corner of the jury box closest to the judge, stands up. "We have, Your Honor."

"Are you ready to read your findings to the court?"

"Yes, Your Honor. I am."

"Accused and counsel, please rise."

There is a shuffling sound as we all stand. Otherwise the courtroom is eerily quiet, despite the number of people present.

The major reads from a tablet that he holds in his hands:

"We find that Lieutenant James Shelley did, on November eighteenth through November twentieth, participate in a conspiracy to kidnap Thelma Sheridan, and that this conspiracy was illegal."

A strange, startled chorus of soft exclamations ignites behind me. Some of the voices are triumphant, others are pitched in clichéd despair. All of them annoy me. There is no cause for outcry or surprise. My dad knows this. He remains utterly quiet as the major hammers the nails in:

"The facts of the case having been stipulated by the defendant, we therefore find Lieutenant Shelley guilty under Article Eighty-One, conspiracy; and guilty under Article One oh Eight, destruction of military property; and guilty of four counts of murder under Article One Eighteen, Part Three, an act inherently dangerous to another; and guilty under Article One Twenty-Two of robbery in the presence of the victim, with force or violence, in an amount exceeding two hundred twenty million dollars; and guilty under Article One Twenty-Eight of twelve counts of aggravated assault; and guilty under Article One Thirty-Four, general article, of the kidnapping of Thelma Sheridan and Ilima LaSalle, and of abusing the good order and discipline of the armed forces."

The major pauses. A sheen of sweat glistens on his cheeks. He swallows a few times and then, without lifting his gaze from the tablet in his hands, he continues:

"We find that Sergeant Jayne Vasquez did, on November eighteenth through November twentieth, participate in a conspiracy to kidnap Thelma Sheridan, and that this conspiracy was illegal. . . ."

He goes on to read the same charges, the same findings that he already read for me, leaving out only the destruction of military property. Sergeant Nolan's verdict is read out next, and then Harvey, Tuttle, Moon, descending through the ranks. Flynn is last. I look at her where she stands across the L of the table from me. She's calm, but her eyes are unfocused. I think she's already checked out.

The major finishes. He finally looks up, but not at us. He looks at the judge. Monteiro gives him a sympathetic nod. "Thank you, Major. Was the verdict unanimous?"

"No, ma'am. It was not."

Another murmur of surprise ignites among the spectators. The judge does not look pleased.

"On your findings of conspiracy, did the court members unanimously agree that the conspiracy was illegal?"

"No, ma'am, that was not the case."

Monteiro gives the panel of officers a dark scowl. "Referring again to your findings of conspiracy, did at least three-quarters of the court members agree that the conspiracy was illegal?"

"Yes, ma'am. That was the case."

"Thank you for your verdict. The defendants may be seated. This court-martial will reconvene Monday morning at ten hundred to consider sentencing. All spectators are asked to remain in their seats until the bailiff dismisses you. Court is now in recess."

"All rise!"

Judge Monteiro abandons the bench, her judicial robes billowing around her legs as she exits the courtroom with an angry stride.

I turn around. My dad is standing behind me. His face is gaunt: He's become an old, exhausted man. Saying nothing, he reaches over the bar with both hands and we embrace.

Then it's time to go.

• • • •

Chudhuri and her squad of MPs are not there to meet us as we exit. They've been replaced by strangers: four men and two women, all with dark suits, farsights, and unreadable faces. They form a gauntlet, with the door of Judge Monteiro's office on the other end. We pile up in a confused knot of prisoners and attorneys as the two closest to us display gold badges, identifying themselves as special agents in the Secret Service.

I wasn't expecting this at all, and I'm not in a mood for surprises. My temper spikes, and I shoulder past Nolan, getting ready for I don't know what. Jaynie comes with me, her fingers a light touch on my arm, though whether she means to caution me or to let me know she'll back me up, I can't tell and there's no chance to find out because Major Ogawa takes over.

"What the hell is going on?" he demands, pushing past me.

The door to Monteiro's office opens; a woman wearing a major's uniform steps out. Her name tag identifies her as Major Perkins. She pushes the door wide. "I want all of you in here *now*."

"What is this about?" Ogawa insists.

"Attorneys may be present," she allows. "Now get in here and sit down."

What's the alternative? Go back to our cells for the weekend? I decide not to pass on another opportunity to be threatened by the president, so I step past Ogawa and enter the office with Jaynie right behind me.

There are paintings on the walls: startlingly beautiful depictions of flowers and leaves. There are shelves too, probably built to contain books, but holding knickknacks and potted plants. Just inside the door is an oval conference table stained to look like rosewood, and straight ahead a large matching desk at a right angle to the window, so that Monteiro should have a view of the Capitol Building when the blinds are open. They're closed now. Afternoon sunlight seeps through the pinholes where the strings pass, and glows around the edges. Monteiro is hanging up her robes in a closet behind the desk. She slaps the closet doors closed with a bang and turns to face us.

Her guest is not the president.

In the little sitting area facing the desk, standing beside a wall-mounted monitor, is the secretary of defense. He's a man of moderate height, lean and well dressed, his gray hair trimmed short and his heavy eyebrows knit in a disapproving scowl as he watches us enter. "Sit down," he orders. Major Perkins gestures at us to take seats around the table.

I go to the far end, where I can see the monitor. It's a feed from the White House briefing room. Bloggers and mediots are assembling, but the podium is empty.

I sit down, with Jaynie beside me. My uncle squeezes my shoulder, then takes the seat on my other side, while Judge Monteiro picks up a sheaf of papers from the desk. Actual paper. The secretary of defense looks on in silence as Monteiro says, "Time is of the essence. We have at most ten minutes. So listen carefully, and do not make me repeat anything."

She crosses the room. Major Perkins meets her halfway and takes the papers.

"The president will grant all of you an immediate pardon, contingent on your acceptance of the terms in the agreements Major Perkins is now distributing."

Shock and hope collide, producing silence. There is only the rustle of paper as Perkins lays a two-page document on the table in front of me. My uncle picks it up before I can read even the first line. The next one goes to Jaynie. More copies are set in front of Nolan, Tuttle, and Harvey. Major Ogawa hijacks Moon's document. Flynn gets the last copy. She's across the table from me, and looks like she doesn't quite understand what's going on, but she picks up the papers, frowns, and starts reading.

The secretary of defense steps forward. "Let it be emphasized," he says in syllables chiseled by anger, "that the president is not granting this pardon for your benefit, and in no way does it imply his approval of what you did. He is acting solely for the good of the country. Read the documents and sign them. *As is.* There will be no negotiation of terms." He directs a curt nod at Monteiro—"Colonel"—and departs.

Monteiro watches him go with an irritated grimace. When the door closes behind him, she turns back to us. "The president *is* acting for the good of the country." She points a small remote control at the windows, triggering the blinds to rise with a smooth electric hum. I stand up to look outside. On the sidewalks along Constitution Avenue and beyond, filling Third Street and spilling over to the lawns fronting the reflecting pool, are tens of thousands of people. I can't see farther down the Mall, but I don't doubt I'm seeing only the edge of a far greater gathering. Monteiro confirms it.

"Seven hundred thousand people. Most of them avid supporters of your cause, demonstrating for your release. Crowd biometrics foresees a high potential for violence when your guilty verdict is announced. Should a riot break out, there is a chance that hundreds, maybe thousands, will die. It is your duty to prevent that."

She triggers the blinds to close again. Jaynie nudges my arm and nods at my chair, reminding me to sit down again.

Monteiro continues, "The spectators who attended the proceedings today are presently being held in the courtroom to prevent word of your convictions going public, pending the outcome of this conference. As soon as your signatures are on the agreements, the president will announce the guilty verdict along with the pardon, which should satisfy your supporters. You have seven minutes remaining."

My uncle speaks without looking up from the paper-work. "Are all these documents the same?"

"They are all the same excepting names and ranks of individuals, and Paragraph Nine pertaining to army property, which differs for Mr. Shelley."

Mr. Shelley.

That would be me. Not an officer anymore. I knew it was coming, but it still feels like reality has been casually kicked to the curb . . . and like I've been casually kicked in the gut. I look up, to find Flynn staring at me from across the table, fear in her wide green eyes. "It'll be okay," I whisper. She nods, looking again at the document in front of her. My uncle slides the first page toward me as he goes on to read page two.

That's when suspicion kicks in and I hear Monteiro again in my head: *Paragraph Nine pertaining to army property.* That has to refer to my legs. They will take my legs.

My gaze skims to the bottom of page one, but Paragraph Nine isn't there. I lean in on my uncle and whisper, "What does it say?"

His head tilts slightly. "A lot, but nothing unfair. Let me finish reading."

"Are they going to take my legs?" I insist.

His mouth curves in a slight, wolfish smile. "That would be bad PR, Jimmy." He's not whispering, not trying to hide anything. "This document is about controlling damage. The president is not interested in making you more of a martyr than you already are."

"He's also not interested in looking weak," Major Ogawa says from the opposite end of the table. He shuffles the order of the pages he's holding. "Here are the terms in sum-mary."

Everyone looks at him to translate what they've already read.

"Upon signing, you will be immediately separated from the army. Your records will show an honorable discharge. You will be required to attend a debriefing session here in the courthouse, to inform you of the classified status of information you are party to. When that session is done, you will be required to attend a twenty-minute press conference, no doubt to prove to the world that you are still alive and that the government has not caused you to disappear. You will be docked all back pay since November eighteenth. You will be allowed to keep your skullcaps, which have been designated as therapeutic medical devices—"

"And you," my uncle interrupts, looking at me, "will get to keep any device presently on or part of your person."

I'm relieved, sure, but it's like I'm in combat. My brain just clicks over to the next issue. "The army's going to give up their access to my overlay?"

He nods. "They will be out of your head forever."

Lissa would have been happy about that.

"And this covers my original offense?" He knows what I mean: my induction contract archived a conviction for an illegal video recording.

"Everything past," he assures me.

"Three minutes," Colonel Monteiro notes.

Unperturbed, Ogawa passes the document he's holding to Moon. "I advise you to sign it."

I skim the first page of my contract while pens start scratching. I go on, pretending to read page two. After all, I've been publicly castigated for not reading documents— but the words don't make any sense to me. It's too bad I don't have my handler Delphi's crisp voice in my head, to read the order aloud.

My uncle holds out a pen. "Sign it, Jimmy."

"Do it, Shelley," Jaynie says. "All you're giving up is the chance to be a martyr."

I think Jaynie and I will have to settle a few issues, preferably in a session of hand-to-hand combat.

I take the pen.

Across the table, Flynn is biting her lip as she concentrates to make her signature—she probably hasn't signed anything since the day she was inducted.

Everyone else is done. They're all watching me.

I sign my name.

My career in the US Army is over.

INTERIM

FALLOUT

"Ladies and gentlemen, the President of the United States."

The voice issues from the monitor mounted on the wall of Judge Monteiro's sitting area.

I'm a civilian now, with no charges pending against me, so I don't need to ask permission. I just get up and, before the applause dies out, I'm standing in front of the monitor. The squad follows my example and gathers behind me, except for Harvey, who decides it's okay to sit in one of the upholstered chairs.

He's a young president, but he still manages to look stern and fatherly behind the podium, framed by the bright red, white, and blue of two American flags. His dark gaze quiets the crowd.

"A guilty verdict has been returned in the case of the Apocalypse Squad—"

There is a gasp from the press audience, a rush of murmuring. The president keeps speaking in his bold voice:

"—but it is the privilege of the president to offer pardons and today I have granted a pardon to all seven members of the Apocalypse Squad, in consideration of their exemplary service at Black Cross, and in acknowledgment of their patriotism. I do not—I cannot—condone the so-called First Light mission, but in extraordinary times, extraordinary measures must sometimes be taken, and that is what I have done today."

He turns and walks out. The startled press pool jumps to their feet, shouting questions at his retreating back. He does not return.

Out on the Mall, cheering erupts, a thunderous sound carried in vibration through the thick glass of the floor-to-ceiling windows. Someone must have grabbed the remote control, because the blinds go up and we get to look at a scene of joy—fists pumping the air, and people hugging, many of them masked.

It's supposed to be about us, but we're just a symbol. It goes deeper. It's about the will of the people; the will of *these* people to take back some small part of the power that is rightfully theirs, and demand change.

Major Perkins tries to hurry things along.

"You are no longer permitted to wear your uniforms," she tells us. "Civilian clothes have been provided for you."

She clutters the table with a collection of white dress shirts and dark slacks, a set for everyone.

"Fuck this," Harvey says unbuttoning her uniform jacket. "I'll walk out in my T-shirt, but I'm not wearing this shit."

With a grim expression, Jaynie picks up the shirt tagged with her name, holding it at a distance like it's unstable explosive ordnance.

"Leave it, Jaynie." I turn to Perkins. "Keep this stuff. We've signed your contract. Now I want our possessions returned, including the clothes we were wearing when we turned ourselves in for arrest."

Perkins looks at Monteiro, but she finds no sympathy

there. "Major Perkins, do not turn your doe eyes on me. You are legally obligated to return all personal possessions seized upon arrest."

"Yes, ma'am."

She steps away. Using her farsights, she holds a low-voiced conference with someone, and then informs us, "It will be a few minutes."

Monteiro returns to the desk and drops into the chair. "Make yourselves at home," she says. "This isn't my office anyway. It belonged to a Judge Kohn, who had the misfortune to be across the river in Alexandria on Coma Day."

She's a colonel. That meant a lot more to me just a few minutes ago. Not anymore. I walk up to the desk and I ask her, "If we'd met back in that courtroom on Monday, you would have sentenced us to life, wouldn't you?"

She studies me for several seconds, then acknowledges this with a nod. "I wouldn't have had a choice, Mr. Shelley."

"When the verdict came back, you didn't like that it wasn't unanimous."

"Two members would not vote to convict, despite my instructions. They were wrong. You did not have a legal basis for what you did. They were responding with emotion, and without regard to the law. That was Ogawa's strategy—to appeal to emotion, to raw patriotism." She raises her voice. "Isn't that right, Major?"

"Yes, ma'am," he calls from where he's standing at the window.

"And it came way too close to working." She drums her fingers on the desktop. "People are fed up, but we need to be able to trust our officers. It should have been a unanimous conviction—and that would have given more meaning to the president's pardon."

"Ma'am?" I ask, sure I've misunderstood. "I thought you hated the idea of this pardon."

"Negative, Mr. Shelley. What you did gave hope to a people in shock. We are all revolutionaries at heart, or we'd like to be. It's our cultural mythology, that a few individuals can make a difference. The Apocalypse Squad has made a difference. I don't know if it will be a lasting difference. I hope so. But there are many forces at play. The president is no innocent, but I do believe he has the best interests of the country at heart. And I believe he was correct to pardon you for reason of your past service and in consideration of your motives—though not to avoid a mob scene on the Mall."

There is no mob scene. Outside the window, crowds of people—half of them wearing masks—are walking up Third Street, heading for the metro maybe, or for a bus stop. Everyone is being civil, patient. There are only a few cars around and it's weirdly peaceful.

Suspicion stirs.

It feels almost . . . orchestrated.

Then again, after a week of demonstrations, maybe people are just happy to be going home with a victory.

"When did this fashion for masks start?" I ask no one in particular.

"A couple of months after the Coma," Ogawa says with a sly smile, as if the question amuses him. "Security's been . . . well, a little heavy handed. So a few patriots started wearing masks—a symbolic protest against street surveillance and tracking through facial recognition. The idea went viral, and homemade masks became a thing, at least here in DC. New York too. A few other big cities. Homeland Security doesn't like it, of course. It slows down their recognition system, so they're trying to make it illegal to cover the face in public. But I'll show you what's really got them complaining."

He gets his satchel and pulls out what looks like coarse, iridescent fabric. Rainbows slide across its surface. "The latest fashion. Made in Germany." He toggles a switch at the cloth's edge and it's not cloth anymore. It takes on a solid shape in the form of a face. Everyone gathers around as Ogawa hands the mask to me. I run my fingers over the surface. It's made of tiny scales, with clouds of color floating across them.

"Wait a second . . . are the scales moving?"

I swear I can feel their edges slowly pinching against my fingertips.

"Can I see it?" Jaynie asks.

I pass the mask to her as Ogawa says, "The scales are constantly moving, reshaping the face, shifting the colors. It blurs IR recognition too."

Jaynie holds up the mask, gazing at it suspiciously. "In the Sahel, we didn't need to see a face to make a positive ID. Kinetic data and full-body biometrics are just as good."

She passes the mask to Harvey, who points out, "Body biometrics only work if you have the data. You think cops keep those kinds of records?"

"I don't know."

"Cops don't," Ogawa says. "Or they're not supposed to. Homeland Security does have a biometric database, but it's limited by law. So facial recognition is still important."

Harvey puts on the mask and it's as if she has put on a veil, with eyes looking through the slot where farsights would go. "I think you should get one of these, Shelley. I mean, the Lion of Black Cross isn't going to be able to walk down the street without getting mobbed."

Shit, she's probably right.

I don't have time to worry over it, though. The door opens and I jump—PTSD—but it's just Chudhuri, coming in with Phelps, Omer, and Vitali behind her. They're bringing our gear—and not just our uniforms. Nolan chuckles when he sees what they're carrying. Flynn gives a little whoop of victory.

We left our weapons in Niamey, but we brought our packs back with us, along with the dead sisters and the helmets we used on the First Light mission—all of it equipment provided to us privately, by the organization, and not by the army. So the MPs are following Monteiro's instruction and giving it all back—the helmets in their padded sacks, and the dead sisters folded into compact bundles so they're easy to carry.

"The exoskeletons are illegal to use within the Capitol district," Major Perkins informs us. "Any attempt to use them will have severe repercussions."

"I'm hoping we won't need them," I answer back.

We are required to inventory everything, but at the end of it we're wearing the anonymous gray summer-weight combat uniforms we had in Niamey, with no insignia of rank or affiliation anywhere on them.

The debrief is a prolonged affair that details the obvious. We are not allowed to discuss any classified information. Specifically, we are not allowed to discuss the contents of the classified report that Colonel Kendrick had in his possession, the one none of us has ever seen. We are not allowed to discuss the action at Black Cross until a public report is officially issued and then any comments we make must be limited to information included in the report. We are not allowed to discuss any electronic security breaches we may have experienced or suspected during our service.

That's it.

"What about the Red?" Jaynie asks Major Perkins. "*Not* classified? Shelley says it's public knowledge."

"You will not discuss any incidents involving a breach of electronic security," Perkins repeats. "The army does not designate popular mythologies with a classified status."

Jaynie turns to me with a questioning look, unconcerned with Perkins's condescending tone. "So the army has opted for denial, and we're free to talk about it—or go after it."

I shrug. This is not the time to discuss her vendetta against the Red.

"Understand," Major Perkins adds, "that while your pardon forgives all past transgressions, you can certainly be prosecuted for any new violations of the law. Questions?"

I don't have any questions for her, but I do have a demand. "I want my overlay turned back to my control, with full Cloud access."

"Do you understand the restrictions I've explained to you?"

"Yes, ma'am, I do."

"Link him up," she says. "And yield control."

A green circle flares in my overlay, symbol of an open network. The dot-mil account connects first and I half expect to hear Delphi greet me—but of course she's not my handler anymore. I haven't even talked to her since my equipment blew out at Black Cross. I promise myself that I'll find her when this is over, thank her for being there for me, for keeping me alive more times than I can remember—though that quest would be made easier if I knew her real name.

The dot-mil download aborts, and then the account deletes itself. A log pops up, detailing the army's other programs and files as each one is erased. When it's done, I dive into my apps and check the recording function. It's been switched off. I wonder if it will stay that way.

The press conference is a mixture of astute questions and idiocy, throughout which our civilian status is conveniently ignored.

"Lieutenant Shelley, what were you feeling when Colonel Kendrick proposed the First Light mission?"

"Sergeant Vasquez, do you still feel the Red is a threat to humanity?"

"Private Flynn, on the flight to Niamey you tried to take Lieutenant Shelley's handgun. Do you regret betraying him?"

From the look on Flynn's face, she'd shoot her interrogator if only she had a gun. Harvey tackles the answer for her, suggesting in a casual tone, "Go fuck yourself."

Afterward, we gather one more time at the conference table in Judge Monteiro's office, though she's already gone home. Major Ogawa addresses us. "This is it for me. You're on your own now, and Godspeed. You will each need to decide where you are going and what you will do." He gives everyone a business card. "Expect to be inundated with requests for interviews and public appearances. Be careful before signing anything, and if you need an attorney, call me, and I'll help you find one." He steps back, nods, and smiles. "It's been an honor and a privilege."

We shake hands and thank him, and then he goes. My uncle is still there but he doesn't offer advice; he's just waiting to take me home. I wonder where my dad is; suddenly I want to see him—but I'm not going to abandon my squad. We've been to Hell and back. That doesn't mean it's over.

"What do you want to do?" I ask them, worried for their safety, for their ability to adapt to civilian life, for what might be coming next.

They talk quietly, seriously. Harvey and Moon consider going home. So far as I know, Jaynie and Flynn don't have homes to go to. "You going home, LT?" Nolan asks.

"For a while."

"Then what?" Jaynie wants to know.

I look at my uncle. "You want to go find my dad? Tell him what's going on?"

His eyes narrow. "Your dad needs you, Jimmy. He needs you at home."

"I know and I'm coming. It's just . . . we need a few minutes."

As the door closes behind him, everyone is looking at me expectantly. I tap the corner of my eye. They know I mean my overlay. "I've been skimming my civilian e-mail. There's a message from Anne Shima."

"Anne Shima?" Moon asks. "Rawlings's friend? From the organization?"

"Yes." During my incarceration I looked up Anne Shima in my encyclopedia and found only a short bio that reported her retirement from the US Army at the rank of lieutenant colonel after twenty-five years of service. That was all. She and Colonel Rawlings are awaiting their own, civilian, trial where they will face charges of conspiracy and treason and God knows what else. Given the state of the country, it could be years before the trial convenes. In the meantime, they are both free on bond.

"Shima wants all of you to know that the organization has already deposited funds into your accounts equivalent to the back pay that the army just took away. She wants you to know that whoever the fuck the organization is, they are grateful for your service, and value your talents—so much that she would like to extend an offer of employment to all of you. So if you want to be mercs, Shima is hiring."

"Fuck," Jaynie says softly. I can't tell if she's offended or pleased.

Flynn is less complicated. "I'll do it!"

"I want to know more," Harvey says, "but I'm interested."

Moon looks around uneasily. "You know, we survived a

hell of a lot already. I mean, how long can our luck hold out?"

That's the smartest question I've ever heard Moon ask— but no one pays any attention to him.

Tuttle, as usual, is looking to Nolan for guidance, while Nolan is staring at me. After a few seconds, he asks, "What are you going to do, LT?"

"Go home. For a while, anyway."

"But you're not saying no?"

"I'm probably saying no. Moon's got it right. Think hard about this before you sign anything." I stand up. "You've got five months of pay in your accounts. Get a room, get laid, get stoned, whatever. Get a phone or farsights—and call me. Call me in a few days. We'll figure things out."

I make sure they all know how to contact me. Then our packs go on. We take our helmets in hand. "We've started a process," I warn them. "And there's going to be all kinds of fallout. There are people who support Thelma Sheridan, who support what she did on Coma Day, because they're that scared of the Red. Those people are your enemies. So be careful of who you're with and where you go—and don't be surprised if things get crazy when her trial starts on Monday." I pick up the folded bones of my dead sister. "Let's go."

I sit by the window on the evening train to New York, my dad beside me and my uncle across the aisle. I'm on edge, watching the dark reflections of the other passengers in the window. Watching the reflection of my dad as he watches me.

"You've been through a lot, Jimmy," he says. "It's going to take time to process. It'll take time to find a new direction."

"Yes, sir."

I answer absently because I'm thinking about the squad,

already second-guessing my decision to leave DC, to leave them on their own.

"*Jimmy.*"

I turn to look at him.

He gives me a half smile. "I never raised you to call me 'sir,' so don't start now."

I crack a smile of my own, though I'm not really feeling it. "Like you said, sir, it'll take time to process."

"Smartass."

Across the aisle, my uncle nods off.

My dad tells me he's not tired, that he's too wired on the aftermath of adrenaline to sleep, but a few minutes later, he's dozing too.

I stay awake and on watch. We're in first class with just a few other passengers in our car and only the staff wandering through, so the potential risk seems minimal, but I remain alert anyway.

My dad wakes up again. He uses his tablet to answer e-mails. I watch my overlay. It's almost time for the usual daily video upload of my life's adventures, and I'm anxious to know what will happen now that the army's programs are out of my head.

But nothing happens. There's no activity—which means whatever story the Red was telling through me is over.

I should be relieved, but I'm not. I'm scared.

My dad looks up from his tablet as we pull into the station. His eyes are bright; he looks happy. "Almost there," he assures me.

"I'm not looking forward to the crowds."

Like I told my squad, we really do have enemies, and not just random crazies. I know Carl Vanda wants me dead and maybe the president does too, but if the Red is really gone I'll have to handle it on my own, without the pre-scient warning sense that kept me alive in the past.

I never thought I'd miss the King David gig.

"You'll be fine, Jimmy. Give it a week and it'll feel like home again."

I think it might take a little longer than that.

My heart races as we leave the train. The station isn't crowded, but people are moving in so many different directions it's hard to do a threat assessment. So I make sure we move quickly, and in just a few minutes we're in a hired car that's taking us through Manhattan's midnight streets.

The city is changed. The glittering energy I remember on Saturday nights is gone. Only a few people are out and there are more bicycles than cars. "Is there a curfew?" I ask.

"No," my dad says. "But the economy was hard hit on Coma Day."

We say good night to my uncle, then go on to our own building, where a crowd of mediots and video stalkers waits for us at the door.

My dad sees the look on my face and shrugs. "Don't worry too much about it. The celebrity can't last."

He's right, but I still have to get past them. So I do the same thing I did in DC: pretend they're not there. I walk through the throng with my helmet in one hand and my dead sister in the other, using the bulk of my equipment to open the way while I ignore their eager questions. I know I have to expect this. It's going to be routine for a while to have strangers pressing around me, but I hate it. There's no way to know if one of them has a gun or a knife, and I'm not wearing armor.

I should do something about that.

We make it into the lobby.

Overhead, a huge plastic banner greets me: *Welcome home, James Shelley! You have the thanks of a grateful nation.* Fortunately, no one's around, so I don't have to think of anything to say.

I press the button to call the elevator, but nothing happens. Apparently, my fingerprints are no longer in the system.

"We'll get your biometrics reactivated tomorrow," my dad says, pushing the button himself.

As we're riding up, I tell him, "I want to go into the apartment first. Alone."

"Why?"

"Just to check on things."

Things like bombs rigged to go off on our arrival, or waiting assassins.

"There's nothing to be afraid of, Jimmy."

I know he's wrong.

We arrive at our floor. I want to rig up in my dead sister before we go any farther.

"Look, let me show you something," my dad says. He puts down his suitcase and takes out his tablet. On its screen are feeds from security cameras inside the apartment. There is of course no one in any of the rooms. "An AI monitors the apartment at all times. No one's been inside."

"What if the AI's been subverted?"

He gives me a dark look—"You can't live your whole life being paranoid"—and picking up his suitcase he heads down the hall. The apartment door recognizes him and opens. No bombs go off. "Come on in," he calls over his shoulder. "You're home."

My dad is no sentimentalist. He had my room redecorated after I left, new furniture brought in. But the bed is still the same one I shared with Lissa when she stayed over on Saturday nights. It feels like I'm trespassing on someone else's life when I lie there in the dark, remembering how it used to be. Melancholy grows until the flickering of the skullnet icon distracts me, reminds me there is no point in brooding. Why think on the past? I can't change any of it.

Why think at all? Better to sleep. The skullnet helps me with
that. I don't wake up again until past noon.

Then I wake in a panic, sweat-soaked, heart hammering.
I'm out of bed and on my titanium feet before I know where
I am.

I hear my dad talking, happy and relaxed in the living
room, while in my head I hear a ghost voice shouting an
urgent alarm: *Rig up! Armor and bones!*

What the hell is wrong with me?

I cross to the window and cautiously pull aside the heavy
curtain, blinking into bright sunlight, studying the building
across the street, wondering if there's a sniper out there looking for me. I think about opening the curtain all the way,
because I hate being afraid, and anyway, with the proper
equipment, a shooter could see through the curtain and
through the tinted window glass.

I open it and flood the room with sunlight.

But I stay well back from the window.

That afternoon, Sunday, I go through my e-mail and my
phone log. I have my phone set to put live calls through
only from select people. Everything else gets logged. I clear
the log and after a quick scan I dump most of the e-mail,
knowing I'll never catch up. When I check the phone log
again, there are twenty-four new calls. I recognize only one
name: Joby Nakagawa, the brat engineer who made my legs.

Curiosity wins, and I call him back.

He links right away. A little image slides into sight on the
periphery of my vision and I'm looking at his pale face framed
in white-blond hair. "Hey, Joby." Then, because he's sensitive
about his work and I have a bad habit of baiting him, I add,
"I haven't managed to break the legs yet. Still working on that."

"You can't fucking break the legs."

I sure as hell hope he's right.

He adds, "I can't believe the fucking army gave them to you without consulting me."

"Sorry about that."

"I told them I have a program running on your overlay—"

"You do?"

"Of course I do. I have to track performance data on the legs. You didn't erase it, did you?"

"I don't think so, but the army wiped all their stuff."

"I don't put my data where Command can access it."

He talks me through the file tree. It turns out he knows his way around my overlay better than I do.

"You see it?" he asks.

"'Bonedance'?"

I hear a heartfelt sigh of relief. "So it's still there. Okay. Find the settings."

"Why? What do you want?"

"I want my data. It hasn't been able to upload in months, and now the army has cut off my access."

It's nice to have confirmation that the army really is out of my head.

Joby and I have had our differences, but he did a damn fine job on my legs and I don't see any reason to deny him his data. "Tell me what to do."

We set up his access, and the first data package uploads. "Got it," he confirms. "Okay . . . I'm setting the program to upload once a day."

Suspicion kicks in. "Hold on. Is this going to include location data?"

"Is there *anything* you don't complain about?"

"I'm not complaining. I'm asking a question."

He must really want this to happen, because he bites back on his temper. "For the data to be meaningful, I need to know the environment you're operating in."

"Yeah? And what if I don't want to be tracked all over the globe?"

"Why? What have you got to hide? Are you going to work for Carl Vanda?"

This is so out of context, I'm at a loss for words.

"Because I heard you played the hero and saved his life—"

"Ah, *shit*."

"—that you fucking got in the way after somebody set up a guaranteed kill."

"Somebody?"

"Yeah."

I inventory my memory of Joby's menagerie of robot toys . . . and decide not to ask any more questions. "You're right, Joby. I did get in the way, and I'm sorry for it. I really am."

Several seconds pass in silence while he tries to decide if my apology is sincere.

It's totally sincere.

"Yeah, all right. If you're off on some secret mission, you can turn off the geopositioning. It's just a check box."

"Okay. I'll do that if I need to."

"Don't forget to turn it on again."

"Yeah."

"Or I'll reach in and do it for you. And if the legs ever do break? No one works on them but me. You got that?"

"Understood."

I go through the closet and the drawers, pulling out my old civilian clothes, the leftovers of another life, from before I went into the army. I put all the slacks in a pile to be donated because my robot legs are two inches longer than my organic ones used to be. Most of the shirts still fit, though I discard a few that I must have purchased in a state of teenage euphoria.

Then I decide I'm going out.

I pull on a pair of knee-length athletic shorts and a running shirt, no shoes on my gray titanium feet because I don't need them. My heart is thudding at the thought of going outside—which is why I have to go.

"Dad!"

"Yeah?"

I find him in the living room. "I'm going running." I head straight for the door, not giving him a chance to object.

He doesn't try. Just like last night, he's braver than I am. "Don't run over any mediots," he advises me as I step into the hall.

It's not the mediots who scare me. I'm used to being watched. It's the potential for a bullet in my brain that's got my heart racing.

The elevator stops twice to pick up people. Both times, the new arrivals do a double take on my legs before they realize who I am. Then it's all smiles and welcome-homes. I want to be polite, but "Thank you" is all I can manage.

The skullnet icon is glowing steadily by the time I cross the lobby, but I still feel afraid. Outside the door there's a gauntlet of at least fifteen mediots. They've caught sight of me and already their farsights are blinking in recording mode.

Face your fears, right? I step outside. A mob of strangers closes in, shouting questions. I shoulder through them. Feedback from my legs is a jumble of sharp sensation, hard to parse, but I think it's telling me I'm stepping on feet, kicking ankles. I don't care because I'm on the edge of panic, sure that someone in this crowd is not what they seem and that I'm about to take a knife in the ribs or feel the cold muzzle of a gun hard against the back of my neck, my last sensation. Then the sidewalk opens in front of me and I take off at a hard run.

The corner light cooperates with my escape, letting me cross the street. I turn right, then left, cross another street, and put another block behind me before I slow to a walk. I'm sucking for air; my heart's hammering. Despite my daily workouts, the five months I spent in prison have wrecked my aerobic conditioning. I need to start training again, today. But for now I just walk.

The sidewalk is not crowded, but there are people coming and going, some in masks. It makes me uneasy, not seeing their faces. Anonymity shifts the power balance, which is why we always patrolled with our visors opaque.

I try not to make eye contact, but I notice anyway when gazes linger on my legs. Some people even stop and stare, their farsights blinking in recording mode. A few try to stop me, to get me to talk, but I just keep going.

In my logical mind I know it's a beautiful afternoon, sunny and cool, but it's not my logical mind that's in control and I hate everything about being out on the street. I hate the touch of the breeze against my skin and the absurd lightness of my clothes that offer no protection against anything but sunburn; I hate that I don't have the assistance of the squad drone and that I can't tap into its angel vision to look around corners and assess hazards in the surrounding terrain. I hate that I have to turn around to know what's behind me.

To think I used to live like this all the time, vulnerable without even knowing it.

I eye the traffic, study the windows on both sides of the street, check doorways and alleys as I pass. I evaluate the pedestrians, masked and unmasked, and keep my distance from them when I can. I want to be in uniform, anonymous behind my black visor, linked in to a squad willing and able to back me up. I want the counsel and advice of my handler Delphi.

Up ahead I see a new hazard: scaffolding over the side-walk that's holding up an ugly canopy to protect passers-by from an ongoing remodel of the building above. The side-walk beneath the canopy is gloomy and enclosed. I don't want to go there, but I make myself do it anyway. The scaffolding squeezes the pedestrian traffic and I wind up trapped behind two older women who've just come out of a store. On the street, a gray cargo van rolls slowly along-side the curb, falling so far behind the flow of traffic that a taxi driver lays on the horn. It makes me think of the fake FBI van in the parking garage of the federal courthouse . . . and of the merc whose throat I tore out.

I fade back toward the building, watching the van driver who is watching me through an open window. He's a big man, muscular, with a military haircut. He's not wearing a mask, so I get a good look at him. My encyclopedia detects my interest and launches a facial-recognition routine, but it can't come up with an ID so he gets tagged *unknown*.

My paranoia is more creative, and labels him as an Uther-Fen mercenary.

I cut into a corner drugstore, weave between the aisles, go out a different door that opens onto a cross street where there is no scaffolding, waiting there until the van clears the intersection and moves on.

This street is luminous with late-afternoon light. It glints in rearview mirrors and the reflective faces of street signs, and picks out a flight of small objects suspended above the traffic: microdrones, three of them, hovering six meters or so above the center of the street. They look like aerial seekers, the palm-size helicopter drones the army uses for surveillance in urban environments, equipped with camera eyes, audio pickups, and chemical sensors.

I hear a faint buzz and turn to see another microdrone, this one just high enough above the street that it won't be hit by trucks. Looking up, I see even more—gray objects hovering high between the buildings. I try to count them: Seven? Eight?

"More than usual," a man observes.

I whip around, doing a threat assessment, ascertaining the position of potential enemy, but there's just the one guy. No high-fashion mask for him; he's going barefaced. He looks maybe thirty, skinny as a junkie, wearing tight jeans, a tighter shirt, and a lifeless prosthetic arm. He's gazing up into the blue through the lens of his farsights.

"Since when are any of them usual?"

"Since Coma Day. It's a whole new world out here." He brings his gaze back to Earth, looks at me, and gets labeled with the same tag as the other guy: *unknown*. "You're him, aren't you?" He gestures with his dead arm. "I was in Bolivia. You got better equipment than I did."

"The difference a couple years make. Who's running the drones?"

"Police. Private security. Mediots. General snoops."

"It's legal?"

He shrugs. "They're supposed to stay above the buildings. You know how that goes."

A tiny green light winks on in the corner of his farsights. He's recording me. I return the favor, logging an image of his face so my system will know him if we ever meet again. As I walk away, the microdrones retreat ahead of me like a flight of fairies.

Up ahead, I catch sight of the imposing bulk of an armored personnel carrier, rolling through the next inter-section surrounded by civilian traffic. It's an urban APC, with four wheels and four doors, marked with police insig-nia. So it's come to this? The police riding in military equip-ment on a beautiful, peaceful spring day?

I cross the street and jog the next block, walk the one

after that, alternating, but always looking around, evaluating threats. There's so much going on, so much in motion, cars and pedestrians and drones and bicycles, with uncountable windows and rooftops for snipers to inhabit. I need an AI to track it all.

Calm down, I think. *Calm down.* Too bad my skullnet doesn't know that command. The icon glows, but it's only taking the edge off, because in my profession—my former profession—a healthy fear can be the difference between life and death . . . but this isn't a healthy fear. If Delphi were with me, she'd adjust the biometrics, but I don't have a way to do that.

I stop wishing for it when I hear a shot—*bang!*—echoing off the buildings. I scramble for cover, shouldering open the door of a deli. Standing well back behind the window display, I try to guess where the shot came from, where it hit. *Bang!* I flinch as another gunshot rings out—except it's not a gunshot. Across the street, a pair of overenthusiastic kids helping out on a remodel are hurling old plywood panels into a steel truck bed.

My hands are shaking, but I make myself go outside again. The gray van I saw before is waiting at the curb, hazard lights flashing. The sliding door is ajar. Two muscular men stand on the sidewalk beside it, arguing in Russian. They wear civilian clothes but have military haircuts. Both look up at me. "Hey," one says, switching to English as the van door slides open wider on remote control.

I don't stay to find out what he has to say, or what's inside the van. Uptown traffic is stalled, so I make my escape by cutting in front of the van and then weaving between the cars until I'm in the middle of the street. I scare the shit out of an oncoming bicyclist as I dart in front of him to get to the opposite sidewalk. A block uptown a siren goes off. I look over my shoulder. One of the Russians is in the street, glaring at me, but his hands are empty. He's not carrying a weapon. Maybe he's not Uther-Fen after all. Maybe he's just a civilian who wants to tell his friends he got to meet the fucking Lion of Black Cross.

The siren is getting louder. The Russian glances uptown, scowls, and retreats, jumping into his van as a police APC like the one I saw before heads our way, lumbering across the intersection under lights and siren. I turn and walk fast for the corner. I want to get around it and out of sight, but the cops have other ideas.

The APC swoops up to the curb in a no-parking zone just ahead of me. Doors open. The cop riding shotgun jumps out, along with two more from the backseat. They head straight for me and I know I'm in trouble again for jaywalking in this town.

The first cop grins at his fellow officers. "I told you it was him. Lieutenant Shelley, sir, it is an honor to meet you—"

I glance back at the van, in time to see it turning the corner.

"—but I need to warn you not to cross the street like that. Tickets for pedestrian violations get issued automatically now, and there's nothing I can do to help you out."

"What?"

"You know, street cameras, they ID you with facial recognition and a ticket shows up in your city account if you're a resident, last known address otherwise." He sticks out his hand; his name tag says *Sutherland*. "Welcome home."

Officer Sutherland is carrying a gun, but I estimate the odds of him shooting me are low and I don't want the NYPD pissed off at me, so I shake his hand and then I shake hands with the other cops, trying not to show how messed up I am.

I think they suspect. Sutherland says, "It must be a shock for you, being in the big city again."

I ask about the microdrones. "Is it always like this?"

They turn to look at my flock of hovering fairies and as they do, the drones move away, rising higher between the buildings. "Shit," Officer Sutherland says. "Let me get the meter."

While he returns to the APC, one of the other cops explains. "All the drones emit IDs, so we can cite their registered owners for harassment, and seize the equipment on a repeat offense."

But by the time Sutherland is back with the meter, the drones are out of sight. "We'll log you into the system," he promises me. "Then our drones can monitor the situation."

I guess that means it's only police drones that are going to be pursuing me from now on, but I don't ask.

They let me go on my way, but I'm done. I need to get off the street.

I start to flag down a cab. Then I get a better idea. A few more blocks will bring me to Elliot Weber's apartment building. Elliot's a journalist, and he's been my friend since before I went in the army—though now that I think about it, his name wasn't in my phone log. It's possible he doesn't want to see me. During our last conversation, he was trying to tell me something important, and I wasn't listening. We didn't part on the best of terms.

It would be smart to call ahead, but I don't.

Maybe he's not even home.

I get to the lobby, and then I make the call.

He startles me by picking up right away. "Shelley? Where are you?"

"Downstairs."

"Stay there. I'm coming."

His apartment hasn't changed much: notes and papers on every horizontal surface; a stack of old tablets; a large monitor on the wall; a collection of long lenses for a digital SLR I've never seen him use. He sprawls on the couch, long and wiry, his tightly curled black hair cut short and his eyes veiled by the tinted lens of his farsights. I stand at the side of the window, studying the windows across the street, and the cars and people below. Looking up, I see a microdrone floating against the pale blue sky.

"Don't take this the wrong way," Elliot tells me, "but this needs to be said up front, so we understand each other. I appreciate your intentions on the First Light mission, but I think what you did was absolutely crazy. And wrong. There was no excuse for it. People *died*."

Lissa died.

The Uther-Fens we killed? I don't care about them. They were the enemy, and they were in our way.

Still, after being treated like a hero ever since the pardon, I'm almost relieved to hear a different opinion.

"I'm glad you got off," Elliot adds.

A gray van rolls slowly down the street, but I'm sure now that the Russian who tried to talk to me wasn't working for Carl Vanda.

Elliot gets up, walks to the window, looks down at the traffic. "What's up, Shelley?"

"I walked here and it was crazy. *I* was crazy. I was scared to be out there. I thought I'd get over it if I kept going, but it just got worse."

"Like a King David thing? A warning from the Red?"

"No." I try to laugh at myself, but the truth is I feel like I've been abandoned. "It hasn't messed with my head since I got back from First Light. I'm on my own now. I think my character's been cut from the show."

"Shelley . . ."

"I sound kind of crazy, don't I?" The van moves on, nothing suspicious about it. "It's just PTSD. I'm not the scary prick behind the black mask anymore, you know? I'm just scared I'm going to run into that guy. But it's stupid. No one came after me."

"I hate to break it to you," Elliot says. "But it's not stupid. You've got enemies. You have to know that."

I tense as I see someone move behind one of the windows across the street.

"I've got neighbors," Elliot reminds me. "Not all of them are killers."

"Sorry." I tell myself there's nothing outside I need to worry about, but I'm not convinced.

"You want to sit down?" Elliot asks, gesturing at the couch.

No. I want to watch the street and I want to know what's going on around me. It occurs to me that Elliot likes to know what's going on too. That's what makes him a good journalist. Once he latches on to a subject, it's hard to get him to let go—and he was interested in me. "Did you find out if there was anyone else like me?" I ask him.

"Like you? Another King David?"

"Yeah. Right before Coma Day, you were telling me you'd already heard a rumor about the Red, that there were soldiers in the linked combat squads who'd been hacked."

"Oh, okay. I remember that. I was doing a lot of research at the time—the unreliable sort that involves fringe sites and crazy speculation."

"So was it real? Were there others like me?"

"I don't know. I never got any names or details, if that's what you're asking. But you know what? I've got something better. How would you like to meet the film editor who put together the reality shows?"

I turn to him in astonishment. "Is that a hypothetical question?"

"No. I've met her. She's here in the city. I can probably set up a time to see her tomorrow, if you can make it."

"I can make it. How did she get the contract? Who dictated the script?"

He starts in on an involved explanation of how she came to handle the show, but I get a call on my overlay. It's an unknown number but it's got my passcode extension, so it rings through. "Hold on," I tell Elliot. And with my gaze I accept the call.

"LT?"

"Flynn?" I turn away from the window. "Flynn, is that you? Are you okay?"

"When are you coming back, LT?" She doesn't sound okay; she sounds like she's been crying. "'Cause I don't want to stay here anymore."

"Where are you, Flynn?"

"In a hotel."

I'm imagining that some asshole she picked up in a bar has been beating up on her, but then I check myself. This is Flynn. She tries to take after Harvey. If a guy pushed her around, she'd probably gut him. Fuck, maybe she did.

"Flynn, are you alone?"

"Sort of. Sergeant Vasquez is next door."

"You haven't been in any fights?"

"No."

"Okay. You stay out of trouble. I know it's a hard transition, but it's going to work out."

"It's just . . . I'm scared shitless every time I step outside. I feel like I'm gonna get slammed every time I go around a corner. I hate it here. I hate it."

"It's just the first day. It's going to get better." I hear her ragged breathing. "Flynn?"

"You're not coming back, are you?"

"I *am*. I'll see you in a day or two. It'll be okay."

Afterward, Elliot emerges from the kitchen where he retreated out of politeness. "Flynn of the Apocalypse Squad?"

he asks, handing me a glass of water. "Flynn who pulled a gun on you?"

"That wasn't her fault. That was Rawlings." I drink the water in one go. "I should head home."

"You're going to call a cab, right?"

"No." It's strange, but I feel a little less scared after talking to Flynn. "I'm going to walk. Nothing happened on my way here. Nothing is going to happen if I walk home."

He shakes his head. "That's a dangerous assumption. You're not going to get your old life back, Shelley. It's not a matter of will. Your world has changed."

I head for the door. "Let me know what time tomorrow."

"Stubborn as ever. Hold on a second. I'll go downstairs with you and show you a back way out."

We go to the first floor. I follow him to a fire door on the side of the building. "It's not as obvious as leaving by the front . . . I mean, if you think there's a chance the bad guys followed you here?"

"I don't know."

I don't know what's real and what's paranoia, but I'll play the game. I ease the door open just wide enough to get through. "See you tomorrow," I tell Elliot. Then I take off, running flat out to the corner, where the light's against me. I look back, I look around, I look for someone, anyone out to kill me, but there's nobody. I don't even see the micro-drones anymore. Maybe the cops got rid of them after all. The light turns and I walk across the street.

Twenty-five minutes later I'm two blocks from home and no one's tried to slam me yet. It looks like I might make it.

The sun has set, but there's still plenty of light as I approach the corner. The traffic light's against me, so I slow my pace, waiting for it to change. On the opposite corner a group of four is waiting to cross. One of them is an older man. He's chatting with two women, both of them wearing pretty white masks with gold filigree. A third woman stands a few feet away, half turned, looking back toward my dad's apartment building. She's slender, dressed in boots, dark slacks, and a gray coat, with blond hair down to her shoulders. I follow her gaze to where four or five mediots are still loitering on the sidewalk.

If I were going to set up an ambush, it would be here, where sooner or later my target would show.

I change my mind, deciding I'm not ready to go home yet. I step around the corner and into a shadow, to wait and watch.

The light changes. The pedestrians on the other side of the street step into the crosswalk. The man and the two masked women walk and talk together, but the other woman, the blonde without a mask, walks by herself. I catch my breath as my overlay identifies her.

Her eyes look gray in the waning light. She's three-quarters of the way across the street when she sees me. She hesitates. Her lips part in an expression of disbelief. Still in the street, she turns to look again at the mediots. Then she hurries to the curb. Her face is smooth, unmarred by smile lines.

"Delphi." My heart is beating hard again, but it's a good thing this time.

"Hi, Shelley." Her voice is magical. It's comfort. Delphi's no-nonsense guidance kept me alive more times than the Red. She cocks her head; still no smile. I want to move in, sweep her up in my arms, let her know how happy I am to see her, but I don't quite dare. I don't know what our boundaries are.

A faint blush in her cheeks hints that she's feeling awkward too. She says, "I was waiting with the paparazzi, hoping I'd get to see you, but it started to feel like a bad idea. . . . You're not still recording everything, are you?"

"No. Not since the army got deleted from my overlay. You want to get dinner?"

She looks me up and down, eyeing my titanium legs and my running clothes. "You're not really dressed for it."

I do not want her to go away. "Can we just walk?"

She lifts her chin to indicate the cross street, and that's the way we go. As we walk, she studies the street, the buildings overhead; she eyes the traffic. Every few steps, she looks over her shoulder. After the first block I ask her, "Have you seen the microdrones?"

"Yes." We walk another half block in silence. Then, "You probably don't know this, but after Black Cross I resigned my position."

That catches me by surprise. I think about the other soldiers she handled, feeling sorry for them.

"I moved back home to Madison, but when I heard about your pardon, well . . ." She looks up at me—she only comes up to my shoulder—and for the first time she gives me a little smile. "I worry about you, and I just . . . I really wanted to see you one more time. That's why I'm here."

I think if I could convey to her the truth about how glad I am she's here, I'd scare her away. So I just tell her part of it. "Geez, Delphi, if I could have picked one person, one living person, to magically appear on the street in front of me tonight, it would have been you."

She overlooks my joy and reacts to my grief. "I'm sorry for your girlfriend, Shelley. And I'm sorry for Ransom. He was a hell of a soldier. And Colonel Kendrick too."

"Do me a favor?"

She looks back over her shoulder. "I can try. What do you need?"

"Tell me your name."

• • • •

It's Karin Larsen. A name as smart and no-nonsense as she is. Walking with her, I feel my nervousness leach away. I stop looking at everything with suspicion. I start to relax.

We hit one of those lulls when, for a few seconds, the sidewalk is empty. The street is clear. Delphi points down the block. "That's my hotel on the corner."

I don't want to let her go. "Is there a bar? Maybe we could sit for a few minutes."

"Do you drink?" she asks, sounding surprised.

"No."

She laughs, looking up at the buildings across the street, looking over her shoulder. "Glad to hear it, because that's what I remember from your personnel—"

There's a catch in her breath. "Drop!"

I do it just like I would on patrol. She's still standing, looking up at something behind us when I hit the concrete. In the field, I'd take the impact on the struts of my dead sister, but here it's my forearms. I have just enough time to register how much it hurts when a little crater bursts open in the sidewalk a meter in front of me. Concrete chips and hot metal fragments tear into my face. I roll toward the building as another bullet bites the sidewalk where I was until half a second ago. I roll to my feet.

"Shelley, get in here!"

Delphi has retreated into an alcove with a glass door. She's got the door open. I hurl myself after her and we stumble together into the building.

She looks at me. "You're bleeding."

We're in the hotel lobby, near the elevator. On the other side of the lobby, the desk clerk is busy checking in two guests and hasn't noticed us. No one else is in sight. I pull Delphi away from the door. "They could shoot through it."

"They could *come* through it. I'm calling the police."

"No, hold on." My dad's been through enough. He doesn't

need to know about this. "I don't want to deal with the police. They're going to use words like 'protective custody.' And anyway, there's nothing they can do. The shooter will be long gone. These things get done in secret or they don't get done at all. No one is coming through that door."

I feel a warm trickle on my face and wipe it away.

Delphi looks like she wants to argue, but instead she grabs my arm and drags me toward the elevator, which opens at her touch. "If anyone asks, you fell down."

No one asks. We get to the fourteenth floor and into her room without meeting anyone.

It's a standard hotel room, with a king bed, two night-stands, a small desk, and a monitor on the wall above a set of drawers. The curtains are open, but the window looks out onto the cross street, not onto the street where the shooter waited for us.

Of course, a second shooter could be on this side of the hotel.

Delphi uses a remote control to close the blinds and the room goes black. Only after a few seconds can I see the green glow of a night-light from the bathroom.

"Even with the blinds closed, we need to stay away from the window," I warn her. "A good surveillance drone can see through . . ." I catch myself, as it occurs to me that Delphi knows exactly what a good surveillance drone can see through. "Sorry. You're the expert."

Her voice comes out of the dark, low, annoyed. "Get in the shower and wash off the blood. I'll be right back."

She returns with skin glue from the hotel convenience store.

We put a chair in the bathroom, and I sit in my running shorts looking up at the bright makeup lights while she glues the broken parts of my face back together, using her eyebrow tweezers to dig out bits of concrete I missed when I washed out the cuts in the shower.

It hurts, which is the only thing keeping my head clear.

My shirt is hanging up in the shower, drying after I washed the blood out. With the lights and the lingering steam there's already a fine sheen of sweat across my bare chest. Delphi has taken off her coat and her boots. She's leaning over me, wearing a silky white sleeveless pullover so sheer that every time she inhales I can see the contours of her bra as it cups her small breasts. Her skin's scent is magnetic and my brain is soaked with it. I stare at her from six inches away, committing an assault with my eyes, trespassing with my gaze against her features: her pale, creamy skin, pink lips parted in concentration, blond hair hooked behind petite ears, glistening brown lashes, and her bright blue eyes firmly focused on the task of minimizing my scars.

"Stop," she says without looking away from what she's doing, "staring at me."

"I can't help it."

She smiles, which does not improve my predicament. It's all I can do to keep my hands off her.

Too soon, she's done. I look in the mirror, to see each little cut glued neatly closed. "You're really good," I say, honestly impressed.

Her blue eyes meet my dark brown ones in the mirror. "Every handler gets three weeks' training in first aid and trauma. We can't coach you if we don't know how it's done."

"Training, huh? I always thought of you as a magic genie who was there whenever I called your name." I smile, gazing into her reflected eyes. "I guess I still think of you that way."

There's a flush in her pale cheeks as she looks away. "Too hot in here for me," she whispers, and walks out into the room.

I'm thinking of her and that big bed out there with its creamy sheets when I should be thinking about a sniper outside the window or a death squad outside the door . . . but I guess every man has his priorities.

The room is dark except for the light from the bathroom. Delphi is half sitting, half leaning on the dresser, her arms crossed, looking at me with grave eyes. "You had no idea that bullet was coming, did you? You always used to know these things, Shelley. What happened to King David?"

"Gone." If not for Delphi, I'd be dead. "I think it's not my story anymore."

If not for Delphi, I would never have walked down the street outside this hotel, and into an ambush. I give her a puzzled look, my heart running a little fast. "How the hell did they know I'd be here?"

Her arms are crossed tight just beneath her breasts. "I think it was a backup plan." She frowns at the floor. "My guess: They had their primary shooter at your apartment. Then some analyst ID'd me while I was waiting there for you, and decided I might work as bait."

People are predictable, and the more that's known about them, the easier it is to call their next move. My life is an open book, so it wouldn't have been hard for a skilled analyst to know how I feel about Delphi.

"If that was the plan, it was a good one." I sit down on the bed. "I expected a sniper at the apartment—hell, I've been expecting a sniper all day—but when it finally happened, I was distracted." I get up again and move closer to her. I touch her cheek. She looks up, surprising me with an angry glint in her eyes. I don't understand what's going on, what she wants, what she doesn't want. "Delphi . . . *Karin* . . . are you sorry I'm here? Do you want me to go?"

She answers with a little, exasperated laugh. *"No."*

"Then tell me what you're thinking, because if you make me guess I'm going to get it wrong."

"You've been expecting a sniper all day, but you've been walking around on the street. Why, Shelley? Do you have a death wish?"

This is not the conversation I want to have. "Look, I've been reading this whole thing wrong. I'm going to go." My shirt is still wet, but what the hell.

"I thought you died at Black Cross," she says, stopping me as I head for the bathroom.

I turn back, sure that I'm missing something, that there is more behind her words than I'm wired to understand.

Her voice and her gaze are steady. "You do crazy things, Shelley, and I can't tell how much of it's you and how much of it is the Red playing you. At Black Cross, when you went outside, I was there with you. Remember? I was looking through your eyes. I saw the flash when that nuke went off. I saw the analysis—and I knew it was over. You were dead. You had to be, and it didn't make any sense to me." She looks away. "That whole mission, I'd been so scared. And then we won . . . it seemed like we won . . . until you walked outside *for no reason* and then you were gone. All contact lost."

She has started to tremble, though she's trying not to show it. Her arms are still crossed, her shoulders hunched. She won't look at me. I go back to her, touch her shoulder. I have no idea what to say. Black Cross was a lifetime ago.

She looks up at me with her somber eyes. "I couldn't handle it." Looks away again. "I went home and I cried for hours. I sent in my resignation. And no one bothered to tell me you were still alive. When episode two came out, I thought it was propaganda. It wasn't until you came back from First Light that I started to think it might be true, that you really had survived. It's stupid, but that's why

I came here. Just to be sure you're not some figment of government propaganda or a generated character conjured up by the Red."

"I am so damn sorry. I didn't know."

"I'm not looking for an apology. It's not your fault. And you don't owe me anything—"

"Yes, I do."

She looks up at me again. "Then stop making yourself a target. Stop daring God or the Red or whoever or whatever it is. I've already seen you die once for no reason. Once is enough."

I put my arms around her. She's still got her arms crossed, but she leans into me a little.

"Being a civilian is a raw deal," I tell her.

She scoffs. "You've decided that already?"

"Hell, yeah. I hated being out on that street today. I never felt so vulnerable in my life. I don't want to go out without my armor and bones, my weapons, my angel eyes. Without *you*, looking over my shoulder. At Dassari, we hunted down and we killed anyone who tried to kill us. . . . NYPD is being nice to me, but I don't think they're going to let me get away with that here."

"Probably not. So what are you going to do?"

I tell her about the e-mail from Anne Shima. "I haven't talked to her yet, but most of the squad is kind of interested and Flynn's all for it. She's had enough of civilian life. She's having trouble adjusting. I am too."

"You've been out one day."

"One day, and somebody tried to blow my head open. I want to be in a position to hit back."

"There is that." She sighs and shifts, yielding at last. Her arm goes around my waist as she rests her head against my chest like she's listening to my heart beating. "So you've already decided?"

"I think so. I think it's my best choice. And I want you to be part of it—I mean, if you don't mind working with me again and you need a job that may or may not be legal."

"Oh, a chance to watch you die again?"

"Well, that's not the goal."

She laughs, soft and cynical and deep in her throat. It's like she's already seen everything that's going to unfold between us and she knows what an idiot I'm going to be.

And I want her.

So badly.

I give up on being a gentleman. I scoop her up, making her gasp, and then I collapse on the bed with her, kissing her face, her neck, waiting for her to protest, to tell me to get the fuck out of there, but she doesn't so I unhook the little pearl button at the back of her shirt and she helps me to get it off and then I get her bra unhooked and out of the way and kiss her pink nipples, my brown hands looking so dark against her pale, pale skin. She makes a little mewling noise as she unbuttons her pants. I pull back just long enough to help her get them off, to get her panties off, to get my shorts off, and then I'm against her again, skin to skin, pushing into her but slowly, making myself go slowly, I don't want to hurt her. She pulls my head down, bringing my mouth to her mouth and we kiss, deep and wet and I'm all the way inside her and I don't think I could stop now if she told me to, but she doesn't. She throws her head back and we fuck and I hold out as long as I can and she comes, I come, we come together.

By the middle of the night we're exhausted and paranoid. Fear of death squads makes us ask for a different room.

• • • •

"Hey, Shelley. I guess you're still alive."

I don't remember answering the call, but it's Elliot, speaking through my audio implants. I blink my eyes, trying to wake up, trying to focus on the time displayed in my overlay: 0932. Jesus.

I have a vague memory of calling my dad sometime last night, letting him know I'd met someone and not to worry. I'm struggling to figure out where Elliot comes into the equation. Delphi is curled up next to me, breathing softly, still asleep, but her eyes blink open when I ask Elliot, "Uh . . . yeah, what's up?"

He sounds irritated. "You remember we were going to see the film editor behind *Linked Combat Squad*?"

I do remember that.

"Shelley, what the hell is wrong with you?"

"Nothing. I just woke up. What time is the appointment?"

"Ten thirty. You okay with that?"

"Yeah. I'm going to bring a friend."

"Who?"

I trade a gaze with Delphi. "Where should I meet you?" I ask him.

"I'll text you the address. Make sure you show up." Then he adds, "Thelma Sheridan's trial started today, in case you forgot about that too." The link closes.

I frown, reaching past Delphi to the nightstand for the TV remote.

"Where are we going?" she wants to know, stretching beautifully with her arms over her head.

I give up on the remote and reach for her breast instead. "To see a filmmaker."

She catches my wrist, giving me a dark look. "A film-maker? You haven't had enough exposure lately?"

• • • •

When I get out of the shower the TV is on, with a blond mediot made up to plastic perfection reading lines from behind a news desk. ". . . the so-called trial of kidnapped American Thelma Sheridan began today. Sheridan is accused of crimes against humanity for alleged involvement in the Coma Day atrocities in the United States."

Delphi, dressed in a white hotel robe, is packing her suitcase. She gives me a suspicious look as I sit down at the foot of the bed. It's like she can see the skullnet icon, flickering in the corner of my vision.

"She has refused all legal counsel or representation, and this morning she faced a hostile courtroom as she delivered a stirring opening statement."

In Niamey, it's already afternoon.

The video shifts to a courtroom. The camera pans across a panel of seven judges, middle aged to elderly: four women, three men; Asian, European, African, the flags of many countries draped from poles behind them.

Next we see Thelma Sheridan. It's a close-up shot designed to make her look noble, brave. She's gazing off camera, her expression fiercely determined. Her hair has been freshly trimmed but not colored, and the new growth coming in is gray. There is a shadow that could be a bruise across one flat cheekbone. I flash on a memory of her with Ransom's blood splattered on her face. The hair on the back of my neck stands up.

The clip cuts to her speaking, midsentence: ". . . sought no representation. I will make no defense. To do so would only legitimize an illegal proceeding. I have been held here against my will, punished for a crime I did not commit. My true offense, the offense that made me a pariah among powerful elements in the American government, was my well-known opposition to the invasive artificial intelligence known as the Red.

"Under secret orders issued extraconstitutionally, the so-called Apocalypse Squad was tasked to remove me from my home and transport me here to face a mock trial on false charges. But I will not be silenced.

"The world is facing a threat unlike any other. The Red is real. It is an invading entity, born of our hubris, and now taking control over all human systems. It is our duty to resist."

Extreme words, but not all untrue. Jaynie might say the same thing. Like Sheridan, she has a vendetta against the Red. It offends her to imagine her life plotted and manipulated. If Jaynie could eliminate the AI, she would—but not at the cost of burning down the world.

Thelma Sheridan doesn't share that restraint. "Any action taken to limit or destroy the Red is justified, in defense of the future existence and autonomy of humanity."

"So she was justified in what she did." I turn to Delphi.

She meets my gaze with a wary frown.

"That's what she's saying," I insist.

"Yes."

It's not the Red that frightens me.

The clip ends and we're looking again at the blond mediot, nodding her perfect face in sympathy with the accused. "The prosecution began presenting evidence today, though our legal consultants tell us that by the standards of American courts, this evidence is tainted—"

The TV turns off. Delphi tosses the remote onto the bed. "You look like you're about to take a swing at someone."

"Sorry." I lie back and stare at the ceiling.

"Ten thirty," she reminds me.

I get up again.

She heads for the bathroom. "I'm going to take a shower," she says over her shoulder. "And then we need to stop by your place so you can change clothes."

All I have with me are running clothes. "There's a store downstairs. I'll just buy something."

I wait until the bathroom door closes behind her, then I call my dad. He sounds relieved to hear from me. "Jimmy, you okay?"

"I'm good. I'm going to come by the apartment later."

"Call me when you do. I'm at work, but we can get lunch."

"Sure. That sounds good."

There's an awkward pause. I want to reassure him, but there's not much I can say. "We'll talk later," I promise, and we leave it at that.

Delphi is still in the shower when I go downstairs. There's a self-serve boutique in the hotel lobby where I pick out a collared shirt and slacks. I scan the tags at the checkout. Then, using my overlay, I call up my bank account number—I can never remember it—and tap it in on the touch screen. The amount shows up on my overlay. I approve it, and the transaction is done.

I try to get back upstairs, but the room was reserved under the name of Karin Larsen. The elevator doesn't know me and won't open at my touch, so I change clothes in the lobby restroom. Delphi is at the desk, checking out, when I reemerge in the guise of a respectable civilian. She's wearing farsights today. She looks me up and down through their clear lens, her gaze lingering extra seconds on my bare titanium feet before returning to my face. With a flicker of a smile she tells me, "I approve."

From that point, she assumes control of the operation, directing me to stay inside while she surveys the street and summons a cab. I'm not even allowed to carry her suitcase. "It will slow you down." Only when she's in the backseat does she turn and crook a finger at me. I shove the door open and bolt, rocking the cab as I drop onto the seat beside her, slamming the door behind me.

"Get down!" she orders, manhandling me until my head is in her lap. She glares at the driver, a small, black-skinned woman who is scowling at us over the back of the seat. "Let's go," Delphi says. "Before the mediots find out he's here."

The driver eyes me suspiciously, and then recognition sparks. "Hey, you're—"

Delphi isn't one to be trifled with. "Let's *go*."

The address Elliot gave me is an office building on West Fifty-Fourth. On the way over, we research the building and study the directory of tenants. Delphi is annoyed that I don't have the company name, but there's only one likely candidate: Koi Reisman Productions. They do most of their work for charitable organizations, editing raw digital footage to develop docudramas with maximum emotional appeal. Nowhere in their company profile is it mentioned that they've worked on *Linked Combat Squad*.

Elliot meets us in the lobby, looking surprised when he sees me. "What happened to your face?"

I forgot about the cuts. "Nothing's bleeding, right?"

"No."

I decide not to answer his question, and turn instead to Delphi, to make the introductions. "Elliot, this is Karin Larsen. Karin, Elliot Weber."

Delphi is surveying everyone present, using her farsights to log faces, masked and unmasked, into a database so she'll have a record of who was present if trouble finds us. This keeps her busy, so she doesn't bother with chitchat. Glancing at Elliot, she asks, "What led you to Koi Reisman Productions?"

Elliot has watched *Linked Combat Squad* many times— enough that he recognizes her voice. "You're Delphi!"

"Come on, Shelley," she says. "I don't like being in the

open, especially when I can't identify everyone." She strides to the security desk, pulling her little rolling suitcase. On the desk is a prominent sign: *Security Requires Masks to Be Removed.* Fine with me.

We present ourselves, and have our faces scanned and our appointment confirmed. During the process, Elliot gives me a questioning look. "Doesn't she work for Guidance?"

I smile. "Not anymore."

We're admitted through the security gate, to the bank of elevators. One is standing open. We step aboard and Delphi touches the key for the nineteenth floor.

"It's on the twentieth," Elliot says as the doors close.

She gives him an arch look. "Shelley will wait on the floor below until I've assessed the situation on the twentieth. Did you tell anyone else about this appointment?"

"No. No, I don't think so." Elliot looks at me. "What the hell is going on?"

"I wasn't just being paranoid yesterday," I tell him.

"Someone came after you?"

I nod.

"Who?"

"I don't know. Lots of candidates, though. Carl Vanda. Rogue Uther-Fen. Nativists offended by what I've done to US sovereignty. Any dragon who resents losing privilege. The president?"

"So what happened? Did you call the police?"

I don't want to scare him with the details, so all I say is, "The police can't help."

The elevator stops on the nineteenth floor. No one is in sight, so I step off. Elliot starts to follow, than changes his mind and stays with Delphi. I wait by a window, looking down on the city. A minute later, Delphi calls. "We're clear." I take the stairwell up.

. . . .

Koi Reisman Productions is a small firm with a staff of three. Koi herself is an older woman with a dancer's petite figure. She wears her thick gray hair in a braid on her shoulder and speaks in a low, precise voice. "I need to let you know there's an NDA, a nondisclosure agreement. I know why you're here, but there's not much I can talk about."

FaceValue suggests she is nervous. I screenshot the report and send it to Delphi.

"This is all off the record," Elliot assures her. "Just like before."

We're in a sitting area in the front office, furnished with a couch and armchairs. The two assistant editors and the office manager have disappeared into the back.

Koi glances at the door before returning her gaze to me. "Elliot took advantage of my vanity. No one was supposed to know we were the firm doing the work on this project, and I was okay with that when we started. The money was good, *is* good." She sighs and shakes her head. "I've worked on a lot of meaningful projects in my career, but *Linked Combat Squad* is easily the best work I've ever done—and no one knows I've done it except my staff and Elliot, who let me believe"—she gives him a dirty look—"that he already knew what was going on, leading me to share more than I should have."

Elliot is concerned. "Did someone find out you talked to me?"

"It was bound to get out," she says in a cautious voice.

She's clearly uncomfortable, worried about what she can say, so before she decides to say nothing, I ask what I want to know the most: "How many episodes are planned? Is it just episode four?"

She frowns, not meeting my gaze. "There isn't going to

be an episode four. *Linked Combat Squad* has finished its run. That's been reported in all the media."

I don't believe her. In my cell, I watched my overlay send uploads almost every night for five months. "It's not over," I insist. "There's been more digital footage. You've seen it, haven't you? Video from the courthouse?"

She bites her lip, and after a few seconds she whispers, "Oh, screw the NDA. You deserve to know, if anybody does. It's not episode four. It's a new series. The contract is for three shows—"

"*Three?*" I start to sweat, thinking about where the material for three shows might come from, and wondering if I'm going to get pulled back in.

She watches me with wide, wary eyes. "The first episode was finished over the weekend. It'll be released tonight in a special showing. The series is called *Against the Beast*. My staff and I, we think it's a double reference—to dragons like Thelma Sheridan who imperil the world, and to Revelation, where the dragon summons the beasts of the Apocalypse—a metaphor for nuclear weapons. At least that's how we interpret it." She sighs, and then she smiles an apologetic smile. "We live in a crazy quilt of cultural traditions. Our mythologies are as blended as we are. It doesn't really matter if we've got the interpretation right. It only matters that the name resonates with the people who watch the show."

I want to know everything about the new series: who's involved and how the process works. Because then, maybe, I can understand the purpose behind the shows, and maybe I can guess what's coming.

"Who's your contact person?"

"There is no one, beyond the federal contracting officer, and that's just financial. I've talked to her. She doesn't know what we're doing here. She gets a notice to approve the payments, and she does."

"So there's no direct oversight?"

"None."

"And how much material do you receive? Do you have to fast-forward through all twenty-four hours of every day?"

"No! No, no, no. We'd never be able to handle that in the time we're given. We get extended clips, and we work from those. We don't see the boring stuff—the quiet time, the sleep periods, the personal hygiene that no one wants to see."

"You don't know who selects the clips?"

"No."

"Do you get daily updates?"

"No, they come in every few days, a package of files with digital footage from multiple cameras. The record from your overlay is only part of it. There's a lot more going on, especially in the new episode. It's called *The Trials*, plural, because the integrity of all the main characters is tested."

"What about the next two episodes? Have you seen scripts or story outlines or anything like that?"

"No. There's never a script. It's up to me to make a coherent story out of the material I receive."

"Out of my life?"

"For *Linked Combat Squad*, yes."

Delphi speaks for the first time. "Why do you think *Linked Combat Squad* was your best work?"

I think it's a peculiar question, but Koi doesn't. "Because it told an important story that spoke to many different people. These days, most programming is aimed at a narrow audience. *LCS* was different. It was aimed at a wide range of narrow audiences. It had universal elements that appealed across demographic bubbles, elements that affected a range of people, inspired them, united them . . . let people know that individuals can make a difference, even if there's a heavy price to pay."

"The demonstration on the National Mall," Elliot said. "That only happened because of the show."

Koi leans forward, resting her elbows on her knees so her braid sways free. In a conspiratorial whisper she says, "That's the aim of the show—to shift the direction of the culture. That's how I see it. The story is expanding, Lieutenant Shelley. Your court-martial is part of the new episode of course, but it's just a small part. I don't think you need to worry about the other two shows, because your role appears to end with the pardon."

So I was right.

"Does the new show include any other soldiers?" I ask. "Anyone like me?"

I feel Delphi stiffen beside me. She puts her hand on my arm, making me wonder what she knows, but I can ask her later. For now, I keep my gaze on Koi, who says, "No, there are no other soldiers. But there are new adventures and new heroes—on the Mall, in the streets, among the witnesses. Heroes who endure their own ordeals, their own trials, who have protected you without your knowledge, Lieutenant Shelley, and prevented a reprise of Coma Day."

I stumble over what she just said. "What do you mean, 'a reprise'? Are you saying there was another nuclear device? One that was close to us? To the courthouse in DC?"

Her lips press together as if to contain the secret, but she affirms it anyway with a nod. As if she can't help herself, she adds, "I believe the title tells us the theme of the new series."

"Nukes?" Delphi asks in a weary voice.

Koi leans back, presses her knuckles to her lips, clearly struggling with how much to say. "It's just my guess." Then she stands abruptly. "And I'm not going to say any more than that, because I don't want this project taken away from me. I want to be part of it. I want to do the next two episodes—and that means you need to go."

No one argues. We move toward the door. It's a strange feeling, a combination of relief and a poignant sort of nostalgia to have confirmation that it's over, that I've been cut loose—no more King David because the Red is not telling my story anymore. Whatever plot twist I have to face next, I'll face on my own.

"I don't like it," Elliot says when we're all tucked into the back of a cab with me in the middle. "If Koi's right, your adventures should be over. So why is someone trying to kill you?"

"Because happily-ever-after is always a fiction."

"Huh. So what are you going to do?"

"Go home."

"Is that safe?"

"Probably not, but I need my gear. I need breakfast. I need to make some phone calls." I need to talk to my dad too, but I'm not in a hurry to have that conversation.

I look at Delphi. "I need to know what you're going to do."

She turns a pointed gaze on Elliot.

"What?" he asks, looking offended.

I take her hand. "Delphi and I have things to talk about."

"Like how you're going to avoid getting killed?"

"I guess that's part of it."

"No more secret missions, though? That's not what you need to talk about, right?"

I'm not sure how to answer that one. My hesitation ignites his suspicion.

"Damn it, Shelley! This is just like that last time we talked in San Antonio, when you said you weren't going to do anything stupid."

"I don't know what I'm going to do. I need to figure things out."

"Figure things out with the help of your partner in war?" He's glaring at Delphi.

She turns to look out the window.

"Leave Delphi out of this," I warn him. "It's like you said yesterday, Elliot. I can't get my old life back. So I have to adapt."

The cab pulls up in front of my building. The crowd of mediots has thinned to three. They eye the cab suspiciously, waiting to see who will emerge from behind the tinted windows. Delphi looks them over. "They were here yesterday. ID as freelancers. Long histories."

"So they probably won't try to kill me?" I ask as I pay the cabdriver.

She gives me a dark look past the clear lens of her far-sights. "You never know. I'll go first, get my bag from the trunk. When they turn to look at me, I want you to move— straight into the building."

She gets out. The driver does too. I turn to Elliot. "Thanks for taking me to see Koi."

"You're taking off, aren't you?"

He's angry. I don't blame him. "Take care, okay?"

"That's good advice, Shelley. Advice you should follow."

I open the door, step from the cab into the shelter of the canopy, and in three strides I'm at the front door, with the mediots shouting questions behind me. I reach for the lock pad, remembering too late that I never confirmed with my dad that he'd reactivated my access—but that's not the kind of thing he forgets. The lock clicks and, ignoring the mediots, I push into the lobby. When it's clear I've escaped, the mediots converge on Delphi, but she's only a step behind me, and she gets past them unmolested.

On the elevator it's only us, so my arms go around her. I kiss her hair. "My dad's at his office," I whisper. "But he's got surveillance cameras in the apartment."

"Awkward," she says regretfully. "I'll just have to kiss you now."

She does.

I'm on the phone with Anne Shima when my dad shows up at the apartment, so furious he's shaking.

"When were you going to tell me?" he demands.

Delphi and I both stand up from the couch. She circles around him, moving toward the door, while I tell Shima I'll call her later. Keeping my voice calm, I ask, "What's the matter, Dad?"

"Your friend Elliot Weber came to see me at my office. He said you ran into trouble last night. By the condition of your face, he wasn't lying. He's under the impression you're about to do something stupid. Take on another secret mission? Gamble your life again?"

I believed I could trust Elliot to be discreet. I know the truth now. "I didn't want you to worry, Dad, but I was going to let you know. I'm leaving New York. I have to."

"You don't have to."

"Someone tried to kill me yesterday."

"And you didn't even call the police—because you want to take care of it yourself? Where the hell did you get the idea that it's okay for you to be part of some vigilante crew?"

"That's not what this is about. And I want this to be over too, but it's not over. You have to see that."

"No. No. What I see is you throwing your life away, again. Look at you! You're standing there on artificial legs. You have just narrowly escaped spending the rest of your life in prison. And Lissa is dead. She's dead because of your adventurism, and you've already replaced her?" He gestures at Delphi, who is poised by the door, on the verge of slipping away.

"Dad, this is Karin Larsen."

"Elliot told me who she is."

"None of this is her fault. She wasn't part of First Light."

"You're really leaving, aren't you?"

"Yes."

"Then don't come back."

At first I can't process it, too stunned by these words I never imagined I'd hear. Then instinctively, I move toward him. "Dad . . ."

He raises his hand, palm out. "No. I love you more than anything in this world, Jimmy, but I cannot do this again. I don't know where I went wrong. I don't know what the hell happened that made you like this. I'd blame it on the wiring in your head, but you've been like this since you were nineteen." He gazes at me, old and gray, but not a weak man, never that. "I won't go through it again, waiting to learn if you're going to live or die. If you leave now, you leave for good."

Silence falls between us. The skullnet icon flickers. Inchoate plans form and die in my mind. But I already know what I need to say. "I want you to leave with me, Dad. You're not safe here either." I take one more step closer. "Come with me. Please."

"So your friends can protect me the way they protected Lissa? No, thank you. I've got my own security. I'll take my chances here."

That's it. He turns and walks out. Delphi watches him go, her face locked, no expression, no presence, until the door closes behind him. Then she leans against the wall, squeezing her eyes shut. "Are you sure?" she whispers.

No.

But I can't stay here.

• • •

One big lesson I learned from my time in service: Focus on what needs to be done *now*.

So I get Shima back on the phone.

The quintessential American male is supposed to be independent, able to handle his own shit, but me? I'm used to being under the protection of a very large and intimidating organization. My day-to-day life in the army tended to be hazardous, but I lived in secure housing, I had access to weapons, and I was in a position to protect myself and those who mattered to me. After only forty hours on my own, I can't wait to get myself back under that kind of organizational security.

I try to talk details with Shima—what she wants, what her organization of mysterious assholes is after, what I get out of it, but the phone connection is intermittent, her voice chopped and cut by blocks of silence until, after a minute, the call drops.

It's been less than six months since Coma Day—not nearly enough time to restore what was destroyed. In the end she e-mails me, inviting me to come see her, no obligation.

Delphi is sitting at the end of the couch, a tablet in her lap, engrossed in some project, her fingers dancing across the screen, unaware of my gaze as I watch her for half a minute or more. I'm thinking of her, thinking of Lissa, weighing my dad's words—and I know he's wrong. This thing between me and Delphi is too new to define. No way to know where it's going. But I know this much: Lissa is part of me and always will be. No matter what comes to pass between Delphi and me, what I shared with Lissa won't be rewritten.

If she were still alive—

No.

I won't pretend.

Lissa is gone. I will never have her back again.

But as I watch Delphi with the light from the window wrapped around the curves of her face, my heart fills with gratitude that she's here with me. "Delphi?"

"Uh-huh?"

"Things are moving kind of fast between us. . . ."

Her fingers freeze above the virtual keyboard. Then she slips off her farsights and turns to look at me, cool judgment in her eyes. "Second thoughts, Shelley?"

A better man would answer *yes*.

"I was just going to ask if you'd consider going to the ends of the Earth with me."

She cocks her head. "And where exactly would that be?"

I forward Shima's e-mail to her. "Northern Wyoming."

"That's a long way." Her gaze scans back and forth across the screen of her tablet before she looks again at me. "We're going to need a car."

"That's your way of saying yes?"

"Yes."

We trade a smile.

Elliot called her my partner in war and that's true. Me and Delphi have been together a long time. I think I've come to know her pretty well and she knows everything there is to know about me—who I am, what I've been through—she's gone through a lot of it with me. We know how to operate together.

She goes to work on a plan that will get us out of the city; I work on reconnecting with the squad. The only number I have is Flynn's, so I link to that. I'm caught off guard when Jaynie picks up.

No greeting; Shima must have messaged her, because she gets straight to business. "Shelley, you made up your mind? You're going to Wyoming?"

"Yes."

"Have you had any trouble?"

"A sniper—"

"*Shit*. You're not hit?"

"No."

"Was the Red looking out for you?"

"No. There was no warning." I look at Delphi. "Just got lucky." She bares her teeth at me. To Jaynie I say, "What about you? Anything happen on your side?"

"Small-time stuff compared to you."

"Trust me to grab all the dramatic scenes."

"I've noticed. Are you safe where you are?"

"For now. But—"

"No 'buts.' Just stay where you are. Stay under cover. We're coming to get you."

My relief is real. No matter how smart our next move, Delphi and I are vulnerable on our own. I hold my hand out to her and she takes it, giving me a questioning look. "We need to get you armor," I tell her.

"I've got armor," Jaynie says, unaware Delphi is there. "I've got our angel too. Chudhuri pried it out of storage somewhere and turned it over."

Our squad drone—I wish I had that here. "So who's in?"

"Everybody."

"Even Moon? I thought he was smarter than the rest of you."

"It didn't last. He reverted to type. I've got a stop scheduled to pick up weapons—"

"Jaynie, you can't bring weapons into the city."

"I don't give a shit, Shelley. I'm bringing weapons."

Right. I hope the police drones don't give a shit either.

She says, "Send your address. I'm putting our ETA at ninety minutes."

That takes me by surprise. "Ninety minutes? It takes almost four hours to drive here from DC."

"We left early."

"What if I said I wasn't coming?"

I swear I can hear her smile. "You're predictable, Shelley. Shima's got you modeled. She knew what your decision would be."

Shima is not the first to pull that off. "Jaynie, Delphi's with me. She's coming to Wyoming with us."

Two seconds of silence go by, then, "Wait . . . *Delphi?* Your handler?"

"Yeah. She quit Guidance."

"And came to New York to look you up?"

I hear the suspicion in her voice, and I don't like it. "I trust her, Jaynie. All the way."

The suspicion is still there when she tells me, "Glad to hear it, but it's going to take me some time to catch up with you on that one. We're at the gun shop. I've got to go. Send the address." She breaks the link.

Delphi is watching me.

"They're coming," I tell her.

"I worked that one out. If you're having any doubts about me coming along—"

"*No.* No, I am not, and you're part of the squad anyway, even if Jaynie doesn't know you." I reach for her. She puts aside her tablet and her farsights, and then she comes into my arms. "But I have to ask you, why would you want to do this?"

She leans against my chest and thinks about it. "I don't have a good reason, except that you're alive and I'd like to see you stay that way. And besides, I've been out of work for months, and I'm bored out of my mind."

This is flattering. "So you're going to go rogue with me and turn into a merc because you're bored?"

"Who said anything about being a merc? I haven't heard there's a job on offer for me."

"There's a job. *I'm* offering."

"You?" She looks up; her eyebrows arch. "And what kind of job would that be?"

Those blue eyes, daring me.

I have to look away. "There's a surveillance camera in here."

She crawls into my lap anyway, kisses me on the mouth. We need to be getting ready to go, but we spend a few minutes at it anyway. We break off only when the building shudders. Delphi pulls back, looks around. A second later we hear the rumble of an explosion.

I propel myself off the couch, sliding to the floor, carrying Delphi with me. Her eyes flare in surprise, and then she's lying on the carpet beneath me, her hand gentle against my cheek. "Hey, take it easy. That was far away."

"Not that far," I growl.

A faint wail of sirens and angry car horns seeps through the apartment's insulation. Delphi tilts her head back to look at the window. I follow her gaze. Blocks away, a fat plume of black smoke is churning into the sky. We get up to look, standing carefully to the side of the window. The smoke is from somewhere near Penn Station. I turn on the recording function in my overlay because I want to remember this. Delphi grabs her farsights and does the same thing.

"This isn't uncommon," she says in a low voice. "Bombs go off somewhere in the country almost every day—although that's a big one."

"I thought the country was recovering."

"You didn't get much news when you were in custody, did you?"

"No."

"The official line, and what most of the mediots preach, is that the Red isn't real. But the paranoid types know that's a lie. Thelma Sheridan is their hero. They want to get rid of the Red, and they don't care about the cost. Critical targets like the remaining data exchanges and undersea cables have massive security now, so terrorists go for smaller targets like cell towers, and server farms when they can get to them. But more and more it's just random."

"Like a nuke in DC?"

"That isn't hard for me to believe. Not at all."

On the street below the window, traffic is stopped, generating a faint chorus of bleating horns. One vehicle at the end of the block isn't willing to wait: A shoddy old van with rust stains on the roof surges up onto the sidewalk, startling two pedestrians, who jump clear. With two wheels still in the gutter, the van guns down the sidewalk—and I know a slam is coming. I grab Delphi's arm, dragging her from the window as the van stops right below us. "Get away! Get into the hall!"

I wish I could scream a warning to the other residents and to all the people stuck in traffic.

Delphi's a handler and a damn good one. She doesn't waste time with questions or protests as we fall back across the living room, through the foyer. I open the door and shove her ahead of me into the hall, yanking the door closed behind us just at the moment of the explosion.

The blast wave hurls me across the hallway. The pressure is like a glass spike in my ears. I can't breathe. I'm down on the floor and it's vibrating under me, unnatural motion accompanied by an avalanche of noise. Dust everywhere, so thick I can't see. Concrete dust, a cold wind, muffled screaming beyond the deafening ringing in my ears.

The floor stops quivering and the dust begins to clear, some of it sifting out of the air, more carried away by the wind.

Both walls of the hallway are intact, but the apartment door is hanging open on broken hinges, with torn black wiring protruding from the frame. Past the door, the apartment glows with spring sunlight softened by a glittering haze of dust settling out across the tumbled furniture. The outer wall is gone, and in the building across the street the windows I can see are shattered.

I turn to look for Delphi. She's on the floor, a fallen statue molded of gray dust, coming slowly to life, raising her head, pulling off her farsights, coughing hard as she pushes up to hands and knees.

Why the fuck did I bring her here? I should never have gone near her. I should never have come home at all. I should have broken with my dad first thing Saturday night and headed straight for Anne Shima, armed myself with every piece of firepower she could give me, and gone hunting for Carl Vanda.

I'm going after him now. I swear it.

Fuck me, anyway.

I get up—at least the legs still work—and help Delphi to her feet. She has all her limbs; nothing looks broken; I don't see blood.

I put my arm around her shoulders. I need to get her out of the building—"Come on"—my own voice sounding muffled in my shocked ears.

As we head for the stairs, a door opens in the hallway. A woman staggers out, covered in gray dust so I can't tell her age. An older man emerges from another apartment. "My God," he wails. "My God." We all get to the stairs and join an exodus heading down. "The gas lines," a woman calls out. "What if they catch on fire?"

We get to the street. It's chaos. Cars are still jammed bumper to bumper. Some of them are burning. People are screaming for help. Where the front of my building used to be, there's a slope of debris: broken concrete, drywall, wood paneling, shattered furniture, and pipes, with water spraying over all of it. God knows who's crushed beneath. What's left of the sidewalk is paved in shards of glass.

People come running in from nearby streets, wide eyed, looking to help; others are fleeing. Sirens scream in the distance, but the police can't get here because traffic on the cross streets is at a standstill. A single motorcycle cop appears at the end of the block, rolling in along the opposite sidewalk.

Across the street, all the lower windows in a thirty-eight-story condominium are shattered, the front doors reduced to warped steel frames. A man in a gray business suit is making his way out past the wreckage, moving carefully but calmly. I watch him past the smoke, the flames, the dust settling out of the air.

My overlay can't identify him because of his headgear: an old-fashioned fedora, tinted farsights, and an iridescent mask like the one Major Ogawa showed me.

But I don't need to see his face. I know him anyway. His brief appearance in the courtroom made a lasting impression on me. I know him by his biometrics—his height, his gaunt build, his severely straight posture. And by his kinetics—the particular way he walks, favoring his right hip. *Carl Vanda.*

He's clutching a hard-walled, dull-gray case, one that's just long enough to hold a sniper rifle if the weapon is broken down to stock and barrel. He gets past the broken door and pauses, showing no concern for the risk of falling glass as his masked face looks across the street—right at me.

I grab Delphi as Vanda uses his free hand to reach inside his coat. I drag her down with me behind the cover of the burning cars just as a gun goes off. Silver bees—the payload of a fléchette shell—whine through the air we just occupied, throwing themselves in suicidal rage against the wreckage of my building.

Delphi struggles in my arms. She tries to get free. "Stay down!" I plead as someone—it has to be the motorcycle cop—shouts, *"Drop the weapon!"* It sounds just like a movie.

I can't see what happens next, but I hear a second shot from Vanda's gun. Someone starts screaming: an adrenaline-fueled howl of pain. The hair on my arms stands on end as I remember other times and other wounded, screaming just like that.

I get up on my knees, lifting my head just high enough to peer over the hood of the nearest car. Heat from the fires fans shimmering ripples of air that distort but don't disguise Vanda's gray-suited figure as he trots away down the sidewalk.

Past him, at the corner, a man stands waiting: a still point in the chaos of the street.

I duck back down, trying to decide what I just saw. The man on the corner was a stranger, too far away for my over-lay to identify. He looked to be six feet tall, an athletic figure dressed in a crewneck shirt, slacks, and a casual brown jacket. Gray hair in a military cut. Was he watching me? No. He was watching Vanda—and he was holding a gray case like the one Vanda is carrying. That's what caught my eye.

I look again. The man in brown is gone from the corner—I think I see him farther down the street—while Vanda is moving in the same direction, weaving through gridlocked traffic to reach the next block.

"Is the shooter still there?" Delphi asks, a high edge to her voice.

"No, he's moving out. It was Vanda—"

"*Carl Vanda?* You know that?"

"Yes."

"He had a mask on."

"It was him. Are you injured? Can you stand up?"

"I'm okay."

We get up together, look across the street.

"Did Vanda shoot that police officer?"

"Yeah."

And the cop isn't screaming anymore.

I cut between the burning cars with Delphi right behind me.

We find the cop on the opposite sidewalk. He's on his side, moaning, clutching at the bloody pulp of his face that's been shredded by steel fléchettes. Beside him is his police-issue sidearm. I stoop to pick it up. "Delphi, do what you can for him."

She gives me a look of searing blue fury, knowing as well as I do that he'll be dead in another minute—but I take off before she can say, *Stay*.

This is my chance. Carl Vanda is not alone, but he is on foot and he's a broken man. I know I can outrun him.

Sirens wail. Helicopters turn and swoop in manic paths above the buildings. Microdrones shoot past me, racing toward the blast site to harvest digital footage. I'm going the opposite way.

All along the street, people are emptying out of the buildings. They stand in small groups on the sidewalks and in the gridlocked traffic, watching smoke rise, relating their experiences, debating the danger. A bold few rush toward the disaster. I weave past, holding the gun close to my side. No one notices it. There is just too much to look at, too much going on.

I don't see the man in brown, but I get a glimpse of Vanda on the next block. He's slowed to a walk, but it's a New York pace that covers ground at a furious rate. He doesn't look back. I don't think he has any idea that I'm following. He ducks around a corner—

And it happens a third time: The air shifts, and then the thunder of another massive explosion rolls across the city. This one comes from somewhere uptown, the blast reverberating between the towers. People scream. They evaporate from the sidewalks, fleeing inside, leaving no obstacles to slow me down.

I sprint to the corner, peer around the black marble base of the building.

The next street is just like the last street: crammed with cars all going nowhere. A few people mill between them. Horns honk. A middle-aged woman runs toward me along the sidewalk, awkward in high heels. Vanda is beyond her, almost at the end of the block. I step around the corner.

Maybe he's got a handler using a microdrone to watch over him. Maybe the man in brown is hunkered down somewhere out of my sight, watching to see if anyone is following the boss. I don't know. But I'm halfway down the block when Vanda gets the word that I'm coming.

He's crossing the next street, surrounded by stalled cars, when he turns to face me. I see the iridescent glimmer of his anonymous mask. He lets the rifle case drop to the ground as he uses both hands to aim a massive handgun in my direction. I can't fire back, not with civilians on the sidewalk and in the cars. Some of them see his weapon and scream. I duck into the recessed entry of a pastry shop, praying he won't shoot if he doesn't have a target.

No shot comes.

Is he waiting for me? Or is he running?

I scan the cars, their drivers, the fleeing pedestrians across the street, looking for the man in brown because I do not want him to get behind me.

I wish to God I had my HITR—the M-CL1a Harkin Integrated Tactical Rifle is equipped with onboard muzzle cams that let it look around corners—but all I've got is a police pistol with no electronic sights. It's a museum piece. All of NYPD's budget must have gone to armored personnel carriers—but at least the pistol doesn't lock up when an unregistered user handles it.

Ten seconds go by. Eleven. Twelve. I lean out, all too aware I'm not wearing a helmet. My helmet is in my dad's ruined apartment, along with my dead sister. Too bad I didn't have a chance to rig up. I peer around the edge of the concrete, imagining my forehead shattering—but nothing happens. Vanda is out of sight and the only civilians left are hunched down in their cars, most of them yelling into phones.

I wish to God I had the squad's angel.

I expend three more seconds debating what to do. If Carl Vanda's priority is to see me dead, he'll wait for me somewhere and hit me from ambush, and I'll never know it's coming. But I don't think that's his priority. He gunned down a cop. NYPD is going to put out every effort to discover who's behind the veil. The current chaos and carnage won't stop them from coming hard after him and he knows it. They're probably tracking him right now with a microdrone.

They're probably tracking me.

Fuck it.

I make my decision and go, running hard to catch up to Vanda again, calculating that he must have turned onto the cross street to disappear so quickly, but when I reach the corner, he's nowhere in sight.

"Where did he go?" I shout at a cabdriver who's made the mistake of leaving his window open. "Which way?"

The man hunches deeper into his seat, but he gestures down the block. "Next corner." It's a short block.

I dart between the cars, reach the sidewalk, and run hard. I'm almost there when a fourth explosion rips into the city.

This one too is far away, but for a moment all sound vanishes except death's thundering roar as it claims more souls.

With the sound of my footsteps covered by that cloud of noise, I hurtle around the corner—and discover that my assessment of Carl Vanda's priorities is wrong. He's waiting for me, just a few feet away, along with the man in brown.

Vanda is standing half hidden behind a scalloped column that's part of the façade of a new condominium. He's got his gun out, but he's not looking at me. He's looking at the man in brown, who's crouched behind a concrete planter close to the curb. Brown has one hand raised to his farsights. He looks like a man still organizing his assets. Maybe he's lost contact with the drone. Maybe he's lost contact with his handler. But it's certain that he doesn't expect me quite that soon. When I pop into sight, he recoils in surprise.

Vanda doesn't. Stepping clear of the column, he turns to target me with the fléchette gun.

I can't stop. I'm going too fast. So I keep going and dive for his knees.

Vanda's gun goes off. The fléchettes fan out, but my dive has put me under the trajectory of the spray. A barb clips my shoulder. Another pings against my titanium foot. I wrap an arm around Vanda's legs and take him to the ground.

He hits the sidewalk with his shoulder and that saves his head, but his weapon is pinned under him. I still have the cop's gun. I try to jam it against his throat, but he grabs my wrist with his free hand. We're grappling, rolling across the sidewalk. He loses the hat, and the mask goes with it, but his gun hand is free.

His face is inches from mine: teeth bared, eyes squinting, every muscle engaged. I pitch my pistol away and use two hands to go after his weapon, slamming the back of his

gunhand into the concrete. His grip breaks, the fléchette
gun falls loose, and I grab for it—but the man in brown
has found an opening. He kicks the gun away. Kicks me
in the ribs. Then in the belly. Maybe in the head, because
I miss a second or two. By the time I check back in, Vanda
is up, talking in a low, growling voice:

"She is out of control."

He's not talking to me. I'm already dead as far as he's
concerned.

"I'm putting an end to this chaos. Niamey is glass."

Somehow I'm on my back. I glimpse the fat muzzle of
the fléchette gun centering on my face. I see it like a still
image, frozen in time, gripped by a large hand, tanned skin
darker than Vanda's, a smoky, pale-blue sky beyond. I kick
at that hand. I propel my robot feet up like a gymnast initiating a backward somersault, titanium impacting flesh just
as the little steel arrows are released. The deadly fléchettes
buzz away into the sky, the gun spins into the street in a
shower of blood, and the man in brown retreats, cursing,
"*Fucking* hell, fucking hell."

I roll over onto my shoulder, then scramble on hands
and knees to the shelter of a parked car, expecting to die
at any moment, but when I look back, they're gone. Both
gone. The sidewalk is deserted.

I squat in the gutter for a few seconds, hunched over
my bruised ribs, with my shoulder bleeding and my eye
starting to swell shut. But I have enough vision left to see
a glistening trail of blood on the concrete, leading to fancy
brass doors at the foot of a skyscraper.

Where the fuck is my gun?

Maybe they took it, but if so, why didn't they stay long
enough to shoot me with it?

I lean out around the car that's hiding me and look for
the gun in the street. Next I look under the car—and that's

where I find it. I have to get down on my belly to reach it, trying not to breathe too hard because my ribs fucking hurt.

Armed once again, I eye the building, but it's a luxury tower, the security system is not going to let me inside, and right now I'm an easy target from any window overlooking the street.

Sense kicks in and I backtrack to the corner. I wait there, watching—and a minute later a helicopter lifts off the roof five hundred feet above my head.

It has to be him. I retreat again, in case he's thinking of taking a wild shot at me, but the helicopter speeds away toward the Hudson.

And I remember his furious threat: *Niamey is glass.*

That's what I remember. But did I hear it right? Because to do something like that . . . it doesn't make any fucking sense to me.

I try to call Delphi, but the city's network is overwhelmed and I can't get a link. So I text her instead—*I'm coming back*—hoping the text won't take too long to go through.

My shirt is torn and bloody where the fléchette grazed me, but the bleeding has mostly stopped. I'll deal with the wound later. For now, I just jam the gun into my pant pocket—but the pocket isn't deep enough to hold it. So I try sticking it into the waistband of my pants at the small of my back, the way I've seen it done in movies. It's damn uncomfortable, but at least the gun is out of sight under my shirt as I walk back past gridlocked traffic.

People have come out onto the sidewalk again, gathering in pensive knots. Bits of conversation reach me as I pass, escaping a background noise of sirens and the low, pounding roar of helicopters:

". . . phone went out with the second blast . . ."

"How many did you count? Four?"

"What's been hit?"

". . . seven bombs on Coma Day."

Sirens rise in an earsplitting howl right behind me. I turn to see a convoy of emergency vehicles creep into the intersection I just crossed. Leading the way is a pair of motorcycle cops rapping knuckles on car windows, directing the drivers to move their vehicles to the sides of the street and onto the sidewalks if they have to. A center lane slowly opens, wide enough to allow a fire truck to pass. Four squad cars follow, their sirens wailing.

I shove my fingers in my ears and keep going, thinking more about what Vanda said: *She is out of control.*

She.

His wife, Thelma Sheridan?

Though she's a prisoner in Niamey, she's also a hero to the paranoid types who want to get rid of the Red at any cost. Delphi said there are bombings somewhere in the country almost every day—but today is different. Today is the first day of Sheridan's trial. It's the day to make a statement.

Vanda must have concluded the bomb that almost killed him was placed by Thelma Sheridan's supporters. He couldn't have been involved. He couldn't have known it was going to happen or he wouldn't have been in the building across the street. He came to kill me in person—a lesson to anyone else thinking of fucking with him—but he was taken by surprise.

She is out of control.

A car bomb in the street was a stupid way to try to kill me. The terrorists who did it couldn't have known if the blast would be the correct scale or channel in the proper direction, or if I would even be in the apartment. But terrorism isn't science. It doesn't have to be smart, it doesn't have to be logical. It just has to fuck with your head.

My head is telling me I'm dangerous for anyone to be around, that innocents die when they get near me. Lissa died. Delphi almost died. I wonder how many blameless civilians are buried in the rubble that used to be my building?

It's not like this operation was even centered on me. Four bombs went off. I was almost an afterthought.

I trot ahead of the fire engine to get away from its brutal siren. As I reach my block, I hear another rumble from somewhere far uptown.

The count of the explosions climbs to five.

Cars are still smoldering, filling the street with stinking, toxic smoke. Someone has draped a jacket over the face of the dead cop. I cross the street, to find seven more bodies laid out in front of my ruined building. These are uncovered; some of them are burned. Ambulances are on scene, their lights flashing but their sirens mercifully silent. I look for Delphi, but it's my dad I see, halfway up the pile of rubble, wearing a now-filthy dress shirt and slacks as he works with three other people to dig someone out.

A text comes in from Jaynie: *No traffic allowed into city. Holland and Lincoln Tunnels closed. Bridge traffic one way only: out.*

"Shelley."

I whip around. It's Delphi. Her face is dirt streaked, her hair dull with dust, her fingers seeping blood, and her clothes filthy. She eyes my bruised face, my half-closed eye. "Did you kill him?"

"No. He got away."

Her gaze shifts to my dad as he and another man lift a concrete slab, sliding it farther down the heap, and she starts trembling. "At least he didn't kill *you* . . . though realistically, it's just a matter of time."

"Delphi . . ." I reach for her and she responds, hugging me, holding me tightly while I tell her the truth. "It's going to be like this. You were at Black Cross. You know the kind of things Vanda-Sheridan is willing to do—and the kind of things we have to do too. And it's only going to get worse. Vanda has more nukes."

She looks up at me, blue eyes even brighter surrounded by dirt. "You know that?"

I nod. "I heard him. He wants to nuke Niamey. Shut down the trial. Shut down his own wife and the crazies who do shit like this in her name. So I'm going after him, but I'll take you home first if you want me to."

This draws a bitter smile. "I don't need help getting home—but you might need help getting to Wyoming in one piece." She half turns in my arms. "Your gear's over there. I got it out of the apartment."

"*Shit*, you went back up there?"

She shrugs. "It took a few trips—your rig is heavy—but I wanted to get your things before the police closed off the building."

"You're amazing."

She's been helping with the search and rescue. That's why her hands look like they do, but as the fire truck arrives civilians are ordered to clear out of the site. My dad climbs down the rubble heap, and sees me. We glare at each other for a second and a half, and then we embrace.

"Why are you still here?" he asks.

"I'm on my way out. You coming with me?"

I'm not surprised when he shakes his head. "This is my home. I want to know who did this. I want to see them burn."

I nod. He has his own mission now, his own purpose, his own story.

So it's just Delphi and me.

I text Jaynie: *Can you get into Brooklyn?*

While I'm waiting for an answer, I get the first-aid kit from my pack and we all clean our cuts and bruises. Delphi glues the gouge on my shoulder, and I put on a clean but stale-smelling T-shirt that I find stashed at the bottom of my pack.

After a few minutes Jaynie's answer comes back: *Roger that. VZ Bridge open.*

We'll walk out over the Manhattan Bridge. Rendezvous.

By this time, the police are getting organized. They come by, barking orders for us to move away, to move back from the ruined building. I turn to my dad—but what is there to say? Nothing that will make a difference. We trade a nod. Leave it at that. I should never have come home.

Hefting my gear, I turn my back on the shattered rubble of his life and I walk away with Delphi beside me, pulling her battered suitcase.

But I get only two and a half blocks before I decide my dead sister is just too damn heavy to carry. "Delphi, give me a minute. I'm going to rig up."

She looks unsure. "Is it legal to wear that on the street?"

I don't really know—but on a day like today, I don't think it matters. "The cops are going to be too busy to worry about me."

The dead sister's power levels prove good, so I strap in, and then we set out again. I'm not in uniform and I'm not using my helmet, so no one seems too bothered by my rig. Soon it's clear we are only a tiny part of an exodus out of the city. It's organized chaos and yet for the first time since I've been back home, I feel safe. There are strangers all around me, but they have their own problems. Only a few bother to comment on the rig, and all of those are just exhausted walkers wishing for their own augmentation. No one cares who I am, and no one tries to kill me.

• • • •

It's late afternoon when we finally rendezvous with the squad. They're at Trinity Park, waiting in and around two new SUVs—one gunmetal gray, the other light brown—and although they're dressed in civilian clothes, I don't think anyone who sees them is fooled. Their close-fitting brown skullcaps are a clear indication that not all is normal here. They're also wearing the audio loops from their helmets, which will let them talk between vehicles.

"You look like a gang of mercs," I tell them as Delphi and I walk up beneath trees thinly clothed in new spring leaves.

Jaynie flashes me a smile from beneath the rim of her skullcap. "You're the one rigged in a dead sister. The cops didn't try to stop you, wearing that?"

"The cops are busy."

She admires my swollen eye. "You look like you got your ass kicked."

"Two against one."

She's wearing a tight-fitting, long-sleeved blue athletic shirt that shows off her muscles and draws the eye to the elegant, alluring shape of her breasts. Her tight black jeans are equally distracting. It's like looking at your sister and realizing how goddamn desirable she really is. Embarrassing.

I introduce Delphi. Everyone shakes hands. Then Delphi slides into the backseat of one of the SUVs to change into clean clothes, while I get out of my rig and load up our gear. There's not much room left in the cargo areas. Nolan gives me a rundown of what's already there: the squad's dead sisters, helmets, and backpacks; our squad drone, a.k.a. our angel; M-CL1a assault rifles, newly purchased; ammunition and grenades for the same; more grenades for distribution by hand; miscellaneous equipment; and enough meal packs to get us through the first couple weeks of the apocalypse. The weapons are surely illegal in every state, even Wyoming.

"How the hell did Jaynie get her hands on this stuff?"

Nolan says, "Shima set it up. We're employed by a licensed security company now. Legit credentials."

"You mean you've got permits for all this?"

"Everything but that piece you're carrying."

I pull the dead cop's gun out of my waistband and show it to him.

"Primitive piece of shit." He turns it over. "No electronics at all. Where'd you get it?"

"Long story, but I need to get rid of it."

"I'll break it down. Scatter the parts." He checks the load, and then makes it disappear into an inside pocket of his jacket.

Jaynie tosses me an ice pack, not yet activated. "Climb in. We need to move."

Harvey gets behind the wheel of the gunmetal-gray SUV; Jaynie is shotgun. I slide into the backseat with Delphi. To my surprise, Nolan comes in behind me, leaving only Tuttle, Moon, and Flynn in the other vehicle. He's a big man and I'm feeling squeezed. It occurs to me that's deliberate.

"What's going on?" I ask as we head out, with Flynn's vehicle following us.

Jaynie turns around to look at me—"We need to work some things out"—and I know we're on dangerous ground.

"Are you talking about you and me? Or the squad?"

"All of us."

"Then let's make sure we're all here." I've still got the communications software Anne Shima loaded into my overlay for First Light, so I use that to log in to gen-com. "Roll call," I say, just to annoy everybody.

Jaynie nods, and carefully pronounces her name, "Vasquez."

The others follow by rank:

"Nolan."

"Harvey."

And from the other car:

"Moon."

"Tuttle."

"Flynn."

"And Delphi's here too," I add. "Though she's not hooked in." I'm watching Jaynie warily; she's watching me. I'm pretty sure I know what this is about, but I want to hear her say it.

She gets right to the point. "Shelley, you're too impulsive to serve as CO of this squad. If we're going to do this, we need to set up a new rank structure."

I turn to Nolan, to gauge his feelings on this. He nods. "If Colonel Kendrick were here, it'd be different."

Harvey glances back over her shoulder. "Nobody's better than you at the front of an assault," she assures me. "No one's going to forget Black Cross. But the CO needs to keep the full scope of the mission in mind."

"And to operate under known parameters," Jaynie adds.

"So this is about the Red? You think it makes decisions for me."

"It's about you *and* the Red."

I glance at Delphi, but she's staring out the window. Staying out of it? Or not objecting because she agrees?

"What's your proposed rank structure?" I ask Jaynie.

Nolan says, "We voted on it."

"This is a fucking democracy?"

Jaynie's finely shaped eyebrows knit in a brief scowl. "It was. Temporarily. But now I'm CO, and you're my second. Can you work with that?"

Taking orders from Jaynie? I've done that before and I didn't like it. I answer honestly, "I don't know. I had an idea I would be establishing mission priorities."

"This outfit isn't Uther-Fen. We pick our missions. Nobody is fucking telling me my priorities without my input."

"Yeah? Well, maybe I can get your input on this: that our first priority should be locating the rest of Carl Vanda's nukes before he uses them on innocent populations, on our allies, on people who have helped us."

Jaynie draws back a little. Her eyes narrow. "Report," she says. "Tell me what you know."

She makes it an order. I play along, summarizing the high points of my encounter with Vanda because I want her to know what happened. When I mention the cop, Nolan swears, "Ah fuck, is that the gun you gave me?"

Harvey throws me a grin over her shoulder. "Nothing impulsive about you, sir! Arming yourself with a murdered cop's gun. *Hoo-yah!* King David! I'd follow you anywhere."

"Harvey," Jaynie warns in a voice endowed with the same quiet threat as a baseball bat. "Keep your eyes on the fucking street."

"Yes, ma'am." But she's still grinning as she turns her full attention back to traffic.

"It wasn't impulsive," I say defensively. "It was the result of a split-second assessment. I had a chance to bring Vanda down and I took it."

Jaynie raises an eyebrow. "Did you kill him?"

Same question Delphi asked. Same answer: "No."

I report on the street brawl, on what I heard.

This earns me the skeptical look that is Jaynie's signature expression whenever I'm involved. "You were barely conscious. You sure you understood what was going on?"

She's pissing me off. "Hold on. I've got video." I avert my gaze and then scroll through my menus.

"You're recording things again? When did you get switched on?"

"I didn't get switched on. I turned it on myself after the

first bomb went off, when we were still in the apartment. Just another one of my fucking impulsive moves."

I check to make sure I turned the recording function off. Then I skim through the video in my overlay, bracket a clip around the time Vanda is speaking, and extract it. "Who's got a tablet?"

Jaynie has one up front. She gives me the address. Delphi rejoins the conversation. "Send me a copy too. The clip first, but I also want the whole record."

When Delphi plays the clip on her farsights, the sound is isolated to her ears, but Jaynie has the volume turned up on her tablet so we all can hear. Mostly it's grunts and thumps and hard breathing as I wrestle with Vanda; then I'm getting kicked in the ribs and Vanda is speaking. He's breathing hard between words, but he says more than I remember, his voice hoarse and dry: "She got in the way of my operation. She is out of control." His words get harder to hear as he walks away. "I'm putting an end to this chaos. Niamey is glass."

The video shows the approach of the fléchette gun, with buildings and blue sky in the background. Then, for a fraction of a second, just at the edge of the video, we glimpse Vanda's partner, the man in brown. He has narrow features—a sharp nose, with prominent cheekbones behind deeply tanned skin. Opaque black farsights hide his eyes, contributing to a cold expression that vanishes as his thin lips part in a scream I don't remember hearing. The clip ends with a spray of blood as I disarm him.

"*Shit*," Nolan breathes as he settles back in his seat. "You cut that one close."

Delphi doesn't say anything, but she has her arms crossed, hugging herself tightly, her shoulders hunched.

I return to the issue that matters. "Vanda has nukes."

My skullnet has tuned out most of the pain, but being

reminded of it lets the pain break through. It shortens my temper. As Jaynie turns around again to look at me, I lean forward, getting in her face. "You get it, Jaynie? *He has nukes* and he's acting like it's nothing to move them around the globe. He could be moving them already."

"I get it, Shelley."

Her gaze warns me to back off, but I don't. "This is our mission," I insist.

Delphi speaks up using her handler's voice: cool and stern. "This is *not* your mission. It's the president's mission. This video needs to get sent up the chain of command."

"We're not part of the chain of command."

"I still have contacts in Guidance. I'll send it there."

I don't object. It's worth a try, but I don't think it will work. "Somewhere along the chain of command, someone is going to make this record disappear, or hold it back until it doesn't matter anymore."

Jaynie looks like she wants to take a swing at me—but she's less impulsive than I am. "I'll call Anne, see if the organization wants to do background on this."

That would be useful, because there's not a damn thing we can do until we know where the nukes are stored. "You might also want to suggest to Anne that she forward that video to Ahab Matugo. Let him know what's coming."

"I'm already on it, Shelley."

I punch the ice pack, blending the chemicals. Then I lean back and lay it against my swollen eye. After a few minutes I pull up the video again. I watch it from the start. I want to know if there was a warning sign, if there was something I should have seen, should have sensed that would have told me a massive bomb would soon go off in the street, killing innocents . . . but there's nothing. God didn't speak to me.

Koi Reisman said it's not my story anymore. The silence

in my head is reason to believe her. But if it's not my story, if the Red has cut me off, why does the plot keep looping back to me?

We escape Brooklyn, and then take Interstate 80 across New Jersey. No one tries to stop us. I study the traffic, noting individual vehicles, wondering if any of them have been assigned to follow us.

There's nothing obvious.

Connectivity is good, so I use my overlay to look for updates on the Manhattan bombings. Details are easy to find. Every aspect of the rescue work is being posted for public consumption, but analysis of the identity, origin, and motivations of the terrorists is almost nonexistent. Next, I skim through transcripts of Thelma Sheridan's first day of trial, but after the opening statements, most of it is legal maneuvering. Finally, I follow up on Koi Reisman's claim that a rogue nuclear device was recovered in the capital. There's nothing solid, but there are rumors and informed speculation that a major terrorist strike was averted just before the start of our court-martial.

"Delphi?"

She turns from staring out the window. Her eyes are red rimmed, from dust or distress, I don't know.

"When we were talking to Koi, and I asked her about other soldiers, you knew something, didn't you?"

A rare, faint smile touches her lips. "It's classified."

I glance at Nolan. He's asleep beside me. I look up front. Jaynie and Harvey are staring at the traffic ahead. Hoping road noise will cover my voice, I whisper in Delphi's ear, "Tell me anyway."

She leans back and sighs. "There's not much to tell. I was interviewed several times by an investigator. He implied you weren't the only one, but how many others there were, and how deep their involvement went, he wouldn't say. You're the only one whose name ever became known."

"It might be worth trying to find out who the others are."

"I did try. After I resigned, I spent time looking into it. I asked myself what set you apart, and the one obvious asset was your overlay. So I looked for other soldiers who used one." She gives a little shake of her head. "I had only civilian access. I didn't get anywhere."

"It's a good lead, though." I lean back, thinking about it. If she's right and an overlay is key, that narrows the prospects. My own overlay, my first one, was a prototype. I got in early because my cousin was on the development team; he's part owner of the company. I decide I'll call him when things calm down, ask him to research the question for me.

Traffic thins as we cross Pennsylvania, and connectivity becomes intermittent. For mile after mile, the interstate is flanked by office parks, distribution centers, and car dealerships—most with empty parking lots and many looking abandoned.

Nolan is awake now, gazing out the window, while Delphi has fallen asleep. For maybe the hundredth time I turn to look behind us. I have no doubt we're being tracked. We've gone too far and we're moving too fast for a microdrone to successfully follow us, but that doesn't mean we've escaped surveillance. No one escapes surveillance these days. The real questions are: Who's looking? And what are their intentions?

It's likely a government agency is monitoring us by drone or by satellite—maybe more than one agency. That's their job. It doesn't mean they're a threat. It doesn't mean anyone human is even paying attention—the feds have a limited budget and a long list of surveillance targets more dangerous than us.

It's possible the domestic terrorists who struck Manhattan are watching us too. If so, they are very much a threat, but

I doubt they have the size or the organization to manage a sophisticated surveillance operation.

Vanda-Sheridan is surely interested—and sophisticated—but I was supposed to die in Manhattan. If Carl Vanda didn't have a plan in place to follow me if I got out of the city, then it's going to take him time to track me down.

The possibility of mediots tailing us doesn't really concern me, because mediots don't chase stories, preferring their victims exposed and helpless.

I study the scattered traffic behind us, but if there's a suspicious vehicle back there, I can't spot it. So I turn around, to look again at the road ahead. And I wonder: Is the organization watching us? Do they have that ability? I'd like to think they do.

I'd like to think they're watching Carl Vanda.

I wonder if he's gone back to his Alaskan stronghold, the Apocalypse Fortress. I wonder if that's where he keeps his nukes. The Apocalypse Fortress extends underground, a home that doubles as a bomb shelter . . . but how mad would he have to be to keep nukes in his basement?

They won't be there. Carl Vanda is not stupid.

Still, if you want to hide something, going underground is a good way to do it. Secrets can stay secret beneath meters of rock and soil, shielded from EM leakage that could be harvested by spies. You'd have to get a camera inside a facility like that to know what was going on. If you could keep cameras out, if you had no direct connection to the surface, your secrets might stay locked away, even from the Red.

That's where the nukes will be: someplace where the Red can't see them.

That night we stop near Pennsylvania's western border, at an old three-story hotel with two long wings skirted by a nearly empty parking lot. Business is bad all around, but at least this place has pride of ownership: The landscaping is perfect, with the hedges around the parking lot lit up by knee-high lights. It occurs to me the owner could be trading the use of a room for maintenance services.

"Let's park away from the door," Jaynie says over gen-com. "Leave one stall open between the vehicles, and back in."

That way we can leave quickly if we need to.

Before I get out, I check myself in the rearview. I look like a criminal with my eye bruised and swollen, but thanks to Delphi, who insisted on a short stop at an anonymous mall, I'm wearing a new shirt. She went in by herself and bought me collared shirts, T-shirts, slacks, shorts, and a light jacket long enough to cover my chest armor. I didn't go with her because the new CO is being a hard-ass, and I am under orders to stay out of the public eye.

Delphi has been driving for the last couple of hours. She parks and slides out from behind the wheel. I get out at the same time and catch her elbow. We've hardly talked since we joined up with the squad.

"What's it going to be?" I whisper. "Do you want your own room? Or do you want to share a room with me?"

She gives me a coy look, then stands on her tiptoes and speaks in my ear, "If it's not going to destroy unit cohesion, I wouldn't say no to a replay of last night."

It *is* bad for unit cohesion. I know that. But I haven't signed a contract yet. I kiss the side of her mouth. "You're on."

On check-in we present IDs for the teenage desk clerk to scan. He watches the records come up, sees our names, but he has no idea who we are. I go last. I'm the only one who's chipped, so instead of groping for a wallet, I press my wrist against a sensor plate. The clerk eyes my bruised face and then reconsiders the record on the screen in front of him. "You're from Texas?" he asks in a soft, nervous voice.

"Just my driver's license. I'm from New York."

He looks relieved.

The great majority of Texans had nothing to do with the insurrection, but that can be hard to remember, and since Coma Day, a lot of people have been carrying a grudge against the Lone Star State.

We get adjacent rooms on the second floor, overlooking the parking lot. Jaynie sets up a watch rotation so that someone will be patrolling the area around the SUVs at all times. Tuttle gets the first shift, while the rest of us crowd onto the elevator. "No one goes out tonight," Jaynie warns. She taps her ear. "And everyone wears their earpiece. We stay linked in to gen-com at all times. Harvey, Moon, figure out something to order for dinner."

"How is all this shit being paid for?" I ask as the elevator door opens onto an empty corridor.

"The organization sent a cash card. Delivered by courier on Sunday afternoon."

I wish I knew more about the organization. I know they have deep pockets and the competence to pull off a complex operation. Rawlings said they were fully funded by donations from individuals who believed in a government by the people, for the people—not for the dragons. I hope it's true.

The room is simple but clean. There's a bed, a set of drawers, a desk, and a monitor. As soon as the door closes, I've got my arms around Delphi.

"Let's take a shower," I murmur in her ear.

Goose bumps rise across her skin as she says, *"Yes."*

Forty minutes later, Moon links on gen-com, letting me know the food has arrived. I get dressed and go out into the hall. It's barbecue. Smells good. Nolan hands me a pistol—

a 9 mm SIG Sauer in a nylon holster—along with a box of ammo to go with dinner. "Just in case."

When I get back inside the room, Delphi is wearing a tank top and panties as she kneels on the bed, puzzling over the remote control. "Don't turn the cable on," I plead.

She gives me an annoyed look. "Koi Reisman said the new show launches tonight, remember? *Against the Beast.* I want to know what time."

"So check the Cloud."

"My network connection is comatose. How's yours?"

"Slow," I admit.

She turns the TV on.

The show is scheduled for later in the evening, so Delphi watches the national news-propaganda channels instead. We sit on the floor, eat our barbecue, and listen to their pseudojournalism. Every time the coverage moves to celebrity babies or sex scandals, Delphi shifts to a different brand.

"I can't believe there's a regular audience for this shit," I grouse as I head into the bathroom to wash up.

When I come back out, two so-called legal analysts are discussing how the case against Thelma Sheridan relies on the preliminary FBI report, which should be inadmissible because it is classified, and that Colonel Kendrick committed an act of treason when he turned it over to Ahab Matugo.

Impulsively, I want to strangle both of them.

"Delphi, can you fucking turn it off, *please.*"

"*No.* We need to know what the enemy is saying. If you don't want to hear it, then listen to some music with the volume turned up."

The skullnet icon is flickering, and I know I should take her advice, but I don't. Instead I sit on the bed and watch, waiting to see how much worse it will get.

The pair of pseudo-intellectuals continue to coach the

audience in outrage for another minute and a half, and then we get to hear the mediot again. "The acts of violence that have plagued the country continued today with a spree of car bombs in Manhattan. Five bombs were detonated within twenty-two minutes, causing widespread damage to transportation and communication infrastructure, as well as to property. The victims are still being counted, but estimates range upward of four hundred dead and twelve hundred wounded in an attack most analysts are attributing to supporters of the Texas Independence Army, the same organization believed responsible for the Coma Day atrocities."

"Fucking liars," I mutter. "The TIA is dead."

"The dragons need a bad guy who is not one of their own."

"If the president wants to be the good guy, he needs to stop these lies."

"Hush, listen."

Because now the mediot is talking about me. ". . . destroying the residence of former army lieutenant James Shelley, popularly known as the Lion of Black Cross. It's not yet clear if Mr. Shelley survived the bombing. Authorities will say only that his present whereabouts are unknown."

"Liars again—but maybe I'm better off if people think I'm dead."

"No, that just means it'll be easier to make you disappear."

I think about that while the mediot reads her lines: "That the timing of this latest terrorist act coincides with the start of the Sheridan trial is very likely no coincidence. Analysts regard it as a protest against the federal government's yielding United States sovereignty by allowing the Sheridan trial to go forward." She sounds like she's starting to get bored by the whole thing. "Street surveillance cameras were able to capture and upload images of two of the bombers seconds before the blasts took place."

I'm looking at my street again: video preceding the blast. The van I saw in real time pulls up to the curb. The driver jumps out. Under his floppy hat he's got a mask like the one Carl Vanda wore, but a mask isn't going to save him. The video contains his full-body biometrics and a nice kinetic sample of the way he moves. The sequence ends abruptly at the moment of the blast.

"There's more than enough in that clip to identify him," I say. "It's just a matter of time."

"If he didn't die in the blast."

Well, yeah. There's that. "I wonder if street surveillance caught my brawl with Vanda?"

Delphi's shoulders roll in a shrug. "The cameras were probably intact, but whether the network was up—who knows?"

While Delphi watches more propaganda, I sit on the carpet and empty my pack for the first time since Niamey. There's the first-aid kit, my arctic camo, sealed rations, a gun-cleaning kit, the armored vest I used for First Light. . . .

The vest smells musty and there's a slug embedded in it, but I put it on anyway over one of the civilian T-shirts Delphi got for me. I rig the holster of my new pistol so it's centered on my chest. My newly purchased jacket goes over it.

Delphi eyes my bulk. "Amazing how fast soldiers put on weight once they're out of the ranks."

"You can help me work it off later."

"Deal."

I head downstairs to relieve Tuttle and take my turn on watch. I've been thinking a lot about Carl Vanda and the assets he has at his disposal. Vanda-Sheridan specializes in satellite surveillance. Most of their equipment is under

government contract, but part of their contractual obligation is processing and analysis, which would allow Vanda
to run searches on the data his satellites collect.

Lights in the lobby are low and no one's at the desk.
The doors slide open as I approach. Outside, the night is
cool and quiet, and though the interstate is just a hundred
meters from the hotel, the only traffic I hear is the distant
static of tire noise from a single electric car. I glance up at a
sky that holds a good collection of stars, though their light
is dulled by humidity in the atmosphere. It's not an ideal
night for seeing, but conditions don't have to be ideal for a
sophisticated satellite to pick out faces on the ground.

Knee-high lights illuminate the handful of cars in the
parking lot. I have to bite down on an urge to chew out
Tuttle when I see him leaning with his ass against the front
grille of the brown SUV, his hands stuffed in the pockets of
his hoodie. *What the fuck do you think you're doing, soldier?*
Stand up straight!

He's wearing farsights, giving him enhanced vision, so
as I cross the parking lot to meet him, it's easy for him to
read me, despite the dark. "Take it easy," he whispers. "I'm
slacking on purpose. Vasquez says we're supposed to look
like civilians."

"You're doing a damn good job. Anything I need to
know about?"

He nods toward the interstate. "You hear how quiet it
is? It's not always like this. Every now and then you'll hear
a convoy of trucks. Twenty or more together—I guess they
have problems with hijackers—but it sounds like a fucking
invasion force when they roll through."

He leaves me a set of keys before he goes. First thing
I do is unlock the gunmetal-gray SUV, the one with my
equipment in it. I rearrange the load so my helmet and
dead sister are within easy reach in case I need them. Then

I open the brown SUV, get out the angel, and unfold its three-foot-long crescent wing.

I still have the software that was loaded into my overlay at the start of the First Light mission. It lets me send a signal to the angel, waking it up. Normally, the angel collects enough solar energy to enable it to fly around the clock, but it's been locked up in storage for months, so I'm worried it will be unusable, the battery drained to wisps—but I underestimate my squad. Someone took the initiative to prep the angel and it's fully charged.

I launch it from the parking lot, sending it in a spiral around the hotel and then up, high above the interstate, and for the first time since we were in the Apocalypse Forest, I have an angel's view of the terrain around me. It's electrifying, like having a lost sense returned to me, a handicap overcome.

But the angel's AI is jumpy. It was trained for the Apocalypse Forest, where any motion at all is a likely threat, so it red-alerts at a lone car on the interstate, and again as a police cruiser moves slowly along a frontage road. I check the default settings, find a template for North American terrain, and start reeducating it on what can be accepted as normal.

If "normal" can be defined anymore.

The angel red-alerts again, highlighting an object low in the sky to the west. It looks more like a reflection than anything real: seven tiny, faintly glowing pearls arranged in a vertical line with no visible link between them. Seen through the humid air, the lights are elusive—twinkling, shimmering, fading from sight only to reappear again. I have no idea what they are and no way to judge their scale or their elevation—they could be high in the sky and far away or much lower and only a few miles down the interstate. All I know for sure is that they're too low for me to see directly from my position on the ground.

I capture an image on my overlay and run a search on it in my encyclopedia. In just a few seconds the encyclopedia launches into a verbal explanation: *"The object identifies as a node in the experimental EXALT communications system, a federal stimulus project launched in January of this year. 'EXALT' is an acronym for 'Expandable Aerial Labyrinth Traffic,' and is intended as a robust, distributed communications system that will use aerial relays to bypass—"*

I cut it off, and instruct the angel to ignore any more sightings of EXALT aerial nodes. It's good to know the feds are working on a new communications infrastructure, but judging by my connectivity it's not working yet.

Impressive though, that a new project has been funded and launched in the five chaotic months since Coma Day. The US economy crashed after the bombs knocked out critical components of the communications system. Jobs were lost as food and fuel prices soared, and recovery won't come soon, but we'd all be worse off without the tireless efforts of people both in and out of government to build on what's left. They are the anonymous heroes of an ongoing story, but there are villains too.

How did Vanda-Sheridan get their nukes?

I think about it, imagining a hypothetical individual: a faceless, nameless link in a nuclear security chain, in this country or another, someone who gave away the ability to immolate thousands in return for a fat payoff.

Hell was made for people like that.

Hell was made at ground zero in San Diego, in Chicago, in Alexandria.

Niamey will have its own ground zero if Vanda's remaining nukes aren't found.

I look up at the sky and wonder if a surveillance satellite has marked my position yet. If Vanda is hunting me, he's got a hell of a lot of territory to scan, a massive amount of data to process. Is his system capable of it?

I'm distracted by a faint roar of engines, far to the west. At first I think it's a jet, but then the angel red-alerts again, this time highlighting a long line of eastbound trucks still a few miles away: one of the convoys Tuttle warned me about.

He was right. It's amazing to hear them. Against the quiet of the night, the slowly building roar of their approach sounds like a prelude to the end of the world.

But it's not the end of the world. Not yet. I reduce the alert status from red to blue and then walk to the end of the parking lot where I have a view of the freeway's on-ramps, and of an overpass that spans the lanes. The trucks' head-lights blaze in the distance. I watch them approach, and as they pass I count them—one, two, three, four—and that's just the beginning.

The drone continues its patrol. As the twelfth truck rumbles by, the drone makes a pass over the parking lot—and flashes a red-alert. I spin around, looking back at the SUVs.

I don't see anything.

I shift to angel sight, so that I'm looking down on the vehicles in green-tinted night vision. There's someone in the empty stall between the two SUVs. He? She? I can't tell, but the intruder is skinny and not very tall—an underfed teenager maybe, with what looks like a crowbar in one hand.

I race back across the parking lot, determined to interfere before any glass gets broken. Joby engineered my padded feet to be quiet, and the little sound I do make is covered by the roar of the convoy—a roar that was no doubt a factor in the timing of this little venture.

A glance at angel sight assures me that the drone has not found any accomplices.

With my pistol in hand, I make a dramatic appearance between the front ends of the two SUVs, boxing the enemy in, with the neatly trimmed hedge blocking a retreat—but the convoy is still rolling past and my appearance goes unnoticed.

It's a girl—I'm pretty sure. She looks coppery in the glow of the streetlights, her smooth, shoulder-length hair bound up in a little ponytail, maybe five six in height, dressed in long, dirty pants, running shoes, and what looks like a badly worn armored jacket—the kind motorcyclists sometimes use. I can see a faint display dancing in the thin lens of her farsights as she cocks her arm, working up her nerve to swing her crowbar at the window in the passenger door of the gray SUV.

"Not your best idea," I say, loud enough to be heard over the trucks.

"Fuck!" She spins around, swinging the crowbar so that it whistles through the air between us. "Touch me and I'll kill you!"

Definitely a girl.

I step aside, giving her room to run. "Why don't you get the fuck out of here?"

She grips the crowbar in two hands. "Don't you touch me!"

"I won't."

She edges sideways, watching me through her farsights, a pinprick green light in the corner indicating she's recording. I expect her to turn and run as soon as she's in the open, but instead she hesitates, asking, "What's going on with your eyes? There's sparks of light flashing in them."

Angel sight is still running in the corner of my vision as the drone takes in the brilliant headlights of the convoy along with our little conflict in the parking lot. I'm impressed she can see well enough to make it out. "It's an implant."

"You're a soldier, aren't you?"

"Not anymore."

"You're the one they call King David."

"*Not* anymore."

She thinks about this for a few seconds, watching me with an anxious gaze. "Sorry," she whispers, edging away. "Sorry I messed with your stuff."

"Are you hungry?"

Just the question, the implication that there might be food, and she looks faint.

But I don't want that crowbar anywhere near me or the trucks. "Go across the parking lot. Wait there. I'll get you something."

She backs away.

I open up the gunmetal-gray SUV, find a case of MREs I remember seeing earlier, and extract a dozen packets while watching her with angel sight. She's retreated thirty feet, toward the opposite end of the parking lot from where I was watching the convoy. Behind her is a vacant lot, overgrown with spindly young trees. I leave the packets on the asphalt between us and return to the vehicles. The last of the convoy has passed, and the night has gone quiet again. She scurries toward the food, setting the crowbar down just long enough to stuff her pockets. Then she turns and sprints for the trees.

It bothers me that the angel missed her presence in its initial survey. I send it to track her, wanting to map her hiding place, but there's no sign of her—so she must be hiding under the concrete shelter of the overpass.

I resolve to stay close to the vehicles, where I spend my time looking for satellites.

Satellites are seen when they reflect light from the sun, so they're easiest to spot early in the night or just before dawn. It's almost 2200, but I see one anyway, gliding in stately silence from the west, so big and bright it makes me curious.

I go back to the gunmetal SUV, sure I saw binoculars stashed with the supplies. I find them and get them out in time to study the object as it fades into shadow. The binoculars are electronically amplified and image stabilized, and what they show me is not just a point of light—it has length and width, a glowing rice grain that has to be a space station. I send an image to my encyclopedia, and it returns an audio article. What I'm looking at is a billion-dollar toy. A company called Sunrise 15 is manufacturing orbital pods to serve as private dwellings, high-tech cabins—dragon lairs. A spaceplane services them. One has been sold to an eccentric hypochondriac, another to a socialite because she can. The money invested in the venture is staggering—billions of dollars—while kids go hungry in rural Pennsylvania.

Motion behind the hotel's glass doors makes me reach for my pistol, but the doors slide open, revealing Nolan coming to take over the watch. He's wearing farsights and a thigh-length jacket like mine to cover his armor.

I search the sky again, wondering how many satellites have looked down on this parking lot since I've been out here.

"You looking for something up there, LT?" Nolan asks.

"I don't have a rank anymore."

He makes a low, skeptical grunt. "Shelley, then. Counting satellites?"

I look at him. His farsights cast a faint glow around his eyes. "Did you know there's a company selling space stations to dragons? They've launched six dragon lairs already."

"No shit?" He looks up.

I pass him the binoculars. "They're looking down on us."

"They always have." He puts the binoculars to his eyes. "We just watched the newest reality show."

"Yeah? How was it?"

"Like you said it would be . . . focused on the people who protected us. Cops and FBI, but mostly these teenage kids in DC who knew something was up and kept poking at it." He lowers the binoculars, frowning. "They almost got themselves killed—but then they found an IND, just like the ones recovered on Coma Day. A nuke in a cheap-ass van. The FBI shut down the trigger mechanism less than two hours before it would have gone off. That would have been the Saturday night before the court-martial."

"That was the night before the president came to see me," I realize. "So when he talked to me, he knew. He knew how close we all came."

"Including him," Nolan agrees.

I think about it. Would the country have survived if that IND had gone off? Our president killed? The government thrown into chaos? I want to believe we would have gone on somehow, with the military remaining loyal to the people, and the people pulling together in support of the Constitution . . . I want to believe it.

But even after the nuke was disarmed, the president kept its existence secret. He knew how close we'd come to disaster, but he didn't trust the people with that knowledge. He didn't trust me. He came after me only hours later, asking for an end to the disruption, the chaos, without ever hinting at what had almost happened.

It's all out in the open now. "Goddamn," I breathe. "Do you know how lucky we are? Not just us. The whole fucking country."

"Thanks to those kids. They're heroes, and not just them. The FBI too."

"And the seven hundred thousand protesters on the Mall."

If not for them, today would have been the start of our

sentencing hearing. A lot of people have been saving my ass lately.

"Hey," Nolan says, "is that one of the dragon lairs?"

I look up to see another bright satellite. For several seconds Nolan studies it through the binoculars. Then he turns to me, scowling. "We're out here without our helmets."

"We want to look like civilians."

"Sure, but we're standing out in the open. A good surveillance satellite can identify us with facial recognition."

I nod. "And Vanda-Sheridan specializes in surveillance satellites."

"*Shit*. You think he'll come after us?"

"He came after me in New York. He came himself. He didn't hire the job out."

"Like it was a personal vendetta."

"He's not like other dragons. He came up through the ranks. It's hands-on with him. And right now it's unfinished business. The job's not done."

Nolan stares at the sky a little bit longer. "I've met assholes like that. Guys who'll go out of their way to finish a grudge match before they transfer."

I'm betting Carl Vanda is one of those guys, and that he's as predictable as I am. "If he does come after us, we need to turn it around on him. Take him alive."

"Alive?"

"Persuade him to tell us all about his nukes. Then we don't have to wait for the organization, or depend on half-truths leaked by corrupt government moles."

"You *want* him to come," Nolan accuses.

I don't deny it.

"So you think it'll be soon?" he asks.

"Yes. If he comes at all, it'll be soon. Probably not tonight, though."

"But if it is tonight?"

"You have any suspicions, put out a call on gen-com."

"Roger that."

I tell him about the girl in the trees, and then I get him set up so his farsights are linked to the angel.

The Red may not be telling my story anymore. That doesn't mean I can't tell one on my own.

As I head back inside, I'm planning to purchase a replay of the new episode, but that changes when I get to the room, because Delphi isn't there. There's no note to say where she's gone. There's nothing. Fear hits. Has she been kidnapped? I didn't hear anything. It doesn't seem possible . . . and no one left the hotel. I know that. I was watching with angel eyes.

I call her.

The cell network is down so the call doesn't go through.

I swear to God I can hear Lissa's ghost whispering, *It's not your fault.*

Panic sends me racing into the hall. I visualize a link to Jaynie. My skullnet picks up the command and tries to connect, even as I pound on her door. "I need your help! Delphi's gone."

The door opens and it's Delphi. She's wearing a tank top and pajama bottoms.

Jaynie is right behind her, dressed in a tank top and panties with a pistol in her hand. "What the fuck, Shelley?" she asks me.

I don't know what to say.

Delphi looks puzzled. "Are you okay?"

"Fuck, no." My heart is hammering, my hands are shaking, and the skullnet icon is aglow. "I didn't know where you were, Delphi! Why the hell didn't you—"

"Stop," she says, putting her hand against my chest. "Just stop."

I back up, shaking my head. "Don't look at me like I'm crazy. He took Lissa out of a secure facility! This is just a fucking hotel."

"Delphi is fine," Jaynie growls, "and you need to calm down."

She's right, but I'm not ready. I go back to our room, letting the door slam behind me.

I tell the skullnet, *Sleep*, but I wake up when Delphi comes in.

She slips into bed beside me, putting her head on my shoulder, her hand on my chest. I don't react. "You said it yourself," she whispers. "It's going to be like this. We're going to be frightened for each other."

Frightened doesn't cover it.

"He can't know about you," I say, keeping my voice low. "We can't let him know."

"He knew before we knew. That's why he had a sniper waiting outside my hotel."

She means I'm predictable. Predictably impulsive.

"What were you talking to Jaynie about?"

"My place in the squad."

"You're going to be our handler, aren't you?"

"If we can get set up for it."

"As long as you're safe."

"None of us is safe, Shelley."

She's right, and it's going to get worse long before it gets better.

At 0500 we're all gathered in the parking lot again, packing up.

"Are we going to secure the handguns?" Moon asks.

"No," I tell him. "I want you to hold on to them, just keep them out of sight and let's try not to get pulled over."

I'd rather take my chances with the highway patrol than be unarmed if we run into trouble on the road.

Moon hesitates, turning with a worried look to Jaynie. She's standing a few steps away, her arms crossed as she eyes me with a critical gaze. I catch on: Moon's question wasn't directed at me. It was meant for the CO.

"Ma'am?" Moon asks her.

"What Shelley said." She unfolds her arms, crooking a finger at me as she walks away.

I glare after her, hating the position she's put me in, but it's not going to help my case to act like an angry kid. So I follow. We meet by a hedge, just out of earshot.

I take charge of the meeting, reminding her, "I haven't agreed to anything."

"Do you doubt my ability to command this squad?"

I take a second to consider her question; then I shake my head. "No. That doesn't mean this is going to work."

"You named a mission yesterday," she says. "If that becomes our first assignment, if we have to go forward with it, I want you along. I need you, especially now that Ransom's gone. But you're no use to me if I don't have your loyalty."

"You promoted yourself over my head, and you want my loyalty?"

"If not me, then who?" She raises her chin, indicating the squad, milling around the vehicles. "Pick one who's ready for command."

It's a trick question. "You're the only one."

"You don't like it," she says. "I understand that. But you are not in a condition to hold the responsibilities of CO. You're not *in command* at all times."

"If you're talking about last night—"

"This goes back farther and you know it. Think about Black Cross. Think about why you went outside."

My glare doesn't waver, but my confidence does. I went outside at Black Cross because the Red got inside my head and walked me out there like a fucking puppet.

She nods, letting me know my thoughts are easy for her to read. "It's for the best," she says. "Now let's roll." She starts back toward the vehicles, but after a few steps she turns to me again. "By the way, it's your turn to drive."

"Hell, no, ma'am." I follow after her. "That is a poor idea."

Everybody's watching now.

"Why? Have you got a concussion?"

"I don't think so."

"Looks like the swelling around your eye is almost gone. You can see okay?"

"Yes."

"So what's the problem?"

I look past her. I look at Delphi watching me in concern, at Harvey smirking, at Nolan who's eyeing me with a puzzled gaze.

"I don't know how to drive."

"Come *on*. You have a driver's license."

"The army made me get it. I haven't been behind a wheel since."

"You drove an ATV at Dassari."

"That was an ATV. Not a massive truck, packed with live bodies and ammunition, on a crazy-ass interstate at eighty miles an hour."

Her brows knit as she tries hard to get her head around this. "You went first down the stairs at Black Cross, but you're scared to drive on the interstate?"

"I didn't say I was scared. I said it was a bad idea."

An idea that could put an end to half of the Apocalypse Squad with no help at all from Carl Vanda.

"You're driving," she concludes. "Sounds like you need the practice."

• • • •

Moon is in charge of the first SUV. I manage to follow
him onto the interstate without getting involved in a major
accident. Jaynie is shotgun, coaching me on how to change
lanes, while Delphi is alone in the back. Everyone else is
riding with Moon in a precautionary measure to minimize
casualties if I really fuck up.

I'm nervous as hell, especially when we catch up with
a long convoy of trucks and I have to pass them all. "Just
follow Moon's lead," Jaynie tells me. "But not too close."

We creep past the trucks, one by one, while I imagine
the huge trailers swaying, swinging into us, the gas cylinders
exploding. . . . My heart is racing, but we get past them
without incident. I move into the right lane. Ahead of us
is open road.

We're rocketing past a small town whose name I didn't
catch when my overlay picks up a network connection.
An upload link opens in my display. I know it's not my
archival program, because that only runs when I'm asleep. I
puzzle over it, concluding it must be Joby's program trans-
mitting data on the performance of my legs—but the link
stays open. Seconds pass.

"Shelley!" Jaynie shouts.

I look up, startled to see that I've swerved onto the
shoulder.

"Turn the display on your overlay *off*," she growls at me.

I try, but I have to keep looking up at the road and every
time I do, the process aborts.

From the backseat, Delphi says, "We've got flashing lights
behind us."

I check the rearview and she's right. *"Fuck."*

Jaynie reaches into my jacket, pulls out my pistol, and
passes it, along with her own, to Delphi. "Secure these."

Then to me, "Pull over. And once you're stopped, get your license out." She switches to gen-com. "Moon, drive on to the next exit, then wait."

"Yes, ma'am."

I bring us to a controlled stop. The upload link is still open in my overlay. While the patrol car pulls in behind us, I check the system log. It's not Joby's program. It's the video of the Manhattan bombing that's uploading—to an address that's just a random string.

Not forgotten. That's what I think. And I'm angry it's back, now, after the silence in New York, but fuck me, I'm relieved too.

Jaynie is still focused on the cop. "Shelley, get your license out!"

"I don't need to," I tell her as the upload finishes. "I'm chipped."

"More machine parts?" she asks with a note of disgust.

"I used to lose my wallet a lot."

We watch the patrol car, using the rearview camera. I watch the traffic too, but I keep my gaze averted as cars shoot past us. I don't want to advertise my face.

"Look across the freeway," Delphi says. "That's the high-way patrol's drone."

I see it. It's an old model—white, cross shaped, flying slowly at a low altitude, keeping an eye on us.

The officer gets out of his car. Jaynie tells me, "Put your window down. Then put your hands on the steering wheel."

As the window goes down, spring warmth rolls in. I watch the rearview screen as the cop approaches. He's a man of average height, chunky, wearing a khaki uniform, his opaque gray farsights like blind robot eyes, and he's got an arsenal around his hips.

I switch my recording function on, and then I turn to look at him. A tiny green light at the corner of his farsights is glowing, indicating he's recording too. We stare at each other for two seconds. His name badge says "Munroe." He's enough of a public figure that my encyclopedia recognizes him and tags him as Terence B. Munroe.

Of course, he's running facial recognition too.

"*Shit*," he whispers when it lets him know who I am. Then he remembers himself, and in a formal voice he says, "Let's see your driver's license, Mr. Shelley."

"Implant," I tell him.

He sighs—"Should have guessed"—and reaches for his shirt pocket, extracting a three-inch-long wand. "Moving slowly, place your hand on the door."

I do as he says. He holds the wand over my wrist, frowning over the report that appears in his farsights. Then he looks at me again. "Do you have a weapon in the car, sir?"

"Yes, sir. I do."

Not the answer he was hoping for. His cheeks pinch and he takes a step back.

I add, "They're secured in the back cargo area."

Jaynie leans over. "They're legally permitted for interstate transport. I have the paperwork."

His forehead wrinkles. "The weapon in question is a police-issue revolver reported missing by the New York City Police Department. Is that in your possession, Mr. Shelley? Ms. Vasquez?"

"No," I say. "That is not in our possession."

He nods. "I heard you tried to chase down that cop killer. NYPD wants to talk to you about that." He waits for my reaction. When I don't give him one, he shrugs. "There's no warrant. You're under no obligation to return."

"Yes, sir."

"Are you planning to stay in this area?"

"No, sir."

Relief floods his face and he gives me a tight smile. "Good.

God knows we've had enough trouble around here since
Coma Day. I'm going to issue you a warning for inattentive
driving and let you go on your way."

"Thank you, sir. I appreciate it."

One of the tools on his belt is a thumb printer. It spits
out a yellow strip of paper, which he tears off and hands to
me. "That's your warning. It also has a contact number for
NYPD, if you'd care to talk to them." He takes a step back.
Then he visibly gathers himself, straightening his shoulders,
settling his lips into a determined line. "One more thing, sir."

It's like some lame line from a movie, spoken right before
the smiling assassin pulls his weapon. Fear shoots through
me and I tense, my gaze locked on his gun hand while I
rehearse in my mind what I'm going to do if he goes for
his weapon.

Jaynie puts her hand on my shoulder. "Take it easy," she
whispers.

"For the record, Mr. Shelley . . . the Red . . . is it bullshit?
Or is it real?"

Not a question I was expecting, but easy enough to
answer: "It's real."

He nods. "Around here, a lot of people want it to be real.
They'd rather have an out-of-control AI running things
than the human nut jobs who let a nuclear bomb go off in
Chicago. You ask me, I'll say no to either choice."

I don't think that's an option, but I keep my opinion
to myself.

He nods again. "You're free to go on your way."

As he walks back to his cruiser, I end the video recording,
and then start the engine. From the backseat, Delphi says,
"Every police department between here and Wyoming is
going to instruct their drones to look for us."

Jaynie shrugs. "Good. With the cops watching, hitting
us gets a little more risky."

"We can't assume every police department is going to have our best interests in mind."

"You're right about that. Pass those weapons back up here."

I get back on the road, rejoining the westbound flow of scattered traffic. After a few minutes, we link up with Moon, and then it's another ten miles before Jaynie asks the inevitable question. "So what distracted you back there?"

She deserves the truth. All of it.

I tap the corner of my eye. "I thought my part was done, but the video I took of the bombing—it uploaded on its own."

"To where?"

"Some anonymous relay."

"Are you carrying leftover software from the army?" she asks, without much hope.

"So far as I know, they're out of my head."

I tell her about the digital footage that went out every night on the cellblock when I was supposed to be locked down, and about my conversation with Joby, who insisted the army no longer had access to my overlay. She already knows about our meeting with Koi Reisman.

"You watched the new episode last night, right?" I ask.

"Yeah, we all did. It streamed while you were outside."

"Koi Reisman said our part in the story was over. Did it look that way to you?"

She considers this for a few seconds, then nods. "Yeah, it did. But things haven't exactly been quiet for you since you left DC—and if the Red's done with you, if you're not King David anymore, then what the fuck is going on?"

I don't know, but it's meaningful to me that there are two more shows.

"Maybe it's just a leftover process," Delphi suggests from the backseat.

I look in the rearview mirror and briefly meet her gaze, wondering if she really believes that, or if she'd just like to.

"We're planning on going after Carl Vanda's nukes," I point out.

"*You're* planning on it," Jaynie counters. "You're the one who wants to do it. You need to think about that."

And Delphi reminds me, "It's not our mission. I reported what we know. An official agency *will* take it."

Jaynie turns to me, channeling sincerity in her voice and her expression as she says, "You're being manipulated, Shelley. You need to get that wiring out of your skull."

I stare at the back of Moon's vehicle, sixty meters ahead. "No. That is not going to happen."

Delphi plays reinforcement on Jaynie's side. "You could go back to using a skullcap. You know the effect is essentially the same, but if the Red endangers you like it did at Black Cross, it doesn't require surgery to take the cap off."

"Come on, Delphi. You were my handler. There's a risk, sure, but you know the skullnet is a hell of a lot more advanced than a cap."

Jaynie hooks her elbow on the back of her seat, turns to Delphi. "He doesn't want the option of taking off the cap. He doesn't want anyone else to have that option." She looks at me again. "That's what you're worried about, right, Shelley? That the cap could be taken away?"

I keep my eyes on the road. "You wouldn't ask me to give up the legs, would you? They're prosthetics that let me walk. The skullnet is a prosthetic that keeps me humming along while people I love die around me and assholes try to blow up my life. Take either of them away, Jaynie, and I'm a cripple. No use to you. So yeah, I'm more worried about losing that functionality than about the Red hacking into my head."

She is unimpressed by my rant. "The real story is you don't mind the Red hacking into your head. It almost killed you at Black Cross, but you trust it anyway."

"Not true. I just deal with it. Part of the terrain. The Red's not going away, Jaynie. Sheridan proved that on Coma Day. You either learn to live with it, or be like her and build yourself an Apocalypse Fortress and lock the Red out."

Jaynie settles back into her seat, her gaze returning to the road ahead. "I thought about that," she concedes. "Be a lot of money to buy that kind of privacy. More than this job is going to pay."

"You wouldn't want to live in a hole in the ground anyway."

She doesn't answer, so I just drive.

In Ohio, young corn crops are already several inches high in some of the fields that flank the freeway—but many more fields have gone unplanted. On both sides of the interstate, miles and miles of land are growing a harvest of bright green weeds.

"What the hell?" I finally say. "People don't need to eat anymore?"

"You ever been hungry, Shelley?" Jaynie asks. "Three-days hungry?"

"No."

I wait for her to say more. She doesn't. When I glance at her, she's staring straight ahead, her back straight, shoulders squared. I return my gaze to the road.

It's Delphi who fills the silence. "Farms like these, they need fuel, fertilizer, machine parts, bank loans. Cash. The system that used to deliver all that got broken on Coma Day."

It's not just the fields. Gas stations are abandoned too. We top up whenever we come across a rare open one. They're all automated. No one is around to talk to.

At one of our stops I spot an EXALT node floating low above an abandoned field, just north of the interstate. At first, I'm not sure what I'm seeing. It looks like a stack of curved blue reflections just a little brighter than the background blue sky. When I look at it through the binoculars, the curves become the visual edge of a series of small spheres. Their smooth surfaces reflect the color of the sky around them, making them hard to see even with magnification. From the article last night, I know they're linked together by a filament, but I can't see it. As I lower the binoculars, a bright white light flashes from the topmost sphere, like a star briefly flaring to life in the daytime sky. A navigation warning light? Maybe. Flynn sees it and wants to know what it is, so I hand her the binoculars and tell her about the EXALT project. "It's supposed to be a new communications grid, but either it's not working yet or it requires its own account"—I tap the corner of my eye—"because I'm not getting a link."

Connectivity is intermittent as we head west, but frequent enough that at least once an hour an e-mail comes in from Shima. It's always the same thing: No news to report in the hunt for Vanda's nukes, and Vanda's own whereabouts are presently unknown. Maybe the same players who tried to cover up the real story at Black Cross are at work again.

We reach Iowa—and drive past more unplanted fields.

Coma Day throws one hell of a long shadow.

We stop for the night half an hour outside of Des Moines at a little commercial development built to capture weary travelers. It includes a three-story hotel—part of a low-priced chain—just off the exit, along with a gas station and a fast-food place. A competing hotel is a hundred meters west along a frontage road that separates the interstate from an abandoned field. There are no other buildings nearby. Jaynie decides we'll stay at the second hotel—she likes the isolation—but first we fill up the tanks, and pick up dinner.

To make Jaynie happy, I wait in the car while Delphi goes inside with Tuttle and Moon to order the food. I've got a feed from Tuttle's farsights running in my overlay. I shift my attention between that and the traffic on the interstate.

The restaurant is clean and bright, but it's a sign of the times that half the slots on the electronic menu behind the counter are blank and all the tables are empty. There are only two other customers—both white kids in their early twenties, maybe a brother and sister. As they wait at the counter, they eye Moon and Tuttle nervously. I think if Delphi weren't there to provide some feminine balance, they'd bolt. "You look like thugs," I mutter in Tuttle's ear.

"Beats looking like a victim," he answers in a low whisper.

When the two kids finally get their food, they leave in a hurry.

Moon steps up to the counter, where a middle-aged woman with short, curly blond hair greets him with an apologetic smile. "I am so sorry to keep you waiting, sir. We don't get anywhere near the traffic we used to, and I'm down to one assistant in the kitchen."

"Not a problem, ma'am"—and Moon rattles off an order that keeps the manager and her assistant busy for the next fifteen minutes.

We drive slowly along the frontage road to the hotel Jaynie has chosen. It's three stories high, built like a box, with a brightly lit company logo near the roof, facing the interstate. Lights are on in several rooms, but when we turn in to the huge parking lot behind the hotel, we see only two cars, both near the main door. It makes me wonder if the manager turned on some room lights so the place will seem busier than it is.

We park close to the building so our vehicles can't be seen from the interstate. The landscaping beside the hotel is neatly tended, but the surrounding field has gone wild. Spillover light shows tall grass and waist-high brush beyond the parking lot—too much for one missed planting. My guess is this section has been sitting idle for a year or more. Maybe it was scheduled to be developed, before Coma Day. Now it's home to a million crickets, chirping and buzzing in the night.

"Tuttle, launch the angel," Jaynie says. "Flynn, you're on watch."

The skullnet icon flickers to life in my display. A vague, restless feeling comes over me. After a few seconds, the icon fades back to invisibility, but the unsettled feeling remains. It's like a reminder to stay alert. I look around again.

To the east, streetlights illuminate the frontage road back to the overpass, where a little Midwestern forest grows in the triangles created by the ramps. In the other direction the frontage road is lit only by the occasional headlights of cars passing on the interstate.

Flynn watches me curiously through the faintly glittering lens of her farsights as the rest of the squad disappears into the hotel.

"You're hooked into the angel?" I ask her.

"Yes, sir."

I link into angel sight too, and take a look at things in night vision. There's scattered traffic on the interstate, but I confirm the frontage road is as empty as it looks from the ground. To the west, maybe 120 meters and beyond the reach of the streetlights, the landscape gets even wilder, overgrown with young trees that branch all the way to the ground. There's no one out there—not that the angel can see—but it was the same last night when that girl popped up out of nowhere.

"I'm going to get checked in," I tell Flynn, "but I'm coming back out again."

"Sir?"

The skullnet icon brightens again. Its glow is faint but steady—and I'm feeling edgy. "Everything looks quiet. I just want to make sure it is."

Behind the desk is a Caucasian man in his fifties with iron-gray hair. Unlike the kid last night, he knows who we are, and he wants us to know we're all on the same side. He talks as he scans our IDs and logs us into the rooms.

"Coma Day ruined me. I used to have a healthy business—I had this place and two other properties. This is the only one still open, but it's just a matter of time. You know what Coma Day did for me? It gave me a full house. For three days after the bombs went off, every room was booked as people left Chicago, but we haven't been more than a quarter full since. People around here are desperate—while the richest of the rich buy playhouses in orbit. Have you heard of Sunrise Fifteen? It's a company launching little prefab space stations, for only a billion dollars or so. Can you imagine having that much money to spend? And there's talk about a resort being planned for the Moon—but not for people like us. The big shots have got everything now. Everything worth having. But at least you made one pay."

In the room, Delphi watches me suspiciously as I put my armor on over my civilian clothes. "I don't understand why you have to go out. You're not on watch until later."

"I just want to keep an eye on things."

"Have you got a feeling about something, Shelley?"

She wants to know if I'm King David again, with the Red riding me, warning me of impending danger. I eye the skullnet icon, its persistent glow an indicator of artificial activity in my head.

Yes, I have a feeling. It's the first time in months I've felt this way.

But I don't tell her. She'll take it the wrong way. She'll ask questions I can't answer.

No way though, that I'm going to ignore the warning. "Just stay inside, okay? If you need me, use gen-com."

In the parking lot, I open the back of the gray SUV and get out one of the new HITR M-CL1a assault rifles, still in its case. I take it into the backseat, switch it on, and run through the initial security sequence that registers it to me. Flynn watches me doubtfully through the partly open door. "LT—"

"Get me some ammo, Flynn."

"LT, if something's happenin', you gotta let me know."

"I don't know that anything is happening. I just want to walk around."

I rig up in my dead sister, using the SUV as cover against a security camera that's keeping watch from the hotel entrance.

"LT, you don't look like a civilian."

"It's okay, Flynn. There's no one here to see."

I put my helmet on so I can use night vision, and then I move swiftly into the cover of the overgrown field, silencing the crickets with my presence.

I stay low, so that the brush and tall grass hide me from the frontage road as I creep toward the thicker cover of the young trees on the western edge of the field. I carry the HITR close to my side to make its profile less obvious to watching satellites. The angel will notify me with a blue alert if a traffic drone gets close, but my goal is to reach the trees before that happens. Four times as I cross the field I freeze within the cover of the weeds, waiting for interstate traffic to pass before I move again.

I take up a position twenty-five meters within the woods, well beyond the angel's patrol route, surrounded by young trees with spindly trunks holding up a dense canopy of spring leaves. The lights of the hotel glint through the brush, but I can see Flynn only when I look with angel sight.

At 2200 Tuttle comes to relieve Flynn.

At 2248 my helmet's audio pickups filter a faint buzzing sound from the rustle of windblown leaves. The anomalous noise is coming from somewhere behind and to my right. I resist the urge to turn around. Moving nothing but my eyes, I summon the feed from my rear helmet cam. Several seconds pass before I spot an aerial seeker—a mini surveillance drone like those that tracked me in Manhattan. It's at least eight meters away and only a meter and a half above the ground as it moves slowly east through the trees alongside the frontage road.

It gives no indication it's detected me, but as it nears the edge of the woods it suddenly descends to the ground. I check my feed. The angel is approaching the western limit of its programmed route, swinging past the seeker's position before circling back toward the hotel. I wait and watch to see if it will pick up the seeker, but it fails to do so, and as it moves off, the seeker rises from the ground, ascending just high enough to achieve a clear view of the hotel across the field.

It's possible the seeker has been fielded by a government

agency, but a seeker requires the oversight of an operator and I can't see an agency expending the manpower when our position can be easily monitored through traffic cams, police drones, and satellite surveillance. It's far more likely the seeker belongs to someone with a special interest in the Apocalypse Squad. I've been expecting Carl Vanda—but I need to confirm it's him and I can't send our angel to look, because any deviation in its route will be a warning to Vanda that we suspect he's there.

I'll have to go myself.

But I'm not going to leave the squad vulnerable. I open a solo link to Tuttle, and then I concentrate on a thought: *Don't make a move.* The simple AI in my skullnet senses my intention, picks up the thought, translates it to words, and then synthesizes a verbal message, which it sends to Tuttle, who is wearing his audio loop.

"LT? Where are you?"

Wary of the seeker's audio pickups, I answer in a barely audible whisper: "West of you. Don't look. Don't move. Don't change the angel's route. Just listen. You're being watched, okay?"

"Okay. By who?"

"I want you to call a general alert. Wake everyone up. Have them evacuate on foot from the hotel's east end. They have to stay out of sight. Got it?"

"Yes, sir?" Not sounding sure at all.

"Your assignment is different. You need to stay where you are and act like nothing is happening."

"Sir, what *is* happening?"

"Now, Tuttle."

I listen to him call the alert. He does a good job, repeating what I told him precisely, insistently: "Evacuate, but stay out of sight. . . . I don't know what's going on, just do it."

When I'm satisfied the squad is on the move, I move too, west through the woods as quietly as I can, my footsteps padded by damp leaves and everything around me bright in night vision.

The ground begins to slope up under my feet. I'm encouraged, because logically, I'll find the enemy at a high point. I move as quickly as I dare. I've advanced over two hundred meters through the woods when I see a two-story house with trees leaning over it. Its white paint is stained by time and neglect. Shingles are missing from the roof, and moss is growing on the ones that remain. It looks abandoned. The only sign of life is a faint glow, visible because I'm using night vision, coming from the second-story window.

I listen for voices, for movement, and hear none. Just the rustle of leaves in the canopy, the chirping of crickets.

Moving on, I circle around the house. The woods have taken the yard for their own, but the driveway is claimed by only a few patches of grass, indicating someone comes now and then to visit the old place.

Someone's here now.

An electric sedan is parked close to the covered porch. The front door is open.

An icon ignites at the edge of my vision: a solo link from Jaynie. But she doesn't say anything. She just wants me to know she's watching through my helmet cams.

I step onto the porch stairs and look inside. Night vision shows me an interior stairway with its banister removed. I cross the porch, treading lightly, and as I reach the open door, I finally hear a voice, its volume boosted by my helmet audio. It's one I know. "Check," Carl Vanda says. "Position data on the third seeker is in."

A second voice answers, also male but younger, less resonant, with a slight country twang. "Triangulating."

In Manhattan, Vanda came after me with a sniper rifle, but there's a bigger operation going on here.

I use the thrust of the exoskeleton to bound up the stairs, requiring only three strides to reach the top. I've got my HITR ready to use if I have to, but I want to take Vanda alive.

Of course they hear me coming.

A figure appears in an open doorway near the top of the stairs. Night vision shows me the narrow face of the man in brown—Carl Vanda's right-hand man in Manhattan, who almost killed me on the sidewalk. A thin honeycomb cast wraps his wrist and hand—I guess I broke bones when I kicked him—but he's working despite the injury. His far-sights help him see in the dark, and he's carrying an assault rifle that he's getting ready to use against me.

I want Carl Vanda alive, but I don't give a shit about this guy. So it's just a question of who can pull the trigger first. My tactical AI takes over, firing a three-round burst into his throat. His head snaps back and I'm jumping over his body as it collapses to the floor.

I burn a half second assessing the room: no furniture, old-fashioned wallpaper, a stained ceiling, a window sash thrown open with the woods beyond. The forest's dense canopy hides the lights of the hotel, but with targeting data from his seekers, Vanda doesn't need to see the hotel to hit it with the portable, programmable missile launcher he's got set up by the window. The device is on a motorized tripod already bolted to the floor. My guess is he meant to pull out, and then pull the trigger remotely, maybe from halfway across the state.

It's too late now to execute that plan, but he's adaptable.

He tosses a luminous tablet at me—probably the one that controls the launcher. The light dazzles my night vision. I dive for the floor. A pistol goes off. The tablet bounces, spraying its bright-green light around the room as the round explodes against the wall behind me with a concussion like a mini grenade. I keep my head up, my HITR ready as I slam against the floor. My tactical AI is ready too. It puts a targeting circle on Vanda's chest.

He's bulky with body armor, so I take the AI's advice and fire two shots that knock him backward against the wall. He's stunned, unable to breathe, glaring at me through his farsights, the pistol still in his hand but only because he can't uncurl his fingers to let it go.

I jump to my feet, twist the pistol out of his grip, and pitch it out the window. Then I grab his farsights off his face and toss them toward the door. He's starting to recover some volition and takes a weak swing at me, so I seize him by the front of his jacket and hurl him facedown on the floor. Shouldering my HITR, I follow him down, planting the knee joint of my dead sister between his shoulder blades with enough pressure to cut off his breathing. I grope in the pockets of my armored vest and a miracle happens: I find a zip tie, left over from First Light. I use it to bind his hands behind his back and then I haul him to his feet. He makes a wheezing sound as he gasps for air.

Outside, past the rustle of leaves, I hear a racing engine. At first I think it's on the interstate, but then I hear the crackle and pop of leaves and twigs crushed beneath tires. Someone is on the frontage road. With a thought, I expand the squad map, but the only soldier noted on it is me. No one else is wearing a helmet.

"Jaynie, I hope that's you coming."

"Roger that. Is your situation secure?"

"Affirmative. I'm moving the prisoner outside."

Vanda is hurting. I hear it in the low, grating fury of his voice when he tells me, "You're going to Hell, Shelley. I'll see to it."

"Been there, asshole, thanks to you."

I push him ahead of me across the room, steering around the black puddle of blood seeping from his compatriot, and then I make him kneel while I recover both his farsights and the ones that belonged to his dead friend. They're probably so tight with security we won't be able to get any data out of them, but I don't want to leave them behind for somebody else to crack.

After that, I half drag, half carry Vanda down the stairs and outside. "Jaynie, I'm taking him out to the frontage road."

"Roger that." Her voice is crisp and cold. It dawns on me she's furious, but she's not going to let that interfere with the operation. "We're almost there."

She comes with lights off. As she brakes, Nolan bails out of the shotgun seat.

"Search him," I order.

While I hold Vanda, Nolan frisks him, finding a knife, a multitool, a small pistol.

"Check his eyes. Make sure he's not wearing an overlay."

"I don't wear an overlay," Vanda growls. "And no chip. Only an idiot would hardwire himself into the Cloud."

Nolan pushes Vanda's head back anyway, shining a light into his eyes to make sure there's nothing there. "He's clear. You detecting any EM?"

My helmet tracks nearby sources, but it's not picking up anything from Vanda. "Negative."

"Move!" Jaynie says. "Get him inside now."

We bundle him into the backseat. I climb in behind him, awkward in my dead sister. Nolan comes in on the other side. As soon as the doors close, Jaynie is driving: over the shoulder, through the wire fence, and onto the interstate, heading west.

I look behind—no traffic—then lean my HITR against the door. "Nolan, you got any zip ties?"

We bind Vanda's ankles together. I want to get him out of his armor so that if I have to shoot him again, it will count. "Try anything and you'll have a concussion," I warn him as Nolan cuts his hands loose.

He's not stupid. He knows that while I'm wearing armor, bones, and helmet, there's nothing he can do to hurt me. Even if he gets his hands on my HITR, it won't fire while it's registered to me. He might be able to take a swing at Nolan before I break his skull or snap his neck, but that's it.

All he has left is talk.

As we work his jacket off, he asks, "Anyone still alive that you care about, Shelley?"

Nolan tells him, "Shut the fuck up."

"You should take this chance to call them and say good-bye."

Nolan waits until Vanda's armor comes off, then he slams a fist into his ribs, making him grunt.

"Don't hit him, Nolan," I say. "The Red sent his plane nose-down in the dirt last year. He's a shattered mess inside. We don't want to start any internal bleeding."

"*Burn in Hell*," Vanda whispers.

We bind his hands again behind his back and then drape his jacket over his head so he can't see where all this is going.

As we head west at exactly the speed limit, I think about what just happened and I wonder, *Why now?* In Manhattan I felt abandoned, it was only luck that let me live, but tonight it was the Red. Was that luck too? It's just a rogue AI, after all. It's not God and it's not omniscient. It can't be. It can't be everywhere at once. It has to allocate resources, so it comes and goes.

Harvey speaks on gen-com. We've been on the road nine minutes, so it surprises me we're still in range. "Second unit loaded and ready. Departing now."

Jaynie and I ask the same question at the same time. "You got the angel?"

"Roger that," Harvey says, managing to insert a note of irony.

"And you've got Delphi?" I ask.

"Yes, sir. All present. Vasquez?"

"Here."

"Shima says to get off the interstate. Take Four Fifteen north and keep your speed legal. She's setting up a safe house."

"Roger that."

The lights of Des Moines loom ahead of us.

I take my helmet off, put it on the floor beside my feet. I want to take off my dead sister too—it's not made for sitting—but I need more room to do that.

This was a successful operation, but there are no *hoo-yahs*, no congratulations. No one says anything. There's only silence, for miles.

AGAINST THE BEAST

EPISODE 2: SHADOW GOVERNMENTS

WE REACH THE SAFE HOUSE AT 0341. IT'S AN ISOLATED farmhouse with a couple of outbuildings and miles of wheat fields all around it. There are no lights on as we roll up, and no vehicles in sight.

Jaynie takes Harvey to check things out. No explosives go off, no commandos fall out of the sky, so we cut the zip tie on Vanda's ankles and get him out of the car, with the jacket still over his head. His legs have gone numb. Nolan and I have to carry him through the front door and into the basement. There's a toilet there. We cut the zip tie on his wrists so he can use it with the door open.

Flynn and Harvey rig up and come downstairs to take over guarding the prisoner. I'm ready to sleep, but Jaynie wants to see me.

There's a small room set up as an office, with a keyboard and monitor and shelves of books on agriculture, business, political philosophy, and the history of war. Jaynie is leaning hip-cocked on the edge of the desk, watching me through her farsights as I come in.

"Close the door."

I do it, and then finally get out of my dead sister, popping the cinches so I can step free. Jaynie waits until I fold up the frame. She's never been to officer candidate school, but she's studied plenty of officers. She knows how to play the role.

"We are a linked combat squad. We are about *communication*. If we do not operate as a unit, we fail."

"It wasn't a mission. It was just a hunch."

"If you had any reason to believe—"

"I didn't have a reason!"

"Just a 'feeling'?"

"Yes," I admit. "I had a feeling, a really strong feeling that it would be a good idea to look around."

"So strong you rigged up and took a weapon—"

"Damn it, Jaynie, you were looking through my eyes. If I hadn't gotten out there when I did—"

"If the Red hadn't sent you out there."

"*Yes.* If it didn't send me out there we would all be dead now, along with the handful of civilians who were in that hotel. I, for one, am fucking grateful."

"And if you had communicated your concerns to me? We could have stopped Vanda's operation before it started. You murdered a man, Shelley. We have all participated in a kidnapping. Those are illegal acts, in case you forgot—and Vanda has a lot of friends. What I'm hearing from Anne is he may have a connection with the president."

"Vanda is done," I say stubbornly. "He is never going to leave that basement alive. And if the president is complicit in protecting him, that's just one more reason he needs to be removed from office."

"Vanda *is* done," she agrees. "So are you. Anne may have a job for you, but I don't. I can't trust you. I have no way to discipline you. You are off my squad."

I think we both knew this was coming, ever since she told me about the new command structure. I don't like the idea of stepping away, of turning over the welfare of my soldiers to another commander, but that happens in the army. I guess it happens with mercs too. Jaynie had damn well better take care of them. . . .

But I know she will.

So what's my place in the world? That's a mystery to me. I don't know if I have one. And I'm too goddamn tired to think any more about it. So I take my helmet and the folded frame of my dead sister, and I head upstairs to shower and to sleep.

Delphi wakes me a couple of hours later, with kisses on my face until I open my eyes. I take my time about it.

Sunlight is seeping past the blinds, casting a warm glow across Delphi's pale face. She is smiling, if only a little.

"Anne Shima is here."

"Yeah?" I sit up, eager to see her.

"And Trevor Rawlings."

"Ah, *fuck.*"

I hate Rawlings. He tried to keep from me the fact of Lissa's kidnapping, and when that failed, he tried to turn my squad against me.

Deep down in a shadowed corner of my mind there's a vault where I've locked up my conscience. On the rare occasion that I take it out I will sometimes find myself admitting that Rawlings might have done the proper thing given the circumstances.

But I hate him anyway.

Delphi sits back on the bed and gives me a look.

"Did you know you participated in a kidnapping?" I ask her. "You're a criminal now."

"I prefer to think of it as a citizen's arrest."

I consider it. "You know, you might be able to sell that if you get the right judge, and I'll testify we're holding you here against your will." It's not funny, though. It's vigilante justice, just like my dad said. "It was a big mistake to hook up with me, Delphi."

"I'm starting to see that . . . but then, I'm not sure what the right path is anymore. Anne's brought a doctor with her, a specialist." She taps the side of her head. "They're going to inject Vanda's brain with neuromodulating microbeads—"

"*What?*"

She nods. "I don't know if it's the same mix you have in your head. With LCS soldiers, the goal is to stabilize emotions while still being able to ramp them up at need. With Vanda—"

"They just want to make him talk."

She nods, watching me with caution in her eyes, waiting to see how I'll react.

I run my hands over my scalp, feeling the bristle of hair that's grown too long. "It's a smart move."

"Uh-huh."

"I bet Intelligence has been doing interrogations this way for a while now."

"I don't know. It's possible."

The organic microbeads come in many types. Some are chemical sensors, others stimulate neurochemical production. I never thought about it before, but it makes sense there's a formula, a pattern of cerebral stimulation that will make Vanda confess everything he knows.

No doubt the same thing could be done to me.

I shrug. The idea would scare me more if I had any secrets left to hide.

•   •   •   •

I put on a clean shirt and slacks, and head downstairs.

The house we've occupied has a modern-country look to it: casual, with smooth lines and basic furnishings. Anne Shima is in the living room talking to Jaynie, who looks like she hasn't slept at all.

"Lieutenant," Shima says. She's wearing an olive-drab pullover and gray cargo pants, with a pistol holstered on her hip. Her smile is warm as she looks at me. Shima is an older woman, early sixties maybe. She wears her thick white hair confined in a braid pinned to the back of her head. Her Japanese ancestry shows in her petite build. Despite her age, she's slim and athletic, and carries herself with a military bearing. I like her. She's no-nonsense, without Rawlings's dominance issues.

"Congratulations on your prisoner," Shima says as she meets me at the bottom of the stairs. We shake hands, and then I look past her to Jaynie, whose face gives away nothing. Shima frowns. "We have a lot to talk about."

"Yes, ma'am. Have you started working on Vanda yet?"

"He's being prepped. It'll be just a few minutes before we begin the procedure."

As she's speaking, Colonel Rawlings—who is retired from the army, but happy to be addressed by his former rank—steps out of the kitchen. He looks much the same as he did when I met him in Alaska: a big man, broad shouldered, though a little stooped now with age. His white hair is buzzed in a military cut.

We trade glares. He presses his lips together and then, skipping over all the accusations and the acrimony and the remembrances of the dead, he says, "We'll know by noon not only where Carl Vanda's nukes are stored, but where we can find the evidence that will prove the president had a hand in protecting Vanda-Sheridan. You did good, Shelley."

I hate Rawlings—but maybe a little less than before.

• • • •

Jaynie, Delphi, and Shima all disappear into the basement. Moon is awake, manning a tactical operations center just off the living room where he can keep an eye on the feeds from a perimeter of security cameras set up around the house and in the surrounding fields. The rest of the squad is off duty, presumably asleep.

I eat breakfast alone in the kitchen—eggs, bacon, fried potatoes, cooked up by Rawlings before he joined Shima and Delphi downstairs. I'm trying not to think about what's going on in the basement.

The house we've occupied is climate controlled. A picture window looks out on green wheat fields and the approaching road. It's a mistake to leave the window uncovered like that. Then again, maybe it's not really a window. Maybe it's a monitor set to display a view of what's going on outside. Or maybe it's not even showing me what's out there now. I could be looking at yesterday or the day before.

God, I need more sleep.

Sleep is easy of course, thanks to the skullnet and the way it interacts with the neuromodulating microbeads implanted in my brain.

When I entered the army, I volunteered for LCS service. It was cutting edge, it promised excitement, and since it was a new specialty, the opportunity was there for fast advancement—so I thought, *Why not?* I went into the army with a chip on my shoulder, wanting to show anyone who doubted me—wanting to show myself—that I could pull it off. Give me a demanding job, because I could do it as well as anyone.

I volunteered. I knew what I was in for—but that didn't kill the fear. The day I had to submit myself to the neurosurgeon to have my brain seeded with artificial control points—the neuromodulating microbeads—I was scared shitless. Just thinking about it now ramps up the adrenaline . . . reporting at 0400 to the surgical center at the training base, being sent to the showers with a depilatory, washing away every hair on my scalp, and then dressing in paper pants, the cold hospital air making the skin on my back and chest prickle.

I walked into the surgery. I was to be conscious for the procedure, so instead of an operating table, a chair waited for me, equipped with straps to secure my arms and legs. As I sat in it, I questioned my own sanity. Why was I here? Why was I allowing this to be done to me?

A nurse secured the straps. He smiled at me, his brows raised. "Are you okay?"

I nodded. I didn't want to show him how scared I was, but he knew.

He spread a topical anesthetic across my scalp. It felt cold at first, but after a few seconds I didn't feel anything. "It's important you keep your head still," he reminded me. "The more you move, the longer the procedure will take."

I nodded again.

"Don't nod. If the doctor asks you a question, use words to answer. Okay?"

"Okay."

Next came twenty minutes of cold waiting until the doctor finally came in. Her name was Dr. Karn. A civilian, midforties. She spent every day implanting control points in the brains of soldiers.

"There will be pain," she assured me, "but nothing worse than a pricking sensation as the injection needle pierces the skull."

She was right: It was a pinprick pain, but drawn out across the entire time it took her ultrathin needles to pass slowly through the barrier of my skull. There were a lot of needles. Enough to keep the doctor busy over the next hour and a half. At each intrusion she would speak: "Position one, injecting. Position two, injecting. Position three . . ." And I would silently question myself: *Can you feel it? What's changed?*

Nothing.

Every few minutes, Dr. Karn would ask me if I was doing okay, and I would lie and answer, "Yes."

During the whole procedure, she worked from behind me, with the instrument tray at her side.

Not once did she let me see those needles.

The memory of that day remains raw because it was burned into my head before I was fitted with a skullcap, which I wore until last September when the army upgraded me to a skullnet. The beads in my brain have no effect on their own. It's the skullcap or the skullnet that triggers them to function. Ever since that day, every traumatic memory I've collected has been detoxified by the alchemy of a precisely engineered sequence of neurochemicals. I clearly remember the events of my past, I just don't feel the full depth of the emotion behind them like any normal person would.

That's why it's easy to put my conscience away in a box.

That's why it's easy to sit here eating eggs and bacon while in the basement a physician forcibly installs control points in Carl Vanda's brain. Pain is part of that process, but nothing he can't handle. It isn't pain that makes the procedure a kind of torture. Sometimes torture is just the shit that gets done to you without your consent.

I'm still staring at that window-that-might-not-be-a-window when Rawlings comes back into the kitchen. He sits across the table from me, blocking my view of the hypothetical outside. "Not stewing in regret, are you?"

I scowl, and shake my head. My plate is empty, so I push it aside. And then I think to ask him, "Is there a warrant out for me yet?"

"For shooting the merc?"

"And kidnapping Vanda, yeah."

Rawlings looks coldly amused. "No one reported hearing gunshots. The incident was not brought to the attention of any legal authority. But there's a team from Uther-Fen at the abandoned house right now, going over the site, looking for evidence."

"So this is a private war?"

"You don't want to sit in a courtroom again, do you?"

"No, sir."

"Nevertheless, you, *we*, are in a difficult position. In the eyes of the law, we are all compromised."

"I understand that, sir."

"It's too late for you to walk away. Do you understand *that*?"

It's beginning to sink in. I take a sip of coffee that's gone cold.

"I'm not going to bullshit you, Shelley. You already belong to the organization. You're part of it. That's a decision you already made."

I put my cup down, meet his gaze, and ask, "What is it you're looking for, sir?"

"An oath of service."

"I swore one of those already."

"To support and defend the Constitution of the United States. Yes, I know."

And that's what I've tried to do, but the system is badly broken and things have not turned out all that well.

"We all swore that oath, Shelley. Everyone here, except the prisoner. And we're still bound by it, even if our activities have become extraconstitutional. But we are a military organization, and as such we have to know we have your loyalty, and that you accept your place in the ranks."

"And if I don't? If I don't agree with what we're doing, then what?"

"You do it anyway, just like in the army."

That means I have to trust those above me. I came into this because of Kendrick, because I trusted him, but Kendrick is dead.

Rawlings is watching me. He doesn't have farsights on. He doesn't need them to read me. "An oath of service will formalize our relationship, and cement the foundation of trust we established during First Light."

"Are you my commanding officer?"

This inspires a tight-lipped smile. "Shima's in command of the field units. I'm her aide."

Good.

"The organization is known to our allies as Cryptic Arrow."

"Cryptic Arrow?"

"Yes."

"And we have allies?"

"Yes, Lieutenant. We are not alone. Cryptic Arrow is an extraconstitutional force, but there are elements within the government and the military who will act to support our missions—even if that only means turning a blind eye."

This is the first time I've been given information on the organization, so while Rawlings is in a mood to talk, I push for more. "You said Shima commands the field units. Are there others besides us?"

"We've put together another squad since First Light. Squad Two. But the reality is, we'll never have a lot of boots on the ground. It's the nature of the game we're playing. We can't compete on scale, so our actions will always be heavily leveraged."

"Meaning the goal is more propaganda actions, like First Light?"

"No. First Light was not propaganda. That was an essential action. That's what we do. Going after Vanda's nukes is an essential action. You proposed the mission, Shelley. Do you intend to be part of it?"

"Yes, sir."

I say it without hesitation because he's right: I'm already in. There is no going back. This is the game I will play until my luck runs out.

"Who is in command of Squad Two, sir?"

"You don't need to know that."

I've missed something. "You're not going to assign me to Squad Two?"

"You are the assault leader of Squad One, the Apocalypse Squad, under the command of Captain Vasquez."

I raise my eyebrows. "*Captain* Vasquez? Sir, Captain Vasquez kicked me off her squad."

"Vasquez gets to deal with the personnel she is assigned, Lieutenant. It's her misfortune that she gets to deal with you."

Rawlings summons Shima and Jaynie from the basement. They stand as witnesses while I take the oath. The words are simple enough. I will not divulge my knowledge of Cryptic Arrow or betray any loyal member.

When I'm done, I salute Jayne Vasquez, my former sergeant, now my commanding officer.

Shima dismisses us both, telling us to catch up on our sleep while we can.

Jaynie departs without comment.

I stay to ask, "Where's Delphi?"

"Downstairs," Shima tells me, "helping with the interrogation. But that space is off-limits except to essential personnel."

"Fine by me. I don't want to know what you're doing down there." And then I remember to add, "Ma'am."

I return to my borrowed bed.

As always, sleep comes when I invite it.

I bolt awake at the sound of a gunshot. It repeats, the concussion muffled by walls but accompanied by a kick that vibrates through the bones of the house.

I grab my pistol and launch myself at the door, throw it open and run to the top of the stairs. Delphi is below in the living room, standing with Rawlings. She looks up at me, wide eyed.

"What the fuck just happened?"

Rawlings's explanation is terse: "We got what we needed from Vanda."

Shima wants us to see the confession. Not the long interrogation, just the summary, after they mapped their way around inside his head and knew exactly how to keep him talking, speaking only the truth. Everyone gathers in the media room.

The video is fixed on Vanda. He's sitting on the floor, on what looks like a mattress, with pillows around him that prop him up as he leans back against a wall. His legs are secured together in a body wrap, with his wrists shackled at his hips. The gray T-shirt he wears is dark with sweat. There's a brown skullcap on his head.

He stares off to the side, his gaze unfocused. He looks stoned with fatigue, dazed, at the failing edge of his strength, his head tipped back, eyes half closed, breathing elevated, sweat gleaming on his skin.

A woman's voice, one I don't recognize, speaks from off

camera in a kindly tone. "The nuclear terrorism that took place on Coma Day—"

"I told ya," he interrupts, his voice a hoarse whisper, his words slurred. I see his eyes shift toward the camera though his head doesn't turn. "I had nothin' to do with that. Nothin'."

"I understand that, but for the record, tell me one more time what happened, in your own words, so I can believe you."

"Yeah? And what's it gonna be after that? A bullet in my head?"

Delphi squeezes my hand. No one in the room says a thing.

"What happened on Coma Day?" the interrogator asks. "What was your involvement?"

He gives a little sideways shake of his head. "Tha' was all hers. She cracked. That whole thing, it was crazy—"

"Who cracked?"

"The Queen. The one we all serve. My wife, Ms. Thelma Sheridan." He turns his head to look beyond the camera. "It wasn't her style to adapt to situations. If she didn't like somethin', she changed it. If she got hit, she hit back hard. Yeah, so she got hit: the company, the main company, Vanda-Sheridan—she put my name first but it was her baby—and it was bleedin' money. But she didn't know who threw the punch. It drove her crazy. Then my plane went down. Left me ninety percent dead, out of it for weeks. Somethin' turned her head during that time. She decided her enemy was this fuckin' invisible monster she called the Red. By the time I heard it, she'd made it her truth. I told her she was crazy. She said I didn't know, I hadn't seen. She said it was the Red that tried to kill me. Anyway, she had an enemy in her sights now, so she hit back."

The interrogator waits a few seconds. When Vanda doesn't

go on, she coaxes him. "So Coma Day was Thelma's way to hit back?"

"Yeah. Nothin' halfway about the Queen. I didn' know what she was plannin'. I didn' know she had the fuckin' nukes. The Queen keeps her secrets, you know?"

"Did she tell you she was responsible for Coma Day?"

"Nah. Need to know, right? It was only after they took her that I found out."

"How did you find out?"

"Enhanced interrogation of her staff. *'Any means.'* That's what they kept saying. They were justified to use any means to bring down the Red." He shakes his head. "They're all fuckin' fanatics, servants of God, fightin' the Devil, and they're willin' to take out civilization if they have to, to get rid of the Red."

His chin lowers, and for the first time he looks fully awake and angry. *"Fuck that!* We've always lived with the Devil! So fuckin' what? You adapt. You don't burn your own house to the ground. My men died at Black Cross. Good men. Because the Queen went crazy."

He breathes in a panting rhythm, staring at nothing. When it becomes obvious his tirade is over, the interrogator pushes again. "When you interrogated Thelma's staff, were you able to learn how she obtained the nuclear material?"

"No."

"Did you learn how many devices she had?"

"I thought she deployed them all on Coma Day. Then those kids in DC turned up another IND. Exact same design—and the fuckin' president lost his shit." He smiles again, bitter humor. "Yeah, he wasn't too happy knowing he came within two hours of being blown to hell. He came after me."

"The president of the United States?"

"That bastard, yeah. He said it had to be me behind it,

because she was in prison. I told him he didn't understand the Queen. She has a court of loyal knights, not just me. He told me to hunt them down. So I did it."

"You were operating under the president's orders?"

"Direct orders. That's right. A little extraconstitutional housecleaning."

I wince at the use of this term, the same term Rawlings used to describe the activities of Cryptic Arrow and the Apocalypse Squad. We are the same as Carl Vanda now.

The interrogator continues her questioning: "Did you find the individuals responsible for the IND?"

"Yes."

"Tell me about it, in your own words."

"What's to tell? We found 'em, interrogated 'em, and eliminated 'em."

"What did they hope to accomplish with the DC nuke?"

"We've talked about this," he growls.

"For the record. What did they hope to accomplish?"

"Blow the president to hell. Payback for letting the Queen be taken. Blow the Apocalypse Squad to hell. Same crime."

"Are there more INDs?"

"Yeah, yeah, like I said before. We recovered two more devices along with the engineer who put them together, 'cause you know, it's not easy to put together a nuke. It takes skill and special equipment and money. Lots of money."

"What did you do with the devices you found?"

"Locked 'em away."

"Did you report their existence to the president?"

"That's not something he'd want to know. Plausible deniability, right? I just told him it was over. Then I went into Manhattan to deal with unfinished business and her fucking crazies almost killed me. 'Take care of her,' he said. I told him I already planned to do that."

The video ends. Silence follows it. I don't like it that Delphi was in the basement, assisting in the interrogation. She's been soiled by it. One of the torturers. I put my arm around her shoulder in denial of the feeling.

Jaynie breaks the silence: "So where are the nukes?"

Time is of the essence. Carl Vanda's nukes need to be secured while our intelligence is fresh. It won't be long until someone in his hierarchy—a senior Uther-Fen officer—decides the boss's absence is a security threat requiring critical assets to be transferred to new facilities.

Anne Shima stands at the front of the room, her shoulders straight, gaze unflinching. "The mission is ours. Our contacts report that the tactics of suppression and cover-up that preceded First Light are in play again. There will be no official action until we force the issue by recovering Carl Vanda's INDs. We have designated this mission Silent Firebreak. A preliminary plan is under review and will be issued shortly. You have forty-five minutes to eat and get your gear together. Shelley!"

I stand up. "Yes, ma'am."

"I do not want to see your bare feet on this mission. You will wear boots to protect your identity."

"Come on, Anne. Boots can't hide what I am. First Light proved that." I was wearing boots in the snow of the Apocalypse Forest, but Carl Vanda identified me by the temperature difference of my machine parts.

"Boots will protect you from casual identification."

"And take away the versatility of the feet."

"Make do."

So I'm already in a bad mood when the newly minted Captain Vasquez intercepts me at the media room door. "Stay a minute," she says while everyone else files out.

Delphi catches my eye. "I'll be in the kitchen."

When we're alone, Jaynie closes the door. I try to cut off the lecture that's coming by speaking first. "This isn't about you and me, Captain. It's about the mission. I intend to do my part, and see that we succeed."

She ignores this. "I don't want the Red deciding the course of this mission. If it starts playing puppeteer in your head, I want to know *immediately*. And if I order you to stand down, you will do so."

"No, ma'am, that is not going to work. If I get a feeling my head is about to be blown off I am not going to take time out to report it before I react. Given that the Red has always been on our side, supporting our missions, I advise you to consider it as a battle asset."

"You would say that."

"Even Kendrick—"

"I am not Kendrick."

"Yes, ma'am. I know you're not."

"I want to know what's going on in your head, Shelley. You will report to me any suspected infiltrations. Is that understood?"

"Yes, ma'am. I will do my best."

Assuming it doesn't jeopardize the mission.

I say good-bye to Delphi in the room where I've been sleeping. She'll stay behind with Rawlings, and maybe she'll be safe.

I kiss her face, regretting everything. I hold her against me, silently berating myself for hooking up with her. It was a stupid, self-indulgent mistake. I knew that at the start and I did it anyway because I'm impulsive.

But she wanted it too.

"I'm sorry I got you into this," I tell her.

She pulls back in my arms, gives me a dark look. "Don't patronize me, Shelley. I'm a handler. I worked three years in Guidance. I knew what I was getting into." She puts her palm against my cheek and pins me with her beautiful blue eyes. "Your pretty face is not the only reason I'm here."

I pull her close again, thinking of the last time I left on a mission, when I said my good-byes to Lissa.

I pray: *If one of us has to die this time, let it be me.*

Let it be me.

The preliminary plan for mission Silent Firebreak arrives by e-mail as we leave the safe house, but Jaynie assigns me to drive one of the SUVs, so I can't read it—and that irritates the fuck out of me. But it's only thirty minutes to a private airfield. We leave the vehicles in a hangar, take seats aboard a waiting commuter jet, and within fifteen minutes we're in the air, bound for Georgia. Shima is our pilot.

I open the mission plan in my overlay and read.

The two nuclear devices have been designated Blue Devil and Gold Devil, named for the colors of the cargo vans they occupy. The vans are stored in the basement of a remote research campus belonging to a biotech firm known as Reyvik Biosystems—one of Thelma Sheridan's hobby companies. It's a sparkling, black-glass facility surrounded by a young, replanted forest. Only one story is above the ground, with two office floors below and then the basement. Communications within the building are limited to a private network, isolated from the Cloud. External communications are allowed only from a soundproof room at ground level, outside the perimeter of the secure area. Upon arrival, all employees are required to turn in phones, tablets, farsights, and any other personal computing devices, and everyone is scanned for implants before being admitted.

We will launch our assault at 0400 when we expect only a few employees to be present—those few researchers who are following their experiments overnight.

We are under strict orders to avoid casualties among both the civilians and the security personnel. I have a feeling the latter will be a challenge.

Outside the building, there are heat and motion sensors, patrolling seekers, and a staff of three Uther-Fen security guards who meet and interview all visitors. There are no guards inside. The interior security at Reyvik Biosystems is entirely automated and relies primarily on the identification of trusted personnel and the use of biometrically coded locks.

It should be easy enough to get to the front door. We'll just come in through the main driveway as if we have an appointment.

This is a mission that should have belonged to the president's forces, but Cryptic Arrow's intelligence team believes that notice of the suspected INDs never reached his office.

So it's ours.

We're not ready for it.

We haven't trained together in months, we're not in shape, and none of us knows how our new command structure is supposed to work. I'm surprised Shima didn't give this mission to Cryptic Arrow's Squad Two. The only conclusion I can draw is that she trusts us more.

We rig up on a cool, Georgia spring night and then, with our helmets under our arms and our HITRs on our shoulders, we assemble for some final words.

We're inside an aircraft hangar lit only by the faint red glow of emergency lights. The bifold door is not quite closed. From outside comes the sound of a light rain pattering on the tarmac. Behind us are two cargo vans of the same make, model, and colors as the vans carrying Blue Devil and Gold Devil. There are no windows in their cargo areas, but there are sliding doors on both right and left.

We'll drive the vans to the remote campus of Reyvik Biosystems and, if all goes as planned, we will exchange them for the ones rigged with INDs, hoping it will look to any watching satellites as if we are leaving in the same vehicles.

Shima stands before us, her shoulders straight, her hands clasped behind her back, a determined expression on her aging face. "Keep this in mind," she says, speaking in an undertone, just loud enough to be heard over the rain. "What Vanda told us was the truth as he knew it about the setup at Reyvik Biosystems. But whether he told us the entire truth, or an expired truth, or a truth subject to change . . . we can't know. As on any mission, expect surprises. And keep us apprised of your progress so we can serve our support functions in a timely manner. To this end, it's imperative you maintain communications if at all possible. Good luck to you, and never doubt that you are serving the good."

There is a whispered chorus of *hoo-yah*s and *yes, ma'am*s. Then Jaynie murmurs, "Moon, Flynn, get your jackets on."

They're assigned to drive, which means they'll be visible to the security cameras on the way in. So they'll both be covered up with a lightweight gray drape to hide their dead sisters. It will be about as inconspicuous as football players on the sidelines covered up in capes on a cold day—but we only need to fool the guards for a few seconds.

"Everyone else, helmets on. Take your positions. Let's get this done."

We're heading into combat conditions, so my helmet's full-face visor is tuned to appear opaque black from the outside, but when I pull it on, the interior display lights up.

Translucent icons assemble on the periphery, confirming links to my skullnet, my M-CL1a HITR assault rifle, and to each soldier in the squad.

Night vision kicks in as I follow Harvey into the windowless cargo area of the lead van. I kneel, facing the right-hand cargo door as it slides shut on its electric motor. I've got my HITR across my thighs, with rubber bullets replacing the regular ammo and flash-bangs substituting for fragmentation grenades. We're all carrying serious ammo too, if it comes to that, but our goal is not to kill anybody.

Harvey kneels next to me, and then Flynn covers us with an IR-blocking tent. I hear a seat creak as she settles in behind the wheel. "Team one ready," she announces over gen-com.

Moon speaks next: "Team two ready."

Then Jaynie: "Initiate operation."

It's 0416. I switch on the record function in my overlay. As the van leaves the hangar, there comes the sound of a soft rain drumming on the roof.

The angel has already been launched. To avoid setting off any alarms and to allow for a quick retrieval, it will hold a stationary position between the airstrip and the perimeter of Reyvik Biosystems' territory. So we will be operating without angel sight. But Cryptic Arrow has reactivated the secure satellite account we used during First Light. With the drone as our satellite relay, we'll have communications—at least until we enter the building. Delphi is our mission handler. She'll be following our progress from her location at the farmhouse, but Jaynie is the CO and will be her primary client.

Not wanting to attract any notice, Flynn drives at a leisurely, legal pace. Seventeen minutes after leaving the hangar, we turn into the Reyvik Biosystems driveway and roll to a stop. I'm sweating under the IR tent. So is Harvey.

"I've reached the gate," Flynn says. "Trying the card lock now."

I hear the window slide open and then the unfiltered drip, dribble, and patter of rain falling through trees. The card lock doesn't work, but it's close enough to legitimate that a human voice—male, young, and slightly annoyed—acknowledges Flynn. "Stand by."

I count the passing seconds. We need to get through the gate without raising an alarm. Beyond the gate we have to navigate another half mile of winding driveway before we reach the facility. If we're forced to, we'll blast the gate open, or go on foot and blow the gate on our way out, but either option gives the Uther-Fen guards a chance to prepare.

After twenty-two seconds, the male voice speaks again. "I'll buzz you through. Vendor codes were reset at two a.m. Your card should update sooner or later."

I hear the gate hum and unlatch. Then we're rolling.

"Both teams inside," Jaynie says.

"Hey," Harvey whispers to me off-com. "It's been a while. You ready for some fun?"

"Cut the chatter. Let's just get this fucking tent off."

On gen-com, Flynn says, "I see the building. Two enemy soldiers waiting out front. Both armed with assault rifles, wearing chest armor. They've got the glass front doors standing open."

It all seems kind of easy.

A new link opens in my visor. It's a solo link from Captain Vasquez. "Set?"

"Yes, ma'am."

"Your call."

"Roger that." I shift to gen-com. "Flynn, I need locations. How far apart are the two guards you can see?"

"Meter and a half."

"Stop the van so you put me between them. Any sign of the third guard?"

"Negative, sir."

"Harvey, when these two go down, you hit the guardhouse."

"Happy to, sir."

"Tuttle, you back her up."

"Got it, LT."

The van stops. I shoulder my weapon as Flynn triggers the door. As soon as I see the figure on the left, I shoot three fast rounds, then I turn and fire to the right. Harvey was delayed by the extra half second it took the door to clear her position, so we both shoot at the same time. Nonlethals pound into the chest armor of a lean kid, knocking him over so that his answering shot goes through the building's portico. He goes down, the back of his head bouncing on concrete.

Flynn rolls out of the driver's seat, stripping off her cloak, while Harvey launches herself out of the van and sprints toward the guardhouse. The second van roars up behind us, its side door already open. Jaynie, Nolan, and Tuttle are out before it slams to a stop. Tuttle darts past us on his way to assist Harvey, while Flynn helps me secure one of the guards. He struggles a little, but a punch to the ribs convinces him to cooperate while we zip-tie his hands behind his back and bind his ankles together. Nolan and Moon secure the second guard. Jaynie strides inside, carrying a breaching shotgun in a sling on her back while holding her HITR in two hands, ready to lay out anyone who might object to her entrance.

"Lobby is empty," she reports over gen-com.

I flinch as shots go off by the guardhouse. Harvey says, "He's holed up, LT."

"Blow the door. Nolan, help them out."

Nolan takes off, leaving Moon on his own.

Jaynie says, "External-communications room is empty."

I search my prisoner, recovering a knife, a handgun, and farsights. "Toss everything in the van," I tell Flynn.

"Door to the building's secure area is locked," Jaynie notes. "Preparing to breach. Shelley, Flynn, with me now. You're the breaching team."

"On my way, ma'am."

Using the arm hook of my dead sister, I grip my prisoner's vest and drag him into the building, abandoning him in the middle of the floor.

I glance around. It's an expansive lobby, ten meters square, with a spectacular glass skylight, expensive flooring, art, and well-tended plants: a display designed to assure visiting investors that there is money to be made here. The lights are minimal, probably to enforce a nocturnal cycle rather than to save money. Against the right-hand wall is a long reception desk like the registration desk at a hotel. On the left, double doors stand open to a room with lockers, desks, and monitors: the external-communications room already cleared by Jaynie. According to our intelligence, it's the only place in the building with outside links.

At the back of the lobby, painted the same color as the walls, is a windowless steel door with hidden hinges. Jaynie is standing beside it, checking the load on her breaching shotgun. Flynn catches up with me. We move in behind Jaynie, our HITRs ready.

"On three," Jaynie says, resting the shotgun's muzzle against the door, above the presumed position of the bolt. "One, two, three."

The shotgun's concussion is muted by my helmet. A hole is punched in the door and an alarm goes off—but the door is not open yet.

"Again," Jaynie says, moving the shotgun a few inches. "On three. One, two, three."

Boom!

This time the door shifts. Jaynie moves to the side and I step in, kicking the door wide. On the other side is a dimly lit hallway running right and left. It's clear of people, but the air is vibrating with the vicious, mechanical buzz of a swarm of tiny drones, at least fifteen of them, speeding toward me in an inverted V. They are just an inch long, their black bodies tapered into blunt cones, with beelike wings to keep them in flight.

No way to tell what kind of hazard they present. I just assume they do.

I raise my HITR. My tactical AI doesn't know what to make of the swarm and offers no targeting circle as the tiny black drones bear down on me. I shoot anyway, three quick rounds, hoping I get lucky. Flynn is crouched by the door, firing alongside me. One of the mechanical bees shatters. The shrapnel takes out another and slows the advance of the swarm, but not for long.

We need a more effective solution.

"Flynn, fall back! Clear the hall!"

I transfer my HITR to one hand. Two bees dive at me. I take a wild swing with the HITR's muzzle and clip one, knocking it into the other. At the same time I try to get a flash-bang out of my vest pocket—but Jaynie moves faster.

"Fire in the hole," she announces, lobbing a grenade past my shoulder.

I pivot out of the hallway, getting the wall to my back.

Flynn screams. The flash-bang goes off, its concussion muffled by my helmet. My visor darkens to compensate for the glare. The dark screen makes it easy to see Flynn's icon. It's shifted from the standard faint, translucent green to strident yellow. Her status posts: *Declining heart rate, elevated body temperature, loss of consciousness.*

I turn to look for her. She's sprawled on the other side

of the doorway, unmoving, her HITR fallen beside her. Embedded in the sleeve covering her left forearm is the little black body of one of the bee drones. There's another stuck in the center of her gloved palm. Jaynie moves in, crouching beside her.

I keep turning until I can peer into the hallway.

All the drones are down. Narrow black wings and glittering bits of glass lie scattered between thimble-size mechanical bodies, some still buzzing faintly and spinning in slow, erratic circles. With their motion stopped or nearly so, details are revealed. At the front of each mechanical bee is a camera button surrounded by a ring of broken glass needles.

When the bees hit Flynn, the needles must have gone right through her clothing, piercing her palm and her arm. Delivering a knockout drug? I don't think it's going to be lethal, because the report on my visor indicates her status has stabilized.

"Hallway clear?" Jaynie asks as she uses her arm hook to knock the quiescent bees off of Flynn.

"Roger that. Advancing."

I step inside, crushing drone bodies beneath my footplates. The alarm is an irritating mechanical bleat accompanied by flashing ceiling lights that illuminate recessed steel doors, set at wide intervals on both sides of the hallway. "Freight elevator to the left," I report. "I'm going to check it out."

"Roger that," Jaynie says.

I head down the hallway at a trot, while Jaynie manages the squad. "Moon, take care of Flynn and do *not* let yourself get stung by these bee drones. Nolan, status?"

He's breathing heavily. "We have just secured the guardhouse, ma'am—*goddamn it, Tuttle, move!*—third prisoner on the way."

I reach the first door, look in through the little window to see ready lights glowing in the darkness. I try the door handle. It's locked. I switch to night vision to get a better look inside. A lab is revealed, but I don't see anyone in it. It's possible someone is hiding, crouched under a long worktable or squeezed into a closet, but we don't have time to breach every door.

I check the lab across the hall. It's locked too, with lights off. I move on.

Jaynie begins assessing the hallway in the opposite direction, checking the first door on the other side of the breach. On gen-com she says, "Nolan, you have your assignment."

"Yes, ma'am. Hold the entrance. Guard the prisoners. Maintain communication."

"And kill that alarm."

"Yes, ma'am. Moon, you're with me."

I pause briefly to confirm the next two rooms are locked and dark.

Jaynie again: "Harvey, Tuttle, ETA?"

Harvey bursts into the hallway. "Here, ma'am!"

"Good. Finish surveying the rooms on this end. Confirm all are locked and quiet."

The alarm switches off; the lights stop flashing. Jaynie's footsteps are loud in the sudden silence as she trots after me through the shadowy hallway.

I reach the freight elevator and punch the call button just to see what happens. Nothing does. Like the elevator in my dad's apartment building, it's keyed to registered users only. "Negative response on the elevator."

Our intelligence stated that the Uther-Fen guards were exterior only, but on a typical night, one to three scientists could be expected to be present. We have to find one of them because odds are good they'll have the authorization to use the freight elevator.

There are two more floors of labs and office space left to search, but first we have to get downstairs.

I try the door to the stairwell.

"Stairway locked."

We can breach every door standing between us and the basement, but to use the freight elevator we need an authorized user—and there is no way we'll be able to extract two vans rigged as improvised nuclear devices if we can't use the freight elevator.

"Let's breach it," Jaynie says as she joins me.

"Roger that."

From the opposite end of the hallway, my helmet audio picks up the heavy click of a door unlatching. I spin around, my HITR ready to fire. Jaynie responds the same way. Then together we lower our weapons because it's Harvey who's in our line of sight.

Just steps away from her, a door is opening, swinging cautiously inward. Harvey lunges at it, hammering the door with the footplate of her dead sister, sending it flying back on its hinges.

"*What the—?*" a woman screams. "*Oh God, it's real.*"

Harvey rolls into the room and three seconds later a civilian is shoved forcefully into the hall.

A registered user.

She's a senior researcher, fiftysomething, dressed in brown slacks and a gray sweater. She has Asian features, with silver highlights in her short black hair. Shock makes her talkative and my helmet picks up every word as Harvey hustles her down the hall. "Oh my God, oh my God. I didn't think it was real. The alarm goes off all the time. We're supposed to stay in the labs, but it's always a false alarm, a simulated attack, some stupid drill. What do you want here? Everything is proprietary, years of research—"

"I want you to listen to me, ma'am," Jaynie interrupts as

the prisoner is brought to the freight elevator. "We need to get downstairs, and we need your help to do it."

Tuttle comes racing down the hallway. The thump of his footplates startles the woman. She twists in Harvey's grip, her lips parted, her breathing swift and shallow—but given that she's surrounded by four hostile mercs rigged out in armor and bones and anonymous black visors, I think she's holding up pretty well.

"The elevator, ma'am," Jaynie encourages her.

She nods, touching the elevator button with a shaking finger. The mechanism responds with a hum, and a few seconds later the double doors pull open.

The floor and walls of the elevator are crosshatched steel. There are doors on the opposite side, and it's easily big enough to take on a large van.

We board. There are three floors below us. Jaynie hits the button for the basement. Nothing happens. "Key it," she tells the prisoner, who has a magic touch. The doors close at her direction, and we descend.

She starts to challenge us: "I don't know what you're expecting to find."

"How many people do you estimate are in the building, ma'am?" Jaynie asks.

"I don't know. It depends who had experiments running overnight. Usually it's just two or three. Everyone will be coming in . . ." She pauses to check her wrist. She's wearing a wristwatch, one with a simple analog face like the kind in old movies. I guess that's what you do to tell the time when you're not allowed to wear farsights. "Oh God, not for another four hours at least. Did you kill the security guards?"

"What's on the bottom floor, ma'am?" Jaynie asks.

She draws a shuddering breath. "Please don't kill me. I have children. Grandchildren—"

"Cooperate, ma'am, and you'll be fine. What's on the bottom floor?

"Storage! And utilities. Labs are only on the three upper floors."

The doors open. We're looking into a cavernous space supported by square concrete columns, floored in concrete, walled in concrete, smelling of concrete. Panel lights on the ceiling cast an even illumination across shrink-wrapped pallets with cryptic labeling, pressurized gas cylinders, a thrumming air-conditioning plant, and a line of six white roll-up doors on room-size storage lockers installed along one wall.

No vehicles anywhere in sight. I step out of the elevator. "Tire tracks on the floor."

"I see them," Jaynie says.

"Looks like a vehicle rolled out of the elevator, and then backed up"—I follow the tracks, pointing to the first storage locker—"right into there."

Jaynie comes after me with the shotgun in her hands. "Harvey, keep the prisoner on the elevator. Tuttle, breach team."

"Yes, ma'am!"

We are almost there. Blue Devil and Gold Devil are almost in our hands.

There is no chance the door is unsecured—there's a keyhole beside the switch that controls its opening mechanism—but I slide the switch anyway just to see what will happen, and to my shock the mechanism triggers and the door rolls open.

I fall back, bringing up my weapon—but nothing is there. The locker is completely empty. Only the black marks of two sets of tire tracks on the smooth concrete indicate the vehicles were ever here.

"*Fucking damn!* Jaynie, they're already gone."

"Next locker!" she barks.

I try it. I slide the switch, but nothing happens. "Locked."

On gen-com, Jaynie says, "Harvey, ask the prisoner if she has keys for these doors."

The answer comes back a few seconds later: "Negative, ma'am. She does not."

Tuttle and I provide backup as Jaynie uses the shotgun to get the door open: two blasts that reverberate around the concrete chamber. I force the door up. The locker is crammed with pallets.

We move on to the next. Breach it. Open the door. More pallets.

And the next.

Every door takes more than a minute to open and it's all wasted time. We need to get back upstairs, report the absent INDs, let Cryptic Arrow's intelligence network get started on tracking them down—but we have to clear this floor first, be absolutely sure we did not overlook the weapons.

The fifth locker is unsecured. Tuttle rolls open the door on another empty space. Jaynie reloads, then moves on to the last locker. "On three. One, two, three."

Boom!

Right away we know something's different, because light is streaming out through the breach hole. Jaynie steps back, letting the shotgun fall behind her on its sling while she takes her HITR in hand. She and I are positioned on opposite sides of the huge door. "Okay, Tuttle," she murmurs. The door shrieks and rattles as he forces it open.

Inside is a housing module. It's similar to the border forts the army used in the Sahel—complete living quarters in a portable package—but this one is small, a size that gets used for emergency housing. It's only a little bigger than a cargo van, but even so, it must have barely fit on the freight elevator.

The module is centered in the locker, filling up most of the space. Its outside walls are a cheery light yellow, there's one step up to a brown front door, and alongside this door is a picture window draped in curtains. Lights are on behind it.

"What the fuck?" Tuttle whispers.

But I think I know exactly what we've got—and Jaynie does too: "We've found our engineer."

"I can encourage him to come out."

"Do it," she says obligingly.

I move in from the side, keeping my HITR pressed against my shoulder, the muzzle trained on the picture window. "You in the box!" I shout in a command voice that echoes around the basement. "Come out now, hands on your head, or I'm going to pump a grenade through that window."

This is a lie, of course. If this really is the nuclear weapons engineer who helped construct Coma Day, I want him alive—but I'm hoping he doesn't open the door, because I want an excuse to go in after him. There wouldn't be much hazard to it. Vanda would not have left weapons in the hands of his captive engineer . . . although he *is* an engineer. Maybe he's rigged some kind of electrical bomb inside his little habitat.

"You have ten seconds," I warn—and start counting.

On seven, the door opens, but only a few inches.

"*Eight,*" I insist.

It pulls wider and I can see him looking out, a thin, tall man, a lot younger than I would have guessed, probably near my age. Brown hair in a neat ponytail, brown eyes. Skin that's pale, but with color to it that hints he would tan if he ever saw the sun.

"*Nine,*" I say.

He remembers to put his hands on his head.

"Come out."

He feels for the stair with his foot, then steps down to the concrete. In a thin voice, with a European accent I don't recognize, he asks, "Have you come to kill me?"

It's not going to be that easy, buddy.

We start the interrogation as we march him to the elevator, his hands zip-tied behind his back.

"Where are the remaining INDs?" I ask him.

He looks perplexed. His gaze searches the open locker doors and the far corners of the basement. "They were here." He eyes the tire tracks. "They're gone now."

"How many INDs were there?" Jaynie demands.

"Two! Only two."

We hustle him onto the elevator, where the researcher stares at him like he's a ghost. "What is going on? Why did you say 'INDs'?"

Jaynie directs another question at the engineer. "What kind of vehicles were they in?"

He shakes his head like he's going to refuse to talk. Jaynie grabs his shoulder with her arm hook, squeezing gently. "What kind of vehicles?"

This guy isn't one of Thelma Sheridan's devoted fanatics. I watch the shift in his eyes and I imagine him calculating the parameters of his situation, concluding he might as well talk now because he *will* talk before we're done with him.

In a quiet voice, he describes the make, model, and colors of the vans, exactly the same as Vanda reported. Blue Devil and Gold Devil.

"That's like Coma Day," the researcher says. "Improvised nuclear devices . . . in vans."

"Have you seen any vans around here?" Jaynie asks her, still gripping the engineer with her arm hook.

"No, no. I don't know what *he's* doing here, or how he got here. Who *is* he?"

"Tell her who you are," Jaynie says, a vicious note in her voice.

He speaks to the expressionless black surface of her visor. "My name is—"

"Not your name!"

His face is gaunt with fear; I can smell the stink of his sweat. He stammers: "I . . . I don't want . . . to say anything . . . else. I have a right . . . to an—"

Letting go of his shoulder, Jaynie draws a pistol, puts it to the side of his head.

He pulls back, eyes squeezed shut. The researcher turns away, hiding her face behind her palms.

"Tell her who you are," Jaynie repeats.

"I . . . I . . . I designed the weapons used on Coma Day."

The researcher lowers her palms to look at him, horror on her face.

"The weapons?" Jaynie asks.

"The INDs."

"The nukes?"

"Yes."

"You designed the nukes. Who built them?"

"I . . . I oversaw the assembly."

"So *you* built them."

The researcher looks like she wants to put a knife in his throat. "It was *you*?" she whispers. "You *fucking* son of a bitch. You fucking *murderer*. I have friends who died in San Diego! Who would do that? *Why?*"

I have to admire Jaynie's strategy. She now has an impassioned witness who can testify as to why we were here and what we found.

"Why don't you answer the lady's question?" Jaynie suggests, pressing the muzzle of her pistol a little more firmly against the side of his skull. "Why did you do it?"

He's shaking now, his eyes still closed. "It was a job!"

"A job? And who were you working for?"

"You know already! You know!"

"Who?"

"Thelma Sheridan! Thelma . . . Sheridan. *Please*. I have money. I was well paid. I'll give it all to you. Just please don't kill me."

"Who took the last two nukes?" Jaynie asks.

"I don't know. I swear. They were here when I was brought here, but it's been days since they locked me up."

I decide to ask a question of my own. "Who brought you here?"

His eyes open. He looks around like he's trying to decide which of the anonymous faces spoke to him. "The security people."

"From what company?"

"Uther-Fen Protective Services."

Jaynie lowers her pistol, telling him, "We'll talk more later." As she holsters the weapon, she turns to the researcher. "Could you please have the elevator take us up?"

"I want to stop on every floor," I say. "Confirm it's all actually lab space."

"Roger that."

The next floor is identical to the ground-level floor where we came in. The hallway is wide enough to drive a van through, but all the doors are standard size, not big enough to admit a vehicle.

We go up one more floor. This time the elevator opens on both sides. One side is lab space. The other is a parking garage. I step out into the garage. Five vehicles are there, but none of them are vans.

"Let's get the fuck out of here," Jaynie says.

On the way out through the ground-floor hallway, I pick

up a fallen bee drone, holding it gingerly by one intact wing.
"What the hell are you going to do with that?" Harvey wants
to know.

"Send it to a friend."

I know Joby will want to see this.

The researcher gets her hands zip-tied behind her back,
but after what she's learned, she's on our side and makes no
complaint. We secure her in the lobby along with the three
Uther-Fen guards, but the engineer we take with us.

Thirteen minutes and forty seconds have elapsed since
the first shot was fired.

As I get in the van, an icon ignites in my overlay and the
video of our operation uploads through the local civilian
network.

I don't mention it to Jaynie.

The highway is quiet. No police, no FBI, nothing—because
when Uther-Fen mercs call for help, they don't call the
authorities, they call their own.

The interrogation of the prisoner continues in the van.
With the squad drone still in the air, Jaynie is linked to
Cryptic Arrow's satellite account, and through that to
Delphi, who relays questions from our intelligence team.

Crouched at the prisoner's side, the anonymous black
shield of her visor inches from his face, Jaynie speaks in a
low, clipped voice: "When did Uther-Fen personnel take
charge of the INDs?"

The prisoner is eager to cooperate. "That was . . . the
twenty-fourth. April twenty-fourth." He's sitting cross-
legged on the floor of the van, hunched over, his hands
zip-tied behind his back. He understands his situation,
that there is no one in the world on his side anymore, that
his only hope is to ingratiate himself with us. "They came

in the morning. We had no warning. They killed people."

"You're alive."

"I told them who . . . who I was. That they . . . needed me."

"What did they need you for?"

"You know . . . if they wanted to . . . to use the nukes."

"Did they indicate that was the case? That they wanted to use the nukes?"

"No! No. *Insurance.* That's what they said. *Bring him. It's insurance.*"

"Is it true?" Jaynie asks. "*Are* you necessary?"

The prisoner hesitates.

"Can the weapons be detonated without your oversight?" Jaynie insists.

He stares at the floor. There's a tremor in his bound hands. His answer is whispered, but my helmet audio filters his voice and boosts the volume. "I told them how to do it. I didn't want to! But they were going to kill me."

I'm surprised they left him alive.

He gives us the vans' license plate numbers, but he doesn't have the VINs—the vehicle identification numbers.

The interrogation shifts to Uther-Fen procedures and how the INDs have been handled in the past. The prisoner claims over and over again that he doesn't know where Blue Devil and Gold Devil were taken and FaceValue indicates he's telling the truth—but we know Vanda intended to take them to Niamey.

As far as I'm concerned, we have to assume they're on their way . . . or maybe they've already arrived. It's been days since the engineer last saw the vehicles. The nukes could be anywhere.

At the airstrip, we leave our vans in the hangar. Shima has the jet ready. Our packs and our dead sisters go into the cargo compartment, and then we hustle the prisoner aboard. Flynn is awake but nauseated from the poison the bee drone injected into her. She staggers to a rear seat, and collapses into it. Moon follows with a first-aid kit.

Three minutes later we're in the air, although I don't think anyone knows where we're going. Then, only twenty minutes after takeoff, Shima announces over the intercom: "Our intelligence team claims to have tracked the nukes."

We are directed to a public airport in Brunswick, Georgia, with the promise that a mission plan is being developed for phase two of Silent Firebreak.

"Eat now," Shima warns us. "Piss if you need to, because this mission begins again when we're on the ground."

The new mission plan arrives in my overlay as the jet descends. The introductory paragraph is not what I'm expecting:

Blue Devil and Gold Devil are believed to be aboard the Non-Negotiable, *a privately owned Kai-Stratford Ultrafast— a merchant marine vessel leased to Uther-Fen Protective Services and used by that company to transport heavy supplies.*

I look across the aisle at Jaynie. "They're on a fucking boat?"

She's wearing farsights. The lights in the cabin are dim enough that I can see the sparkle of the display. "Yeah. I thought it would be a plane."

She sounds as unsettled as I feel. We're infantry. We don't do boats.

"Why would he put them on a boat?" she asks. "Why not a plane?"

"Because we took his plane?" That was part of First Light, when we hijacked Vanda-Sheridan's C-17 and left it in Niamey.

Jaynie really doesn't like the idea of a boat. "He could hire another plane. Why the fuck didn't he hire another plane?"

I think about it, and shake my head. "You'd have to hire

a flight crew to go with it. I don't think either Vanda or the Uther-Fen culture would allow strangers that close to a critical operation."

She shrugs, and we both return to reading the report.

The *Non-Negotiable* is a roll-on/roll-off cargo-carrying catamaran designed to transport personnel and equipment. It's a hundred meters in length and built for speed, able to run at over forty knots. Yesterday evening, around the time Carl Vanda was executed in the basement of Cryptic Arrow's safe house, it completed a domestic run from Virginia to the port of Brunswick. As the *Non-Negotiable* docked, a gate camera recorded the arrival of two cargo vans that matched the description of the vans known to be carrying Blue Devil and Gold Devil, although the license plate numbers were different. A port worker claimed to have witnessed the vans being driven aboard the *Non-Negotiable*. Dock-usage records and harbor surveillance cameras agree the ship left the port of Brunswick at 0044—over five hours ago now. Coast guard surveillance tracked it for the first three hours as it headed out to sea.

I pause in my reading to wonder: Who in the organization has access to the port's surveillance cameras? Who interviewed the worker? Who was allowed to examine the coast guard's records? Of course the report doesn't say.

The mission plan calls for us to rig up as soon as we land, and then board a contracted helicopter, presently being equipped with external fuel tanks to extend its range. We will be ferried out to sea, in the expectation that the precise location of the *Non-Negotiable* will be determined by satellite surveillance while we transit.

We will board the ship. (There are no specifics of how this will be accomplished, no indication of the defenses we will face.)

We will subdue the crew and security personnel. (No

mention of how many, their training or experience, the arms they will be carrying.)

We will take possession of the ship and return it to port. (I would feel better about this if Flynn were going with us. She's flown a C-17 and I'd like to see her drive a boat. But Flynn is disabled. She'll be staying behind.)

There is a closing notation that the mission plan for Silent Firebreak will continue to be revised as we approach the target. Good to know.

"Nonlethal ammo, Anne? Come on. That is an Uther-Fen ship. It's going to be crawling with mercs."

Shima gives me an annoyed look. "Our intelligence doesn't support that."

We're in a hangar in Brunswick, sandwiched between Shima's jet on one side and a no-frills Bell helicopter outfitted for industrial work on the other. The prisoner is being held aboard the jet. Flynn, who still feels like shit, is assigned to guard him.

I've already rigged up and collected additional equipment in my pack, including a satellite relay to boost signals to and from my helmet, since we'll be going in without the angel. Though I've loaded plenty of lethal ammo, the mission plan calls for us to go in with the stuff used for crowd control and I don't like it.

Shima thinks I'm being a drama queen. "Uther-Fen is a well-run company," she says, going over a checklist on a tablet she's holding in the crook of her arm. "They don't ferry personnel around the world for the hell of it. That ship is on a mission to deliver Gold and Blue. It will have a security contingent to protect that cargo. We don't have hard numbers, but a reasonable estimate suggests ten to fifteen security personnel at the most."

"Ten to fifteen mercs compared to six of us? I guarantee you Uther-Fen is not going to be using nonlethal ammo."

"No, but the ship's crew will not be carrying any weapons at all. They are a civilian crew, and you're far more likely to win their cooperation if you don't kill them. If and when you get into a battle with Uther-Fen security, you can utilize lethal ammo, but your first goal is to take the bridge without shedding any civilian blood, and get that ship turned around."

"This is not a mission we've trained for."

She glares up at me. "I am aware of that. And I would not ask you to do it if this were not the direst emergency, and if I did not have confidence in the ability of this squad to adapt and innovate. That said, this is a voluntary mission. Anyone who chooses not to participate, please stand aside now."

Silence descends as everyone in the hangar stops what they're doing and turns to stare—at me. Jaynie looks up from loading ammunition into her pack. "What's it going to be, Shelley?"

Nolan racks a magazine of nonlethal ammo, and scowls. "How sure are we that the nukes are on that ship? When the license tags on the vans don't match?"

"A license plate is easy to change," Shima says.

True. But we are about to commit an act of piracy.

"We can't know with one hundred percent certainty," Shima goes on, looking around from Nolan, to me, to Harvey, Tuttle, Moon, and Captain Vasquez. "It's true the vans we're looking for are common, and it's possible the ones loaded onto the *Non-Negotiable* are not the same vans described by our captured engineer. But reason says otherwise, and our chain of evidence is convincing enough that we have allies in this operation. We are not alone. On this mission we are acting as a shadow agency, but our activities are known, and supported."

"So let's hear it!" Jaynie barks. "Shelley, are you in?"

I look for the skullnet icon, wondering if the Red is riding me, but I don't see it. I realize I haven't seen it the entire mission—maybe because I don't need help making up my mind. "Yes, I'm in."

"Nolan?" Jaynie asks.

His scowl deepens and I'm worried he'll say no—but this is Nolan. "I'm in."

Where Nolan goes, Tuttle goes, while Harvey lives for crazy-ass missions, and Moon goes along because that's how our squad dynamics work.

The mission is on.

"You think maybe we should be wearing life vests?" Moon wonders.

"Check the helicopter," Shima says. "There should be life vests aboard."

The helicopter pilot pulls them out for us. They're civilian issue, a brilliant, reflective yellow designed to stand out against the ocean's vast, textured surface. There is no way I'm going to put one on and mark myself as a target.

"We can't wear those," Jaynie says—and the neatly rolled vests go back into storage.

Just before we board, I remember the broken bee drone I picked up on the way out of Reyvik Biosystems. I stashed the device inside a plastic box scavenged from my first-aid kit. I hand the box to Shima. "Do me a favor? There's a guy, an engineer, in San Antonio who built my legs—"

"Joby Nakagawa."

"Yeah. Can you get this to him? Ask him if he can build something like it. Tell him I think this one is better."

"Better than what?"

"Just tell him I said that, okay?"

• • • •

The pilot is alone up front. Two unpadded bench seats have been rigged in the back, facing each other, just clear of the dual sliding doors. I sit between Jaynie and Moon, awkward and uncomfortable in my rig.

It's past sunrise when we lift off, but we don't get to see the sun. A spring storm is churning off the coast and rain hammers at the windows. We fly low, beneath the ragged skirts of gray clouds whipped by a gale-force wind that turns the flight into a stomach-churning thrill ride.

Over the intercom the pilot keeps promising everything is fine, he's handled worse than this, no reason to worry, no reason at all. Then we hit an updraft from hell and shoot straight up, an ear-popping thousand feet, the pilot swearing the whole way, reading off our altitude and having a religious experience—"Holy shit! Holy *shit!*"

In those seconds I am certain we are going to wind up in the water, weighed down by the bones of our dead sisters.

But we live.

And our unplanned elevator ride has the positive side effect of silencing our pilot. He stops his patter of reassurance to concentrate on flying. Or maybe he's saying his prayers.

I think happy thoughts, knowing I can't afford to be exhausted from fear if and when we do find the *Non-Negotiable*.

What a stupid fucking name.

For almost two hours we head straight out to sea.

I feel like we've left the world, like we will never see land again.

Every few minutes I turn around to peer out a window, gazing at the gray clouds racing above us and the giant swells rolling below, white foam torn off their peaks.

Even with external tanks, there can't be enough fuel to fly us back through this storm. Can there?

No one has spoken in so long it's a shock to hear the pilot's voice over the intercom: "We're about three minutes away."

I turn again to look out the window, but I don't see a ship, just empty ocean.

"The deck is going to be heaving," the pilot warns. "There's no way I can put down on it."

"So it's the backup plan," Jaynie says grimly. "This is a no-choice mission. We go in on cables."

It's probably a one-way mission, but I keep that opinion to myself because she's right. We don't have a choice. The nukes cannot be allowed to move beyond our reach. It's our duty to all those who died on Coma Day to ensure they are never used.

Harvey says, "Too bad we don't have mounted rocket launchers on this bird. It'd be a hell of a lot easier just to sink that ship."

That would be my choice too.

But it's not a choice.

I unbuckle my safety harness. "Harvey?"

"Yeah?"

Jaynie is CO, but I'm assault leader. I go in first, and the initial tactical choices are mine.

"I want you with me on the initial assault."

"Roger that, LT! I said I'd follow you anywhere—just swear you won't make me babysit any prisoners this time."

"I'll do my best—and don't unhook from the cable until you are firmly planted on that ship. Got it?"

"Yes, sir! Let's slam some Uther-Fen mercs. *Hoo-yah!*"

The *Non-Negotiable* is almost certainly scanning for other vessels, to avoid both collisions and pirates. We are gambling that their security is not rigged to detect a pirate assault that comes from the air . . . in the midst of a howling gale.

As I hesitate in the open doorway, staring down at the gray waves, I wonder if the depth of the water below me is best measured in miles. I don't consult my encyclopedia, though. I don't really want to know.

My helmet is on. My HITR is on my shoulder. I've got a pistol in a chest holster, a collection of grenades, and a knife on my belt because you never know. One thing is for sure: If I end up in the water, I'm going down fast.

I link into the satellite relay I'm carrying in my pack. "Delphi, you there?"

"Gotcha, Shelley."

"Moving out," I say.

And I step out the doorway and into the storm.

The wind rattles my sleeves and the legs of my pants. It spins me on the cable. That's how I get my first glimpse of the *Non-Negotiable*: As I'm spinning clockwise, the ship appears beneath me. It's a gray rectangle, the bow as blunt as the stern. The forward third of the ship is a smooth and nearly featureless top deck that ends at the bridge housing. On either side of the bridge are narrow observation decks that span the width of the ship. Except for antennas, the bridge is the highest point. Like the top floor of an aircraft control tower, it's ringed with windows looking out in every direction—except up.

So far, no one is shooting at us.

Behind the bridge, gray photovoltaic panels form a roof over an open-air deck designed to carry shipping containers. According to the harbor surveillance images, it's empty under there. Underneath the container deck is an enclosed deck. That's where the INDs are supposed to be—if we have the right ship, the right intelligence, the right luck. In any case, we're pirates.

Maybe Jaynie is right and the Red *is* playing puppeteer inside my head.

Maybe it's in all of us.

Because this is fucking crazy.

I'm soaked before I descend halfway. Blasted by the gale, I should be freezing, but there is so much adrenaline pumping through my system I don't feel a goddamn thing except a fatalistic excitement. I'm flying with the speed of a superhero, with Harvey just a few meters away. Together we swoop in toward the port observation deck. Despite the storm, our pilot manages to briefly match speeds with the *Non-Negotiable.*

"Harvey, get ready!"

"Roger that!"

The deck heaves, the cable pays out, and the distance from impact narrows with terrifying speed. I decide to hit my release early and drop the last meter, meeting the deck with a ringing, metal-on-metal clang just as the bow drops over the summit of a wave.

Wasn't expecting that.

I hurtle forward into a three-strand cable fence that saves me from plummeting to the foredeck. A geyser of white spray explodes into the air as the bow plunges into the next wave. A shower of seawater falls over me, mixing with the rain.

As the ship climbs the next swell, I turn. Six meters separate me from the bridge, where three figures in khaki uniforms are looking at me through the heavy blue-green glass, shocked expressions on their faces. Holding on to the cable fence for balance, I swing my HITR up and fire one-handed right at them. It takes six shots before my nonlethal ammo manages to crack the window. Harvey appears beside me and together we hammer the glass until it shatters into fat cubes. By this time the bridge crew has dropped out of sight and the ship is plunging again into a wave trough.

"Harvey, come in behind me!"

"Roger that!"

One bound in the dead sister takes me most of the way. A second jump leaves me crouching in the frame of the shattered window. The ship hits the trough. The impact jars me out of the window frame. I slide on the hip joint of my dead sister across an instrument board, breaking God knows what switches, but at least I'm out of Harvey's way. A one-handed grab at the arm of a chair keeps me on my feet as the tilt of the deck reverses.

Our window-breaking fusillade has cleared the immediate area. The bridge crew has retreated—either down a metal stairway aft or behind a large central console, I can't tell. There's only one crew member in sight, crouched at the aft end of the console and marked as a target by my AI. I don't ask why. My finger just flexes on the trigger while my brain is still processing an image of a woman in a khaki uniform, Caucasian, brown hair pulled back in a tight bun, maybe forty-five years old, holding a pistol in a two-handed grip aimed in my general direction.

She's not wearing armor.

My round slams into her sternum at a range of under two meters. Her pistol goes off in a wild shot as the impact knocks her down. Her head cracks against the edge of an instrument panel. Screams of outrage and terror erupt from behind the console as she collapses bonelessly to the floor— but the others don't show themselves or try to help her.

Delphi is silent, too skilled a handler to intrude when the action is moving this fast. She must have silenced gen-com too, because I don't hear any chatter from the helicopter.

I let go of my death grip on the chair, stepping around

the end of the console just as Harvey comes in behind me. She arrives with more grace than I did, vaulting on purpose from the window frame to land with a thump against the rubberized floor. Water drips off her clothes and off the gray bones of her dead sister. She grips her HITR in two hands despite the angle of the deck, swinging the weapon from right to left as she searches for a target.

With my HITR braced against my shoulder, I round the console. Behind it are two more of the bridge crew, a man and a woman huddled together. They hold each other. Neither has a weapon. I hook an elbow over a chair to stabilize myself as the ship plunges again.

Delphi finally speaks: "Identifications confirmed as civilian crew. He's the navigator. She's the helmsman."

Something's not right.

"Delphi, mission plan said we'd find four personnel serving on the bridge." I use a whispered undertone so our prisoners can't hear me, leaving it to gen-com to amplify my voice. "So someone's missing."

"Checking. . . . We imaged only three when you landed."

Was there a fourth? Did someone rabbit down the stairway when they first saw me dropping out of the sky?

My guess is yes.

"We assume the fourth has reported in to Uther-Fen," I say. "Harvey, secure the door to the stairway."

"Yes, sir."

Behind me a door chunks shut. It's not steel. It's a bullet-resistant composite.

"Bridge secure," Harvey reports. "For now, anyway. We could use some backup, Captain Vasquez."

"Right behind you, Harvey," Jaynie answers.

I sure as fuck hope so, because we have maybe twenty seconds before the ship's security personnel figure out what just happened.

There's also the problem that no one is driving right now.

I shift my gaze to an icon that activates a voice synthesizer and address my concerns to the woman Delphi has designated as the helmsman, remembering to whisper so I don't give away my identity by voice analysis. "You're the helmsman, right? I need you at your post. Get on your feet." There is a pause, and then the synthesizer echoes my words in a booming, authoritarian male voice, *"You're the helmsman, right? I need you at your post. Get on your feet."*

The pair just look at me, too shocked by the artificial voice to make an answer.

"On your feet!"

"On your feet!"

I hate the fucking synthesizer.

"Don't kill me," the woman whispers. "I'll cooperate."

The only reason I can hear her frightened voice is because my helmet amplifies it.

She rises tentatively. I step back so she can make her way to the end of the console. "I'm going to straighten us out," she tells me in a trembling voice.

"No. Turn us around. Take us back to the coast."

"What?" She looks at me, wide eyed. I can see her thoughts churning. She has no idea what cargo this ship is carrying. She's thinking that if we go back, there will be help. The coast guard, the US Navy, the port authority. She nods. "It's going to be rough as we come around."

"Understood." I turn to her companion, the navigator. "You! Facedown on the floor."

The floor is wet with rain and spray blown in through the broken window, but he goes down anyway. I kneel beside him and zip-tie his wrists behind his back. "How many people have you got on this ship?" I ask him.

"Eight crew. Maybe twelve security people."

"The mercs don't always make it official, huh?"

"We are a security company. We are *not* a military ship—"

"You're the navigator, right? We might need you, but until then, don't move." I start to get up.

"Who the fuck are you?" he asks. "What are you after?"

"The nukes on your cargo deck."

He rolls his eyes to look up at me. "You're crazy!"

An arguable point, but not about the nukes, and I want him to know it. If we get killed, I want someone here to know what is being transported on this ship. So I ask him, "What did you pick up in Brunswick?"

"Not much. Personnel. Some vehicles."

"What vehicles?"

"Just some vans. I don't know."

"Did you check inside them?"

"The security people handle the cargo."

"Just so you know, the vans have nukes inside them. You're delivering the leftover Coma Day nukes to Africa. I hope you get paid well for it."

"It's just cargo! You killed the captain over cargo."

I turn to look at the captain. She's sprawled unconscious on the floor, but I can see she's breathing. "Your captain's not dead. I hit her with a nonlethal round—but I'm switching out my magazine. The next person I shoot is going to die—and you don't want to die for Carl Vanda."

Harvey takes this as permission to swap out her nonlethals too. She jacks in the real thing, then nods at the forward windows. "Our backup's here."

I stand, to see Jaynie and Nolan beyond the bow, swinging crazily on cables as the helicopter fights the wind to get them to the bridge. But the ship has already begun to turn, angling across the face of the next swell so that the deck rolls beneath them at a crazy angle—and shooting starts outside.

"Harvey, go, go! Find that!"

"Yes, sir!"

She vaults to the window, catches the frame with one hand, and crouches there, her HITR in the crook of her right arm as she tries to locate the shooter.

The helmsman glances at me with cautious eyes, while on the floor the captain finally stirs. Harvey drops out of sight, and a second later I hear her shooting.

We're broadside to the waves now. The ship rolls hard, Harvey swears over gen-com, while out the front window, the foredeck rises under Jaynie and Nolan. Like the observation deck, the foredeck is fenced in by a three-strand cable barrier. Jaynie just misses swinging into it. She knows she's not going to get a better chance, so she hits her release. Nolan follows. They drop to the deck, but it's at a forty-degree lateral angle, and they slide.

Nolan is halfway across the span of the foredeck when he gets an arm hook around a tie-down loop and jerks to a stop.

Jaynie finds nothing to grab. She skates on her side all the way across the deck, under the cabling, and over the edge, catching herself just before she drops out of sight, with an arm hook on the lowest strand. She's hanging on by that hook when we hit the trough. White water roars up around her, floods the foredeck, and for three seconds I can't tell if she's still there. Then the bow starts to climb, the water drains away, and I see her again with her HITR over her shoulder and a second arm hook gripping the highest cable as she levers herself up.

"Holy fucking shit, Vasquez!" Harvey yells over gen-com.

I think she speaks for us all.

But I need to restore order.

"Captain Vasquez, do you need assistance?"

"Negative," Jaynie growls. "Nolan, get the fuck to the bridge. Harvey, what's your status?"

"Just outside the bridge, waiting for our shooter to—"

There is an eruption of gunfire. Then Harvey says, "That one drew blood. Can't tell if it was a kill."

The ship has come almost all the way around. The swells are rolling in behind us now and the ride is smoother. Nolan uses the opportunity to cross the foredeck, disappearing from my sight below the bridge.

"Nolan, you climbing up?"

"Roger that, LT."

"Harvey, don't shoot him."

"Got a better target, LT."

I check the feed from her helmet cam. She's looking under the PV panels, at someone huddled by a recessed elevator door on the port side of the container deck. Harvey starts shooting, right through the aluminum corner that's sheltering her target. Boots kick out, and then crawl away. "Damn it," she whispers.

Nolan finishes his climb to the observation deck. Jaynie is still below, advancing along the edge of the foredeck, gripping the cable, with the sea running in white foam below her.

I scan the sky for the helicopter. "Tuttle, Moon, what's your ETA?"

Delphi answers, "They're not coming."

"What? Why? We can't run this operation with just the four of us."

Jaynie breaks in. "We *are* going to run the operation. We've got no choice."

"Well, what the fuck happened?"

"The pilot called it off," Delphi explains. "He felt it was too dangerous to approach the ship again, and he claimed he was running out of fuel."

The *Non-Negotiable* completes its U-turn. We are heading back to the coast. Wind is howling through the broken window and white spray is spinning off the wave crests, but the rain has lightened enough that I can see a distant object beneath the clouds, moving west ahead of us. The helicopter. A second later, it disappears.

Nolan drops in through the broken window. "The pilot tried to pull out after dropping you and Harvey. Vasquez let him know that was not going to happen."

I wonder how persuasive she was, but I don't ask because it doesn't matter. We aren't getting Tuttle and Moon. It will be just the four of us against twelve mercs who know the ship better than we do and who are sure to be better armed—but Jaynie is right. This is still a no-choice mission.

A new sound grabs my attention. My helmet audio amplifies the rustling and creaking of movement on the other side of the closed door to the stairs. I see the door handle jiggle. "Back up!" I warn, gesturing at Nolan. "Back up, they're going to blow the door."

I turn my back, putting my arms around the helmsman to shield her just as the grenade goes off. The concussion kicks hard. A chunk of debris slams against my helmet, leaving my skull vibrating, while searing heat rolls around me. I shove the helmsman to the floor, then turn, bringing my HITR to my shoulder as I assess the situation:

The security door is hanging on its hinges, singed, its lock blown. The aluminum stairway beyond is empty, but at the bottom of the stairs are two armored soldiers, their assault rifles aimed at me. They could have lobbed a second grenade through the doorway and destroyed us, but that would have taken out the bridge crew too and damaged the equipment. It's good to know they have some restraint.

I don't.

My finger squeezes the second trigger of my M-CL1a, launching a grenade right between them. The brightness and the concussion of the explosion are filtered by my helmet.

As my visor clears, I look again down the stairway. The walls are charred, but I don't see any bodies.

"Behind you," Nolan warns.

I spin around to see the captain creeping on her belly. Following her gaze, I see her pistol still lying on the deck. When I step in front of her, she stops. The helmsman is still crouched on the floor by her station, weeping, her palms pressed against her ears, while outside there's a firefight. I want to send Nolan outside to help. I want to go down those stairs and pursue the enemy. But we have to stay with the prisoners. We have to hold the bridge.

I pick up the stray pistol, check the safety, and drop the weapon into my vest while Nolan moves to the window. He has his HITR ready, but he's not shooting.

I pull the helmsman to her feet and return her to her station. Then I zip-tie the captain's hands behind her back, finishing off with a push against her shoulder blades to encourage her to stay on the floor.

My helmet filters what I hear, muting the sound of the firefight, amplifying a noise from below, like something being dragged. I make a decision. "Nolan, I'm going downstairs."

"What's downstairs, Shelley?" Jaynie asks in terse syllables.

"Half-dead merc, I think. Also, Blue and Gold. Fucking hope so, anyway. We need to confirm it, Jaynie. We need to make sure the nukes don't go overboard on the way back to port."

The pace of shooting picks up and she doesn't answer. Then the shooting stops. I scan my squad icons. Moon and Tuttle display as missing. Harvey and Nolan are nominal. But Jaynie is yellow. She's showing a rapid heart rate and declining blood pressure.

"Goddamn it, Jaynie, are you hit?"

"Roger that," she says in a strained whisper amplified by my audio.

"I'm coming after you."

"No, I'm coming in."

"I'm with her, LT," Harvey says.

"Get the door," Delphi orders.

I open the door to the observation deck, just wide enough for them to slip in.

Though Jaynie is still moving under her own momentum, the upper half of her right arm is a bloody mess.

"Hope the other guy looks worse," Nolan says.

"Damn straight he does," Harvey answers, kicking the door shut behind her.

"Harvey, Nolan," I say. "Make sure nobody moves out there."

The deck rolls and Jaynie staggers. I catch her by an arm strut before she can go down. "Come over here, and sit."

"I can fucking take care of myself!"

"Endorphins pumping, huh?"

"Go fuck yourself, Shelley."

"*Sit*," I insist.

To my relief, she does.

I get out my first-aid kit and go to work while Harvey and Nolan keep watch. Jaynie's arm is broken. I hook her up with artificial blood and antibiotics. Then I clean up the wound and set the bone using an air splint. "You're not going to pass out on me, are you, Jaynie?"

"Like I said, Shelley. Go fuck yourself."

"I love you too." I slap a stimulant patch on her neck. "But you've got to go back to work. Try to stand."

"I can fucking stand!"

And she does. She turns her head, scanning the back of the ship. Her rig will hold her up; it'll help her hold her weapon, and her tactical AI will help her aim it; it will even shoot if she lets it. She should be functional for a while. "Shelley," she says. Gen-com boosts her voice, but I can tell she's whispering through gritted teeth. "You need to move. Like you said. Secure Blue and Gold."

"Roger that, ma'am. I'm taking Harvey with me."

"Go. Do it."

"Jaynie, you damn well better not pass out while I'm gone. I don't want to get back here and find Nolan on his own."

"Just find Blue and Gold."

"I will."

"And don't let them push the nukes overboard—and don't get Harvey killed."

There are three paths to the cargo hold:

The first is an interior assault, down the stairs from the bridge and through the personnel deck—territory we know is held by the enemy.

The second is outside: down a ladder from the observation deck to the roof of the personnel deck, and then down another ladder. After that it's a run halfway across the open-air container deck to the elevator—which is also held by the enemy, with the further drawback that even if we get aboard the elevator, we will have to ride it down past the personnel deck.

The third route skips the elevator. We run all the way across the container deck to where an uncovered stairway drops two stories down the side of the ship to a stern access door that opens directly into the hold.

I opt for the third route, betting it will give me the best chance to get close to Blue and Gold before Uther-Fen intercepts me—but to get across the container deck, Harvey and I are going to need covering fire. The bridge commands a view of almost all of the empty deck, so it makes a good vantage—except the heavy glass windows are in the way. Nolan has the breaching shotgun. He uses it to take out two of the panes.

A freezing wind howls in as he reloads and hands the shotgun to me. "Might be a good idea to take this."

"Thanks."

Our prisoners are shivering, so I spend a minute getting an emergency blanket out of my pack. I wrap that around the captain, and hand an IR-blocking cloak to the helmsman, while Harvey takes care of the navigator. Better than nothing.

"Get going, Shelley," Jaynie says as she and Nolan set up by the empty window frames.

"Yes, ma'am."

I get my pack on and sling the shotgun behind it. My HITR I hold in two hands. "Delphi, you there?"

"I'm here," she says in her handler's businesslike voice.

I turn to Harvey. "Ready?"

"Born ready, sir."

"Let's go, then."

We crouch by the starboard door.

"On three," Jaynie whispers. "One, two, *three*."

I push the door open. Then I run bent over to the first ladder. It's a two-meter jump to the roof of the personnel deck. I hit with a *clang!* then cross the roof in three strides. Harvey bangs down behind me as I make the second jump, down to the container deck. The shooting starts while I'm still in the air. I can't tell where it's coming from, but there's nowhere to hide anyway. The shocks on my dead sister soften the impact when I hit, and then I'm running all out beneath a roof of photovoltaic panels, my footplates banging against the aluminum deck. I hear Harvey pounding behind me. "One down," Delphi says calmly as someone starts screaming. I don't look to see who it is.

Halfway across the deck, I spot a figure at the top of the

stairs. More shooting. This time I hear rounds whizzing from behind me, passing just above my shoulder; got to be coming from the bridge. I sure as fuck hope Jaynie's aim is steady. I never ever want to go out by friendly fire.

The fusillade serves its purpose, forcing the figure to retreat down the stairs and out of sight. Seconds later I'm there, my HITR covering the stairway. The first flight drops to a platform, part of a catwalk on the side of the ship. The catwalk leads back to a second flight of stairs that's aligned beneath the first. When I see my target turning to bound down the second flight, I shoot a three-round burst. The bullets punch through the upper stairs, knocking the target down. But when I peer between the stairs I can still see motion, so I shoot again. The movement stops.

"One down," I report.

"Stairs clear?" Harvey asks as she pounds up beside me.

"No enemy in sight."

"This one's mine."

"Harvey, no!"

Too late. She grabs the rail with her arm hook and uses it to pivot, launching herself from the container deck down to the first platform. A wave lifts the stern, showering her with spray as she hits with a loud *bang!* that shakes the whole stairway. She pivots, darting along the catwalk to the top of the next flight. I follow her lead, cursing silently because it's my job to go first and Harvey damn well knows it.

When I reach the platform, I duck back against the side of the ship. A glance down shows me a body in a black Uther-Fen uniform draped on the stairs below. Harvey vaults it. She's about to land at the foot of the stairs when someone out of my line of sight, no doubt assigned to guard the stern cargo doors, fires a three-shot burst that catches her in the air.

The only thing between her and the sea is a pipe railing.

The bullets impact her chest armor, spinning her around just as the stern drops away. She slams into the top rail, taking the impact on the lumbar struts of her dead sister and she flips over, dropping shoulders-down into the water with hardly a splash, her footplates disappearing last beneath the opaque gray surface and she is gone.

The ship moves on, while on my visor Harvey's status icon updates to orange—*missing*. Not deceased. Just lost—gone too deep for her transmission to reach me.

But she is still alive.

She has to be. The bullets would not have penetrated her armor. The impact might have stopped her heart though. Certainly, it would have temporarily stopped her breathing.

She might not be conscious.

If she's not conscious, she won't be able to get out of her gear.

And her gear is pulling her straight to the bottom.

And if I go after her, my gear will pull me to the bottom too.

But she is alive.

All this in a half second of horror.

"Jaynie, cut the engines."

Even as I say it, it's done: The engines run idle, the wake ceases to churn, and the ship settles into the water, heaving in the swells, surrounded by the slow breathing of the sea.

"Thirty seconds," Jaynie says. "If she doesn't surface in thirty seconds, she's gone."

With my back to the ship's side, I edge along the catwalk until I can peer down and around at the stern. No one's in sight. This is the roll-on/roll-off access point. The closed doors to the cargo hold are recessed. Whoever shot Harvey is back there, where I can't see them without exposing myself.

I look around at the ocean, look for some sign of Harvey, anything, a dark spot rising with the coming swell. "Delphi? Do you see her?"

"No."

There's nothing but blowing sea spray.

I tap into the feed from the muzzle cam of my HITR. Steadying my shoulder against the side of the ship, I reach with my weapon around the corner and do a quick sweep, faster than I can process, but my AI can handle the pace. It marks a target. I line up, and the AI fires a grenade.

As the explosion goes off I look again at the ocean.

Nothing.

I use my HITR to check around the corner again. My AI doesn't find a target this time. I lean over to check for myself. There's a burned body slumped against the closed cargo door.

I take one more look at the ocean. Nothing's out there. I wonder if Harvey has drowned yet or if she's still fighting for her life a hundred feet down.

In a tone of quiet fury Jaynie says, "She's gone." The ship's engines engage again. "Shelley?"

"I'm here."

She's whispering, but gen-com boosts the volume. "We're pinned down here. We can't help you. But this is still a no-choice mission."

"Roger that."

"I want evidence that Blue and Gold are really here. I want at least that."

"Roger that, Jaynie. I'm going in."

"For Harvey," she says.

"For Harvey."

I get a hip up on the top railing, pivot over the top, and drop to the narrow stern deck, the noise I make mostly covered by the churning white wake behind the ship. "Delphi, you with me?"

"I'm with you, Shelley." Her voice is soft, but controlled.

I step over the body to reach the access door and then, cautiously, I test the handle. The door is locked. I consider using the breaching shotgun, but I want my HITR in my hands when that door opens. So I copy the Uther-Fen strategy of rigging a grenade on the door handle, stepping away around the corner while it goes off. When I look again, the door is ajar.

Nolan speaks calmly over gen-com: "Enemy on the interior stairs."

Jaynie answers: "Enemy on deck."

The assault is on.

Masked by the rumble of the engines, the shooting that erupts sounds like distant firecrackers. I move swiftly, jamming the muzzle of my HITR through the smoking doorway to let my AI take a look inside. It marks no targets and no one shoots at me. Delphi says, "Clear to advance." I push the door wider and go inside.

The lights are off, so night vision kicks in.

The green glow reveals a nearly empty bay. Two long rows of support columns divide the space lengthwise into thirds. Metal tie-downs form parallel rows in the floor. At the far end of the bay, close to the elevator door, is a stack of shipping pallets. A forklift is strapped down beside them. Closer to the middle are three armored personnel carriers, urban models like the ones rolling around in Manhattan. And closer to me, backed up against the port side and tied down with mesh chains, are two cargo vans. I can't tell their color because in night vision they're just different shades of green and white.

Jaynie and Nolan trade matter-of-fact phrases:

"Three more in the shadows."

"I've got an angle."

"Fire in the hole."

Delphi says, "I'm taking you out of gen-com." She doesn't want me distracted.

My link icons update and I don't hear the battle narration anymore.

I look around the bay one more time. My AI still doesn't find a target so I have to conclude that only the two soldiers, already dead, were left to defend the stern while everyone else—every merc still alive—is engaged in the firefight upstairs.

So long as Uther-Fen doesn't start lobbing grenades into the bridge, Jaynie and Nolan have a good chance of holding them off.

"Delphi, I'm moving in."

"Roger that. Cleared to advance."

I sprint for the vans, my footplates pounding against the deck.

Nothing happens. No one shoots at me.

I reach the first van. I think it's the blue one. I grab the handle on the sliding door and jam it down. It's locked. So I swap my HITR for the shotgun. Holding it parallel to the van and angled down on the lock, I fire. A car alarm goes off, echoing in the bay as the door pops out a couple of inches. I slide it open. My helmet cams record everything. The video data flows to the satellite relay in my pack, which boosts the signal to Cryptic Arrow's account, and from there it shoots around the globe to Delphi. My overlay records too.

"Fuck," I whisper, staring at the van's cargo area. "Delphi, is that it?"

My helmet mutes the bleating alarm while enhancing her voice. "Stand by."

Inside the van is a massive gray cylinder, close to a meter in diameter and almost as high, bolted to the floor. There's a keypad—my guess is that it's a digital lock—placed next to a seam that probably marks the edge of a door.

Delphi says, "We have confirmation." She's trying hard to hold on to her handler's calm diction, but I can hear a tremor in her voice. "The container you're looking at is a lead shielding to limit leakage of detectable radiation. It's the same structure used in the unexploded weapons recovered on Coma Day. The nuclear device is within. Don't try to open it."

"I won't."

"They want you to check the other van."

"Roger that."

"Please be careful."

I don't want to stand in the tight place between the two vehicles, so I walk around to the other side. On the way, I eye the APCs and the forklift; I scowl at the elevator . . . but nothing moves except the deck as it rolls with the waves. Again, I use the breaching shotgun—and set another alarm blaring.

Inside the second van is another gray cylinder.

Whatever else happens, we did the right thing coming here. That's what I tell myself. Then I flash on Harvey, floating head-down in lightless, freezing waters.

Did we do the right thing?

My focus has slipped. Delphi has to jar me back to the present. "What's that sound? Shelley, do you hear it?"

The helmet brings me the hum of an electric motor. I swing around to see the elevator doors sliding open. Instinct takes over. I bring my weapon up, ready to launch a grenade— but it's not my HITR I'm holding. It's the shotgun. The unfamiliar shape of the weapon makes me hesitate.

"Shoot!" Delphi orders.

I pull the trigger—too late. A barrage of shots hammers into my visor—an impact that puts me on the floor. I hear Delphi yelling at me, "Get up, Shelley. Now. Now. Get up!"

I would like to.

I just don't remember how.

"Can't see," I whisper.

"Your visor's broken. Take your helmet off."

I'm not supposed to do that. I can't remember how to do it anyway.

"You've got a bad concussion, Shelley."

I hear something. Running footsteps. Heavy steps. At least two people.

From somewhere above me, a man says, "Stunned."

I feel the press of cold steel against my throat, a sensation that has the positive effect of nailing me back into my body. I'm on my side, propped up by the mass of my backpack.

"No." The same man. "Don't kill him. Not yet."

I feel my hands again. I flex my fingers.

The pressure of steel withdraws, but not the pressure from Delphi: "Shelley, goddamn it! You need to move now! There's a pistol in a holster on your chest."

She's right. I reach for it. Someone grabs my wrist—a bad move on their part, since I'm still in my dead sister. I swing my arm as hard as I can and feel a satisfying impact, accompanied by a gasp, a moan. I hammer whatever it is again and the moaning stops.

A gun goes off. Sensory feedback hammers up my left thigh, into my spine—a special kind of pain, the kind that comes from my robot legs. I sit up, wrenching off my helmet and screaming, a five-second roar of agony. My legs shouldn't generate pain at this level. This is more than maximum. I stare at the slider icon at the bottom of my overlay, the one that lets me control the level of pain I feel from the legs, and I slide it down to fucking nothing—

The gun goes off again. I see it this time: He shoots out my right knee.

I should feel nothing.

But my nerves catch fire. I swear they turn molten, burn

the inside of my body to ash. I writhe and reach for the legs, wanting to jettison them, to remove them, to make them stop telling me what I don't want to know, that they are scrap metal. Twisted, broken, circuit-melted scrap metal—

"You're Shelley, aren't you?" the man's voice says. It's an American accent. "King David himself. Those legs give you away every time."

My shoulders are heaving, I'm trembling, but the pain has peaked. I assess my position. The only light is what's spilling through the doorway where I came in, but it's enough to tell me I'm on the floor alongside the second van. The merc I hit is an unconscious heap of meat beside me. He looks in bad shape: his nose broken, front teeth missing, blood pooling in his open mouth.

I look up at the surviving merc. I've never seen him before. He's at least six feet, broad shouldered, darkly tanned skin, maybe Hispanic, maybe Greek. I don't know, I don't care.

"Get your pack off," he says.

I do it.

"Now strip out of that exoskeleton, nice and slow, or I'll blow your elbow next and that will hurt even more."

I nod.

"Start with the arms."

I do what he says, uncinching my arms, thinking, *See, Jaynie? I don't want to die.*

The shoulder frame doesn't fall to the ground, but it also doesn't move with me when I lean forward to uncinch my robot legs. I try to assess the damage. There's not much to see: just holes in the pant legs. No blood, of course. Also, no machine parts. I stretch farther to uncinch my ankles. That's when I know for sure my legs are broken. The lower legs are loose inside my pants, no longer attached to my thighs.

I hesitate too long. He raps the muzzle of his weapon

against the back of my head, igniting a blinding wave of pain inside my skull and I almost puke. I try to sit up straight again, but he won't let me. He's got his hand pressed against the back of my head and his gun in my ear. If he pulls the trigger, maybe that will stop the hammering agony in my skull.

"Very slowly. Take the pistol out. Two fingers. And pitch it."

He's worried about the pistol in my chest holster. I do exactly what he says. The pistol rattles away under the van.

"Now the knife."

I pull out the knife on my belt. I've never used a knife in combat anyway. I pitch it away, but he doesn't let me sit up. He wants to talk. That's fine with me.

"I knew the men you killed at Black Cross, and the ones who died in Alaska."

My left hand is still curled under my chest. Slowly, very slowly, I use it to reach inside my vest.

"You'd be dead already, Shelley, except I heard a nasty rumor your friends are holding my boss."

Inside my vest, I feel the stock of the handgun that I took from the ship's captain.

"You think maybe they'd trade Vanda for you? You've got to have some value. The great war hero. The Lion of Black Cross."

I'm pretty sure that's a deal that won't go through.

I brush my fingers against the pistol until I find the safety; I push a little harder and move the switch.

"I'm going to let you up, and when I do, I want you to roll over, out of this rig and onto your belly, facedown, with your hands behind your back. Understood?"

I nod. As he steps away, I pull the gun.

He swears and shoots a round into my side. I get one into his throat. Given that we're both wearing armored vests, I win.

It fucking hurts, of course. Not just my ribs, but my skull too, my pulse pounding through my head like artillery. The pain pisses me off. It makes me a little crazy, makes me want to pay him back for it, to pay someone back, and the next thing I know I've got the muzzle of my pistol jammed against the forehead of the merc whose face I broke—but I don't shoot. I remember who I used to be, and I don't shoot. The cumwad is probably going to die anyway, drowning in his own blood. I decide to push him over onto his side so the blood can drain. Maybe he'll live.

Time to evaluate my own injuries.

Leaning forward again, I pull up my right pant leg, dreading to see what's left of my knee.

And I think:

Holy fuck.

And:

Joby is a fucking genius.

Because my knee doesn't look broken at all. I mean, it's not like I could walk. The lower leg has disconnected from the knee joint, but the joint doesn't look broken. It's not shattered, it's not penetrated.

The lower leg was always designed to disconnect. Joby made it that way. When the bullet hit, it must have detached on its own, failing gracefully with a reaction time faster than an air bag. And the pain I felt? That must have been the heat, the momentum of the bullet impact playing chase up my spine.

Joby promised me I couldn't break the legs.

I pick up the leg—it feels heavy with the boot attached—and fit it carefully back into the knee joint. It locks right in and I'm able to move the foot that's still inside the boot. Where my knee was resting, there's a hole punched into the deck.

I pull up my other pant leg. The left socket is scarred,

but the leg still clicks into place. It still works. I move the slider icon back up again so I can get some sensation from my legs, enough to let me know where they are and what they're doing.

I have a feeling I'm going to hear from Joby when he gets a look at this data set.

My head still hurts like hell and I'm dizzy and nauseated, but I cinch up anyway, and then I stand. My balance is almost defeated by the shifting deck; it's only the struts of my dead sister that keep me on my feet. I manage to pick up my HITR and the shotgun. Then I have to kneel to bind the feet and wrists of the merc with the broken face. My pulse hammers in my head as I bend over him, but I get the job done. Next, I go hunting in the dark for my helmet. When I find it, I pull it on, but I can't see a damn thing. Delphi said the display was broken. I take it off again, pull out the audio loop, and hook it over my ear. "Delphi?"

"*Oh my God, Shelley!*"

"Are Jaynie and Nolan still alive?"

"Yes. The enemy has withdrawn again. Shelley . . ."

Her voice breaks. Of course she thought I was dead. What else could she think?

"I love you, Delphi."

Wrong thing to say; wrong time to say it. She starts crying.

"Delphi, I've got another problem."

Shima's voice cuts in. "Shelley, go ahead."

"There's got to be cameras down here. That means there's a record of who I am."

"Don't worry about it. We've got a deal set up. Navy helicopters are incoming. You will be evacuated and all records of your identities erased. You're still with Blue and Gold?"

"Yes."

"You need to stay there. Guard the targets. There is still resistance on the ship."

"ETA?"

"Seventy minutes."

Halfway to forever.

"Is Jaynie going to make it?"

"We'll do our best."

Not the answer I want to hear. "Can you link me back to gen-com?"

"Stand by. . . . Done."

"Nolan?" I ask. "You there?"

"*Fuck me*," he answers in an incredulous whisper. "Shelley? I thought you were dead."

Jaynie murmurs, "How many lives you planning to burn through, Shelley?"

"I don't know, but I'm giving you one of them, okay? Jaynie? Don't cut out on me."

"Story's not over yet, huh?"

"Not yet. But when we're back on land? I'm done, Jaynie. I swear, I'm done."

Wind and wave and engine noise combine to cloak the approach of the helicopters. From my position just inside the door of the cargo hold, I don't hear them arrive. I only know they've come because Nolan describes the special-forces unit dropping in on cables just like we did. The gun battle heats up following their arrival. A few minutes later, Jaynie gets evacuated, flown away to a navy ship.

The fight's not over. I hear sporadic gunfire for over fifteen minutes as the decks are secured. Then I'm ordered to the foredeck. Nolan and I get extracted the same way we went in: swinging in storm winds on the ends of cables.

We're both given crew helmets to wear on the long flight

back to the coast. There's an intercom, but the flight crew doesn't speak. Neither do we. The less said the better, because officially, we're not here and what we did aboard the *Non-Negotiable* never happened. An alternate history will be substituted in which the US Navy, acting on a credible anonymous report, performed an interdiction resulting in the recovery of two INDs.

But unofficially?

An upload icon winks on in my overlay.

Koi Reisman may have another story to tell.

I hope so, only because it might be a solace for Harvey's mom to know what happened. She was sitting beside my dad during our court-martial. Now her daughter is dead and she won't have a body to bury, she won't have an explanation, because we can't talk about Silent Firebreak—but Koi Reisman can.

We're out of the storm sooner than I expect—or I'm losing track of time. Delphi said I had a bad concussion and I believe her. I'm dizzy and sick and my anxiety is ramping up. I close my eyes, and watch the skullnet icon glow.

I've got a bad feeling . . . about what happened to Harvey, about this mission, about what's to come.

I'm still wearing the audio loop from my squad helmet; the satellite uplink is in the pack under my seat. I use the gear to reach out to Shima. "Anne, you there?"

Nolan is similarly wired. I know because he turns to look at me.

Shima links in. "I'm here, Shelley. Sitrep?"

"Nothing to report. Conditions nominal. Things look okay on your end?"

"Roger that. We're minutes from takeoff. We're just waiting for you, Nolan, and Flynn to return."

"Where the fuck is Flynn?"

"On an errand. Take it easy, Shelley. You'll be here soon."

The sun is shining when the navy helicopter sets down. I peer out the window. We're outside the hangar where our plane is stashed, but no one comes to meet us. The hangar door is closed.

One of the flight crew speaks. "Orders are to keep your crew helmets on. Make sure you've got the visors pulled down. Wear them until you're inside the building. I'll come behind you to collect them."

You never know who's looking, right? I guess Shima is feeling anxious too.

I lower the visor on the helmet and then stand up. Dizziness swamps me; my head hammers worse than before. I get my pack on anyway and sling my HITR over my shoulder. With my broken helmet in one hand and the folded rig of my dead sister in the other, I move out.

Even through the tinted visor, daylight is like a knife in my eyes. The pain leaves me swaying on the tarmac.

Nolan catches my arm. "You doing okay, LT?"

I whisper some obscenity as he steers me toward the hangar. A staff door on the side opens. My rig bangs against the doorframe as Nolan shoves me through. Inside, most of the lights are off and it's as hot as the Sahel. Two shadowy figures converge on me, backlit by a glow spilling from the open door of the commuter jet. One turns out to be Tuttle. He takes away my dead sister. The other is Moon. He grabs the broken helmet I've got clutched under my arm and then deprives me of my HITR. "LT," he says as I pry the navy's helmet off my head, "you know we wanted to be there, but the fucking helicopter pilot, he wouldn't drop us off."

"I know that. It's not your fault."

"I'm sorry, sir," Tuttle adds. "And I'm real, real sorry about Harvey."

"Yeah." I turn and hand the navy helmet to the crew-man. Silent Firebreak is over. "Let's get the fuck out of here. Where the hell is Anne?"

"I'm right here," she says from behind me. I turn, then duck my head against the painful outside glare. Shima closes the door, leaving only a dusky light inside the hangar, spillover from a glass-walled office at the back. Her olive-drab pullover is gone. In the heat, she's peeled down to a tank top with her gray cargo pants. A sheen of sweat glints on her cheeks beneath the rim of her farsights. "Your last status update indicated a nasty concussion, so we're keep-ing the lights low."

The dim light is easing my headache, but not my anxi-ety. "Thank you, ma'am, but we need to go." Anxiety can be a side effect of concussion—but I'm pretty sure that's not what's going on inside my head. "What about Jaynie? What's her status? Are we going to recover her now or later?"

"Vasquez is safe in a hospital and she'll stay there for now, but her prognosis is good. You can relax about that."

From outside, I hear the navy helicopter lift off with a roar. "And the prisoner?" I ask.

"Not our concern anymore. He's been transferred to a more official venue."

"Then we need to go."

"Stow your gear and get cleaned up. We're still waiting on Flynn. She took your package to a courier's office, but she'll be back—"

"Are you in touch with her? Anne, she needs to get back *now*. Something's wrong. I don't know what. Not for sure. But I can feel it."

Shima knows my history. She looks at me warily from behind the glimmer of her farsights. "You're saying the Red wants us to move out ASAP?"

"*Yes.*"

"Lieutenant, are you asking me to leave Flynn behind?"

"No, ma'am. But you could tell her to hurry."

"I will do that. Now stow your gear. Nolan, you too!"

"Yes, ma'am!"

"But keep your weapons with you," she adds as she strides toward the plane.

Moon's got my HITR. I shrug out of my pack and go after it. As he hands me the weapon, an upload link winks on in my overlay. It's Joby's program, sending out the daily report on my robot legs. My gaze causes a status tag to slide out, telling me: *Upload complete.* But the link doesn't close. Instead, the tag updates, informing me, *Download in progress.*

That's never happened before.

"You okay, LT?" Moon asks.

"No. Something's going on. Get your weapon."

Moon is right beside me. Tuttle is a few steps away. Nolan is already beside the jet, loading his dead sister into the cargo compartment. Shima is halfway up the stairs, but she hesitates, turning back to look at me like she's worried about what I'm going to do.

She should be worried.

"Get on the plane!" I shout at her. "*Now!* Before it's too late!"

Maybe it was always too late.

INTERIM

DIVINE FAVOR

SOMETHING HAPPENED—

What?

—and now everything is wrong, broken.

I don't know where I am.

I can't see anything around me.

I can't move—not even to lift a finger. I can feel the presence of my body, its mass, the sensation of breathing, but it's a one-way flow of information, incoming only. Signals aren't getting out, and I can't move.

This should frighten me, but I don't feel it. I don't feel much of anything. I think my eyes are closed, because the only things in my field of view are icons, and there are only two of them, so I know my overlay is broken too. One icon tells me I'm linked to an irregular network. I stare at it, willing a menu to appear. Nothing happens.

The other icon is my familiar skullnet icon. It's glowing brightly in the corner of my vision, its steady luminosity a measure of the massive, real-time interference presently occurring in my brain.

Someone on the irregular network is fucking around in there and it's not the Red. I'm certain of that, even if I don't know why. And it's not the army. They never dug this deep.

Someone else. Someone clever. I decide what I'm experiencing right now is something like sleep paralysis—my brain cut off from my motor nerves. The army didn't know how to do that . . . or if they did, they never did it to me. Then I remember what we did to Carl Vanda, what Delphi helped to do, and my anesthetized emotions start to twitch, and I get scared.

Where the fuck is my squad?

I think maybe they're dead.

Are they dead?

I stare at the glow of the skullnet icon and I try to remember what happened, why I'm here, why I have this feeling my squad is dead. Nothing comes.

But I don't need to rely on organic memory. I've got a digital memory too that contains video of everything I witnessed on the mission. I shift my gaze, seeking a menu. I wait for it to surface.

There's nothing.

Is this a dream?

I grope for a recollection, anything. I remember being aboard the navy helicopter. I clearly remember that. I think I fell asleep on the flight back, but later . . . I saw Shima. I know I saw her. I wanted her to get on the jet—unless that was a dream?

I remember thin shafts of sunlight piercing the shadows of the hangar, and the thick, sticky smell of blood.

Why can't I remember more?

The glowing skullnet icon is my clue. They're fucking with my short-term memory. They don't want me to remember what they did to my squad.

They?

Not the army, not the Red. I've established that. And not Uther-Fen, because if the mercs were inside my head they'd make it hurt worse. They'd make sure I remembered exactly what went down. They'd burn it into my brain in high-def detail.

Who then?

I think I know. My long-term memory is still in good shape. I have a clear recollection of the kidnap attempt in the basement of the DC federal courthouse. I think these are the same people. On that first try, they used nonlethal ammo. We speculated it was because they wanted my cooperation. I think they still do, and that's why they're trying to ensure I don't remember what happened to my squad. Another miscalculation on their part. I remember enough.

Twenty or thirty minutes go by. Maybe an hour. With no time display on my overlay, I don't really know, but things change. First, the skullnet icon winks out. Brain metabolism is fast, so in only a few seconds I'm in communication with my body again. I've been slumped in a cushioned seat, but now I try to straighten up. My hands and feet are all asleep, my side aches where I've been leaning. Everything hurts, especially my head, and I still can't see anything, though I can blink my eyes—so I know they're open. The air I'm breathing is hot and stale. My guess is there's a hood over my head. I try to lift my hands to test this theory, and discover my wrists are loosely bound behind my back.

I notice the vibration of an engine only when it stops. I hear a rustle of movement. Then a woman speaks. "Crow, be careful. He's a dangerous man."

American accent. Southern. Georgia, probably. A voice of authority.

Crow answers, a deep male voice, also American, but not regionally specific. Crow sounds annoyed. "Why don't you wait outside?"

She doesn't answer, but I think she leaves. Several seconds later, there's a grunt behind me. Hands close around my upper arms and I'm lifted to my feet. I try a head butt just for the hell of it. This effort earns me a muscular arm around my throat. I try to kick, only to discover my robot legs are shackled. The arm around my throat squeezes until I pass out.

Thin shafts of sunlight stab through my shadowy dreams, each bright ray the diameter of a 7.62-millimeter round. When I smell blood, I jerk awake and find myself in near darkness—but at least the hood is off my head and I can see again, by the dim red glow of round ceiling lights recessed behind thick glass faces. I sit up slowly, my skull pounding and my throat so dry it's hard to swallow. I swear every muscle in my body hurts.

I'm in a windowless concrete room furnished in a familiar fashion, with a prison-style toilet and sink combo in one corner, and a narrow bunk covered in a soft flannel blanket against the opposite wall. I'm sitting on the bunk, still dressed in the trousers of my combat uniform, along with my T-shirt which reeks of stale sweat, the stench more noticeable because my surroundings are pristine. I look down, and confirm the bed frame is bolted to the floor. I also notice my robot feet are bare. The boots I wore during Silent Firebreak are gone. So are the leg shackles and wrist cuffs I remember from before. I eye the door. It's steel, with no door handle and no hinges showing.

I return my gaze to the ceiling. Fresh air is flowing from a central vent surrounded by the dim night-lights.

I check my overlay and realize with surprise that most of my missing icons are restored—the time display, the emotional-analysis app, even the communications apps—though when I dive into the menus, I find there's no data and no history. My e-mail, texts, phone log, videos—all of it is gone.

The encyclopedia is still there, though. I pop it open, just to be sure, confirming that its local library of hundreds of thousands of articles is still intact.

The standard network icon has also been restored. It displays as a red circle with an X in it, meaning there's no connection available, but I'm not locked down. They can't lock me down because they need access to my overlay to manipulate my skullnet. So I'm linked to a nonstandard network, one with no outside connections. Realistically, I'll probably never have an outside connection again. I'm like Carl Vanda in that basement. Once Anne Shima sent him down there, we all knew he'd never see the light of day again.

Despite this certain knowledge, I'm hungry. I can't remember the last time I ate, and I hope my captors will consider a final meal.

I swing my bare titanium feet to the floor. The skullnet icon is invisible, indicating my skullnet is quiescent, but it doesn't matter. The damage is done. They've been inside my head deleting organic memories, and they've emptied my overlay of digital memories too.

The skullnet icon revives with these thoughts, flickering faintly as the embedded AI launches an automatic routine, ensuring I won't feel too bad.

Jaynie warned me I needed to get rid of the skullnet. Guess I should have listened.

I look again at the time on my overlay. Assuming they haven't fucked with my internal clock, assuming I remember right, nine hours and maybe twelve minutes have passed since the US Navy returned me and Nolan to the Brunswick airfield. Something happened after that. I don't remember what it was, I just know my squad is dead.

I heave myself up with a groan. The lights respond to my movement, brightening slowly, revealing the glassy glint of camera buttons in the four corners of my cell.

I piss, wash my face, drink water, swear vengeance.

First step, I want to start my overlay recording—but that turns out to be a no-go. Though I can see the video icon, there's nothing behind it. The program that handles videos has been wiped. Determined to make something happen anyway, I move to the center of the room and address the walls. "I'm awake. So let's get on with it."

Someone is paying attention, because less than a minute later, the door opens, revealing two guards on the other side. Dressed in dark-blue uniforms without insignia, rigged in dead sisters, wearing chest armor and helmets with black visors, they are anonymous. They're not carrying any firearms that I can see, but then they don't need to, not while they're powered by exoskeletons.

"You going to be stupid?" one of them asks me. "Or are you going to cooperate?"

I recognize the voice. It's Crow. The one who had his arm around my throat.

"Cooperate with what?" I ask him.

"Whatever you're told. Right now she wants you cleaned up and fed."

"She? The woman with the Southern accent?"

"You going to make a fight out of it?"

It's a temptation. "Who the fuck are you people?"

"Your new owners." He gestures to his silent companion—a shorter figure, by a good eight inches—but man or woman? Beneath the rig, I can't tell.

Both the Silent One and Crow take a step back, leaving the doorway clear.

"Into the hall," Crow orders.

I consider making a show of resistance. They could either

come after me and haul me into the hallway, or close the door and leave me to starve for another twelve hours.

My head still hurts. I don't want to aggravate my concussion by getting my skull slammed against the wall and I don't want to starve. So I do as I'm told and step into the hall. The passage is short, barely twenty-five feet in length. On my left are two doors facing each other, before the hallway dead-ends. On my right, the hallway is closed off by a steel door with no handle. Directly across from me is an open doorway into a brightly lit shower room.

Crow gestures at it. "You've got three minutes to shower and change. Clean clothes are hanging on the wall. If you get done in time, you get to eat. *Go.*"

I decide I don't like Crow. Despite my recent resolve, I play out in my mind what would happen if I went for him.

"You're thinking too hard, Shelley."

My gaze shifts to Crow's silent companion. "Was that your operation in the basement of the DC courthouse?"

"That fiasco?" Crow asks. "Shit, no. That was hers. I just signed on. You've got two and a half minutes."

Even if a miracle came to pass and I managed to kill both Crow and the Silent One, I'd still have to get past a locked door. So I give it up and do what Crow wants, stripping off my reeking clothes, and washing away the salt spray and the sweat in a blissfully hot shower. There's no razor or depilatory, so I'm stuck with the stubble of my beard. After I towel off, I step into a loose-fitting pair of electric-green canvas pants, and then pull on a matching T-shirt. I feel like a lime glow stick. "Afraid you're going to lose me?" I ask.

"Can't be too careful. I hear God's on your side."

Is that why I'm here? Is that why I'm alive and my squad is dead? Bitterness slams me. The Red let this happen. Why? Because it doesn't see everything? Because it's not always there? Because there's room for chance? Or because this is a necessary part of the story?

It dismays me to think that's what it might be.

"Step into the hall," Crow says, "and present your hands."

I'm well practiced at the prison routine. Handcuffs go on my wrists and we march to the steel door at the end of the hall. It opens for us with an electronic buzz. The hallway continues beyond it, but instead of being sealed off with another imposing steel door, there's an elevator, and an ordinary fire door marked with an exit sign.

"In here," Crow says, his hand on my arm as he steers me into a side room.

The room is furnished with a plastic table and two chairs. On the table is Greek takeout, for fuck's sake. The food is barely warm—it's probably been forty minutes or more since it was picked up—but now I know I'm still in North America. While Crow watches from the door, I eat—gyros, spanakopita, salad, and even an order of fries. I eat everything, despite my headache; the handcuffs don't slow me down at all. Afterward, I'm marched back to my cell.

"Don't I get to see the Southern woman?"

"Her name's Shiloh. You'll get to see her later."

The truth is, I'm exhausted. I lie down on the bunk, the lights dim to faint red, and I sleep.

The pattern repeats—a shower, food, and then sleep. My beard grows and my body heals. Exhaustion recedes until sleep doesn't come so easily anymore. I lie in my bunk and think about Delphi, wondering if she's safe, if she knows what happened to me. I wonder if the organization has any plans to retrieve me or if they'll just assume I'm dead. It's not like I know enough to compromise them.

After three days, Crow brings news: "Shiloh is ready to see you."

Per usual, my hands are shackled, and then Crow and the Silent One escort me to the room where my fast-food meals are delivered. This time the table is empty. Crow sits me down at one end, taking up a position behind me while the Silent One stands just to the side of the door.

In less than a minute the door opens. A woman comes in dressed in brown slacks and a black, long-sleeved shirt. Her Caucasian skin is tanned golden, with a scattering of faint freckles on her nose, her hair is trimmed in a brown-velvet buzz cut, and she's used brown eyeliner to emphasize her brown eyes. Physically, she looks soft, a little pudgy. Not an athlete.

Shiloh is not her name of course, any more than Crow is the name of my warden.

As she sits at the opposite end of the table, my encyclopedia posts the results of its automatic facial-recognition routine. It's identified her from its local library of articles. Her real name is Jasmine Harris. She's thirty-four years old, an acclaimed specialist in adaptive artificial intelligence and a major stockholder in Exalt Communications—the same company I researched after seeing their aerial network nodes along Interstate 80.

Maybe it's just a coincidence that I've already heard of her operation—but more likely, there are connections between us I'm not seeing yet.

I say nothing, waiting for her to speak. As we study each other across the table, there is a glint of light in her right eye. It's enough to tell me she's wearing an overlay. As if this observation has freed her to speak, she asks, "So you know who I am?" Her voice is soft, a little husky, very assured. Her question is not a casual one. It's designed to make me think about the facts of our relationship: that she has hacked into my overlay, that she can see what I see there, that she knows of everything I do, and that she can control the activity in my skullnet and by extension, she can control me.

So there's no sense in denying the truth. I nod and admit, "I know your real name."

Deception cannot benefit me in this relationship. Truth and lies arise from different regions of the brain, and since Shiloh can access the data from my skullnet, she'll always know if I'm lying.

With this matter clear between us, she moves on. "I'd like you to meet my partners. Say hello, John."

A man's voice issues from a speaker in the ceiling. "Hello, Shelley."

"And Mary?"

A woman this time: "Hello."

Fake names. Maybe they're fake people, but Shiloh wants me to believe they're real and that she's not acting alone. "For reasons of security and continuity, John and Mary will remain remote observers. I'll be your only point of inter-action. Your handler, we could say."

It's a struggle, but I manage to keep my smartass mouth in check. "Why don't you just tell me why I'm here?"

"I'd first like to tell you about EXALT."

A word pops up in the center of my overlay, rendered in huge, bold text. It's like having something thrown in my face. I'm so startled I flinch, jerking my head back, but the word is still there, written out as an acronym: *EXALT*.

I slam my fists down on the table. "Get the *fuck* out of my head."

The text disappears. Shiloh looks apologetic. Through the speaker, John says, "Sorry, I'm new at this."

Asshole. At least I know he's real.

I lean forward, glaring at Shiloh. "What the hell do you people want with me?"

"The world is changing, Shelley."

"Look around, Shiloh. The world *has* changed."

She dismisses this with a shrug. "What we've seen so far is just the beginning. New rules are being rolled out. You're already operating under them. So is this partnership. We are beginning to understand the algorithms that determine the behavior of the Red. That's how we succeeded in bringing you here, Shelley. Understanding is power. We're learning to predict and influence what the Red will do, which means we'll be able to turn conflicts and competitions in our favor."

Yeah, okay. I get it now. Jaynie pointed it out to me months ago when we were prepping for First Light: *I think most of the people who know anything about this stuff don't want to get rid of the Red. They want to control it, because whoever figures out first how to do that gets to run things.*

Shiloh is one of those people, confident in her own brilliance.

"You want to be a dragon?" I ask her.

"Who doesn't?"

I don't, but I don't tell her that. People who want to rule the world tend not to believe that some of us would say no to the privilege. I think about Jaynie quietly calculating what it might cost to construct her own Apocalypse Fortress: *Be a lot of money to buy that kind of privacy.* She'd like to have the choice, but when the Coma Day bomb maker offered to trade a fortune for his life? She didn't even blink.

Money and power mean a lot, but they're not everything.

I remind Shiloh, "Being a dragon didn't do Thelma Sheridan any good."

"It's given her a worldwide audience. The testimony coming out of Niamey is damning for a lot of powerful people. It's a miracle that trial hasn't been shut down."

I don't tell her what Carl Vanda intended. I don't want to bring him up.

"If you want to know," Shiloh says gently like she's conveying delicate news, "no one who's been following the trial can doubt Sheridan's guilt. The evidence you provided—"

"Colonel Kendrick made that happen, not me."

She nods to acknowledge this. "Unless the panel of judges is utterly corrupt, Sheridan will be convicted."

So there's that. We achieved at least this one thing. It's a relief. Even in my present circumstances, it makes me glad.

I push Shiloh. "Knowing that, you and your partners still want to be dragons? Because there's one rule of the Red I *have* worked out, and that's if you stand up too high, you'll get hammered down."

She shrugs, unimpressed. "It happened once, to Sheridan, but there are still a lot of dragons operating in the world."

It happened to Vanda too, but all I say is, "It's early yet."

"True. But Thelma Sheridan had nasty ambitions. She did some very bad things."

"Like mass murder."

"Yes. Don't think I'm naïve, Shelley. I used to work for her. So did my partners. We all heard the diatribes, and I had a firsthand view of her paranoia. I put up with it because I was being paid a fortune to do what I would have done for free—try to understand the Red."

"You were one of the software engineers in her consortium? That was real?"

"Very real. But then you kidnapped her and the money dried up."

"I hope you're not expecting me to apologize."

That earns a smile. "No. It was for the best, really. It led us to establish our own consortium. It's the frontier out there, Shelley. Wide-open opportunities."

Given that I'm imprisoned in a radio-opaque basement, I'm less than impressed by the opportunities available to me.

But I want more information, so I keep up my end of the conversation. "Opportunities for what?"

"To devise new stories."

We stare at each other like this is some significant, revelatory moment, but that's bullshit. She's playing me, working to pique my interest, to get me involved. I hate these games. "Just give me the sitrep."

"I need you to understand what's already been accomplished. John's going to show you another image."

I'm ready for it this time. It's an artist's rendering of an EXALT aerial node: seven floating spheres reflecting the sky around them, arranged in a vertical line and linked by a filament. "Your company's putting those up, right? It's a federal work project."

"It's a new communications system."

I delete the image. "EXALT. Expandable Aerial Labyrinth Traffic."

"You remember," she says, sounding impressed—because she can see my overlay, so she knows I'm not reading from the encyclopedia. "EXALT is a communications system intended to replace the bottlenecks of satellite and cable, and to eliminate the vulnerabilities that were clearly demonstrated on Coma Day. What you're looking at is, of course, only one node in a distributed network of aerial communications towers. Each node is self-powered by solar and wind."

"Don't they blow away?"

"They do, but not easily, and they can change altitude to avoid wind currents or use them to migrate. As you said, it's officially a federal stimulus project—funded to shore up infrastructure while putting people back to work—but the funding and the federal oversight are . . . complex to trace. Much like your reality show."

I understand now why she's telling me about her work. "You're saying the Red is behind EXALT."

She acknowledges this with a gracious nod, a regal gesture oddly enhanced by the nontraditional boldness of her buzz cut. "Exalt Communications was built around an existing design and suddenly we had funding, permits, permission to issue subcontracts. So yes, I'd say the Red wants this. Badly. No more Coma Days, and lots of new ways to observe and interact. We used EXALT to find you, Shelley. We don't have access to satellite surveillance, but we've developed an efficient observation network. We picked you up in the parking lot of a hotel in western Pennsylvania a week ago. Your identity was logged by a facial-recognition routine that runs on the farsights of EXALT users."

I flash on that night, the first night out of New York, making it . . . seven days ago? Is that possible? I'm burning through my life—but then, these days I have left aren't really mine. My time ended with shafts of blazing sunlight lasering through the bullet-perforated walls of a shadowy hangar reeking of blood. Everything since has been borrowed time.

"What are you thinking about, Shelley?"

I tell her the truth: "I don't know." I draw a deep breath and bring myself back on track. The best thing I can do now, the only thing, is gather information. "It was the girl with the crowbar," I say. "She had new farsights, but she was starving."

"It began there, yes, but there were other observers." The girl doesn't matter to Shiloh beyond her function as a mobile platform for EXALT data collection. "Once we had your vehicle type, we were able to track you through public traffic cams." She smiles a condescending smile. "The license plate images are automatically obscured to protect 'privacy,' but it's a joke. Any good image-analysis program can identify specific vehicles, especially when two are traveling together."

There it is. I knew we were being watched. I just thought it would be through drones and satellites, not traffic cams. That's what comes of spending too much time in remote locations. I forget to be wary of the basics.

"We lost track of you in northern Iowa."

She waits, like I'm supposed to say where we went. I'm surprised she doesn't already know. Then I remember: I didn't record our road trip, or my assault on Carl Vanda, so there was no digital memory in my overlay for her to steal. Of course, she could make me talk, the same way Carl Vanda was made to spill his secrets. I look away as my heart rate ramps up, but Shiloh and her partners can read every twitch in my vitals, so it's not like I can hide my anxiety.

She watches me thoughtfully, as if she's trying to guess the details of what's going on in my head. "Another EXALT node picked you up at the Brunswick airfield. You took off again shortly after that. You know we have the video you recorded?"

"If you use it against me, you'll just incriminate yourself."

"That's not our intention. The action you took aboard that ship was impressive, important—but at the time, we didn't know where you'd gone. I didn't think you'd return. I thought the Red would try to keep you out of our reach. But it didn't. And that implies you are meant to be here, that this is a planned association. *Not* something you should be fighting."

Yeah. I'm already haunted by that idea.

"We're working to develop a radical, innovative new episode to your story, Shelley. In your story you've been a servant of the Red, striking down its enemies, protecting its interests, exposing political corruption to weaken the positions of the very powerful. We've served the Red too, by building EXALT."

I despise the smug certainty on her face. "Are you thinking

that buys you karma points? That it puts the Red on your side?"

"All our simulations show the odds of success go up for those who serve the goals and interests of the Red. *Way* up. But we've never been able to simulate *you*. Your story is an outlier. It doesn't fit with anything else we've seen. Our best theory is that yours is a meta story."

That was Lissa's theory too. She believed *Linked Combat Squad* was a reality show meant to influence the emotions and choices of the millions who watched it.

Shiloh pulls me back to the present. "Surveys have been done showing that your story resonates across widely divergent groups. People interpret it differently and they come to different conclusions, but those conclusions empower individuals by leading them to take action in their own lives. But why was it you? Your qualities are right. You're sufficiently intelligent without being intimidating, you're bold, irreverent when it comes to authority, you look good in front of a camera—"

"Is this a fucking casting call?"

"The same traits could be found in a hundred thousand other Americans. My pet theory is that the Red picked you because you parse out as a keystone according to some presently inscrutable machine logic extrapolated a million moves ahead."

I may not be smart enough to be intimidating, but I do know some things. "It's not possible to calculate the future."

"True, but it *is* possible to calculate probabilities. And when you have thousands, possibly millions, of candidates— as the Red does—some of those probabilities are going to play out just as predicted. Your importance to us though, doesn't hinge on *why* the Red set a meta story around you. But just that it has. That you exist in a state of divine favor."

Divine favor? For a few seconds I'm not sure I heard her

right—and then fury rolls in, because what I've done, what I've witnessed, what I've suffered, what I've survived that others have not, my certainty that Shiloh and her friends *murdered my squad* to make it easier to grab me—that's not divine favor. It's a curse and these are trials that I've lived through, that I have to live with. I am not going to sit quietly and listen to her call it divine favor. "You're fucked, lady. You're twisted just as bad as Sheridan."

I stand. So far as I'm concerned, this interview is over— but Crow has a different opinion. Powered by his arm struts, he slams me back into the chair. I don't stay there. I pivot out, crouched this time and moving fast. Weaving my fingers together, I swing my shackled hands in an upward stroke, hammering Crow's balls. His breath whooshes out of his lungs and he doubles over. I swing again and catch him under the chin, sending him over backward though I cut my left hand on the bottom of his visor. That's all I achieve because the Silent One hits me with a Taser.

It hurts.

It fucking hurts.

It hurts like getting my robot knees shot out.

Next thing I know, I'm on the floor, staring at the ceiling, scared because I can't move my legs and I can't see any icons in my overlay. *Fuck.* Did my electronics get fried?

A black visor leans over me.

"Get the fuck up," Crow growls. He's still bent at the waist, his hand at his crotch, and judging from the tone of his voice, he's holding himself back from tearing my head off.

"My legs don't fucking work."

But then my right leg twitches, shooting a bolt of pain into my spine. The left leg follows. For a few seconds I can't breathe for the pain, and then I whisper, *"Fuck me."*

"Don't tempt me. Now *move.*" He grabs me with his arm hooks just below my shoulders and hauls me up, dropping me back into the chair. My left hand is covered in blood. It drips on my lime-green pant leg as the pain in my thighs recedes. The system stabilizes, and I can move my robot toes again. Ignoring Crow, I watch my toes under the table as I make them stretch and curl.

My overlay wakes up too, the icons neatly arranging themselves around the periphery of my vision, before fading to near invisibility.

"Want to tell me what that was about?" Crow asks from his position behind me.

I look up to where Shiloh should be sitting at the other end of the table, but she's not there. I look around to find she's left the room. It's only me and Crow and the Silent One, who has returned to her—his?—post by the door.

"I thought we had an understanding," Crow goes on, "that there's no way out for you, so you got nothing to fight for."

The pain has faded, but not the anger, so I give him a smartass answer. "Escape isn't the only prize I'm after."

"You'd like to kill me?"

"And her."

"That kind of talk will get you put down, Shelley."

"Just a matter of time anyway."

"Listen, brother. It's not like that, or it doesn't need to be. They've got plans for you. What'd Shiloh call you? A keystone? But they're not sentimental. They aren't going to keep you around if you can't control yourself."

He's still standing behind me, sparing me the chore of looking at him. Instead, I flex my legs and inventory the programs on my overlay. The system looks like it's working again. "Next time, I'll control myself long enough to go for the Silent One first."

"Yeah? I'd appreciate that. So what was it that set you off, Shelley? That crack about divine favor?"

I watch the blood still seeping from the back of my left hand, and I don't answer. He doesn't really expect me to.

"She doesn't get it," he tells me. "She's a civilian. She sees the glory, the hero. And the bodies that line up behind you? Those are just props to her. The pain? That's just a minor chord in the soundtrack."

"Go fuck yourself."

"Don't bring it to the point that I have to put a bullet in your brain. I really don't want to do that."

I guess I'm supposed to believe Crow's a nice guy, that we have things in common, but it's hard for me to get past the certainty that he designed the mission that led to the murder of my squad.

The door opens. Shiloh leans in long enough to hand a white plastic box to the Silent One. It's a first-aid kit. Crow gives me a minute to clean up my hand and glue the cut closed. Then he says, "Let's go. Back to your cell."

The Silent One exits first. I'm supposed to follow and Crow will come behind me. He moves gingerly. He's still hurting and it's a good bet he's not as focused as he might be. I'm not in great shape either, my muscles are quivering and empty from the Taser episode, but as I follow the Silent One into the hall it occurs to me I may never have a better opportunity to make a break for the exit. It's not like I expect to escape, but if I can at least get out of this radio-opaque basement, maybe I can hook up with an outside connection.

So I try it.

I throw myself at the Silent One, knocking him—her?—off-balance, and then I run as fast as I've ever run in my life, reaching the fire door before Crow makes it out of the room. A precious half second is lost getting the door open. Then I'm lunging up the stairs, taking three at a time, using my shackled hands to haul myself along the railing. I'm rounding the first landing when someone bursts after me into the stairwell.

I don't take time to figure out who it is. What I do notice as I sprint up the next flight is that my pursuer is not all that experienced at climbing stairs in an exoskeleton. The footplate misses the first step, and whoever it is almost goes down. This is encouraging. I reach the top and round the corner to the next flight. I don't look down again. I don't even listen for them coming. I just push myself and make it up another flight, and another, eyeing my overlay in the desperate hope it will pick up an outside network.

Turns out it's easier to run away from Crow and the Silent One than it is to slip the shackle of my skullnet. I'm halfway up the next flight when my brain is hit with a neurochemical shit storm. I reel and hug the railing to keep from falling. I try to force myself to take another step, but my body is not listening. One of my guards reaches the flight below, turns a black visor my way. I'm pretty sure it's Crow. Three long strides and he's reached the landing, and I can't move, and I have no outside connection.

A titanium hook closes around my already bruised arm. "Goddamn you, Shelley."

At the same time, the door on the landing above opens and the Silent One steps through. I'm incapacitated *and* surrounded. But with the steel door above me open, I get a weak connection to the Cloud—and an automatic upload initiates.

God *damn* it. It's Joby's stupid program hogging the bandwidth. Given all the programs Shiloh wiped, why didn't she wipe that one? But that's easy to guess: She must have thought it was necessary for the operation of my legs.

My own frantic message is caught in the queue and fails to send.

My overlay blanks.

I'm shut down.

• • • •

My captors are unhappy with me. I'm given a day of solitary fasting to think about my sins. They decide to liven things up by playing with my skullnet.

I'm lying on my bunk half asleep when the skullnet icon blazes to life. Within seconds my mood slides into a happy zone so intense I wonder if the Heavenly Spirit has taken up residence inside of me and for sure there should be fluffy bunnies dyed in Easter colors and beds of bright spring flowers with blue skies above them. Fuck these blank concrete walls. They're not real. They're a projection of some asshole's negative energy.

A laugh bubbles up from my belly. Not a guffaw, just a quiet chuckle, a safety valve to release the overburden of joy that threatens to suffocate me. It's a chuckle that goes on and on until my whole body is shaking with it, eyes watering, and as I curl up on the bed, curl around this burden of searing happiness, I'm not sure anymore if I'm laughing or crying.

I just want it to be over.

"Get the fuck out of my head," I whisper.

Maybe they hear me. Or maybe they just decide this experiment is a bad idea. Whatever the reason, the skullnet icon winks out. My joy drains away. Within seconds I return to a familiar neutral misery. The icon flickers, but this time it's just the skullnet's embedded AI running an automated routine to arrest my mood swing and hold me back from the hopeless dark.

I roll over and stare at the ceiling. In their how-to-survive-as-a-prisoner-of-war advice, the army suggests developing a motivational image that can be held in the mind during times of torture or emotional distress. My motivation is an image of a hangar, its shadowy interior shot through with lasers of sunlight blazing from bullet holes in the closed hangar door.

Shiloh and her faceless partners ordered the murder of my squad. I hold on to that. I don't remember what happened— all I remember is that image—but that image is enough.

They try again to mess with my head and they get better at it. By the time my day of penance is over, I'm quietly obedient when Crow hands me leg shackles and tells me to put them on. I don't eat much. I ask if I can go back to my cell and sleep.

Shiloh is not in the room, but Crow addresses her anyway. "Give it up, Shiloh. He's a man, not a puppet, and he's no good to you like this. If you want his cooperation you're going to have to get it the old-fashioned way—by striking a deal."

After that the experiments come to an end.

I hold in my mind an image of narrow shafts of sunlight as I face Shiloh for the second time across the plastic table. Today she's wearing a white blouse with pearl buttons up the front. Artful highlights of green eye shadow enhance her brown eyes. "We can benefit each other," she tells me. "Our goals are not in opposition."

"My goal is to get the fuck out of here." I raise my shackled hands from my lap. "You people seem opposed to that." I'm wearing leg shackles too, and I'm all too aware of the chemical shackle in my brain—it's not active now, but that could change at Shiloh's whim. Crow, rigged in his dead sister, looms behind me, positioned to enforce her will.

"Don't be simpleminded, Shelley. You are not just a cog

in some military machine. Not anymore. You have a role, a duty, to undertake missions that serve the goals of the Red."

"Bullshit. My squad did what needed to be done. That's all. Sometimes the Red helped, but you're wrong if you think it's on my side, or your side, or anyone's side, and if that's why you and your consortium brought me here, then you've got nothing."

She doesn't smile, but she looks relieved and relaxed as she leans back in her chair. "So you do understand the basics. The Red isn't human, it isn't bound by human values, and it doesn't operate on human concepts like justice and loyalty. Its primary purpose is to create environments that both challenge and reward. In part that means encouraging the balkanization of societies, sorting people into groups small enough that individuals matter, so success isn't a one-in-a-hundred-million prospect."

"Maximizing the potential of the greatest number of individuals."

"No, we think it's more that it gives the greatest number of people a chance to live their own story. But to be compelling, a story requires hardship, challenges. That could be as simple as a child overcoming her fear of speaking in front of her class, or as harrowing as retrieving a working nuclear device from the hands of terrorists." She finishes with the banal truth. "Not all stories have happy endings."

"Yeah. I've worked that one out."

"The other purpose of the Red is to ensure continuity. Our theory says Thelma Sheridan got hammered down not because she stood too high, but because she attacked the infrastructure and threatened the very future of the planet."

"You'd want to believe that, because your goal is to be a dragon, but the fallout from my court-martial is threatening the position of a lot of powerful people and I'm pretty sure the Red is involved with that."

"The Red encourages managed chaos and the frothing possibilities that brings."

"Managed chaos? Is that what you call this mess we're in?"

She smiles. "It's my term. What's happening to us is not about justice. It's about potential, even at cross-purposes. The Red isn't in pursuit of a peaceful world, because people do not *want* peace. They want challenges. Look at you, the noble warrior, driven by honor and righteousness. You're an archetype, Shelley, but in a peaceful world there would be no need for you. No purpose.

"A lot of people are like you. They want a chance to be a hero. To save others. To make a difference. The Red allows it. Let the world get rocked, destabilized. That opens up opportunities for social experiments and adventure games played on the edge of chaos. Real-life games, where real lives are risked and often lost.

"But it's *managed* chaos, meaning the game is moderated, the scope of any conflict limited, and no one gets to destroy the world—or at least it will be that way. We're not there yet. Getting us there—getting rid of stray nukes for example—that's your game, your story."

"So you want me to play a game for you? That's why I'm here?"

To my surprise, she nods. Leaning forward, with a fresh intensity in her gaze, she says, "The consortium has developed a scenario that will let us hook into your meta story. We'll ally with King David, aid you on a mission that will serve the purpose of the Red, while we pursue our own goal."

"And that goal is?"

Disappointment creases her brow as if she expected me to already know. "You said it before. We want to be dragons, and this mission will let us gain a dragon's fortune."

"Crow?" I ask without turning around.

"Yeah, Shelley?"

"Is she crazy?"

He chuckles. "Not more than any of us. Not more than you."

I know I should say nothing, give her nothing, but I want to disturb the quiet confidence in her eyes. "I'm going to have to spoil your plan, Shiloh. It's like this: I'm not the one you want anymore. I have it on good authority that I'm done, that my part in the story is over, that the Red is finished with me. Maybe that's why you were able to pick me up."

Several seconds pass as she considers this, her head cocked, fingernails rapping at the tabletop.

"What authority?" she asks at last.

"Just take my word on it: You need to rethink your plans."

The focus in her eyes shifts as she checks something on her overlay.

"You know I'm not lying."

Her focus returns to me. "You're repeating what you've been told. That doesn't make it true. We wouldn't have gotten this far if the Red weren't behind us."

"You want to believe that. But the Red doesn't give a shit. Not about me, not about you. That's just the way it is."

"Okay, then. Let's talk about something else. Let's talk about Eduard Semak." She cocks her head. "Have you heard of him?"

Eduard Semak.

I don't know that name. But I react anyway. It's like the name is a trigger. Hearing it kicks off a reaction in my skullnet. The icon flicks on and a sense of mindfulness sweeps over me, telling me that Eduard Semak is a subject I need to pursue.

My focus shifts briefly to the encyclopedia icon, long enough to induce a menu to pop out. But what I need to learn about Eduard Semak won't be in the encyclopedia.

So I return my attention to Shiloh. "What should I know about him?"

She's happy to fill me in. "He's a Russian industrialist, one of the wealthiest people in the world and insane by any practical measure. Paranoid, hypochondriac, sure that God and his children are out to kill him. He's become the ultimate recluse, literally withdrawing from the world to live in a cramped and ugly orbital habitat."

The skullnet icon fades, but my interest doesn't. "You mean a Sunrise Fifteen habitat?"

"You've heard of the company?"

"They build dragon lairs."

The term must amuse her, because she smiles. "And you're the dragon slayer."

I hesitate, reviewing my sins—and she's wrong. I've never slain a dragon. Sheridan isn't dead, and I didn't actually pull the trigger on Vanda.

"I'm speaking in a metaphorical sense," she says, halfway between amusement and irritation. "You brought Thelma Sheridan to justice. Now I want you to go after Eduard Semak."

"Why? What's he done?"

"It's what he *could* do. You went after Thelma Sheridan because she used nuclear weapons, but she isn't the only dragon to possess them. She was small time compared with Semak. You've heard of Cold War weapons that went missing? Semak was part of that. He's got a cache. No one knows quite where."

"You mean no one knows but Semak."

"Yes."

I accept what Shiloh is telling me. I assume the weapons are real, a doomsday hazard that needs to be found. I want to make sure they *are* found. Found and eliminated. Not found and turned over to Shiloh's control.

She speaks to my suspicion. "This would be your mission, Shelley. Not mine. I'm just here to tell you how you could do it."

I want to do it. I'm supposed to do it. The faint glow of the skullnet icon is a dim reflection of the obsession building inside my head.

Shiloh gives me a worried look as she hurries on with her explanation. "Semak has an overlay, Shelley, like you and me. That's where he keeps all his critical data. You're going to extract that data and then you'll know where the nukes are, and you can turn the information over to a responsible authority."

"You know how to extract that data?"

"Yes, of course. I got inside your head, didn't I?"

"Don't bullshit me." Shiloh never told me how she cracked my system, but I can guess. "Just because one of your people found a security hole in my setup doesn't mean Semak will have the same vulnerability."

"I *can* crack his overlay," she says, definitely irritated now. "You don't need to worry about how."

"Then let's worry about why. You're on the side of the angels, you want to eliminate rogue nukes from the world. Right?"

"Of course I do. We're all in danger."

"That's the mission you want to send me on, but it's a cover story for the part you care about. You're after *all* his critical data. Meaning account numbers? Passcodes?"

She nods. "Also, the means to update his will and his powers of attorney."

"His will? You're not expecting him to survive my interview?"

"I expect he'll succumb to the stress. No need to feel sorry for him, though. He's an old man with a lot to account for. Ruthless murders, and the slow killing of tens of thousands through environmental destruction on a massive scale. The fate of the world could be determined by the nukes he controls. Eduard Semak is a bad, bad man."

"How do you know what data he keeps in his overlay?"

"One of the partners has high-level access to sensitive federal investigations."

I want this mission. Or anyway, there is a program running in my skullnet that tells me I want it. But Eduard Semak is beyond my reach.

"You said Semak is in orbit."

"Yes."

"Then how can this mission be for me? I don't know shit about space, or operating in orbit. You should have kidnapped an astronaut."

"King David has a better chance to make this mission work than any astronaut. The Red will back you, Shelley. You know it will. I don't care what you've been told. Your story isn't over. This needs to happen and you'll have a better chance than anyone else to make it work."

The skullnet icon fades to invisibility. It doesn't make sense I should get this mission—but it feels like something I need to do.

For a moment I wonder if Shiloh and her partners are the force behind my conversion—but I don't believe it. Not after enduring their sledgehammer attempts to rewrite my disposition. I don't believe she has the skill to mimic the emotional guidance I get from the Red.

A shift in her gaze tells me she's looking at her overlay again. Her tone is sharp when she asks, "What's going on with his skullnet? Who's manipulating him?" I don't answer. She's not talking to me. Seconds pass. I imagine John and Mary explaining to her that they don't know what the fuck is going on. Finally, Shiloh returns her gaze to me. "You are *not* connected to the Cloud."

I don't want her prying into my head, so I tell her the truth. "The phrase 'Eduard Semak' triggered a reaction in the simple AI that regulates my skullnet."

She cocks her head, her mouth open in wonder, beginning to realize she's won. "Approval?" she asks. "Preloaded?"

I shudder, wondering who the fuck I am, what I'm doing. I can't meet her gaze, so I look away. I *want* this mission. It feels right. But how can it be right when my squad is dead because of her ambitions? Did the Red let that happen in order to put me here, preloaded to cooperate in her scheme?

"Shelley," she says, speaking now with easy confidence. "Don't fight it. You know what you need to do."

I want to deny that. Deny her, because this is wrong.

Jaynie took over my squad because she believed I was not always in command of myself and she was right. I am running on a program. But knowing it doesn't change my mind. I'm going to do the mission anyway.

The mission plan is simple. Every dragon lair is sold with a habitation contract that acts like a condominium association agreement. The contract stipulates that Sunrise 15 technicians will visit each habitat at regular intervals to deliver supplies and perform mandatory maintenance. I will accompany the next maintenance run to Eduard Semak's habitat, which is technically known as Orbital-4, or O-4 in the company logs, but is more commonly called the Semak Hermitage. We will stay at the hermitage for as long as it traditionally takes to transfer supplies and perform maintenance—mostly swapping out modules—and then we will depart.

"We" means me and a spaceplane pilot flying for Sidereal Transit Systems, the company contracted to provide Earth-to-orbit transport for Sunrise 15. The STS pilot is code-named

Amity. Shiloh assures me there is a second accomplice at Sidereal Transit Systems who will counterfeit the flight data, erasing my presence and making it appear as if a qualified, authorized technician accompanied Amity on the flight and performed all scheduled maintenance.

Simple.

After I'm introduced to the basics of the mission, Crow and his silent companion escort me one floor up, to a large room containing two mock-ups: one of a dragon lair, the other of the spaceplane's cockpit. The room's walls are radio opaque, and Shiloh is ensconced safely out of my reach in a "control station" behind a thick pane of bulletproof glass, so the shackles come off.

As my guards leave, Shiloh speaks. "We will look first at the habitat," she says, her voice arriving through speakers in the ceiling.

"That's not life size, is it?"

"It is. It looks small because it replicates only the interior dimensions."

Those dimensions are cramped: The mock-up is just two meters high, with a length I guesstimate at less than eight meters. Several protrusions show on the outside—probably bins or closet space when viewed from the interior. There's a closed hatch at one end. "What if Crazy Eduard decides against visitors and refuses to open the door?"

"Crazy Eduard won't have a choice. Maintenance is mandatory, so the hatch isn't locked. Once Amity has docked the spaceplane, you'll be able to open the hatch whether Semak wants to see you or not. So open it."

I follow her directions as she describes how to work the mechanism. When the oval door swings open, I stoop to look inside.

There are four flat walls, joined together by rounded corners. The walls are clean-white molded plastic. Just inside, a ring has been inscribed with a black marker. It's labeled "cupola." Beyond that, grab bars and handles stud the walls.

"Go inside," Shiloh urges.

I duck, and step past the hatch. The floor is too smooth; it feels slippery beneath my robot feet. When I straighten up, my head scrapes the ceiling. The interior feels confined, claustrophobic. I don't like it at all.

"Imagine you're in free fall," Shiloh says. "You're floating, with a wall always in reach."

What I imagine is the deadly nothingness of airless space lurking on the other side of the dragon lair's pristine walls.

There is so much that could go wrong.

"What about radiation?" I ask. "Isn't radiation a hazard in space?"

"Not for the short duration of your visit. You'll be at the hermitage only about thirty minutes. You get in, get the data in Semak's head, and get out."

I move deeper into the pod, trying to understand why anyone would choose to live in a dragon lair. That's like choosing to live in a fallout shelter when there is all the beautiful world to wander in. *Crazy.* No other way to look at it. Eduard Semak is crazy.

Of course, my life is crazy too.

Six meters in, there's another hatch. I open it and clamber into a second, much smaller space, only about a meter and a half in length.

"The bedroom," Shiloh explains. "Also, an emergency evacuation capsule."

I open a closet door. A sleeping bag hangs inside. I find three more sleeping chambers, and a toilet. Then I make my way back through the main chamber, step out through the hatch, and look up at Shiloh. "What kinds of weapons does Semak have?"

"None that we know of."

"None?"

"That we know of. But this is Eduard Semak. He hasn't lived this long by being a trusting soul. He will have weapons. Darts, gases, garrotes, are all possible. A blackjack maybe—"

"Poison drones?"

"Possibly, but he almost certainly won't have guns."

I guess that's reassuring.

"What'll I have?"

"Body armor."

I shake my head. "You've got me confused with special ops. I'm not trained for this."

"The mission is simple," she insists. "All you have to do is secure the dragon lair, its communications, and its sole occupant. Amity will take it from there."

Simple.

I turn around and look again at the absurd habitat, the Semak Hermitage, a billion-dollar prison for a hypochondriac dragon—and I wonder again, *Why me?* Why is this my mission? There has to be an angle to this story I'm not seeing yet.

I move on to the mock-up of the spaceplane. It's very simple, just a cylinder of white plastic less than three meters long, with two high-backed seats mounted inside it. Behind the seats, a cutout in the wall of the cylinder simulates a hatch, and in front of them, a featureless plastic board poses as an instrument panel. The cylinder is suspended from the ceiling by four mechanical arms—the most expensive part of the setup, I suspect. Right now, it's oriented vertically, with the cockpit facing the ceiling as if the spaceplane is ready for launch, but the arms can shift, moving it to a horizontal orientation.

"Enter through the hatch and climb into the right-hand seat," Shiloh tells me.

It's awkward, but I do it, and then I buckle in.

"For you the flight is the easy part," Shiloh says. "Nothing for you to do but enjoy the view."

It's a clever setup, cheap and functional, but it leaves out an important factor. "What about zero gee, Shiloh? You have a way for me to train for that?"

"Ah, no, sorry, Shelley," she says in a coddling voice. "No swimming pool, no wind tunnel, no high-altitude plane rides. But you're adaptable. I know you'll do your best."

Over the next seven days I spend hours inside the training room, developing an intimate familiarity with the interior of the hermitage, and learning how to get in and out of the spaceplane in both its vertical and its horizontal orientations. I spend even more hours with a VR visor on my head, immersed in cheaply made scenarios that let me rehearse what to do if Semak tries to block me from shutting down communications, or if he comes after me with a knife or poison darts or bee drones, or if he has a gun, or tries to jam the hatch to the evacuation capsule.

"He *will* be wearing a face mask," Shiloh warns me, her voice emanating from wall speakers. "He always does during the maintenance runs, because he doesn't want to breathe the same air the technicians are breathing. So the presence of a face mask doesn't mean he's overtly hostile or that he's poisoned the air."

I push back the visor so I can see her at her post behind the glass. "Should I be wearing a face mask?"

She shakes her head. "He'd know right away you weren't maintenance and he'd send an alarm before you could get the com link shut down."

"How am I supposed to subdue him?" I gesture at my eyes. "He's got an overlay, so just tying him up won't stop him from sending an alarm." I scowl, remembering when she called me the dragon slayer. "You didn't expect me to murder him outright?"

She cocks her head. "Would you have a problem with that?"

"Yes."

"You were willing to assassinate Thelma Sheridan."

True enough—an inglorious segment of my history displayed to the world during the last episode of *Linked Combat Squad*.

"We didn't assassinate Sheridan, and we don't need to murder Semak."

I've ended lives—a lot of lives—but that was always a necessity of the mission. If I don't have to kill Semak, I won't. I'd rather bring him back for trial than be his executioner.

Shiloh smiles, entertained by my hypocrisy. "I was only curious. We don't want Semak dead—not right away. If he dies before communications are shut down, it's sure to set off an alarm."

My training continues. We run every scenario over and over again. At the end of each day, Crow comes for me with hand and leg shackles. I put them on myself, not wanting to get involved in another fight.

Then a day comes when, instead of leaving me alone in the training room, Crow takes up a post by the door. I throw him a questioning look, but of course his anonymous visor betrays nothing. "What's up?"

Shiloh is behind the glass. She answers over the room's speakers. "Amity has flown in today. Your mission partner, the spaceplane pilot. This is the only chance you'll have to train with her."

I look again at Crow. "And you're worried I'm going to kill her?"

"And what good would that do you?" he asks.

This gets me thinking, which is not always a good thing. I haven't tried to escape since I accepted this mission—Crow hasn't allowed an opportunity—but if an opportunity presented itself, would I take it?

It's my duty to make every effort to escape, that's how I was trained, but I want to do this mission.

I want it.

Because Jaynie is right and I'm a fucking puppet operating on a program written into my skullnet.

The door opens. Amity comes in. Anyway, I assume it's Amity. She's a woman of moderate height, middle-aged, her full figure gone a little soft beneath a black, long-sleeved pullover and jeans. Her hair is an interesting, dark artificial red. She wears it short, trimmed in layers. My encyclopedia contains no record that will allow it to identify her, so it tags her as *unknown*.

"Honored to meet you, Lieutenant Shelley," she says in a cold voice with a light Russian accent. "I'm here only a few hours. Let's not waste time."

I hesitate. I'm supposed to be the muscle on this mission. That means I should be able to take her, use her as a hostage, a human shield to buy my way out of here.

I run a few scenarios through my head:

I jump her, she proves to be more than she seems, and breaks my neck.

I jump her, and while she's fighting back, Crow breaks my neck.

I jump her, get the best of her, get past Crow—but before we can escape the building he shoots us both, because it's better to call off the mission than to let me go, knowing I will expose their operation.

They will never let me go.

I'll be a prisoner even when I'm on the spaceplane, because

it's not like I can hit Amity over the head and fly the plane myself.

So I do the sensible thing. I look her in the eye and say, "Tell me what I need to know."

I want to escape, but I also want a chance to do this mission. Those two goals should be in conflict but they're not, because right now there is no way for me to get away. That could change. My interpretation of Shiloh's "managed chaos" is to keep things moving and see what shakes loose.

We run through the mission, beginning with the climb into the spaceplane's cockpit. Amity comes in behind me, watching critically as I strap in. "You need to be faster," she growls. "There is no way to know what might go wrong at the habitat. If we need to exit swiftly, you must be prepared. Know how to get the harness on with one hand, in the dark!"

She drops into the pilot's seat, her body language communicating a sullen anger out of proportion to my poor performance—and I begin to sense discord in the mission plans. Or maybe I'm not the only one conscripted into service?

"You sure you want to be part of this mission?" I ask.

The gaze she turns on me promises dire consequences if I don't proceed with care, but I probe anyway. "Maybe you know something I don't? A reason to call it off?"

Her brows knit in an indignant scowl that tells me I've got it all wrong. "You understand this conversation is not private? That both Shiloh and Crow listen to all we say?"

"Standard procedure."

"Of course." She turns away. "*You* would be used to it."

"You're not?"

"Only when I'm in the cockpit." She raises the volume of her voice, declaiming to the ceiling. "But I don't care that you're listening, Shiloh. You know my opinion." She turns to me. "I don't trust you. I don't trust your motives. I am the architect of this mission and you are not my choice to fly in the second seat."

Her anger is cold. Mine is not as I consider again the sacrifice of my squad. "So why am I here?"

It's Shiloh who answers, through the room's speakers. "Because the mission plan was revised after we failed to launch twice. The first time, there were mechanical issues with the spaceplane and the flight was rescheduled. Then we missed the rescheduled launch because a ridiculous sequence of delays kept Amity from reaching the launch complex. It was clear to me the Red had shut down our mission."

"So you decided you needed me."

"Yes, and I was right. It's *your* story. King David's meta story. So we help you, and reap our own reward."

Shiloh is confident in herself and in her vision of reality, believing she understands the Red well enough to run this ruthless gamble. She calls me King David. I see her as a would-be Solomon, endowed with the gift of wisdom and expecting a massive payoff from it when she's boosted into wealth and power by the deus ex machina of the Red.

That's assuming the story plays out the way she hopes. I've got a feeling she's going to be disappointed—and the scorn on Amity's face suggests I'm not the only one who thinks Shiloh is a little too confident.

"Let's start again," Amity says. "I have to fly home in a few hours. We don't have time to waste."

That night I lie awake until late, rereading the article in my encyclopedia on Eduard Semak, and then moving on to a web of articles on failures and cover-ups in nuclear weapons security. It's near midnight when I finally sleep, but I'm up again at 0400, disturbed by a noise I haven't heard before.

It's a faint, rhythmic knocking, like a toothpick tapping against a metal plate, just audible above the whisper of the air-conditioning. I don't move. I just listen. The sound is coming from overhead. It's probably a beetle knocking around in the AC ducts . . . but beetles don't usually tap out a complex rhythm: *Tap! Tap-tap-tap, tap-tap-tap, tap-tap-tap, tap!* Repeating.

Moving only my eyes, I look up, taking in the faint-red familiar glow of the ceiling lights. I see nothing else.

I stand up. Good time for a piss.

As if disturbed by my movement, the pace of the tapping picks up, becoming faster, more urgent. I decide it really is coming from the air-conditioning vent, so I step up onto the bed to get a closer look. That lets me peer past the louvers, where I see a faint amber glow. At first I can't make out what it is, but then my brain gets creative filling in the shadows and I decide I'm staring at a robo-bug like the one that came after Carl Vanda in the courtroom. The amber light seeps from twin slots on either side of a cylindrical body smaller than my little finger. Caught against the undersides of its resting dragonfly wings, the light bounces down, defining the microdrone's curved, needle-thin legs. The wings make the robo-bug just a little too big to fit through the louvers. The noise is being produced by one of its legs tapping frantically, working through the rhythmic pattern, but it stops before it reaches the end—and the network icon in my overlay goes green.

Again, it's Joby's program that launches first. The upload goes before I can stop it, and then a download comes in. That's a sequence I've seen before. The memory surfaces. It was in the hangar, right before . . . what followed.

Panic kicks in. I try to cancel, but I'm not in control of

my overlay. A program executes without my permission and seconds later an icon is added to my display.

It's a link to gen-com.

Speaking with a handler's calm inflection, Delphi says, "Shelley, confirm link."

"*Delphi*. Link confirmed! My God, are you okay? How . . . ?"

But I know how: The robo-bug is acting as a relay. There must be a string of them up to the surface, and Joby's program offered a way in.

"Status?" Delphi demands. "Are you injured?"

"No. I'm fine. I'm confined in a cell."

"Are you shackled?"

"No. Get the door open and I can go."

"Stand by."

The network icon goes red. No connection.

I jump down from the bed and look around, look for anything I can use as a weapon, but I've done that a hundred times before and I already know there's nothing.

I stand beside the door and listen.

There's only silence.

I worry Crow might look in through the camera eyes in the corners of my cell. I don't want to give him a reason for suspicion, so I return to the bed, lie down again, close my eyes, and try to slow my racing heart.

Joby sent his bugs to find me. He used his own program to establish a communications link.

I'm kind of astonished at that. Joby's not exactly fond of me and as far as I know he isn't part of Cryptic Arrow. But on that day I ran up the stairs—knowing I couldn't escape, just wanting to get far enough to find an outside network—his program launched, uploading the data on my legs, along with GPS coordinates of where I'd been, because I forgot to turn that function off when we headed out after the *Non-Negotiable* . . . a security lapse that might just save me.

The faint glow of the night-lights cuts out, leaving me in total darkness. The whisper of the air-conditioning ceases. Electricity out. I hope the basement's network nodes are out too. I don't want Shiloh fucking around in my head.

It's so quiet I hear my heart. I count each beat to mark the time. When I reach 473, I hear small-arms fire.

That puts me back on my feet.

The shots are distant, echoing off concrete walls. They come singly or in bursts of three, with intervals of silence between. Several times, multiple weapons fire at once. I estimate five, maybe six, automatic rifles. Crow is earning his money now.

I want to know who's out there. Who's coming for me?

The walls tremble as a grenade goes off.

Silence follows.

I cross the lightless room, taking up a position by the door. If Crow makes it down here first, it's a good bet he'll come to kill me. Odds are there won't be anything I can do to stop him . . . but I can still try to seize a weapon, go down shooting.

My network icon goes green again. The link to gen-com opens. "Status?" Delphi demands as I hear the sound of clomping footplates approaching, at least two sets, maybe three.

"I'm fine! What the hell is going on out there?"

"The building has been secured."

"Is the basement network out?"

"Roger that. The only live network down there is ours."

Relief sweeps over me, knowing Shiloh can't reach into my skullnet to hit me again.

"Which cell are you in?" Delphi asks.

"The first on the left."

Jaynie's voice cuts in: "Got it."

The thudding steps stop outside the door.

"Don't jump me, Shelley, when I open this door."

"I won't, ma'am," I say in a voice suddenly hoarse.

The heavy lock clicks and releases. The door swings open, admitting a slice of red light along with the smell of gunpowder and fresh sweat. I peer outside. Three shadowy figures look back at me, all of them rigged in armor and bones, and carrying HITRs which they hold pointed at the ground. Their faces are hidden by the black visors of their helmets, but I know them anyway. It's Jaynie who's closest to me.

Jaynie wasn't in the hangar. She'd been evacuated to a navy hospital after the *Non-Negotiable*. I wonder if her arm is still in a splint, under her gear.

Flynn is next to her, the smallest of our squad. She's got a tiny LED flashlight with a red beam clipped to her thigh pocket; it's the only light source in the hall. Flynn was poisoned by bee drones when we hit Reyvik Biosystems. She didn't make it to the *Non-Negotiable*, staying behind at the hangar with Shima . . . but she wasn't in the hangar, was she? Shima had sent her on an errand.

I look at the third figure—

"Clear the doorway," Jaynie orders. I hear her voice twice: directly, and over gen-com. "Step into the hall."

I do it. There's a faint creak and hiss from her dead sister as she moves past me into the cell. "Room's clear."

"Roger that," Delphi says, while I take a shuddering breath and ask what is surely not possible.

"Nolan, is that you?"

He answers in his familiar, gentle voice. "Hey, LT. I guess you thought I was dead."

If Nolan is still alive . . . have I been wrong all this time about what happened? "Moon and Tuttle? Did they make it? And Shima?"

Jaynie's voice takes on a hard edge as she returns to the hall. "You saw what happened to Moon. He was gunned down right in front of you. So was Shima."

I shake my head. I don't remember it. "What about Tuttle?"

"Dead," she confirms, turning to look toward the end of the hall. "Any reason to think these other cells are occupied?"

"No. I've never seen the doors open. I've never seen other prisoners."

"Stay where you are while we clear them."

The doors aren't locked, and the cells are empty.

"Anything we need to take care of before we pull out?" Jaynie asks me.

I think of the mission to slam Eduard Semak . . . the mission I agreed to do, wanted to do, still want to do. Fuck me, anyway. "No. There's nothing."

"Hold position in the basement for now," Delphi instructs. "Still waiting on an all clear."

Jaynie responds, "Roger that."

"Who's upstairs?" I want to know. "Who are you working with?"

"Squad Two. Cryptic Arrow's second field unit. We came in together against minimal defenses. The enemy thought they were safe, thought we couldn't find them."

"It was Joby Nakagawa who figured out where I was. Right?"

She goes still. A few seconds slip past. Then, "I guess you could say that. Course, it was Nakagawa who opened up a hole in your head that let the enemy walk right in."

I feel an echo of the panic that hit me minutes ago, when a program downloaded and launched without my permission.

"Shima was watching you when it happened," Jaynie continues. "Her farsights were recording. The video shows you falling like you were hit, but none of the blood on scene was yours. None of the shots taken were at an angle to hit you. The enemy got inside your head through Nakagawa's access, and they brought you down using the skullnet."

I scowl, struggling to remember, but nothing else comes. "They fucked with my short-term memory. All I remember about it is the smell of blood—lots of blood—and beams of sunlight stabbing through what must have been bullet holes in the hangar door . . . and being certain, absolutely *fucking* certain, that everyone in there was dead." I turn to Nolan. "You were in the hangar. How the hell are you still alive?"

He raises his hand, touches the side of his helmet. "I got hit here. Creased. It was a bloody mess, a real Hollywood close shave. I was out cold for three hours."

Bitterly, Jaynie says, "The squad never had a chance. The shooter was a robotic sniper, set up in another hangar. Delivered ten precision shots in seven seconds using a sensor system that could see through the walls. Programmed to gun down everyone but you. They wanted you because of your connection to the Red, didn't they?"

"Yes." Moon and Tuttle and Shima are dead because of me. "They're the same group who hit us in the courthouse basement. They got a new merc since then. Changed tactics."

"They don't got him no more," Flynn says, speaking for the first time. "Not if he's one of them we met coming down. LT, I wasn't no part of what happened in that hangar. I want you to know that. I wasn't there only 'cause I had to drop off your package, that's all."

"Hey, take it easy. Who said you were part of it?"

"Everyone's actions were evaluated," Jaynie explains. "Mine too. I wasn't there either. Both of us could have been conspirators."

Flynn again, in an icy voice: "I'm no fucking conspirator, sir."

"I never thought you were, Flynn."

But she's carrying a burden of guilt and my reassurance doesn't help. "When I got back to the hangar, an' saw what they did . . ." She breaks off, turns her helmeted head to gaze at the empty hall. "They gunned down Moon, sir, just to get him out of the way. They slaughtered Tuttle. I thought it had to be Uther-Fen that hit us, an' I swore I'd see every one of 'em dead."

I swore vengeance too, but I traded that oath for a mission that will never happen now. The disappointment runs deep—and it makes me feel out of control, like I'm a windup toy: Point me at an objective, turn me on, and I'll go after it.

Not this time. My rescue came too soon.

"What happened to us in that hangar . . . it never made the news, did it?"

"Hell no," Jaynie says. "And this operation won't either. Black Phoenix. That's the mission name."

Delphi breaks in. "You're cleared to head out."

We jog for the stairs. The first corpse we pass is just inside the fire door. "Flynn, give me your flashlight."

She hands it over. I use its dim red beam to examine the body. It's a big man. He's barefoot, dressed only in shorts and an armored vest like he was caught sleeping when the hammer came down. His throat is shot out. Someone has laid him out neatly on his back, with his blood-spattered helmet removed and placed beside his head, portrait-style, to ensure a clear photographic record of the dead. He has a sun-darkened Caucasian face with glazed eyes staring from beneath a heavy brow, buzz-cut silver hair, a crooked nose, blood from his mouth drying across a one-day growth of stubble.

I've never seen his face, but I know him. "That's got to be Crow. He was always wearing a helmet and dead sister—but

I guess he didn't have time to rig up tonight. He was there at the hangar, Flynn. That was his operation."

"Fucking merc," she mutters. "Burn in Hell."

One floor up, there's a second body, this one rigged in an exoskeleton. Like Crow, this merc has been turned faceup, the helmet placed near the head. The Silent One, judging by the body size. I shine my light on the face, but I still can't tell if this was a man or a woman. Someone less sortable, maybe. It's a youthful, smooth-featured, black-skinned face, with thick eyebrows and dark irises just visible behind half-closed eyes. There's no hint of beard growth on the smooth, pale cheeks, but a good depilatory could explain that as easily as gender.

It doesn't matter though.

I move on.

One more floor and Flynn opens the door to a parking garage, but there's another body on the landing above, so I break away to take a look.

It's Shiloh. She's laid out like the others. Exit wounds have ripped open her chest. She's dressed in civilian clothes and she wasn't wearing armor. She never had a chance—just like Moon, and Tuttle, and Shima.

Nolan explains, "She didn't go down when we told her to. She tried to run."

"She believed the Red would be on her side."

Hooking into King David's meta story is a fool's game.

I head back down the stairs.

"We're pulling out in three minutes!" a commanding voice—male—announces as we enter the parking garage. "Get your rigs and your weapons stowed *now*."

The only light is what spills from the open doors of two cargo vans, but that's enough to show me the tense faces of the Squad Two soldiers—ten of them, all strangers to me, and all dressed in anonymous charcoal-colored combat uniforms and black skullcaps. There's a pause in their quiet, coordinated haste as curious faces turn in my direction— and I'm suddenly conscious of my neon-green prison attire, scruffy beard, and slovenly hair. They pretend not to notice. Nods and smiles greet me, and then they're back to work, folding their dead sisters, bagging their helmets, and loading everything into the backs of the vans.

Jaynie gestures at one of the vehicles. "Get inside. I'll be right back."

Nolan and Flynn follow her behind the van. I start to get in, but then I hear a familiar low buzz. It makes the hair on my arms stand on end. I turn, ready to fight or flee, but all I see is one of Joby's robo-bugs buzzing out of the hallway past the propped-open fire door. A plastic equipment case is lying open on the floor. Five robo-bugs are already nestled into slots in the gray packing material that fills both sides of the case. The last robo-bug lands on the case, walks to the empty slot, settles into it, and goes quiescent. One of the Squad Two soldiers closes the case and picks it up.

"Lieutenant Shelley."

I recoil, the voice is so unexpected. I've let my guard down; I've let a stranger get within arm's reach of me without realizing he was there. The skullnet icon lights up, schooling me to calm as I turn to see Squad Two's CO.

He's watching me cautiously: a lean man of moderate height, carrying twice my years. "Didn't mean to startle you, Lieutenant," he says in a gentler voice. "I just wanted to say it's an honor to meet you."

I gather myself enough that I can provide the ritual answer: "Thank you, sir. Thank you for coming after me."

Nolan shows up at my side. His helmet and bones have been exchanged for farsights. "Let's go, LT."

I nod and follow him into the van's third seat. Jaynie climbs in behind me. Two strangers come in next. They look at me with triumphant smiles as they slide into the middle seat.

"Welcome back, Lieutenant."

"It was a fucking joy to help get you out of there, sir."

The door slides shut and the light goes out. There are no windows in the back of the van. It feels like a prison cell.

But another light comes on when the front doors open. Flynn gets into the shotgun seat. Her gloved hands grip her HITR as she holds it muzzle-down between her legs. Her seat is pushed back far enough that she has room to swing it into action if she needs to.

The driver looks at us as she gets in. "All secure?"

"Roger that," Jaynie answers. "Let's get the fuck out of here."

A ramp takes us out of the garage, into predawn darkness. I have no idea where we are. I can see only a little through the front windshield, enough to know we're driving past empty parking lots and the glass-block buildings of an office park. The streetlights are out and there are no lights behind the office windows, no lights in the parking lots. Just moonlight, gleaming against intact glass, but swallowed up by the depthless dark that marks a scattering of broken windows, some in every building we pass.

I spot a real-estate sign standing in a garden of weeds, boldly proclaiming premium office space available January 4 of this year—that would have been less than two months after Coma Day.

A feral cat dashes across a sidewalk shot through with weeds—and a new worry kicks in. God knows what Shiloh packed into my head . . . an electronic IED maybe, programmed to automatically overload my skullnet and bring me down if I get away. I tense. Maybe I start breathing a little fast, sweating, I don't know, but Jaynie turns to look at me. "Easy, Shelley. We're doing okay."

"My overlay is a mess. Completely compromised."

Delphi speaks over gen-com. "Roger that. We're going to reformat your system. But that means you'll lose anything personal—"

"I'll get it from backup."

"—and you'll be isolated for at least an hour."

"*Shit.*"

"It needs to be done," she insists. "Like you said—"

"I know, I'm compromised, so do it—but Jesus, I miss you, Delphi. Have you been okay?"

Her response is strictly professional. "Initiating reformat."

It leaves me with a hollow feeling in my gut. "Wait—"

I'm kicked out of gen-com. My display blanks except for a tiny orange-yellow counter in the lower left: *1%*, it tells me. And after many seconds pass, *2%*.

That feeling when you know your lover has started cutting the bonds? Yeah, I have that.

"It's been really hard on her," Jaynie says, "not knowing if you were dead or alive . . . or being tortured."

"I understand." I keep my gaze fixed on the night beyond the windshield as the van climbs a ramp to a freeway. No one else says anything. "Thanks for coming after me, by the way."

"We're in this together."

"Not many of us left," Nolan adds.

After a few minutes, I think to ask where we're going.

"Wyoming," Jaynie answers. "That's our headquarters. With luck, you'll get there this time."

Maybe it's luck or maybe it's in the script, but we get there, arriving by chartered jet late that afternoon. At the airfield where we land, there's a single hangar and two fuel tanks, one labeled *Aviation*. On the opposite side of the runway, sheep graze in pastures fenced with barbed wire. It's hot outside and the terrain is mostly flat, but the air feels thin in my lungs, confirming we're on the high plains.

Set back from the airfield is a large garage with four roll-up doors, all closed. Farther away but linked to the airfield by an asphalt driveway is a sprawling, two-story ranch house. It has a wraparound veranda and an encircling lawn planted with shade trees. There's a greenhouse on the far side of the lawn. When people talk about the American dream, I think they mean a place like this.

Squad Two forms a line to offload the gear into two waiting pickup trucks. Jaynie leaves the work to them. "Come on," she says, and the four of us walk together to the house.

AGAINST THE BEAST

EPISODE 3:
VERTIGO GATE

COLONEL RAWLINGS MEETS US ON THE VERANDA. He ignores my county-jail attire and sticks out his hand. "It's good to have you back, Lieutenant. One less gone than we first believed."

I clasp his hand. "Too many gone, sir."

His eyes narrow in anger, but it's not directed at me. He's looking into the past. "Harvey's death was tragic, but it was a risk of the mission—a mission that proved successful, and saved God knows how many thousands of lives. But what happened in Brunswick"—his gaze fixes on me again—"there is no excuse for it. We failed. Our intelligence failed." He turns to Jaynie. "We were blindsided, and your squad paid the price."

Rawlings is a pompous old fart, and while I know he's willing to sacrifice the soldiers under his command, I also know he will never sell out or betray the mission. Maybe I don't like him personally, but I can respect that.

He steps back, holding the door open. "Come inside. Vasquez, you and Shelley have fifteen minutes to shower and change. Then I want you both downstairs to debrief Black Phoenix."

I follow Jaynie into the house. The interior surprises me with an absence of faux-Western trappings. Instead the decor is modern, with steel accents and a black, gray, and white color scheme. I look around the great room, hoping to see Delphi, but she isn't there, so I ask Rawlings. "Sir, I need to see Delphi—Karin—where is she?"

"Downstairs, involved in the intelligence analysis. I'll make sure she knows you're here."

We don't go upstairs. "Squad Two's quartered up there," Nolan explains as he shows me to a hallway off the great room. I assumed this was a family home, but the interior is laid out more like a guest lodge or a small hotel. Most of the rooms are upstairs, but off the downstairs hallway are four bedrooms, each with its own bath. Nolan opens the door to my assigned quarters. "All yours," he says. A fresh combat uniform, anonymous gray, is waiting for me on the bed.

I'm in the shower, washing a depilatory off my face along with two weeks' growth of beard when Delphi comes in, so quiet it takes me a few seconds to realize she's there, her blond hair pulled back in a ponytail, no smile, her bright blue eyes watching me warily through the steam. "Jesus, Delphi." I shut off the water, open the shower door, grab a towel, and use it to dry off as much as I can in the two steps it takes me to reach her. Then I've got my arms around her, and if she's not holding me as closely as I'd like, at least she's not pushing me away. "Are you glad I came back?"

"Don't be an asshole! Of course I'm glad . . . and Rawlings is expecting you downstairs in six minutes." She's on the verge of tears; I can hear it in her voice, but she tries to hide it behind her scolding. "For God's sake, would you buzz your hair? You look like a derelict. Here. There should be clippers in one of the drawers."

She pulls away from me and goes to look for the clippers, slamming drawers until she finds them.

"Why are you angry?"

"Take care of your hair." She retreats to the bathroom doorway, watching with her arms crossed as I begin to restore a military discipline to my hair. I'm halfway done when she speaks over the clippers' soft buzz. "Do you remember what I told you about Black Cross? That I thought you'd died there?"

I watch myself in the mirror as more black hair falls into the sink. "I remember."

"It was like déjà vu when you disappeared from all my sensors on the cargo deck of the *Non-Negotiable*."

"I reported in as soon—"

"And then the incident at Brunswick. We had no idea who took you. They wore masks and we couldn't identify the voices. But we knew exactly how they slammed you, because your friend Joby called and told us."

I don't think Joby really qualifies as my friend, but I don't correct her. "Jaynie said something about that."

"Are you done with your hair? Get dressed."

She moves out of the doorway so I can get to the fresh uniform laid out on the bed.

"Nakagawa tried to call you, to let you know the program he had running on your overlay was compromised. An assistant had reset the access and sold the key—that's what he said, anyway. But you didn't answer calls or respond to e-mails. Then he got the package, the one Flynn posted for you, so he called the number on the packing slip. That was Shima's number, but it forwarded to Rawlings. So we knew. Someone with money and determination and an insider's technical skills had taken you. We assumed Uther-Fen, or the president's private army. Either way, we'd never get you back."

"There was no way I was ever going to escape, Delphi. They had me locked down tight. But I tried to get word out to you. I got far enough one day to get an outside link."

I'm pulling on the jacket of my uniform when I'm finally rewarded with a little smile. "You did," she whispers. "That was Joby's program too. That was the start of mission planning for Black Phoenix."

She lets me kiss her after that, but it's not the same. It's like I can taste her reluctance. I don't think I'm forgiven. Maybe I never will be.

Jaynie is waiting for us at the end of the hall. We head down to the basement, where I'm impressed to find a dedicated briefing room with three short rows of theater seats, a podium, and a large monitor on the wall. All that's lacking is analysts, but it turns out they're attending virtually over what the organization must believe is a secure line.

Good luck with that.

Rawlings is already there, in the front row. I sit at the opposite end, leaving a seat between us for Delphi, but she doesn't sit down. Instead, she takes up a post under one of the glassy camera eyes in the front corner of the room, leaning against the wall, her arms crossed. I wait to catch her eye, but she doesn't look at me.

Jaynie slides into the second row, taking the center seat.

A soothing, androgynous voice issues from a hidden speaker. "For security purposes, we want to limit knowledge of the analysts who are participating in this debriefing, so we will be using a shared synthetic voice. You can address us as Jones."

I don't like synthetic voices, they irritate me, but at least this one isn't a booming masculine threat like the voice I used aboard the *Non-Negotiable*.

First, Jones asks me to describe what happened in the hangar. I don't have much to offer. I go into more detail about waking up, first with a hood on, and then later, in my cell. The analysts ask questions, backtracking over and over again. They want to know everything I can remember about Crow and the Silent One. They question me closely about the manipulation of my skullnet, about the effect of the Taser on my equipment, about my escape attempt, and about Shiloh's knowledge of the Red and what she believed its goals to be. None of my experience was recorded—not by me, anyway—so I do my best to remember all the details I can.

Maybe it's my imagination, but it seems to me that despite the synthetic voice, I can hear a growing excitement in the cadence of the questions, as if we're getting closer to the subject that really interests them. We're two hours into the debriefing when the monitor lights up with an image of the mock-up of the Semak Hermitage.

"Let's talk about this," Jones says.

I look at Delphi. She's not looking at the screen and she's not wearing farsights. She's watching me. That tells me she's seen the image before, she's had time to think about it, and maybe she's guessed its purpose.

I feel ashamed that I agreed to do the mission, that I was training to do it—but shame or not, the compulsion is still there. I ask myself: Is it only because of the Red, playing puppet master? Or do I go along with the prompts because I'm an adrenaline junkie out to be the hero no matter how crazy the mission? Shiloh said people like me don't want peace. We want challenges. Maybe she was right.

I watch anger build in Delphi's eyes and I swear to God she can read my mind. So I look away. I look at the screen.

"Lieutenant Shelley," Jones prompts, "can you identify the image?"

"Yes. It's a mock-up of the Sunrise Fifteen orbital habitat owned and occupied by a dragon named Eduard Semak."

"What was Exalt Communications' interest in the Semak Hermitage?"

The skullnet icon remains dark, but a feeling comes over me anyway that I should be very careful just how much I say.

"They believed Semak was in control of a number of nuclear devices, and that intel on the location of his weapons cache could be recovered from his overlay. So Shiloh developed a mission to visit him in orbit and extract the data. The mock-up was created so I could familiarize myself with the layout and components of the habitat."

"You?" Jaynie asks, catching me by surprise. It's the first time she's spoken since we entered the briefing room.

I turn to look at her, sitting in the row behind me. Her elegant eyebrows are raised and there's a cold half smile on her full lips that tells me she already knows what Exalt, and Shiloh, were really after.

It's not a subject I want to talk about in front of Rawlings and his analysts.

"Listen," I say, standing up. "I need a break. I've got to get some air."

I give Jaynie a nod, hoping she'll follow me as I head out. Delphi looks startled. I signal her too and then trot up the stairs, ignoring the objections of both Rawlings and Jones. At the top, I glance back. Jaynie and Delphi are behind me. Both look puzzled, but they're following, just as I hoped.

I head outside to the veranda, and then down the stairs to the driveway. Twilight is settling in. I slow my pace until Jaynie and Delphi catch up, and then we walk together toward the airfield, my titanium feet padding against the driveway as crickets bombard the evening with their buzzing and chirping competitions. Without being told, Jaynie takes off her farsights and turns them off. I check my overlay to confirm it's not recording.

"What is going on with you?" Delphi demands in an angry whisper.

I keep my voice low as I tell her the truth. "Shiloh wanted me to take the mission because she believed the Red would back me."

"And you agreed to do it?"

She's furious, but I'm not going to lie. "You know how it is, Delphi. I had a feeling."

"Fucking King David," Jaynie says softly. "You know, Shelley, I was half dead on that ship, but I swear I remember you promising you were done. No more, you said. But now the Red wants to play you—run you like a puppet again—and you're okay with it."

Sometimes you're called to do a thing. That's just the way it is. But it's not an argument I can win, so I skip it and go on to the mission specifics. "With the organization's backing, we can still do the mission. It needs doing, and it's only a two-person op. Me, and the spaceplane pilot. So the risk to life is minimal."

"Fuck that," Jaynie says. "If Cryptic Arrow gets behind this, *I'm* going."

"You can't. The mission plan specifies—"

"Are the nukes real?"

I sigh, postponing the argument. "They have to be real. The Red would know, right? But the nukes were just Shiloh's excuse. The cover action."

Jaynie nods. She already had the motive figured out back in the briefing room. "It was Semak's fortune they were after."

"Yes, and we can go after it now, if we want to."

Delphi comes to an abrupt halt.

Jaynie steps away, staring at me. "Joking, right?"

"No."

Delphi looks to be in shock. "You can't be thinking of stealing that money. It doesn't fit your psych profile. Not at all."

The crickets are chirping and buzzing, and a light wind is rustling the grass. Ten years ago that might have been enough to cover our conversation. Now? A good processor could filter out everything but our whispers—but only if Rawlings has listening devices set up along the road. I'm guessing he doesn't.

"I started thinking Eduard Semak isn't as crazy as he seems. He's made his own little world up there. That's what you want to do, isn't it, Jaynie?" I turn to her. "You want your own little world where the Red can't reach out and play you like a puppet. But you're going to need dragon money to make it."

"Shelley, that is *crazy*," Delphi concludes, and she's not whispering.

"So what if it is? That doesn't mean we can't do it."

"Why, Shelley?" Jaynie wants to know. "Why would you want to try it? Why take the chance?"

"Because we *have* the chance. The chance to do something different. You don't want the Red telling your story for you, Jaynie, then tell your own."

I turn to Delphi. "You're going to be my handler—"

"*Our* handler," Jaynie corrects. "If we're doing this, I'm in on it too."

I keep my focus on Delphi. "So you need to figure out how to make it work. Send any data on the nukes to the intelligence team, keep the financial data on the side."

Past the chorus of crickets, I hear the faint buzz of an approaching seeker. Our time is up, so I change the tone of the conversation. Putting my arm around Delphi, I kiss her cheek. "Please, don't be angry. You know how it is." We all turn to watch the seeker swoop around us. "This is just like Black Cross, just like the *Non-Negotiable*—sometimes you just have to do it, whether you want to or not."

"You *want* to," she accuses, stepping away from me. Her bitter tone not just for the benefit of Rawlings listening in. "You believe your own legend. *King David.* You can't wait."

She's right, though in a situation like this it would be a mistake to confirm or to deny. So we walk back to the house in silence.

During Black Phoenix, Squad Two collected all the tablets, laptops, farsights, and data storage devices they could find. Analysis of Exalt Communications' operations has barely begun, but as the debriefing continues, Jones confirms that records have been found supporting my account of a planned mission to recover intel on the location of Eduard Semak's weapons cache. "There will be an evaluation of the Exalt mission plan," Jones tells us, communicating the enthusiasm of the analysts, despite the synthetic nature of the voice.

To date, Cryptic Arrow has pulled off three successful missions: First Light, Silent Firebreak, and now, Black Phoenix. Confidence is growing.

That evening, after a late dinner, Rawlings pulls me aside. "You've lit a fuse, Lieutenant. The organization wants this mission. A lot of questions remain, but the early consensus is that we have the skills and the personnel to carry it out."

Wanting to lend my approval without pushing too hard, I tell him: "I think it's something we need to seriously consider, sir."

"We will be looking at every element in the coming days. This is the kind of mission we exist to do—a critical project outside the reach of constituted authority. You might not be aware of this, Lieutenant, but rumors of Semak's nukes have existed for years. If we can recover the location of the cache and some knowledge of the security around it, then something might finally be done."

It's nearly midnight by the time I leave Rawlings. The house is quiet. There are only a couple of lights on in the living room. That's where I find Delphi. She's been sitting in a recliner, but when she sees me, she stands up, crosses her arms. "Good news?" she asks as I approach.

"All of Rawlings's patriot friends want to do it."

"If the intelligence is real, it needs to be done." Each word is crisp and deliberate. She's locked down in handler mode, but she's been so distant in the hours since I got back that even a cold statement of approval feels like a peace offering.

"So are you in? For all of it?"

"It's not that simple. We need to talk."

Nothing pleasant ever follows that phrase.

My thoughts shoot back to that first night we spent together in her hotel room. I wish we were there again. "Delphi, I love you. I do."

Her gaze cuts away. "I love you too—and that's a problem. Shelley—"

"Look at me."

She does, but she's locked down tight. "Let's go outside."

I follow her onto the porch where we're met by a soft chorus of crickets and the dusty scent of night air. No one's around. Dim light seeps through the blinds, enough to show her shape as she walks to the railing and turns around.

"You know Rawlings will have this porch under surveillance," I remind her.

"That way I won't have to say this twice."

"I thought this was about you and me."

"This is about the mission."

I don't know if that bodes well for me or not—but I'll find out soon. I join her, leaning against the railing, hip cocked, with the star-spangled dark beyond. "Go ahead."

"I told you before you left that I knew what I was doing by getting involved with you—and I did know. I believed I could handle it. But I was wrong."

Okay, I know where this is going. "You're thinking about what happened on the *Non-Negotiable*." Delphi broke down near the end of that mission, forcing Shima to take over as my handler. "You need to let that go. Silent Firebreak was a success and you were a big part of that."

"Colonel Rawlings thinks you need a new handler."

"Rawlings can go to hell. I want you. And we *need* you if we're going to do this the way we discussed."

"I understand that. But I don't know if I can do it again. It was bad, Shelley. When I lost contact with you on that cargo deck, it was just like Black Cross. I *knew* you were dead and I was dying inside."

"You didn't quit, though. You were still there when I checked back in. Delphi, you're the best handler I've ever had."

"I used to be." She reaches out, tentative in the dark, to run her palm across my freshly buzzed hair. "Maybe I should get wired up like you."

I catch her hand, pull it down to my mouth, and kiss her palm. "You don't need that shit."

I hear her sigh. "This is . . . hard to convey. When we run a mission, it's not my life on the line. No one is shooting at me. But I need you to understand what an unbearable anguish it is to sit in a room and watch passively, *helplessly*, as death strikes out at someone you love . . . to hear it happening and not be able to change anything."

I do know what that's like. I flash on the sick, consuming horror I felt when I knew Lissa was dead.

"When you went missing and I didn't know—"

"Shhh . . ." I pull her against me. Stroke her hair, kiss her face. "That's over now. We got through it. And this next mission, if we go at all—"

"Shelley, you just don't get it!" She pulls back. "What I'm trying to tell you is that Rawlings is right. You need a new handler."

"No. If we're going to do what we talked about, we need you. For just this one more mission. An easy mission. No guns, no grenades. Just a crazy old man all on his own. You can do that, Delphi. And afterward, you can retire. You and Jaynie. If that's what you want."

"And you? What do you want?"

It's late, so I go for the direct approach. "I want to stop thinking about all this shit tonight. I want to be in bed with you, Delphi. I want to be having sex with you."

She's silent for a few seconds. Then she leans in to kiss the corner of my mouth. "Okay. I want that too."

We wake up to news of a verdict in Sheridan's trial.

She has been found guilty of crimes against humanity for her involvement in the nuclear terrorism of Coma Day. In deference to those judges on the international panel whose countries prohibit the death penalty, the recommended sentence is life in prison.

Colonel Kendrick would have been pleased to know it.

Most court observers are commending Ahab Matugo for overseeing an exemplary proceeding. In an interview, a mediot from Japan asks his opinion of Sheridan's allegations about the Red. "Is it real, sir?"

Matugo sits in an upholstered chair in what looks to be

an opulent library decorated in African prints and dark hardwoods. He is a soldier and a scholar, his innate dignity reflected in his posture and in a reserved expression that makes him seem older than he is. There is no gray yet in his short, tightly curled hair, and his black skin is smooth over strong, balanced features. He answers the mediot's question without any hesitation, speaking with a crisp accent: "Studies I've commissioned indicate that it is, that there is something out there, something of vast reach and influence, skilled at engineering coincidence—and frightening in the way of all things that hold immense power."

"Then you feel Ms. Sheridan was right in her concern?" the mediot asks. "Even if she was wrong in her actions?"

"No, that is not my opinion at all. Power must reside somewhere. Accept that, and the question becomes, whom do we trust? This endeavor at justice"—he waves his hand vaguely—"which has earned such accolades, would not have come about without the subtle interference of this hidden entity, the Red."

He leans forward in his chair. "The Red is real, and it is, in any practical sense, beyond our ability to eradicate, supposing we should want to do so. Make no mistake—it is a dangerous thing. No one truly understands its intentions. We do not know that it *has* intentions in the aggregate beyond this one: to maintain a thriving marketplace—or market*places*, many arenas in which we may seek and perhaps find that which wakens our souls. Not always a good thing, that—the human soul is as often corrupt as it is beautiful—but it is surely better than nuclear annihilation, environmental contamination, or the climate change that is already killing us, here in the equatorial world.

"The tragedy of the human race is that we need this thing, that we are not brave enough or wise enough to live to our potentials on our own."

Later, we gather over coffee to celebrate the guilty verdict. Rawlings makes a short speech about how those who died did not die in vain. We congratulate one another. And then it's back to business.

Delphi heads to the basement to help Jones with the ongoing analysis of evidence recovered during Black Phoenix. I spend the next two hours in a PT session with both squads, where the decline in my physical condition becomes abundantly clear. I'm near death when we're released. I'm given an hour to shower, eat, and try to convince my body that this is better than prison. Four hours of detailed debriefing follow. After that, Rawlings pulls me aside again and tries to convince me I need a new handler, but I refuse to be persuaded. "Delphi's the best," I insist. "If we get to do this, I want the best behind me."

It's late afternoon before I get any free time, and by then all I want is to sit on the porch in a rocking chair—which is what I do.

From my vantage on the porch I can look down a one-lane asphalt road that climbs a rise maybe seven hundred meters away, and disappears. Tall trees in bright green leaf grow in the low ground on the eastern side of the road, their canopies shimmering in a soft, steady breeze. My overlay tags them as cottonwoods. The sky is bright blue with only a few clouds and two hawks idly circling. I watch them for a minute, until something else catches my eye: a blue glint, hard to see, like a hairline fracture in the sky.

It's a surveillance drone. Delphi restored all my command privileges when she reformatted me, so I link into angel sight. The angel is following the road from the south. Far behind it I can see a highway with scattered traffic. Thunderclouds are gathering to the east. As the angel floats silently above the cottonwood grove, I look down at a sparkling stream running beneath the trees. There are fish in the water, and birds flitting in the tree branches, and one lone human following what looks like a well-worn path out from under the trees to the road. The angel identifies the subject of observation as Mandy Flynn. She's dressed in brown uniform pants, a T-shirt, farsights, and her skullcap. She looks up at me on the porch, squares her shoulders, and picks up her pace, closing the distance to the house.

Something's up.

I watch her with angel sight until the angel moves off on its route. A minute later she's standing on the lawn in front of me.

"LT?"

There's anxiety in her wide green eyes. It's contagious. I get up and move to the stairs.

"You think you could come look at something with me, sir? It won't take long."

"Something wrong, Flynn?"

"No, sir. No. Not like you mean. If you could just come."

"Where?"

"Not far."

She leads me back down the asphalt one-lane, glancing at me every few steps, but refusing to meet my gaze. It puts me on edge. Anything unexpected or unexplained puts me there.

"Flynn, what—?"

"Just a little farther, sir."

She doesn't want to talk about it. I tell myself I need to respect that, because it's trust that binds us together, loyalty that defines us. Flynn wasn't with us in the hangar, but to let myself consider that she might have betrayed us would itself be a betrayal of who we are. So I follow in silence, shamed by my doubt.

She brings us to the path I saw with angel sight. The spring grass growing beneath the trees has been cut to make it easy to walk. The stream is ahead of us, but before we get there, we come to an open space where the grass has been trimmed and trampled. There's a monument at the center of it, a gray granite obelisk six feet high set on a smooth, round base made of some kind of resin that looks like black glass.

Sitting on that base with his back to the monument is Matt Ransom, wearing the gray-and-white Arctic uniform we used during First Light. He looks up at me, meets my gaze, and then he's gone.

I rear back, reaching for a weapon that I'm not carrying. *"Holy shit!"* My heart is hammering as I turn away, rubbing my eyes as if I can reboot them. I thought I was doing okay handling all this shit, but if I'm starting to hallucinate—

Flynn touches my arm. "LT, it's okay. It's this place. It's for us. To remember them, you know?"

"What are you saying?"

"You saw Ransom, right? That's how it works."

Together we circle the monument. I look for the names of the dead, but it's the mission names I see—*First Light* and *Silent Firebreak*.

Flynn sounds like she's apologizing when she says, "Silent Firebreak is always going to be secret—that's what Colonel Rawlings said—so we didn't put any names at all on the memorial." She taps her farsights. "But they're here. We can see them. You and me, and Sergeant Nolan and Captain Vasquez. And Rawlings. Only us."

I look up, and glimpse Jayden Moon among the trees, alongside the path we followed to get here. Tall and skinny, with his arms crossed over his chest, he smiles at me. It's a half second of forgiveness, and then he's gone, no trace left behind.

I breathe again.

"It's a projection in your overlay," Flynn explains quietly.

"Yeah. How did you get the access?"

"Delphi set it up."

We sit on the monument's black resin base. The trees rustle overhead, the stream whispers, birds sing to one another, and slowly, as the day draws to a close, I see the rest of them: Vanessa Harvey, Samuel Tuttle, Anne Shima, and Steven Kendrick.

Flynn tells me, "When you were gone . . . those first days, we didn't think we'd get you back."

"Did you put me here, Flynn?"

She shrugs. Not a question she's willing to answer.

"This memorial . . . it was your idea, wasn't it?"

She shrugs again, refusing to meet my gaze.

"You did good," I tell her.

Technically, Eduard Semak is not an American problem, but no one likes the idea of rogue nukes that might some-day be used against us. So after fifteen days spent evaluating captured files, the analysts declare a new mission, designated Vertigo Gate.

The plan is tentative and pieces are missing.

One of the missing pieces is Amity.

During the initial debrief, I told Jones about her visit on the day before the raid. "We called her Amity, but that wasn't her name. I couldn't ID her, but she had a slight Russian accent."

At a later meeting, the analysts had shown me a photo.

"Yes," I confirmed for them. "That's her."

They told me her real name is Ulyana Kurnakova. She's the new hire among six pilots flying for Sidereal Transit Systems. Prior to that, she claims to have served twenty-five years in the Russian air force. The analysts still don't have details.

"Her career is a black box," Jones concedes when we meet again in the briefing room to discuss Vertigo Gate. "Her personal history is unknown, so we can't even guess at her motive. She might have conceived the plan to hijack Semak's life and lifestyle because of a grudge or for purely mercenary reasons or with some other purpose in mind."

The synthesized voice doesn't communicate frustration, but I imagine I hear it anyway.

The analysts also haven't been able to link Kurnakova to Exalt Communications. She's not a company director, shareholder, or employee, and she's not associated with anyone who is, so Jones thinks she was an outsider, engaged in a partnership of convenience: "So she could be open to forming a new partnership, with us."

I'm skeptical, reminding them of her animosity toward me. "She didn't want me there. She wasn't buying Shiloh's King David tactic."

Delphi says, "But even if she didn't like it, she was still willing to deal with your presence. So she's motivated."

"We killed Shiloh and Crow since then. That might put her off."

"She hasn't gone to ground. She hasn't disappeared."

"Twenty-five years of service off the record," Jaynie muses. "She would know how to disappear if she wanted to—don't you think so, Jones?"

"A reasonable guess," Jones answers.

"But she hasn't disappeared. That means she doesn't scare easy. And Shelley, she wanted to make sure you knew the mission was her idea. Wouldn't surprise me if she recruited Shiloh, instead of the other way around. A woman like that is practical. She'll do what she needs to do to get what she wants—which means we can turn her if we do it right."

If we do it wrong, Vertigo Gate is not going to happen.

It's marginally possible we could bribe another pilot, but I prefer one who has already dispensed with moral qualms.

A long discussion follows on the best way to approach Kurnakova. In the end, it's agreed I should recruit her because she has a history with me—even if it's not a positive one. "It doesn't matter if she likes you," Jones concludes. "It's your legitimacy that matters, and the organization behind you. If she wants this enough, she'll work with you. If she doesn't, if she's already decided it was a mistake, it doesn't matter who we send. She won't cooperate."

So I'm going to San Antonio.

"Not alone," Rawlings insists. "You're a target out there. That's been proved more than once. So Squad Two is going with you, to make sure you get back."

"Negative, Colonel. Not a good idea."

Jaynie backs me. "Kurnakova will think it's a death squad. I'll go with Shelley. Two's enough. And if we get into trouble? Then you can send Squad Two."

"I'm going too," Delphi announces.

Just like that, my heart is hammering.

"You're not trained for field duty," Jaynie says, puzzled.

Delphi leans back in her chair, looking relaxed. "This is not a combat situation. It's just a trip to San Antonio."

I watch her, waiting for the inevitable flickering of the skullnet icon.

Rawlings doesn't like it. "Essential personnel only. There's no need for you to go."

"I want to go."

Jaynie crosses her arms and leans back in her seat, tilting her head to look at me. "You got an opinion?"

Logically, Rawlings is right—but I left Lissa behind and I lost her.

Delphi knows what I'm thinking. "None of us is safe,"

she reminds me. "*Anywhere.* That said, this is a diplomatic mission, and neither you nor Vasquez is known for your diplomacy. So I'm going."

We don't leave right away. I need more time to heal and to recover my fitness, so another ten days go by before a little chartered four-seater propeller plane brings us into San Antonio.

Delphi has been busy working with Cryptic Arrow's intelligence team, and the team has been busy spying on Kurnakova. So we know she's in town, we know where she lives, we know her usual schedule transiting between her high-end apartment and the Sidereal Transit Systems launch complex—and we know her phone number.

I call her as we're landing, using a phone Rawlings supplied. The call routes to voice mail. I keep it simple. "We can still do this thing, Amity. Call me. Let's talk."

We've just picked up the rental car when Kurnakova calls back. Her voice is soft with tension. "Almost a month of silence, and then *you* call. Did they stand down? Or did they get burned?"

"They got burned."

"By who?"

"My people."

"She said you were alone."

"She hoped I was."

Several seconds pass as Kurnakova considers this. Then, contemptuously, "You call me now because you think you can get rich."

"Why are *you* doing it?"

Again, she hesitates. Then softly, "Eduard is the reason I'm flying for STS. He got me the job . . . and he thinks it is all okay, you know?"

"But it's not okay?"

"It will never be okay."

So she's on a quest for justice. I know something about that. I understand how it feels. She will hesitate and negotiate, but she wants this desperately, so eventually there will be a fragile trust. And the mission? If we can assemble all the pieces, it's a go.

We do a face-to-face in an anonymous office rented for the day from a business park. Kurnakova explains the situation. "What I bring to this business is transportation, yes? Access? Everything else, you bring."

We're seated around a bland table, with cream-colored blinds closed against the fierce Texas sun. Delphi takes the lead. "We do ground support, guidance, postmission support including legal aspects—and of course Shelley has trained for the actual assault."

"I am a soldier too," she says, looking at me. "I will do what needs to be done."

I nod. That's the definition of the business we've taken on. I don't want to think too hard about the right or wrong of it. Doubt seeps like water into the tiny fissures of our beliefs, and when we're left out in the cold, brooding on what it all means, that doubt can freeze and shatter the foundation of our purpose. So I tell myself as often as I need to what Shiloh told me, and what I've since confirmed for myself: that Eduard Semak is a bad, bad man.

Jaynie makes her move. Leaning forward, one elbow on the table, she says, "I will be going on this mission too."

"No," Kurnakova says. "That's not possible. There can be only one."

"You need to make room for two."

"No. This cannot be done. Shelley will take the place of

the scheduled technician. To add another passenger would require changing the flight plan—and a change would draw attention that we do not want, questions that we cannot answer. So, no. There can be only one."

"Then that one will be me," Jaynie says. She holds up her hand to forestall my objection. "I'm pulling rank."

I object anyway. "You haven't trained for it."

"There's time."

"There's no training facility."

Delphi interjects, an edge to her voice. "The decision doesn't reside with either of you. It will be made by the mission planners."

"It will be made by me," Kurnakova counters, rapping the table with her neatly groomed fingernails. She turns her gaze on me. "Shiloh chose you. I did not approve. I thought it was an irrational decision—but now she is dead, while you, King David, are alive and free—"

"And willing."

Kurnakova nods. "As you say." She turns to Jaynie. "I respect the privilege of rank, but in this we follow the original mission plan. It will be Shelley—assuming we go at all." Her gaze returns to me. She raises a hand, touches a finger beside her eye. "Semak wears an overlay. You understand this technology?"

I hedge. "Shiloh talked about it."

"The data we're after is contained in the overlay." Her hand returns to the table. "Shiloh knew how to extract it. That's what made her useful to me." She gestures again, this time moving her hand in a half circle, though whether she's indicating all of the table or all of the world, it's not clear. "None of our talk matters if we can't take over control of Eduard Semak's overlay, take over all of his passcodes and private files. That skill, your people must bring to this mission—or there is no mission."

Delphi leans forward with a calculating smile. "We have a contractor who is acquainted with these data extractions. So yes, we will be able to supply that skill."

I glance at Jaynie. She has a fighting look on her face that tells me the discussion of who is going on this mission is not over yet, but when I raise a questioning eyebrow, wanting to know if she's familiar with Delphi's claim, she answers with a minute shake of her head.

Kurnakova catches the exchange. She raps the table again. "I will want proof you can do this thing."

"Within a week," Delphi assures her.

Given that the Sidereal Transit Systems flight to visit Eduard Semak is scheduled to leave in twelve days, that's cutting it close, but to my surprise, Kurnakova agrees. "Let it be so." Her gaze drops; her fingers tap in a slow, clicking beat. "The mission has been delayed twice already. I think it is dangerous to delay again. He is a very old man, very frail."

She looks up at me. "You want to do this thing, King David. I want to do it. But if he is dead before we get there, it will be too late. Neither of us will get what we want."

And what does she want? I am putting my life in her hands, so I want to understand her. "This isn't just about the money, is it, Ulyana? Not for you. There's something else you're not saying. Why do you hate him?"

She draws back, a combative look in her eyes. "Who would not hate him? He is a man deserving of hate. A man who amuses himself by corrupting all those around him. His children hate him. His grandchildren hate him. There is not one person in this world who will grieve when he is gone."

Her gaze warns me to ask no more questions—but I ask anyway. "Are you going there to kill him?"

She regards me for a few seconds more. Then, "I told you once before, Lieutenant Shelley: I am the architect of this mission and we will carry it out as planned. It is my goal to see Eduard Semak stripped of power. I want him to know what it is to be helpless. I want him to know he can do no more harm to the world. What happens after that"— she turns her right hand palm-up—"fate will decide."

A nice speech—but she is still not telling me everything.

Jaynie seizes on my hesitation. "Are you backing out, Shelley?"

"No."

I tell myself that so long as Kurnakova is carrying out the mission as planned, it doesn't really matter why she's doing it.

"Then let's move on," Delphi says in a clipped voice. "We need to discuss communications and logistics before we're through."

It's mid-June in San Antonio and the city is scorching, 115 degrees American. I can't directly feel the burning surface of the asphalt parking lot with my robot feet, but I can feel the heat rising through the titanium shafts that splice with the living bone of my thighs. The air in the car is unbreathable and the seats are searing hot. Delphi starts the engine, and flips the air-conditioning to max. Jaynie takes the shotgun seat, and I'm the junior officer stuck in the back.

No bombs went off in San Antonio, but seven months after Coma Day the trauma still shows. It's late morning on a weekday, but the parking lot of this office complex is only half full. As we head for the exit, we pass several parked cars covered in dust and sitting on flat tires—abandoned by owners who will likely never return.

As we leave the parking lot and turn into light traffic, Jaynie says, "I don't like yielding control of this mission to Kurnakova."

"And I don't want Shelley to go," Delphi answers. "But the fact stands that he's had the training, not you. And I did not get the impression Kurnakova considered the matter open for debate. Our options are to let Shelley go, or to call off the mission altogether."

I lean forward, my hand on the back of Jaynie's seat. "I don't want to call off the mission. We need to do this."

Jaynie looks over her shoulder at me, an accusing gaze, though what she's accusing me of, I'm not sure. Turning to Delphi, she says, "What contractor were you talking about who handled these data extractions?"

In the rearview mirror, I watch Delphi frown. "He hasn't *handled* them—not yet—but he understands the process."

This is not what I want to hear. "What's that mean? Can we do this or not? From what you told Kurnakova—"

"We still have a week to work out the details."

"Who is this contractor?" Jaynie insists.

Delphi stretches her shoulders the way people do when they're feeling uncomfortable but want to look casual. "Joby Nakagawa has been working with us on data forensics—"

"Nakagawa?" Jaynie interrupts. "That's a hell of a security risk. It was his program that let Shiloh crack Shelley's head."

Thinking about the implications of that, I'm kind of awestruck. Joby takes his work very seriously, he has a fiery temper, and he likes to think he's the smartest fish in the pond. But he made a basic mistake. He trusted the wrong person. He let his assistant get access to my overlay, and that assistant sold me out to Shiloh.

I say, "He must have been seriously pissed off when he realized what happened."

"Stone-cold fury," Delphi confirms. "He deduced your location from the program data you managed to upload, and when he figured out we were going in on our own, he gave us the robo-bugs to use on the mission." She glances at Jaynie. "They worked perfectly, by the way. No security breaches."

"Lucky for us."

"He wanted to see Shiloh slammed."

No one ever told me what happened to Joby's assistant. I don't bring it up. I don't really want to know. Instead, I ask, "Does Joby know how to extract the data from Semak's overlay?"

"In theory, yes," Delphi says. "In practice? I haven't been able to get a straight answer out of him, but when I told him we were coming to San Antonio, he said to bring you by the lab." A slight, worried smile twitches her lips. "He said he could use a subject to experiment on."

Neighborhoods along the freeway are looking tired and worn. Electricity is expensive and a lot of people are out of work. Those who can't afford air-conditioning have moved outside, setting up cots and tables and propane stoves under canopies stitched from bedsheets. Vegetable gardens are shaded too, and everywhere, kids play under sprinklers.

Fortunately for us, air-conditioning won't be lacking at Kelly Army Medical Center, where Joby keeps his lab. The energy-independent building was an oasis during the chaos that followed Coma Day. After Black Cross, I spent a week there with Lissa while my cyborg enhancements were repaired. Then I left on the First Light mission, and I never saw Lissa again.

So much has happened since then it feels like a lifetime ago. As we turn into the driveway I brace myself, expecting an onrush of memories, but it's not the past that comes for me. It's the future—the void of Lissa's lost future, all that she might have given to the world, to me . . . reduced to nothing. Not even ashes.

Delphi's blue eyes inspect me in the rearview mirror as she brings us to a stop beside the guard booth. "You okay?"

Jaynie glances over her shoulder, wondering what's up, while I assume a stonewall expression.

War steals the future. On Coma Day it voided the potential of ninety-three thousand lives.

It could happen again. But I'll be damned if it happens on my watch.

"I'm okay," I assure Delphi. "I just want to know for sure that Vertigo Gate is a go. That's all."

The MP at the guard booth confirms our identities and matches our names to a visitor roster that lists our appointment with Joby. "You're cleared to proceed, ma'am," he tells Delphi. And then he adds, "Thank you for your service, Lieutenant Shelley, Sergeant Vasquez. And Lieutenant? Welcome back."

We move with all practical speed from the merciless heat of the parking lot to the shade beneath the portico, and then in past the medical center's glass front doors—where we're enfolded by the heaven of air-conditioning and by a smiling squad of nurses and nursing assistants, all of them familiar faces. A lot of people helped me out while I was here. As we make our way across the lobby, I trade hugs and handshakes and greetings:

"Welcome back, Lieutenant Shelley."

"Glad to see you're in one piece this time, sir!"

"Best move the president ever made was to pardon you."

"We know what you've done for us, sir, and we don't care what the mediots say about you."

• • • •

We take the elevator to the basement. The corridor is deserted. We walk past the morgue to Joby's lab. I try the door, find it unlocked. "Brace yourselves," I warn. Pushing the door open, I peer cautiously inside.

The lab's main room looks just as I remember it. There's a clutter of model airplanes, dirigibles, and rocket ships hanging from the ceiling, and racks on the walls holding cyborg body parts. Workbenches on the side are heaped with equipment, but the center floor is open and uncluttered, the back half cushioned with a beige carpet.

I don't see Joby, but there's an open door in the far corner.

I go in first. Delphi and Jaynie follow. All is quiet until the door clicks shut. Then a low buzzing kicks on. It's a sound I've heard before and I react involuntarily, ducking and turning as a squad of three tiny black bee drones lofts from a workbench and zips toward us. Or toward me. The devices are replicas of the little security drones that attacked us and poisoned Flynn in the Reyvik Biosystems building. I step away from Jaynie and Delphi. The drones track my movement, assuming an inverted V formation as they target my face.

"Goddamn it, Joby!" I swear, ducking low.

The squad sweeps over my head.

"You said you like these better."

I glimpse Joby standing in the back doorway, but I don't dare take my eyes off the bee drones as they double back, targeting my face. There is only one part of my body that isn't threatened by the drones' glass needles, so I use it. Shifting my weight, I launch a high kick at the closest one. My robot toes connect, sending the bee hard into the ceiling. To my surprise, the other two drones follow it up, circling around it as it stabilizes in a bobbing hover above my head.

"That's solid engineering," Jaynie observes. "And I mean the legs *and* the poison drones. Now call them off."

"I didn't make the drones," Joby says irritably. "They're mass-produced, with really simplistic flocking behaviors."

As he's speaking, the three little drones form a line and withdraw, buzzing over his head to disappear into the back.

Quiet descends. Joby looks at me, his pale eyebrows knit in a scowl under a fringe of white-blond hair. He's only five three, but he's got an athlete's build, with health-club muscles. "Sorry about the hack," he says.

An apology is so unexpected I almost ask him to repeat it just to make sure I heard him right—but I catch myself, and try for something more diplomatic. "I didn't know you had that kind of access to my overlay."

He shrugs. "That's what we're here to talk about."

He comes into the room, looks around, spots a folding chair, and carries it to the center of the carpet. "Sit here."

"What are you going to do?"

"Just *sit*."

I sit because I want to get this over with.

Jaynie stands a few steps away, her arms crossed, a comforting presence. She doesn't trust Joby and she looks poised to intervene if she has to, while Delphi has gone into handler mode. She's turning in a slow circle, scanning the lab for hazards, while every few seconds her restless gaze shifts to Joby to assess threats from that direction.

From his pocket, Joby produces a small device—not something I've seen before. It's a white plastic cylinder, two inches long and half an inch in diameter. At one end is a black, flared soft-plastic cup. "Every overlay is manufactured with a back door that can be opened if you have the right keys—"

"Wait. What?" I've read the documentation on security vulnerabilities. "I never heard even a rumor of a standard back door."

Joby shrugs. "Not something the manufacturer wants to advertise."

"How did you find out?"

"That's a proprietary secret."

"Asshole."

"Dickhead. But anyway"—he holds up the device for me to see—"this is proof that Jasmine Harris knew."

Jasmine Harris? Oh, right: That was Shiloh's real name.

"This is called an optical trigger," Joby says, holding the device upright like a white-stemmed, black-petaled flower. "It was recovered from the building where you were held. Illegal for Exalt Communications to possess it of course, but then it was illegal for them to possess you, and they didn't give a shit about that."

"Yeah." I'm not sure if Joby knows that Shiloh's people gunned down half my squad just to make it easier to grab me, but it's not something I want to bring up. "Thanks for helping to get me out of there."

Joby scoffs. "Like I was going to stand by and let someone fuck with one of my projects?"

"Yeah, whatever." I reach for the optical trigger, not sure if he'll give it to me, but he does. I turn it over in my hands. There's a slider on the side of the cylinder and lenses at both ends, one of them nested at the bottom of the flared black plastic fitting, which I'm almost certain is an eyecup. I look up at Joby. "So what does this have to do with cracking an overlay?"

Making a circle of his thumb and forefinger, he peers out through the loop. "Place it against your eye."

"No fucking way." I hand the device back to him. "Put it on *your* eye. You've got an overlay."

He takes it back with a sly half smile that lets me know I'm not even close to escaping whatever he's got in mind for me. He holds the optical trigger up to his eye. A flash of light leaks out around the edge of the cup. He lowers the device and shrugs. "Nothing—because it's keyed for you." He hands it back. "Try it, you dick. It's not going to kill you."

It's like I'm twelve years old. He dares me to do it, so I do. I put the device up to my eye. A light flashes for half a second, just long enough for me to perceive an image of a long string of letters, numbers, symbols, and bar codes projected in white on black. I yank it away, but it's too late. All the latent icons are wiped from my overlay, replaced by a single icon that flowers in the center of my vision, expanding until I can't see around it. *What the fuck?*

Delphi moves in so close I can sense her gravity. "What's going on?"

"You've been unlocked," Joby says.

I feel Delphi's hand grip my shoulder. "Shelley, tell me what's happening."

"That thing, that optical trigger, it wiped my display and introduced a new icon, a red circle with three blunt arrows inside the ring, pointing outward. It's sitting right in the center of my field of view and I can't see through it."

"Don't get up," Joby advises. "You might fall down."

"Joby, what the *fuck* did that thing do to my overlay?"

"Triggered the feds' back door. It's there in case some FBI agent wants to take a look at what you've got stored in your head. Now take it easy, okay? I'm going to put the trigger on your eye again. Don't hit me."

"*Fuck,*" I whisper. Delphi's hand tightens on my shoulder. But I sit quietly while Joby gently presses the device against my left eye. The red arrows turn green. "What's going on?"

"Upload. Everything in your overlay is being mirrored on the stick."

"*Hey!*" I pull away from the trigger and the arrows go red again. "That's *my* data."

"I've seen it before and it's not that interesting."

"Get these fucking arrows out of my face."

"*Don't* hit me." He covers my eye again with the device. I see the white-on-black character string flash past and then the alien icon is gone. My own display returns.

"It would take a lot more time to mirror everything," Joby says as he takes the optical trigger away. "But you can see how it works."

"So the idea is, I stick that thing in Semak's face, and it'll extract a copy of everything he's got in his overlay?"

"Fuck no. It won't extract a thing."

"Nakagawa said it's keyed to you," Jaynie reminds me.

"Right." Joby twirls the optical trigger in his fingers. "Every overlay is manufactured with a unique access code that has to be scanned into the optical trigger before the connection can work."

Okay, I see where this is going. "And you don't have Semak's code?"

"I don't even have mine."

"Wait . . . then how come you have *my* access code? Where'd that come from?"

Joby cracks a cynical smile. "Your army personnel file. When your new overlay was installed after Black Cross, someone decided to record your supposedly secret access code. I don't know how they got it or why, but at least now we know it's the right code and the system works."

Jaynie doesn't have a lot of patience for bullshit. "So just to be clear," she says in an icy voice. "No record of Semak's access code was found in the intel retrieved during Black Phoenix?"

"No. I've run searches through all of it and found nothing. If Jasmine Harris had the code, she probably kept it in her overlay."

"*If* she had it," Delphi says thoughtfully. "Do you think that piece was missing?"

"Evidence-free guess?" Joby asks. "No. Harris had it, and she had it early in the game. It would be stupid to take the risks she did if she wasn't sure she could crack Semak's overlay. She hit the federal courthouse and when that didn't work, she gunned down the Apocalypse Squad—"

So he does know.

"—so she must have been sure."

"Then how do we get it?" Jaynie asks.

Joby turns the question around. "How did Harris get it?"

"Bribed somebody, I would guess."

"I think it's more likely it was an inside job, that she had someone in her conspiracy who worked for the manufacturer—someone with high-level access who could copy the code without being detected."

"We can reassess the recovered data," Delphi says, moving around the room in her restless manner. "There might be hints about who that was. . . ."

As they discuss it, I get up, fold the chair, and return it to the side of the room, silenced by an unsettling suspicion that all this was meant to be, that it was planned years ago.

I interrupt their discussion. "Joby." All three turn to look at me. "How high in the corporate hierarchy do you think you'd have to be to have access to those codes?"

He hands the optical trigger to Jaynie. "Why? You know someone? Got a favor you can call in?"

He's joking, but in fact I do. "My cousin Mark Graham is a cybernetics engineer. He's one of the company founders. Set me up with my first overlay a year before the product was officially released."

For maybe the first time ever, Joby looks impressed. "No shit?"

We trade stares, like neither one of us can believe the coincidence. Adrenaline sprints through my system as I weigh the odds that I would know one of the few people in the world who can get the code we need—and I ask myself: Is this scheme coming together like puzzle pieces because the Red set it up to work that way when I was still a naïve kid, nineteen years old? Surely that's impossible. We don't live in a clockwork universe. No entity could look forward in time more than five years and predict that we would be here, now.

"It's not really a coincidence," I decide.

"It's really fucking weird," Joby says.

"No, it's not that weird." I want it to be explainable, so I explain it. "It's straight-up cause and effect. The only reason I have an overlay is because my cousin helped design them. He got me interested and he got me in early—"

"Gave you what you needed to bring the cops down on you," Jaynie says, looking thoughtful.

"Hey, that wasn't his fault."

She cocks an eyebrow. "That illegal video you made with your overlay is the only reason you ended up in the army."

"Yeah, but that was my doing. Not his."

"Geez," Joby says. "She's *agreeing* with you. It's not some fucking one-in-a-billion coincidence that you know Graham. It's because you know Graham that you're here at all."

Delphi crosses her arms, looking impatient. "Shelley, can we just please set up a secure call with your cousin and get this done?"

I'm grateful to her for the change of subject, but this isn't going to be as easy as she hopes. "Mark won't do this over the phone. This isn't a little favor. The only way he'll consider it is if he can look me in the eye, log my overlay's serial number, and know that he's not being spoofed and that no one is holding a gun to my head. So we have to go see him."

Jaynie looks resigned. "Back to New York?"

"Back to DC. Mark lives in a Maryland suburb, just outside the capital."

• • • •

Airline seats are rationed and booked up for months, so we take a train. Rawlings isn't happy. He says we have too many enemies, we're too vulnerable. But during the two days it takes to reach the Capitol, no one tries to kill or kidnap us. It's kind of nice.

On the way we watch the second episode of *Against the Beast*. It's titled "Shadow Governments," and Koi Reisman has put it together to look like a political drama. The story centers on the FBI agents, introduced during the first episode, as they pursue a relentless investigation of the DC nuke. Undaunted by power plays and stonewalling from above, they persist—until a credible informant whispers of an old and long-buried scandal linking the president to Carl Vanda and, by implication, to the Coma Day cover-up.

It's an association that could bring down the administration.

As the senior agent contemplates her next best move, fresh intel arrives. Two more INDs have been tentatively located. Fearing a cover-up in her chain of command, the agent defies protocol and organizes her resources to back an illegal mission by a secret militia on its way to confirm the presence of the INDs aboard the *Non-Negotiable*.

The bloody, tragic gun battle that follows consumes less than forty seconds of the show. It's all blazing muzzle shots, heavy breathing, and first-person viewpoints—an anonymous militia to the end—but the nukes are recovered, with the promise that they will be removed to a secure facility and disassembled.

Koi Reisman said it wasn't my show anymore. She was right and I'm glad for it, but that doesn't mean my story is over.

• • • •

My cousin Mark picks us up at the station in an electric sedan with tinted windows. He's twelve years older than me and a few pounds heavier, with a neatly trimmed beard and dark brown hair already beginning to show a little gray. As I slide into the passenger seat beside him, he gives me a nervous smile.

I introduce him to Jaynie and Delphi.

"Let's not talk until we get to the house," he says.

He's had a shielded, soundproof room built into his basement to use when he's working at home. There are monitors on the walls, a stand-up desk, a couple of sofas, and pillows on the carpeted floor. Mark closes the door, cutting off the faint hum of appliances running upstairs. He turns to me. "You are seriously scaring the fuck out of me, Jimmy."

"We need this, Mark. I wouldn't ask if it wasn't critical."

"I saw 'Shadow Governments.' It looks like fiction, but the rumor mill is buzzing. Chatter says the president is stitching his golden parachute. I don't know if you meant to bring down the administration when you pulled off First Light, but it looks like you might do it."

"The president," I say noncommittally, "is a complicated man."

"So are you, cousin. That battle at the end of the show? I had a feeling I was seeing part of it through your eyes."

"Good guess," Jaynie says. She takes off her jacket to show him the livid, fresh scar from her bullet wound. She's still wearing a brace on her arm.

"Holy shit," he whispers.

She tells him, "There's another mission in the planning stages, with a similar goal."

I sketch out the highlights. Mark, of course, has his

own overlay and while he's too polite to say so, I know he's using emotional analysis to measure our truthfulness and our sincerity.

Delphi sums things up. "If we can access Eduard Semak's overlay, we'll know the location of his rogue nukes, and we will turn that information over to an agency that can go after them."

Mark looks at me with real worry. "Why is it you, Jimmy? You've done your part. You've done enough. Someone else should go."

Jaynie answers for me. "It's not our decision."

Mark studies her with a thoughtful expression, as if FaceValue is giving him mixed data, but then he shrugs. "Okay. I understand you can't tell me everything." He pulls a hand-size tablet out of his pocket. "You've got the optical trigger?"

Jaynie hands it to him.

He shows us how to use the slider switch to wipe the memory. Then he manipulates the tablet until it displays a long string of letters and numbers and symbols. "My company has reevaluated security, in light of the breach you uncovered, Jimmy."

"So you know who was working with Jasmine Harris?" I ask him.

"Let's just say I know how Harris got the code." He taps the rim of the tablet. "We've closed the loophole that let it happen. I need you to understand that I will not be able to do this again."

"Mark, you know I wouldn't ask for it this time, except—"

"I know." He scans the string with the optical trigger, which beeps in acknowledgment. Then he hands the device back to Jaynie. "That'll let you do what you need to do."

"Mark . . ." I hesitate. I don't want to compromise him,

but there's another question he might be able to help me with. "Do you know of any other LCS soldiers who use an overlay?"

Right away, he's suspicious. "No, but we've sold close to two hundred thousand systems. So I guess it's possible. Why?"

"There are supposed to be others like me." I asked Jones to look into it—more than once—but I got nothing back. "I want to know if it's true. I want to know who they are."

It's an awkward moment as his gaze darts away. When he looks at me again, it's with narrowed eyes. "I'm not going to look that up for you."

"Mark—"

"Leave it, Shelley," Jaynie warns. "We got what we need to support the mission. Pushing for anything else is a security risk and it undermines our integrity."

All true. But I don't want to let it go. Mark is my last, best resource. He has direct access to the names of everyone who has ever been fitted with an overlay. "Look, it's not like I'm asking for more codes. I don't want to hurt anyone. I just need to know if . . ."

I hesitate, wondering why this is so important to me.

Jaynie wants to know the same thing. "If what, Shelley? Why does it matter?"

I just want to know I'm not the only soldier on call in the Red's network. If there are others, soldiers who've held on to their anonymity, I want to believe they have my back, that they'll be in a position to step in and salvage things when I fuck up.

"I'm just asking for names. Nothing else. I just want to know if other soldiers are wired with overlays—and if they're still alive."

Mark crosses his arms. Puts on a stubborn expression. "If they do exist, if they're still alive, I'm not going to compromise their safety or the future of my company by compiling that information. Sorry, Jimmy. But I've got integrity too."

We're not due back at the train station until after midnight, so we order pizza and then sit in the living room and talk. Mark tells me that my dad's doing okay, he's got a new apartment, and he's thinking of getting into city politics, which amazes me. He's always been a private man, but he's angry now, and determined to take back his world.

We've moved on to a discussion of the guilty verdict in the Sheridan trial when a soft, tonal alarm goes off. I look at Mark, who's frowning at something on his overlay. "Black SUV stopped at the curb," he announces. "Right in front of the house. Two women, one man, exiting. Dressed in dark suits, wearing farsights, with handguns under their coats."

"Still holstered, right?" I ask him.

"So far. Okay, two are staying by the car. Just one of the women is coming to the front door—that's a good sign. She identifies with ninety-five percent probability as Secret Service. So does the other woman. The guy must be a rookie. I've got him at only forty-nine percent."

"Nice security system," Delphi says.

"Thanks."

I do not want to be arrested again, but I also don't want to get Mark in trouble. "I'll answer it." He objects politely. I ignore him. Signaling Delphi to stay put, I go to the door. Jaynie comes with me.

Past the curtain, I see the porch light come on. Jaynie stands on the side so she'll be out of sight as I open the door—which I do slowly to avoid startling the agent.

She nods when she sees me, and for a few seconds we study each other, her translucent farsights confirming my identity while my overlay seeks for hers. She looks to be in her forties, maybe five nine, with a neat black perm and strong Latina features—but my encyclopedia fails to come up with a name.

"Lieutenant Shelley," she says, displaying her badge. "May I come in?"

I turn to look at Mark for permission. He shrugs. If he has anything to hide, it's well hidden. So I open the door wider and let her in.

As she enters, she scans the room with her farsights. Her gaze pauses first on Jaynie, who is looking intimidating dressed in a tight black athletic shirt, black skullcap, and farsights. The agent smiles. "Sergeant Vasquez."

"Ma'am."

Her gaze lingers next on Delphi. No doubt she successfully identifies my former handler Karin Larsen, but she has the manners not to say so. Instead she turns to me with an earnest look. "Lieutenant—"

"I'm not an officer anymore, ma'am."

"Of course. My apologies. Mr. Shelley—and Ms. Vasquez—a ceremony of some importance will take place tomorrow at noon, at the White House. The two of you were not expected to be available, but since you are here—"

"We're leaving tonight," Jaynie interrupts.

"In that case, the president requests you delay your departure."

The president requests it?

"What kind of ceremony is it?" I ask.

"I'm not at liberty to say, but be assured it is of crucial importance to the future of the country. A car will pick you up tomorrow morning at oh eight hundred. You will be informed of the nature of the ceremony when you reach the White House. Nothing will be required of you except your appearance."

I wonder if it's a trick, but if so, why go through a charade? They could arrest us now if they wanted to.

I look at Delphi for her opinion. It's easy to see from her expression she doesn't like the idea. "You don't have a suit," she points out. "Neither does Vasquez."

The agent frowns, hesitates. Then her farsights flicker and she relaxes again. "Formal attire will be provided."

I am not the president's favorite war hero, but that doesn't mean Jaynie and I can't be useful to him, our presence a stamp of approval on whatever scheme he's about to announce. I don't want to go. I don't want to be used as propaganda in a regime as corrupt as this one, but if Kendrick were here he would tell me to shut the fuck up and honor the request of my commander in chief.

"You okay with it, Jaynie?"

She crosses her arms. "It's an invite from the *president*. Say no to that, and next time he might not ask nicely."

I think she's wrong. I don't think there will be a next time; I don't think there can be. The video of Carl Vanda's interrogation hasn't gone public yet, but that won't last.

"So you're coming?" the agent concludes drily, one arched eyebrow communicating her opinion. "Very good." She opens the door. "Please do not speak of this to anyone who might leak it to the media."

After the black SUV pulls away, Mark inspects the walkway and the front porch for bugs.

I help Delphi reschedule our train tickets.

By ten hundred the next morning, Jaynie and I are back in DC. I'm wearing a perfectly tailored gray suit; she's in a dusky blue, flowing jacket and loose slacks that somehow make her skullcap look like an intentional part of the outfit and not just the emotional prosthetic that it is.

We take seats in a briefing room with nineteen other puzzled citizens. My overlay identifies most of them as respected and retired politicians and military officers. Clearly, the president is determined to endow this ceremony with all the borrowed legitimacy he can.

When the chief of staff comes in, the low murmur of conversation falls off into silence. She takes the podium— a fair-skinned woman, around forty years old, mostly Caucasian with her African ancestry showing only around her full lips, in her wide eyes, and in her heavy black hair.

"Thank you all for coming on such short notice. Your presence here today will help ensure a smooth transition, and encourage the people of this country to be confident in the president's decision. I am authorized to announce to you that with the president's encouragement, Vice President Thompson has chosen to resign from elected office effective now, at ten hundred, in deference to a suite of charges that will soon be filed against him—charges that have resulted from the ongoing and widespread investigation into the systemic corruption and influence peddling that allowed the treason of Coma Day." Her gaze settles on me and Jaynie. "We have here with us today former lieutenant James Shelley and former sergeant Jayne Vasquez, whose patriotism ignited the search for truth and justice that has led to Mr. Thompson's resignation. Lieutenant Shelley, Sergeant Vasquez, I'm sure I speak for all of us here when I say, thank you both for your service."

She gives us a tight-lipped smile, and then her gaze rises to take in the full audience. "Ladies and gentlemen, the nominee for vice president of the United States is judge and former colonel Susan Monteiro."

I turn to meet Jaynie's incredulous expression. Judge Monteiro, the woman who, less than two months ago, was prepared to sentence us both to life in prison, will be second-in-command of the United States. Jaynie shakes her head, I grin, and we both rise to join in the applause and exclamations of approval that greet Susan Monteiro as she walks in and takes over the podium.

Monteiro is dressed in civilian attire, a formal jacket and skirt, but otherwise she looks much the same as she did in the courtroom, her no-nonsense expression reassuring in troubled times.

Ahead of the public presentation, she speaks to Jaynie and me. We sit in upholstered chairs within the shelter of a shielded alcove while two Secret Service agents stand watch a few steps away.

"Ms. Vasquez, Mr. Shelley." Monteiro eyes us each in turn. "You're here today at my personal request. The president has alluded to some of your recent activities during the discussion of my nomination. I'm assured such activities are necessary in the current circumstances and that you have continued to serve your country—but please do not misconstrue your presence here as an unlimited approval. The United States of America was founded on lawful juris-diction, and I intend to see we return to that."

"I hope so, ma'am." And I mean it.

But this is Washington, DC. No gift is given or privi-lege granted without the expectation of return. Monteiro could not have secured her appointment without agreeing to certain favors.

She props an elbow on the arm of her chair, rests her chin on her hand, and treats us to a self-mocking smile. "The road back is crooked," she concedes. "As you know, we sometimes trade integrity for the stability of the country. Justice is never perfect."

"But the investigation isn't finished," Jaynie says.

"It *is* ongoing," Monteiro agrees.

And eventually it will reach the president. Maybe it already has.

I have to give him credit for the way he's preparing a legal, orderly, and responsible succession. He's used the threat of pending charges to clear the office of the vice president, and now he'll replace the disgraced VP with a nominee known and admired across the country. If the process plays out to the end, Monteiro will become only the second unelected president in the history of the country—and once in office, she'll be free to pardon those who put her there.

"There won't be any more trials, will there?" I ask her.

"The country's been through enough, Mr. Shelley. It's time to heal. To make the country stronger than it was before. Coma Day showed our vulnerability and we don't want to repeat the mistakes of the past, so we're implementing changes in our essential systems. Have you heard of the EXALT communications network?"

The mention of EXALT startles me, but Jaynie leans in, providing cover: "Yes, ma'am. EXALT is a distributed system. Supposed to be more rugged than the communications grid it replaces, without the vulnerable choke points. Harder to take down. Immune to EMP."

Monteiro nods her approval. "Exactly. This is a defense issue—and it exemplifies the creativity we need to ensure there will not be another Coma Day."

Shiloh believed EXALT existed to house the Red. I wonder if Monteiro has been briefed on that. I ask her: "What about the Red, ma'am?"

She sighs and leans back, looking disappointed with my question. "I'm familiar with soldiers in the field. I know it's common to develop your own mythologies. But you can feel assured our cybersecurity is constantly evolving."

So government policy is unchanged since Major Perkins

debriefed us after the pardon, assuring us that the Red was just a popular mythology. I don't try to dissuade Monteiro. In a sense it doesn't matter what she or anyone else believes, because the Red's existence is not dependent on belief. It's there, whether we choose to see it or not.

She stands up. Jaynie and I rise with her, and we shake hands.

"Best of luck to you both."

"And to you, ma'am," Jaynie says. "This is one of the president's decisions that I can agree with."

Monteiro laughs. "You might as well. You two made me famous. You're the reason I'm here."

Interviews follow the ceremony, and I do what I can to assist the nomination, assuring any mediot who asks that I have full confidence in Susan Monteiro, but I don't answer questions on anything else. "This is her day."

As soon as we can get away with it, we slip out and change back into our own clothes. A car takes us to the train station, where Delphi meets us.

We've got what we need to go after Semak. This will be our last mission, I know it for sure this time, because Vice President Monteiro is going to put a stop to operations like ours—and that's a good thing. That's what we want, the rule of real law, by the people, for the people—but we're not there yet.

The days pass too quickly as we roll into early summer on the overheated high plains of Wyoming. The heat in Washington is worse. For the first time in a decade, Congress acts decisively, swiftly approving Susan Monteiro's nomination, and she is sworn in as vice president. Across the country, people wait for the president to resign, shielded by a full pardon to be issued by his appointed successor—but these are earthly considerations and no part of my world anymore.

I say good-bye to Delphi at 0430 outside the hangar at Cryptic Arrow's private airfield. I don't make any promises. Neither does she. Her eyes are dry as she kisses me one more time, and then she says, "Try to come back."

I nod. I'll do what I can.

I've studied every stage of the mission, I've watched videos of the spaceplane launch and the docking sequence, I've spent time with VR simulations—but I'm still ambushed by awe at the sight of my ride, poised on the launchpad.

I get my first look at it as we approach the spaceport thirty miles outside of San Antonio, where Sidereal Transit Systems keeps its launch complex. Ulyana Kurnakova is driving. Good thing, because once I spy the rocket standing coupled to its gantry, I can't take my gaze from it. The closer we get, the bigger it grows.

"Twenty million dollars to low Earth orbit," Kurnakova says in a matter-of-fact voice. "That's a fraction of what it cost just a few years ago."

The gate guard gives me a cursory look-over before waving us through.

Over the past year, flights to low Earth orbit have become routine, financed by dragons who have already conquered the world and are moving on to other things.

As the road swings close to the launchpad, Kurnakova pulls over. We both get out, to stand for a minute beside the fence, gazing at the fantastical machine. The rocket itself has two stages, and it towers nearly two hundred feet. At its top, in place of the classic cone-shaped capsule, is Stellar

Systems' little spaceplane, *Lotus*, perched tail-down, its flat-
tened fuselage only a little wider than the rocket's diameter
and adding only thirty-five feet to its height. With its jaunty
upswept wings, snub nose, white surface, and heat-resistant
black belly, *Lotus* looks like a child's toy fixed to the end of
a monster New Year's firework.

I turn to Kurnakova. "You ever had any paying customers
back out when they reach this point?"

She looks at me through farsights tinted black. "Not yet.
You going to be the first?"

"Am I a paying customer?"

"Of course you are. Shiloh bought your seat."

A bribe, to ensure I appear in the logs as a legitimate
technician. No one will need to ask questions if I have the
proper credentials. At least, that's the theory.

"I will tell you a dirty little secret," Kurnakova says. "Rules
do not mean much to people who can pay twenty million
dollars for a grocery delivery. The fastest way to lose your
job at STS is to say no when one of our customers asks for
a little favor."

"This isn't a little favor."

"The cost of your ticket was no little thing either. Don't
worry. We will be okay."

The staff at STS may be used to operating outside the
boundaries of standard procedure, but as we move through
check-in, I get the impression Kurnakova is pushing the
envelope with the little favor involved in this launch.

We interact with only two personnel. Both are nervous.
Neither will meet my gaze, looking to Kurnakova for direction. I follow their lead and say nothing, just do as I'm
told. If we all pretend this isn't happening, nothing bad will
come of it, right?

Before long, Kurnakova and I are riding the elevator to the top of the gantry, both of us wearing blue coveralls and flexible, fire-retardant booties on our feet. Underneath my coverall, I've got an armored vest with the optical trigger stashed in an inside pocket. I've also got a sealed packet containing a sedative mask. We tested the mask on Nolan and it dropped him in nine seconds.

Lotus is mounted for a vertical takeoff, so we enter through a hatch behind and just below the two forward seats, where the pilot and technician sit. Canisters of cargo are locked down in the back, each sized to fit through the meter-wide hatch. Two jump seats for emergency evacuations have been folded up and locked against the walls.

Kurnakova waves me in first. I pause in the hatch, long enough to slip off the booties. It's a violation of flight rules not to wear them, but those rules weren't written for a cyborg with robot feet. The booties offer fire protection in case of accident, but I don't need that, and wearing any kind of foot covering limits my options. All I can do with shoes on is stand or walk—and I'll be doing neither where we're going—while the feet are capable of so much more.

With my feet free, I climb to the shotgun seat, lie back, and strap in—just like I did weeks ago when I was training in the mock-up Shiloh had created for me. It feels awkward, looking up through the segmented windows at a bright blue sky. Kurnakova pops up beside me, checks my straps, and nods her approval. Then she settles into the pilot's seat.

I'm recording everything, of course.

Kurnakova talks to her handler—a blandly friendly male voice representing ground control. Together they run through the prelaunch checks, while I set up my own communications using the same satellite-relay system we had aboard the *Non-Negotiable*. Opening a link through my overlay, I say, "Hey Delphi, you there?"

"Gotcha, Shelley," she answers in her cool handler's voice. And then, after assessing the data from my skullnet, "You're a little wound up."

"I just want this to happen." I'm riding an electric excitement that I didn't think I could feel anymore. It's like I'm a kid again, thrilled just to be here, poised to do what has always seemed impossible, head into space, low Earth orbit, where fewer than two thousand people have been in all the history of the world. Eduard Semak is so far away I can't worry about him yet, and the postmission fallout is too remote to contemplate. My only fear right now is that a supervisor or some government official will step up and call off the flight—but that doesn't happen. The countdown continues to zero without interference. The main stage of the rocket ignites—and Delphi breaks her handler's reserve to whisper parting words in my ears: "I love you."

No one can stop us now.

We are enfolded in a trembling roar as gravity gives way and we rise slowly into the blue.

Blue deepens and turns to black. Stars come out.

The second-stage rocket fires and we are in orbit, but we are still hours away from rendezvous with Eduard Semak's hermitage in the sky. Kurnakova talks with ground control, but there is nothing for me to do as we circle the world except to admire the overwhelming beauty of this place that we have threatened and corrupted with our wars and our poisons. *Lotus* passes from daylight into a night lit by electric lights that outline the continents and surround the oceans, and in time it is day again, and we are bathed in the bright-blue reflected glow of the Pacific, and I can't stop looking at it all, taking it all in. Astronomers speak of finding Earthlike worlds around other stars, but they are speaking in hyperbole, in meaningless generalities. There is only one Earthlike world. There will only ever be one and it is fragile, and if it takes the cold manipulations of a fathomless AI to bring balance and to protect this precious place from the madness of those who would set it on fire, so be it. I, for one, am proud to serve as a soldier in that war.

"Ready?" Kurnakova asks after she's completed the delicate docking process, locking the hatch of *Lotus* to that of the Semak Hermitage. Semak has not responded to radio hails, but Kurnakova shrugs it off. "He has been here over a year, since long before Coma Day. This is his fourth maintenance visit. He can't live without us, but he does not want us here."

Smart man.

I'm wearing a patch to suppress inner-ear issues, so both my stomach and my brain are responding well to free fall. It's an uncanny sensation to be unmoored from gravity. At first I clutch at the seats and at handholds, but very quickly I give in and let myself believe in the magic act of weightless motion. I practice moving around in the space available within *Lotus*. After a few minutes it starts to feel natural, as if I've dreamed this a hundred times or lived this way in another life.

"I'm ready," I tell Kurnakova and Delphi both. I make my way to the hatch, check the status, and then open it as I've been taught.

It's dark and cold on the other side. Feels near sixty degrees to me, but the chill hasn't wiped out a faint scent of human presence. It's not a bad smell—the filtration system is too evolved for that—it's just a slight, musky vapor marking this place as home to someone, though to my surprise I don't see Eduard Semak.

Just past the hatch is a staging area, lit by a dim glow spilling from *Lotus*. Beyond that is the cupola, a ring of hemispherical windows, each half a meter across and deep enough that if I drifted up into one, I could see the habitat's outer shell and all that lies beyond. From where I am, still within the hatch, I can already see the Earth in all its glittering nightside glory.

It's night within the habitat too. The only lights are pale green dots, six meters away at the other end of the main chamber, placed around a closed interior hatch. Behind that door is a one-time-use emergency evacuation capsule. According to Kurnakova, Semak uses the capsule as a bedroom. I assume he is in there now. There's nowhere else he could be. But why is he hiding? He wasn't supposed to know we're the enemy.

The satellite-relay system I set up brings me Delphi's voice: "Clear to advance."

I move out into the chamber.

The setup here looks different from the mock-up I trained in. It feels smaller, more cramped, an effect I blame on a lining of thick, fuzzy fabric, light brown in color, that covers the traditional white plastic walls. The equipment, access doors, ready lights, and storage containers I expect to see are hidden behind it. Neatly hand drawn all over the fabric, as if with a black marker pen, are chessboards, with cloth chess pieces in play. Alongside each game is a plastic label, handwritten in Cyrillic. My encyclopedia provides a hovering translation as I scan the first few.

"They're names," Delphi says in surprise.

Names from all over the world—does that mean each game represents a different opponent? I don't ask my question aloud though, because I'm supposed to be a technician, intent on my job.

"It's weird that he doesn't play electronic chess," Delphi muses.

Everywhere on the chessboards and between them are bits of trash—crumbs, strands of white hair, scraps of plastic—stuck to the fabric lining. I touch it and it feels sticky.

Not everything is covered by the fabric. Though the light panels are dark, cutouts allow them to show through. There are also four glittering points set around the chamber. Draw a line through them and it would mark out a spiral. As I glide past the first of these, it turns a glassy eye in my direction, causing shards of reflected light to slide across its surface: a camera button on a motorized mount.

Delphi says, "He's watching you."

I'm wondering if the Red is looking too—but it doesn't matter. The Red is here anyway, looking through me.

Still, the knowledge that I'm being watched makes my first task feel more critical: I am to disable the habitat's link to the Cloud, on the pretext that I am replacing a critical communications component. For now, I ignore Semak's presence behind the closed hatch as Delphi helps me hunt for the bin holding the hardware. In the mock-up, the bin's location was obvious, but here it's hidden behind the brown fabric. I guesstimate the location—a few feet beyond the ring of windows—and examine the liner.

"Those look like flaps in the liner," Delphi says. "Try pulling one." I do it, disturbing a chess game attributed to Midori. The flap opens with the ripping sound of Velcro, revealing lockers underneath. "Okay, I know where you are now. Move up, in the direction of your head. Farther. There. Try that one."

I pull the flap she's indicated, bending back a chess

game labeled "Nasir." The bin I'm looking for is revealed underneath.

"Have you got it?" Kurnakova asks anxiously. I look over my shoulder to see her adrift in the hatch, backlit by the spaceplane's instrument board, a halo of fractured light filtered through her swaying dark red hair.

"Yeah, I've got it." I open the bin.

"Looks good," Delphi says.

I share the relief in her voice: The sealed components inside look exactly like those I saw in the mock-up. A glance back at the hatch shows me that Kurnakova is following our script. She has retreated from view, returning to *Lotus*'s console. I reach into the bin as I did so many times in the simulated habitat, grasp the handle of the component labeled "CA-147"—

"Damn it!" Kurnakova swears.

I freeze, startled. She is back in the hatch.

"Why did you unplug the module ahead of schedule? We are not ready! New components still to unpack, and communications already down!" These are the correct words, the words we rehearsed, words that confirm I've successfully switched off the habitat's link to the Cloud—except I haven't.

"I didn't pull the unit yet."

"Wait . . . you found it not working?"

I tug gently on the component. It slips loose without resistance. "Yes, it was already disconnected."

We both glance toward the interior door with its encircling lei of faint green dots.

With artificial confidence Kurnakova says, "That explains why Mr. Semak could not answer my hail!"

Delphi whispers in my ears, "Something's up, Shelley. Proceed with extreme caution."

"Could it have been disconnected by accident?" I wonder aloud.

Maybe Semak wanted more isolation than he'd already purchased. Maybe he was getting too many robo-calls. Maybe his kids were waking him up at all hours to check if he'd passed away yet, freeing them to inherit his fortune.

"I don't think so," Delphi says. "Something else is going on."

Kurnakova is even more anxious. "*Now*, Shelley," she whispers. "You must move now."

Yes. With communications down, the next step is to secure Eduard Semak.

I play my role, for what little it's worth. "I think we need to talk to Mr. Semak."

I tap the wall liner with my robot foot, not too hard, sending myself gliding through the chamber. All around me are chess games. A hundred of them. Two hundred? Maybe Eduard pulled the communications module because he needed time to consider his next move.

Each camera eye shifts its gaze to watch me pass.

I reach the hatch to the evacuation capsule. It's closed, but not locked. No way to know what's on the other side until I open it. I imagine a fléchette gun, like the kind Carl Vanda used. Why didn't I think to bring one of Joby's bugs? I could send it into the room ahead of me to reconnoiter.

"Mr. Semak," I say, just in case we're reading this situation all wrong. "We need to talk to you." There is no response. I have no way to know if he's listening.

"I'm going to open it," I tell Delphi. What choice do I have?

"It's going to be a double hatch," she reminds me. "He probably has the second door closed as well."

She's right. When I open the hatch door, another is revealed behind it. "Mr. Semak! If you can hear me, please come to the door."

If I had my HITR this would not be a problem. I could use the muzzle camera to look beyond the door. This gives me an idea.

"Kurnakova!"

"*Da?*"

I am playing the role of a technician with all the props. "There's a diagnostic camera in the tool kit. Can you grab it?"

"Yes, yes. Turn around. I will glide it to you." I turn to see a rod tumbling in my direction, no thicker than my little finger, with a flared cup at one end, much like the optical trigger. At the other end is the flashing lens of a camera button.

I catch it, give it a quick look-over. The rod bends easily, so I put a right angle in it. Then I unlatch the second door and open it half an inch. Right away I hear Semak talking, talking, talking, a stream of Russian spoken in a panicked old-man's voice which my overlay helpfully translates, whispering its interpretation in my ears: *"They are here for me. They have come! They have come for me!"*

I switch on the camera, slip it through the gap, peer at the image projected in the eyecup, and swear. *"Shit!"*

Pitching the camera away, I shove the door wide.

Semak has no weapon. He's just a pale, undernourished, frightened old man with stringy white hair and a stringy white beard, his age-ravaged face swollen from his long time in zero gravity. He's dressed in shapeless navy-blue flannel pants and a pullover shirt with side flaps velcroed to the pants to keep it from drifting in zero gee. And as Shiloh predicted, his hypochondria is on display: He's wearing a face mask of dull-green, engineered biotissue that covers his nose and mouth. The mask is linked by a flexible tube to a small oxygen canister tucked into the front pocket of his pullover so he doesn't have to breathe my exhalations, which is fine. Not an issue. The mask doesn't even inhibit his speech.

The problem for me is that he's talking on a radio. Not an instrument that's part of the habitat's communications system. This is something else, something older, with dials not digital touch screens, and a handheld mic. The radio is sitting inside an open bin just above the headrests of two reentry couches that crowd the capsule's limited space. It looks wholly out of place there, an object from the wrong century. Despite its age, it works. I know this because a woman is answering him. Her voice is low and I think she must be well into middle age. She speaks with a contemptuous sarcasm plain to hear even in the translated voice: *"They haven't come for you, Papa."*

I launch myself at Semak. He drops the mic and twists away, but there's nowhere to go. I grab him, wrap my arms around him as I collide with the wall. We bounce together back across the tiny capsule. I hit my head. I need to arrest my momentum, but I don't have a free hand. So I use my feet. The robot joints of my right foot curl around a grip, while I use my left foot to grab the armrest of a reentry couch. For a few seconds I sway and bob. Then I'm under control.

Against my arms and chest I feel the creaking fragility of Semak's ancient joints, padded by only a thin cushion of flesh. Worried I'll break his ribs, I ease my grip. He gasps for air behind his face mask while the woman keeps talking, her translated voice speaking in my ears: *"It is maintenance, Papa. You knew. You complained of it all week!"*

Semak squirms, but he's been a year in zero gravity and he has no real strength left. I decide I can hold him in one arm, freeing a hand to strip off his face mask.

"Fine then," the woman says as I get the sedative mask out of my pocket. *"Don't answer me."* I tear open the packet with my teeth, then press the mask against Semak's nose and mouth. Instead of supplying him with oxygen, it will add a sedative to every breath he draws through it. *"I don't have time to talk to you anyway. I have to go out."*

Semak is a fighter and doesn't yield right away. I think he's holding his breath, but it's just a matter of time. He wriggles, makes a short gasp, and as Kurnakova looks in, he goes limp in my arms. I fit the strap of the mask behind his head to ensure he will stay under, and then I let him go.

Kurnakova scowls at the radio. "What the fuck is that?"

Eduard Semak's isolation is not just physical. The old-fashioned radio, the disconnected communications system, the manually administered chessboards: All point to a fear of electronic invasion. Did he imagine himself to be the next dragon targeted by the Red? He probably didn't think that the offensive, when it came, would be in the form of a physical assault.

I leave the radio on. With no one to use it, it should be harmless—and I'm concerned an alert might go out if I start shutting down equipment. Our priority is to proceed to the next stage of the mission.

I get out the optical trigger, preloaded with the access code that will open Eduard Semak's overlay. If it doesn't work, our mission fails and a cache of rogue nukes will continue to be a threat to the world.

It *will* work. It has to.

For every action there is an equal and opposite reaction. With no help from gravity, Semak's inert body floats away when I try to press the optical trigger to his eye.

"Strap him into the seat!" Kurnakova says impatiently, moving in to help.

"No, it's faster if I just hold him."

Again, I use my feet to brace myself, pulling Semak's head against my chest. I hold him there with one hand, using two of my fingers to open his eye. With my other hand, I press the trigger in place. There's a flash of light. A few seconds later Delphi confirms, "It's working. Download in progress."

So far, so good.

Kurnakova looks tense behind her tinted farsights. Her face is flushed. "How long to completion?"

"Unknown," Delphi says.

The trigger doesn't give us any options. It takes a snapshot of everything stored in the overlay, the trash as well as the gold.

"Let it be done quickly," Kurnakova whispers as if it's a prayer. Then she draws a sharp breath, recapturing a stern expression. "I will unload the cargo. We cannot appear innocent if we return with a full hold."

As the download continues, I watch her work. With brisk efficiency, she hauls full canisters out of *Lotus*, swapping them for empty ones stored in racks behind the fabric wall.

Delphi speaks on gen-com. "It's done. We've got it all."

I switch off the trigger and put it away, releasing Semak's unconscious body to float in the limited free space of the capsule.

The mission plan calls for Delphi to copy the download to the Jones intelligence team, but she delays that transfer while she expands the files and sets an AI searching through them. If she can find the financials, she'll cut those files out and send the amended package to Jones.

"It's all unencrypted data," she says in wonder. "He must have had security so tight he didn't think anyone could get inside."

"He probably never linked directly to the Cloud." Hiding instead in his own electronic fortress.

"Things are going well," she says softly.

So she's found the financial data. Whether she and Jaynie can do anything with it is another question. Right now, what I really want to know about is the nukes. "What about the weapons cache? Is the location data there?"

"There's a tangle of files. I can't tell what's—" She interrupts herself. "Hold on. Something went wrong. I need to try resending to Jones."

So she's pulled what she needs.

"The nukes, Delphi. I want to confirm we have the evidence we need to bring Semak in."

"Yes. Yes, the data's here. Goes back years. Looks like more than one cache. That's not good. The weapons are scattered. No telling if this is up to date, but it's enough to—

"Oh my God."

The shock in her voice sets my heart racing. "What? Delphi, what is it?"

"One of the listed weapons caches is the Semak Hermitage. Is that possible?"

Kurnakova looms in the doorway. Her knuckles are white where she grips the frame of the hatch. "It is possible," she says. "And it's true. I flew the device here myself and I will fly it back today if Eduard doesn't kill us and half the world first." She pushes away from the hatch, entering the capsule, and then she pushes Semak's drifting body aside, clearing the way to a closet door, one that faces the reentry couches.

She slides the door open.

There is nothing terrifying inside: just a small aluminum briefcase and a metal cylinder, dull silver in color, roughly a foot in diameter and two and a half feet long. The cylinder is locked in place by two riveted steel straps. Wires connect it to the briefcase.

When we met in San Antonio, I wanted to understand her motivation for this mission. The words she spoke then come back to me:

He is a man deserving of hate. A man who amuses himself by corrupting all those around him.

Bitterly, she says, "I was a fool."

• • • •

Her explanation is rushed, almost breathless: "He got me this job. He owned me. When he asked me to transport his possessions, I did it, no questions. The crate was huge and heavy. He let me believe it was gold. Solid gold." She shakes her head at the absurdity of it. "Who would want gold in orbit? Who? Only a senile, insecure old man. I believed his act. I *did*." She shakes her head, her short hair a dark, drifting frame for her pale face.

"Shelley," Delphi says with artificial calm. "Jones wants you to move in closer. They need a better image."

Despite the chill, sweat breaks out across my skin. I flash back to Black Cross and the nuke that detonated low in the atmosphere. That weapon was ten miles away and it almost killed me.

"Don't touch it," Kurnakova warns. "The old troll probably has the warhead rigged to go off if it's disturbed."

Fuck.

Although, if it happens, I will never know.

I press my sleeve against my face to soak up the sweat. Then I grab the rim of the closet and rotate, bringing my eyes closer to capture a more detailed image. There is a serial number on the metal casing. "Stand by," Delphi says.

Instead, I back away, putting a little breathing room between me and the nuke. Then I turn to Kurnakova. "Why the *fuck* didn't you say something before?"

"Could I be sure you would still take the mission? Now we are here. There is no choice. You are who you are—and you will do what must be done."

She's right, of course. There's a program running inside my head, busily defining a new objective, updating the script I will follow.

Delphi comes back on gen-com, breathless. "It's confirmed,

Shelley. Jones says the serial number identifies the unit as the nuclear component of a disassembled B61 gravity bomb that disappeared from a NATO weapons storage facility in Belgium in 2010—although the weapon is reported as subsequently recovered."

The usual lies to cover up security failures.

"You know what is a dead man's switch?" Kurnakova asks.

More sweat leaps from my pores. "Yes."

She points to her eye. "He has the warhead rigged so that detonation is always a moment away, but continuously delayed by a program in his overlay. If the signal from his overlay fails because he is taken away from the hermitage or because he is dead—"

"The bomb will go off," I finish for her.

Her voice is soft, but there's a grim weight behind each word. "Naturally I have not tested his claims, but I have no reason not to believe him. It's a mistake to think of him as just a criminal. He is more than that. He is a sort of tinkering genius. A *paranoid* genius. Egotistical. Cruel. If they ever came for him, he said, they would get nothing."

"They?"

"Whoever. He has many enemies, some real, some imagined."

"He told you all this?"

"Yes. He flirted with me when I delivered the cargo. He played the role of a sweet old man. But on my next visit he showed me what he had done . . . what *I* had done. He wanted someone to know. He wanted to boast about it."

Semak floats up against her. She looks at him in distaste. "Delphi?" she asks. "Have you found this program that controls the bomb?"

"Waiting on Jones. Stand by."

"*Do not wake up yet,*" she whispers into Semak's ear. She looks at me again. "He told me because he thought I would say nothing. I had taken a large amount of money in payment for delivering his 'gold,' so I was complicit in his crime. He also thought he would live forever." She turns to him again. *"But I think you have very little time."*

The weapon appears innocuous. It is quiet. Lifeless. No glowing lights, no status indicator, no digital countdown to apocalypse. No way to know if Kurnakova's story is true—but FaceValue tells me she believes it.

"This is why I needed Shiloh," she says. "To hack the troll's overlay and neutralize this little weapon of his that I helped him to create."

Semak starts to drift away. She pinches his shirt, holding him close. He looks pathetic, pitiful—just a withered old man. But that's illusion.

The illusion fades as the old dragon starts to twitch. His legs jerk. His eyelids tremble. The sedative mask must be drying up. I move in closer. "Delphi, tell Jones we need that program *now*. Semak's not going to be out much longer."

And if he wakes up? How long before he detonates the weapon?

Kurnakova takes a firmer grip on Semak's shirt. "We cannot let him wake up," she growls. "We *will* not."

"Roger that," Delphi confirms. "Shelley, you will *not* let him wake up. Don't kill him, but otherwise, do what you need to do."

"Delphi . . . you're saying you want me to crack him in the skull?"

"Roger that."

I've done terrible things, but I've done them in the heat of battle. I've never done anything like this.

"You think you might hesitate?" Kurnakova asks me.

"No. I'll do it. Let's get him strapped down."

I know what a nuke in orbit can do. If it goes off, Kurnakova and I die instantly. Millions of others die later. Not only will the detonation destroy hundreds of essential satellites, but at this altitude, the EMP could wipe out electronics across a continent—and start a world war.

Throwing a punch in zero gee is fucking hard, of course. I brace myself and practice a few times on an empty recliner. And when Semak coughs behind the mask and starts to moan, I put a stop to that.

"We're ready to go ahead," Delphi says in a voice so stripped of emotion I know right away how scared she is.

"What do you need me to do?"

Kurnakova is braced in the capsule door, waiting.

"Nothing. There's nothing for you to do. I just thought you'd want to know. Jones has found the program. They're going in through Semak's overlay."

"Now?"

"Now."

The old man is strapped in a recliner, blood bubbling from his nose. I hover over him, listening to his breathing, willing it to continue.

"Done," Delphi says.

I don't understand. Neither does Kurnakova. We both speak in shared confusion. "What? What's done?"

Delphi answers with an uneasy little laugh. "It's anticlimactic, I guess, but Jones shut down the ignition system. And now . . . Jones has deleted the ignition program from Semak's overlay. . . . Okay . . . okay . . . and now they have shut the overlay down. So it's *done*. Semak no longer has access. He cannot control anything within the habitat." Again, that weak little laugh that tells me she's barely holding it together. "I'm going on break, Shelley. Vasquez is taking over."

The link closes before I can say anything, but right away Jaynie links in. "Shelley?"

My answer is automatic—"Here"—but all I'm thinking is that Delphi has never walked out on me before.

"Scary part's over," Jaynie assures me. "But you're not done yet."

My first task is to transfer Semak to *Lotus*. He's still out, his eyes closed. The blood on his nose has dried, and with no more bubbles to assure me he's breathing, I'm not at all sure he's alive. So I lean close, putting my ear beside his mouth where I sense the faint current of a breath, and then he speaks to me, Russian syllables muttered in a hoarse whisper. My overlay translates, its androgynous voice at standard volume in my ear: *"You think you have won. You have not."*

"Not yet," I whisper back to him. "But we'll be back in the world soon."

I guide him out of the capsule into the main chamber. He tries to fight me, grabbing the frame of the hatch and then a handhold, but he's weak. It's easy to pry his long fingers loose. By the time I get him to *Lotus*, Kurnakova has pulled a jump seat from the rack and clipped it to the spaceplane's deck. We strap him into the harness. Then I zip-tie his hands behind the seat.

Even a small nuke can generate an overwhelming EMP if it bursts above the atmosphere, so the stolen nuke will be coming down with us. I eye it doubtfully. "Jaynie, what about radiation? I just want to know the full scope of risk. What is this thing doing to me?"

A pause. Then: "Nothing. Don't worry. Jones says the radiation emitted by an unexploded weapon is very low."

Okay. Good.

Jaynie puts me to work with an electric saw, cutting the straps that hold the nuke in place. It turns out I'm good at this, because I can grip with my feet to hold my position in the tight space, while using both hands to control the saw.

Kurnakova is searching the hermitage. From the main chamber come the sounds of Velcro ripping, bin covers squeaking, and Kurnakova murmuring to herself as she inventories what's there.

Just as I make the last cut to free the warhead, she announces on gen-com, "Found it."

"Found what?" I ask as I stuff both the saw and the metal straps into a plastic bag.

"The rest of the B61."

I go to look.

Kurnakova has uncovered a large closet behind the chess-board liner. Inside is a collection of disassembled machine parts stowed in clear plastic bags strung together with an elastic cord. The parts include cables, gearing, steel hous-ings, and other pieces I can't begin to identify.

"Gather everything," Jaynie instructs. "We don't want any evidence of the nuke left behind."

"This is a cover-up?" I ask. I want it confirmed.

"Roger that."

Rawlings cuts in, overriding mission protocol. "If this gets out, it will be a major incident, and potentially an excuse for militaries to place their own nuclear weapons in orbit—in defiance of global treaty."

Jaynie was wrong when she said the scary part was over.

I help Kurnakova unfasten the ends of the elastic cord that secures the bags. We hook the ends together in a loop and then tug the bags out of the closet. Behind them are larger parts: the shining silver tail section of the bomb's housing, decked out with four angled fins; the hollow mid-section, marked with a serial number; and a gray nose cone, tipped in black.

More than the innocuous-looking warhead, these are the symbols of Armageddon. Handling them is surreal, an experience out of nightmare, weird and terrifying. Perplexing. Why are these components even here? It's no small thing. Every pound of material brought up on the spaceplane comes at enormous cost—but the cost meant nothing to Semak.

What did Kurnakova call him? A tinkering genius. He might have wanted to do the disassembly work himself—or he might have had no choice. If he had ordered the B61 disassembled and only the critical components sent up, would he have been obeyed? Anyone with the skill to do it would surely have known they were putting themselves and their family at risk. Better to promise riches to an underling with no expertise, one who could be trusted to deliver the crate, no questions asked.

We move the pieces to *Lotus* and strap them down.

There's only one item left in the closet: a bundle of tightly bound tan-colored cloth over three feet in length. "Is that part of it?" I ask Jaynie. "Or do we leave it behind?"

"Jones says to take it. It's the parachute."

We load the warhead last. Its mass astonishes me. Kurnakova helps me maneuver it. We take it very, very slowly, afraid it'll get away from us. It would be easy to crush fingers or break limbs or to damage the interior of the hermitage—or more critically, *Lotus*.

Semak is awake, his eyes open, watching us as we bring it in. He's breathing in swift shallow breaths and blood is bubbling from his nose again.

In unspoken agreement, we take the warhead to the back, as far from our position as we can get it. Then we strap it down. Just as we finish, the plane's radio speaks. Kurnakova goes to answer, telling me, "Do a final walk-through."

As I exit *Lotus* I hear her informing ground control that Eduard Semak will be a passenger on the return flight, his poor health requiring him to be evacuated from the hermitage. I leave behind the flurry of questions that follows. This is my last excursion in zero gee, so I make the most of it, gliding unhindered all the way through the main chamber into the cramped capsule. I close all the bin doors, then I grab the bag of discarded metal scraps. I'm about to leave when a voice speaks from the old-fashioned radio. It's not the woman. This is the voice of a young man. He is demanding a response from Semak, confirmation that all is well.

Jaynie speaks over gen-com. "New orders incoming. Delay your departure."

Kurnakova protests. "We have done what we came to do. We are ready to go."

"New orders," Jaynie repeats. "Under no circumstances is Eduard Semak to be transported on an American plane. He will not be allowed to land on American soil."

By this time I'm back in *Lotus*'s hatch. "Whose decision is that, Jaynie?"

"It's from Jones. Relayed from 'highest authorities.'"

The fucking president?

"Do you believe it?"

"*Yes,*" she insists, a rare urgency in her voice.

"I won't leave him to live out his life here," Kurnakova warns. "Semak is a criminal. Shelley, you brought Thelma Sheridan to trial. Semak needs to face trial as well. We have the evidence—"

Jaynie interrupts. "He is to be turned over to Russian authorities—"

"But—"

"Shut the fuck up and listen to me! This is not a game. Your orders are to escort Semak to the evacuation capsule. You will secure him there in a reentry couch. You will seal the capsule, and then you will drop that fucker back into the world. Is that understood?"

Jaynie knows more than she's telling us. The urgency in her voice makes it clear the stakes have gone higher than I want to imagine, but I don't need to know the details. The only question is, do I trust her?

That's an easy question to answer.

"Is that *understood*?" Jaynie repeats.

"Yes, ma'am, it is." I move to free Semak. "Executing orders now."

As we return Semak to the hermitage, he rolls his eyes and shows his worn-out teeth in a grimace of amusement. "You have lost," he whispers, in English this time. But when we strap him into one of the capsule's reentry couches his expression changes. Fear returns to his voice. "What is this? What do you do?"

"You are wanted back home," Kurnakova tells him.

I don't think anyone really wants Semak. I suspect that, like us, the Russians are mostly interested in the data he keeps in his overlay.

We close the doors and seal them. Then we retreat to *Lotus*.

The launch of the capsule is handled from the ground. With Kurnakova, I watch through *Lotus*'s windows as it drifts clear of the hermitage. Rockets fire, and it falls away.

"Our turn," Kurnakova says. "You ready to go home?"

There's regret, knowing I'll never be up here again. But I'm one of the lucky few. At least I got to experience it once.

"Yes, I'm ready."

She completes the separation, fires the rocket motors, and we are away.

After consultation with STS ground control, she executes a deorbit burn and we begin our descent. Africa passes beneath us, remote and beautiful. The deserts of the Middle East roll by. India. We enter the atmosphere, the nose of *Lotus* pitched up.

The speed of our descent compresses the air in front of us, causing it to heat and glow, a plasma that appears pale pink at first, gradually deepening to red orange. The plasma curtains our view and breaks our link to ground control, but our descent remains smooth. There is no shaking.

Minutes pass, and then Kurnakova authorizes the AI pilot to roll *Lotus* on its side and we begin a long bank to control our descent. Another turn, and another. The craft is agile.

"We could slow more quickly," Kurnakova says. "At this point we could land in Hawaii if we needed to, or California, or Mexico."

A map on the instrument panel shows that we have flown from day into night.

"We will follow a gradual glide profile, coming in high and slow over the continent to mitigate sonic—"

The radio wakes up as we emerge from communications blackout. The now-familiar voice of Kurnakova's ground control handler speaks again in the same slow, friendly voice he's used throughout the flight, but his message is no longer nominal.

"*Lotus*, your flight plan has been revised. Sending new navigation sequence now. Landing is redirected to facility at sixteen forty-five north, one sixty-nine thirty-one west."

Kurnakova leans against her restraints, glaring at the instruments as *Lotus* parses the instruction, helpfully marking the location on the map. It's a long way from San Antonio. Just a point in the Pacific Ocean west and south of Hawaii. "Say again, STS."

"Landing is redirected to the emergency runway at Johnston Atoll."

The red curve of a revised flight path appears on the map, and all on its own, *Lotus* begins another steep bank.

Kurnakova abandons the ritualized exchange of communications. "Gene, what are you talking about? There is no emergency. Conditions are nominal."

"Negative, *Lotus*. Emergency conditions dictate an immediate landing. We will reassess once you're on the ground."

The panel lights are reflected in a sheen of sweat on Kurnakova's cheeks as she glares at the map. "STS, what is the condition of the emergency runway?"

"Acceptable, *Lotus*. The runway was rebuilt eighteen months ago."

Her professionalism gives way to disgust. "And how many hurricanes have rolled over it since, Gene? Has it been cleaned? Inspected?"

Gene's official tone shifts to something more personal. "There are no landing lights, Ulyana. But there will be US Navy helicopters present to illuminate the runway."

She switches off the mic. Then she leans back in her seat, gaze frozen on the instrument panel. "I'm sorry, Shelley."

I use my satellite relay to link to gen-com.

"Jaynie?"

"Here."

"We're not coming back. We're being routed to Johnston Atoll on the basis of an undefined and unconfirmed emergency. They say we'll be allowed to land, but there may be an accident."

"Okay," she says. "I'll see what we can find out, what we can do. Can you divert and land somewhere else?"

"Negative," Kurnakova says. "Flight computer has control."

"Roger that."

Our long bank has gone full circle. We are spiraling down through the atmosphere, dumping velocity fast. I can't help myself. I glance over the seat back to check on the warhead, where it's securely strapped to the deck. It looks as harmless as ever, just an unadorned steel cylinder that gives no hint of its terrible potential. But more dangerous now than its physical power are the implications of its existence and its history. The warhead is testimony to failed nuclear security, both past and present, and to the vulnerability of the technological system we have created with our satellites and our ubiquitous electronics.

If Semak had blown the nuke in orbit, he could have ignited a world war. That didn't happen. We brought the device down to ensure it wouldn't happen, but now both the Americans and the Russians have a problem, because if the news gets out that they allowed a nuke into orbit, old treaties will be terminated and a race to militarize space will commence. Even the dreams of dragons will fade as private development is choked off out of concerns for security, leaving companies like Sidereal Transit Systems to crumble into dust.

To prevent that, time is now being unwound, history rewritten, facts force-fitted into a politically convenient narrative. The warhead we found will disappear again, Semak will not survive his precarious descent in the evacuation capsule, Kurnakova will die in a tragic accident at Johnston Atoll, and I will never have been present at all.

The worst part of it is I understand why they need to do this.

Not that I intend to cooperate.

"Jaynie."

"Here, Shelley."

"Talk to Jones. If we can get control of the flight computer—"

The plasma glow is gone, but the night sky lights up again in a blinding white burst. As swift as the light, the realization comes: They are shooting at us. Shock follows: They did not score a direct hit.

Maybe our speed saved us, or maybe the tiny profile of our spaceplane wasn't programmed into their guidance system— or maybe the Red is trying to play this out a little longer?

The shock wave from the explosion collapses that hope. We are still in a steep bank when it slams into us. An alarm launches a buzzing protest as *Lotus* bucks, shimmies, and rolls over, hard and fast so that the horizon line on the instrument panel is upside down and I'm hanging in my harness. The truth hits next: The missile detonated as intended— ahead of us—avoiding the miniscule risk of a direct hit on the nuke, because the shock wave alone is enough to bring us down.

Debris from the blast slams into us with ear-shattering concussions. The flight computer is overwhelmed and aborts its program, yielding to Kurnakova. She grabs the controls. "Fuck!" she screams, working frantically to get us upright again. "Roll for me, sweet one. Try!"

Lotus swoops. I'm thrown sideways in my harness. The fuselage vibrates madly, and from somewhere there comes a high metallic scream as the plane begins to tear apart— but the horizon icon on the instrument panel shows us to be upright again.

Then *Lotus* goes dark as the electrical system fails.

A thin wash of moonlight falls across the instrument panel. The satellite relay is still clipped to it. It's a field unit, independent of *Lotus* and running on batteries. "Jaynie!"

"Stand by. We're talking to STS ground con—"

"Jaynie, we're going down! Tell Delphi I'm sorry."

Kurnakova is alternately cursing at *Lotus* and begging the plane to bring its nose up, up, as she works the flight controls. I flash on Delphi, listening. She doesn't need to hear any more of this. Breathing hard, I reach out and switch the satellite link off.

Lotus continues to shudder and shake. Not long now before we burst apart.

At least the mission succeeded. It was worth doing. We recovered the intel from Semak, and then we went beyond the mission plan and returned a rogue nuke to the world. That nuke will soon be on the bottom of the Pacific, but a submarine crew will surely come to recover it.

I wonder: *Is the story supposed to end this way?*

I think it is. I've had my run. I've played my role. Welcome to the finale.

Fuck that.

I don't want it to end. I don't want it to be over. So I grope for options. I grasp for ideas. Anything. There is no way *Lotus* can hold together long enough to land, but maybe it doesn't have to. I unbuckle my harness. *Lotus* bucks, throwing me into the instrument panel. But then I get myself braced. "Slow us down!" I yell at Kurnakova. "Get our speed down as far as you can!"

She pitches me a look, moonlight glittering in her wild eyes. "I'm trying to make Johnston!"

"We'll never make Johnston! So we're getting out. You remember? The B61? We've got its parachute!"

"You're fucking crazy!"

No shit.

"It *cannot* happen," she insists as if the idea actually offends her. "You say this because you do not comprehend how fast we are going!"

"So slow us the fuck down! Do you want to die?"

I heave myself over the seat just as the plane drops out from under me. It's only my grip on the seat back that keeps me from being hurled against the ceiling. But when I get my feet under me again, Kurnakova has recovered control. The plane is still trembling, shuddering, but we're flying level. It's an interlude of peace compared with what we just went through—but it lasts only seconds. There's a deafening *crack!* and then wind shrieks, prying into the fuselage and I'm in free fall again—but Kurnakova is still doing battle. She gets the nose of the plane up and once more our descent slows. If we were still flying at supersonic velocity, surely we would have ripped apart by now?

I heave myself at the parachute, hammering the quick-release buckles that hold it strapped to the deck. Then I haul it to the jump seat we set up for Semak. I'm gambling the seat has a titanium frame. Holding myself in place with my feet, I couple the parachute to the jump seat using a cargo strap and the swivel from the parachute rig. Then I unclip the seat from the deck. My theory is that when the seat falls with my weight and Kurnakova's in it, it will be enough to trigger the parachute to deploy—or at least things would work that way in a comic-book universe where superheroes rule. In the real world? The seat frame will probably snap.

Like Kurnakova said, I'm fucking crazy.

I grip the seat with my foot to keep it close, then I lean over Kurnakova, screaming to be heard over the wind. "How fast are we going?"

"It does not matter! We are going down!"

"Come with me now!" I reach over the seat to unbuckle her harness.

She shoves my hands away. It's an instinctive defense. She's not fighting me. Not really, because a moment later she hits the release button, wriggles out of her harness, and rolls over the back of the seat.

Lotus starts to roll again. I grab Kurnakova and throw myself into the jump seat before it can slide away. I've got her in my lap while I grip the seat's frame with my robot feet. "Get the harness around us!"

The deck tilts and the fuselage screams. A piece tears out above our heads. Another follows. We are seconds away from catastrophic failure.

Kurnakova twists, grabbing one side of the jump seat's harness. I grab the other just as the fuselage shatters with an ear-rending scream. What I see is like a still shot, composed in moonlight, frozen in time: flakes and shards of the fuselage suspended in the grip of a hurricane wind.

A fraction of a second later the debris hits. Kurnakova's body shields mine. I feel her anguished spasms. I taste her blood in the ripping air. And then she's gone. Vanished in the roaring dark.

I'm still in the chair, my feet locked on its frame, one hand with a death grip on half the harness. And I'm falling backward. God knows if I'm clear of the debris. I wrestle the harness over my shoulders and fight with the buckle, once, twice, and then it locks just as the parachute deploys, a roar of rippling canvas followed by a low *whump!* like mortar fire that puts the stars out. God's hand reaches down out of the empty dark, arresting my momentum so abruptly my bones try to separate at every joint, my lungs collapse, and my brain slams against the inside of my skull.

The world starts up again and I'm still falling. It takes me a few seconds to really register the fact. Surprise follows that I'm not dead—not yet. Can't be much longer though. Fuck.

I try to assess the situation. Wind is racing past me, brutalizing my eyes, roaring in my ears, stripping away my body heat as it hammers the fabric of my coverall into rippling waves and drives a mad feathering in the canvas above my head.

That canvas is my parachute. Is it working? It's deployed, but is it fully deployed or is it just a tangled mess trailing me in my long fall?

My eyes are clamped to slits against the force of the wind but I crane my neck anyway and try to look. Nothing's there. . . . Maybe that's a good sign? If the chute weren't deployed I'd see the stars.

Right?

Maybe I'm looking up at a cloud deck.

Nothing I can do about it anyway.

I look down.

I've seen the world from orbit. This is a well-lit planet. There are only a few places in all the world that are still dark at night. Too bad for me the middle of the Pacific Ocean is one of them. There is not a spark of bright yellow, not a speck of electric white. No ship's lights, no shore. All I can see is a faint glittering of moonlight reflected and refracted in fine, sinuous, broken, watery lines.

I twist around to look behind me. The movement sends me reeling sideways like I'm on a fucking carnival swing but I get a view in the other direction—and it's just more moonlight on water, endless water, nothing else.

I'm spinning, twisting, breathing hard.

How lost am I?

I need to know.

So I check my GPS. I have to close my eyes all the way to do it, to keep out the wind that wants to destroy the lenses of my overlay. Another few seconds slip past while the lenses rehydrate. Then I get the menu open. Pull up a map. A map with nothing on it because I'm falling to Earth in the middle of fucking nowhere. I zoom out, and that reveals islands that might as well be a million miles away. I don't bother to identify them because it doesn't fucking matter. All I care about now is how many seconds I have left before I hit. So I open my eyes to just slits and look down.

I can see texture in the water now.

I have a feeling I'm falling too fast.

Nukes like the B61 use parachutes in part to soften their landing, but mostly the chute serves to slow the bomb's fall so the delivery plane has time to get away before fucking Armageddon ignites. I have been a soldier in the war against Armageddon and that is something I am proud of—but soldiers, of course, are expendable.

Oh, I can easily see the long crests and ridges of swells now, moonlight glittering on their peaks.

Soon.

I am falling too fast, I'm sure of it.

I'm sorry, Delphi.

This time for sure, I won't be coming back.

The closer I get to the glittering dark, the faster it seems I'm falling. With my hand on my harness release, I watch the sparkle of moonlight—so hard to tell how far away the surface is—and then it's not far at all. The scent of the sea envelopes me as spume blows off a wave crest only meters below.

I hit the harness release, kick free of the seat, and drop feetfirst into the water.

It's farther away than I thought. When I hit it's a hammer blow. Whatever air I had in my lungs is expelled on impact. I plunge into utter darkness with a horde of tingling bubbles racing across the skin of my hands and face.

• • • •

I want to breathe, but where is the surface?

Don't panic.

Somewhere above me is the parachute, square meters of canvas coming down on my head. Somewhere in the dark, guylines are sinking beneath the surface, tangling in an invisible web.

I pick a direction and swim. I pull hard at the water and kick—and learn something new. For all their amazing engineering, my robot feet are useless for swimming because they're so well made they slice through the water without any significant resistance.

I kick anyway, I stroke, thinking of Harvey, lost over the side of the *Non-Negotiable*. Her rig pulled her down, but I know she didn't panic. She would have kept her cool, tried to escape—she would have tried, but she never saw the surface again.

I don't know if I've gone far enough to clear the chute, but I've gone as far as I can. I need the surface. So I swim up, up, up, empty lungs lined in fire, offering me no buoyancy. It's all a struggle and for what?

To breathe again.

To breathe. That's all that matters.

I'm going so fast when I reach the surface that I burst through to my waist, throwing off a spray of glittering foam.

There is a gibbous moon above me, a handful of bright stars, and the flashing lights of an airliner so far away its engine noise doesn't reach me. Long swells roll past, lifting me up, ferrying me down, again and again. I breathe.

Breathe.

Embraced by a silence that is not silence because it's broken by the blowing wind and the gurgle of water in my ears as I float with only my face above the surface, all too conscious of the infinite deep below me.

There is no reason in the world I should be alive.

I watch the plane until it disappears.

A little longer.

Strange things happen on the edge of death. There are always stories.

My fingers have become wrinkled and numb, my ears are aching from the cold water, my eyes burning from the salt, and I think I'm owed something before I go. A ghost, a vision, here on the edge of death. Harvey, come to escort me to Valhalla. Or Lissa, come to show me the way to the Elysian fields. Hell, I'd be happy if Matt Ransom showed up, eager to haul me off to Heaven or Hell, I don't give a shit which, just as long as something's there.

They don't come.

But why should they? I'm the one who got them killed.

There's a faint flicker from the skullnet icon, the first I've noticed. Safe bet that I'll be seeing a lot more of that. Wouldn't want to remember my own death as a traumatic experience.

Fuck.

It's too damn bad I don't have a satellite uplink because I've got some hellacious good video recorded. I'd send it out into the world if I could.

Not that it matters.

A hundred years from now, no one will give a shit about anything I've ever done.

Hell, *one* year from now it'll all be ancient history, with some new crisis on the stage.

The world goes on. Not one of us matters all that much. The dragons want to change that, they want to believe they matter.

Hell, we all do.

• • • •

Far, far overhead, an airliner passes. My overlay wakes up, sensing a link to the Cloud. I watch the trembling of the network icon and my heart beats a little faster. But the connection is denied and then the plane is out of range.

I don't need false hope. I don't want it. If I'm going to die, let me die.

I'm cold and exhausted and I want to sleep.

I remember that the skullnet can help me with that.

Am I done then?

Maybe I am.

I've come back from the dead too many times.

I close my salt-swollen eyelids and, using my gaze, I work my way through the overlay's menu tree. First, I shut down network access. No more false hope for me.

Next, sleep.

A word, a thought. That's all it will take.

I don't do it.

Why chase death? It'll get here soon enough.

I hear things: the wind, my heartbeat, fish jumping, the gurgle of water in my ears, a low bass thrumming. I stir, open my eyes, lift my head from the water—and I can't hear the low noise anymore. So I let the water fill my ears again and there it is, the rumble of a distant engine.

No false hope. That's all I ask.

I tread water to keep my head above the surface so I don't have to hear it.

A swell rolls under me, raising me up. As I pass over its crest, motion draws my gaze. Motion far above the ceaseless motion of the waves. A shadow, a shape, moving in the moon-washed sky. It's high, thirty degrees below the zenith. It's not an airliner; it has no lights. I can see it only because moonlight falls gray against its delta wing as it transits swiftly, silently, between horizons.

It's a surveillance drone—a larger, faster, higher-flying aircraft than the angel we used in the LCS.

Why?

Why is it here? If the navy has come to look for the fallen nuke, they should have come with a submarine. A drone won't help them.

Why is it flying so low that I can see it?

I blink against the salt, watching it, until after several seconds it disappears in the distance, leaving me alone again at the empty center of nowhere.

Maybe it will come back.

Doesn't matter.

With only my head above the water I am a speck, a mote in the wave-tossed, glittering vast night, my body as cold as the ocean that cradles me. Even an AI couldn't pick me out against the background noise.

No false hope.

I close my eyes again, so all that's left for me to look at are the icons on my overlay. My gaze settles on the red X, the icon of network isolation, all connections denied. A menu pops out, offering me options. I look away.

In an irritated voice, Lissa says, "Turn it back on, dickhead."

Holy shit. The ghosts are speaking at last.

"Lissa?" I ask in a hoarse whisper, knowing her voice was a hallucination, knowing she's not really here, but I want to play the game. "Baby?"

No answer. But out of habit I do as she says. I gaze at the icon again, the menu pops out, and I turn my network access back on.

Right away I get a connection. It comes up as a closed network, no Cloud access, but there's someone on the other side who knows me, because within seconds I get a text. I don't recognize the source, but it's got my passcode appended, so it gets through: *Reply with your GPS coordinates.*

Jaynie thinks I want to die, but I get to prove her wrong again. I don't know who it is out there hunting me, but I dump my location data into a text and I fucking send it.

SUPPLEMENTARY DOCUMENTATION

EXIT INTERVIEW

LOOMING ABOVE ME, SILHOUETTED AGAINST THE moon-washed sky, is the tall, sharp-edged superstructure of an old-style navy ship, maybe a destroyer. No lights showing, so I can't see the flag. No sound but the wind and the idling engines.

I want to shout, cry out for help, make my presence known, but something tells me not to. I've got a feeling—a strong feeling—that this operation calls for silence. So I tread water, watching the ship as the long swells roll beneath me.

Three minutes and thirty-two seconds slide past on my time display. I hear a quick intake of breath. Turning my head, I see a swimmer treading water less than a meter away. Moonlight reflects off the facets of his face mask. He speaks in a soft voice that identifies him as American: "We're on the same side, okay?"

I wonder what side that is, but I don't ask or argue. I'm okay with it. Everything feels right.

"Quick and quiet," he says, moving closer.

His life vest inflates as he wraps his arms around me and then we're moving, a little wake burbling around us as we're dragged through the water. We submerge twice as swells roll over us and then we're at the ship's side. A basket is waiting.

I know the air can't be as cold as it feels, but in the few seconds it takes to haul us up, I start shivering. I can't make it stop.

The deck is empty except for one man who grips my arm and gets me up before I have time to doubt my ability to stand. He steers me through a doorway into a narrow, air-conditioned passage lit by dull red lights. It's fucking cold.

"Got to move fast," my escort murmurs under his breath. He's a bigger man than me—broad shouldered, dark skinned, dark haired. Polynesian, maybe, with his wide, powerful face. He's dressed in a black long-sleeved pullover with no name tag, and dark cargo pants that might be part of a navy uniform but it's hard to tell in the vague light. There's a glint along the curve of his jaw that looks to me like the tattooed antenna of an overlay.

I hear the swimmer behind us. "Not a mistake, Kanoa," he says in a soft but triumphant voice. "*And* we beat the satellite. Twelve seconds to spare."

"Shut up," Kanoa advises him. "We are not secure."

It's all I can do to stay on my feet as we move swiftly through dark passages. We reach a closed hatch. Kanoa holds his wrist to a sensor plate until an electronic lock clicks, and then he pulls the hatch open.

More dim red lights are on the other side, illuminating shared quarters with four bunks stacked floor to ceiling and a plastic table with side benches bolted to the floor. We enter. The swimmer comes in behind us. When he closes the door, the lock clicks and buzzes. "All secure," he announces as bright white lights come on.

Kanoa steers me past the benches and bunks and into a shower cubicle.

"Get the wet stuff off," he orders as he turns a spray of lukewarm water on me.

I'm allowed a minute to rinse the salt off. Then I clear out so the swimmer—his name is Griffin—can have a turn. It's the first time I get a good look at him. He's a skinny guy, Caucasian with narrow features, light-colored hair shaved to a stubble. Because I'm looking for it, I see the gold tattoo of an antenna on the back of his jawline.

Still shivering, I get dressed in the clothes Kanoa hands me. They're a duplicate of what he's wearing: blue-gray trousers and a black pullover.

Hot coffee waits on the table. I sit at one of the benches, wrapped in a blanket, struggling to keep my hands steady so the coffee doesn't spill. When I try to speak, my throat is so swollen all I can manage is a hoarse whisper as I state the obvious: "You two aren't regular navy."

Kanoa refills my cup. He sits opposite me, his dark eyes locked on mine. "We're like you—professional soldiers wired with a skullnet and overlay, who work for the Red."

It's a jolt to hear it put that bluntly, but FaceValue affirms he's telling the truth—at least as he sees it.

"Like you, we get assigned to address potential existential threats. Make sure no rogue operator has a chance to do what Thelma Sheridan did on Coma Day. It's a covert war, just beginning. Black Cross, First Light, Silent Firebreak, Vertigo Gate—"

"You know about Vertigo Gate?"

"Those missions were some of the early skirmishes. There have been other engagements, ones you've never heard of. And there will be more. You need to decide if you still want to be part of it."

I lean forward, fired by the memory of this world as I saw it from orbit, this beautiful, fragile, irreplaceable planet that is our home. "Of course I want to be part of it."

Griffin, dressed just like us now, sits beside Kanoa. They trade a long look. I've got a feeling there's a conversation playing out, thoughts picked up by their skullnets, translated and then transmitted between them as words, but I can't hear any of it because I'm not linked into their network.

After several seconds, Kanoa nods. He looks across the table at me. "You can go home if you want to. But when Susan Monteiro is sworn in as president, she *will* shut down Cryptic Arrow."

No need to ask how he knows about Cryptic Arrow. He already told me he works for the Red.

Griffin wants to make sure I understand: "If you go home, Shelley, you'll find yourself retired."

Kanoa isn't wearing any rank insignia, but it's clear he's the commanding officer of this outfit, so I direct my question to him. "And if I don't go home?"

"I'm recruiting."

The few who know of Vertigo Gate consider the mission a success, despite the losses. Eduard Semak's cache of rogue nuclear weapons has been secured and the B61 nuclear warhead he kept in orbit is no longer a hazard. It was recovered from the seafloor by a US Navy submarine and is scheduled to be decommissioned.

Semak himself did not survive reentry while certain anonymous funds, in the approximate amount of $2.5 billion, were successfully transferred to new owners.

The tragedy of the mission came in the loss of *Lotus* pilot Ulyana Kurnakova and her technician. Despite an extensive search of surface waters, their bodies were never recovered.

I won't be stepping forward to correct the record.

Guilt cuts when I think of Delphi, but it's better this way. She's been through enough trials, she's seen me die too many times. I won't put her through that again—and it will happen again.

This isn't over.

ACKNOWLEDGMENTS

The Trials had help along the way from many of the same people who so generously provided assistance for its predecessor, *The Red*. They are: Nancy Jane Moore, Edward A. White, Dallas Nagata White, Vonda N. McIntyre, Jeffrey A. Carver, and Chaz Brenchley.

Judith Tarr again served as my initial editor, with additional insight from Joe Monti, my editor at Saga Press.

Thanks to all of you for your assistance, your patience, your wisdom, and your time. Thanks also to my husband, Ronald J. Nagata, Sr., whose continued support makes my writing possible.

A writer, of course, is nothing without readers. Thank you to all who've spent time in my story worlds. Your interest and encouragement are deeply appreciated.

If you enjoyed *The Trials*, please consider reviewing it at a blog or an online bookseller, or mention it on your favorite social media. Don't forget to look for the final book in The Red Trilogy, *Going Dark*, also from Saga Press. To be notified of my latest books and stories, please visit my website at MythicIsland.com and sign up to receive my occasional newsletter.

Linda Nagata, January 2015

ABOUT THE AUTHOR

LINDA NAGATA is the author of many novels and short stories, including *The Bohr Maker*, winner of the Locus Award for best first novel, and the novella "Goddesses," the first online publication to receive a Nebula Award. *The Red: First Light* was a finalist for best novel for both the Nebula and John W. Campbell Awards. She lives with her husband in their longtime home on the island of Maui. Visit her at MythicIsland.com.